T0274017

ignite

Books by Kara Swanson

Heirs of Neverland
Dust
Shadow

The Phoenix Flame
Ignite

KARA SWANSON

For the ones like me –
Where courage is taking the next step, the next breath,
believing the next moment will be better.
That your story does not end here.
I see you. I'm so *proud* of you.
This is for you. <3

To my David –
For being the Eli to my Mara and never letting me go.
You are my safest place and believe in me
when I don't know how to believe in myself.
I love you.

CHAPTER ONE

"You shouldn't be here."

My father's voice cutting through my temples makes me jump. This sprawling, icy wasteland is silent except for the words reverberating in my mind.

I take a cautious step forward, worn boots crunching against the frigid snowfall as I wrap my arms around myself, fingers tucked into my ragged sleeves to ward off the nipping chill. My tangled, black-as-lava-rock hair whips against my nose, reddened by the wind.

I can help, Father.

I lick my lips and tug my heavy-knit coat closer around my shoulders. The worn animal fur brushes against my flushed cheeks as I search the bleak stretches around me. It's eerie and still, as haunting as the dead buried deep beneath the ice. Little survives for long out here.

I shove one scuffed boot after another through the dredges of snow. He was headed this direction when he left to hunt.

"Father? Where are you?" The words are breathless and rough, but I force them out through cracked lips.

I narrow my eyes at the dimmest rays of light glinting off the muffled ridges. No one can hear me for miles out here. But I'm not expecting Father to hear my words spoken aloud.

I know he'll be listening where he always lives. Deep in my thoughts.

My guardian. My mentor. My father.

The one who helps me sort through the volatile whispers to keep my inner inferno in check. To bank the raging phoenix fire in my veins that sometimes surges against my control and makes my joints throb with every movement. My body doesn't know how to hold this blaze dormant. Not without him.

For several stretching seconds, Father doesn't reply, leaving my thoughts empty. Sweat drips down my forehead and heat ripples in my bones. Water sizzles as the sheath of ice trying to form on my sleeve thaws.

"Father?"

My boots are already soaked as I tread a few more careful steps, trudging over the hard-packed snow and toward the pallid crests towering ahead. This stretch of wasteland isn't fully shadowed yet by the angle of the mountains. With the faint whisper of heat from the dissolving sun overhead, I expected Father to have laid his trap here. But he left a quarter sunpass ago to set it, and there's no sign of him. I glance over my shoulder. Fresh drifts cover any footsteps I could have retraced.

It's empty as a tomb out here. No whisper of the phoenix who raised me.

Or the hunt he's out to capture, bringing home one last meal for our tiny village.

I try to slow my breathing. *He hasn't left. Not yet. He wouldn't do that to you.*

He wouldn't let me follow him out into the Forsaken Lands just to turn his back when I need him. He knows how long it would take for me to freeze out here.

Not a quick death.

If my own blood didn't turn my skin to kindling first.

"Mara, I told you to stay back at the temple."

Warmth floods my body, melting the ice underfoot. I pick up the pace. My senses reach out for the familiar tone of his heat signature.

"I know, Father. But I wanted to help." I only have a few precious hours left with him. With any of them. And then I will be as forsaken as these lands.

"You have been well prepared for what you must do, little one. You are not forsaken yet." Father's voice, listening in on the chaos of my *ero*—my thoughts, is like a blanket of snow cooling the fire inside me and bringing clarity. *"If you want to help me hunt, then find me."*

The chilled gust picks up again, trying to rip my face open, but I can't fight back my smile.

"I'm coming, Father."

I'm surprised he hasn't chided me yet for speaking aloud. None of the others like it when I do. But something about using my voice, letting the words linger in the air—it makes the world feel more real.

When you've existed this long, reality starts to feel like a dream.

Hunching my shoulders against the cold, my eyes fall closed. Instead of using the light from the dull sun to guide me forward, I search for the ripple of warmth.

Let it swell from somewhere deep inside me. Let it bring that too-familiar heat along my shoulder blades and twin scars that always burn there. And as the fire inside rises—I can feel the warmth beneath my feet echoing in reflection. A whisper through the interconnecting tunnels buried below me in the snow. There's someone else out here.

I hum quietly to myself, filling my own head with sound to numb how achingly silent my thoughts are.

My feet skim over the divots in the frost, used to deftly gauging the stability of the next step. I've found an echo of his warmth—the faintest whisper that something else breathes out here. Something else fights to exist against this frozen landscape.

The closer I get, the stronger I sense him. Like a beacon that flickers in my mind's eye against a backdrop of grey nothingness. His heat signature is a dull, reddish hue that blurs and dances in contrast to the haunting stillness of the ice. But when I open my eyes, almost on top of where he should be—the world is still empty.

The ridges towering on either side have changed shape, indicating how far I've come. But the small hillocks and faint valleys are devoid of any other life. A large outcropping rises from the snow just ahead, frozen so solid it's almost reflective.

"You're walking too loudly. You'll scare them away." His chiding blasts through my thoughts, and I'd swear he stands right beside me. I soften my steps, pressing my lashes together and searching for those heat signatures again.

This time, I don't just see one. I see three.

Found them!

I drop to a crouch and inch forward, using the ledge of ice as cover. I peer over the frigid spire and can finally make out the small flock of furred birds. They're quickly pecking and eating scattered iceplant in a shallow indentation of snow.

I still feel Father's silhouetted warmth—but it seems dampened somehow. Distant. I'll bring him my spoils when I find his hunting blind. I can practically see the look of pride that will cross his face— especially if I capture all three of the *argots.*

I dig the toes of my boots into the frigid curve of the outcropping of ice, giving myself a little more height, and reach inside my coat pocket for two curving blades. My daggers are made of pockmarked volcanic rock, sharpened to an obsidian point on one end and wrapped with a leather grip on the other.

I focus on the fluttering *argots,* watching their too-thin bodies fall and rise with breath and the way their fur fades into scaly wings.

They've fought so hard to live. Maybe I owe them that much.

No. No. You must prove to Father you can do this.

You can survive on your own. You can protect him.

So, I raise my right hand, perch the blade between my thumb and forefinger, set my sights on the largest bird—and flick the weapon with deadly accuracy.

"Mara—no!"

Father's voice is so sudden and desperate that the second knife I've just unleashed from my other hand spirals to the side, missing the second bird.

"What?" I slide backward down the small shelf of ice. "What's wrong?"

I approach the *argots* to find the first one I'd speared lying on its side. My dark weapon protrudes from its sallow little breast. The other two are long gone. Leaving nothing but a pair of crumbled holes where they burrowed away from their dead friend.

I'll never find them again. Any creature that can still survive in this world has mastered the art of hiding from predators.

"Mara!" Father's angry tone splits through my temples like a headache, and my knees give way. I sink to the ground, arms over my head.

"I'm sorry! What did I do? Where are you?"

When my eyes flutter closed, I can sense the pulsating source of heat just ahead that I'd thought was only the *argots*. But he was hiding behind their heat signature. Stalking them.

Oh, brimstone.

I destroyed his hunt.

Shame crashes over me like a tossed storm and makes my body tremble.

Idiot. Idiot!

Of course he knew where they were. He specifically told me not to scare them away.

I should have asked his permission. Should have waited for him to tell me to move.

"I'm sorry, Father . . ." I whisper, staring at my soggy boots. "It was so foolish of me."

"You are careless." His words boom inside my head. Tears prick at my eyes.

I'm a stupid child.

I run my gaze across the frigid ground in front of me, catching on the edge of something curved and dangerous sticking out of the snow. Something at the base of another sharp cliff of ice—pointed and flickering, almost crystalline.

My shoulders instinctively twinge, but I don't move. I just wait for him to reveal himself.

I should have waited before. Should have listened better.

Why did I think I could go and do this on my own?

The curved edge sticking out from the snow quivers. Ice and slush slide away as a massive ripple of feathers arches out of the snow. A bruise-tinted wing, easily as long as I am tall, cuts upward, shaking off frozen clumps, and reveals a cloaked figure bent over. My father lifts his other buried wing, their full span stretching twelve feet from end to end.

The wings expand, crystallized feathers withered with just a flicker of blue flame within. His gaunt shoulders are bent, but even so, he stands several heads taller than me. Father already seems weary, but seeing those ashen wings arching on either side of him makes the scars along my shoulder blades twinge.

I'll never have wings like his.

But he's always said that was for the best.

"I was waiting for the rest of the flock . . ." Even though his crackling grey eyes meet mine, he still chooses to communicate telepathically. *"And now they will never resurface here."*

My chin drops to my chest. "I should never have acted on my own. I'm sorry. I only wanted to help."

He takes a limping step, letting his wings drag in the snow behind him, creating dual, scar-like indentations. His eyes are bloodshot, dark bags beneath them. His heavy, ragged coat hangs loosely around his too-thin limbs and shuddering chest, those wings sweeping out of slits in the material that wraps his spine. He looks even worse than yesterday. *"How can I trust you to guard us if you spoil a simple hunt?"*

My throat tightens. I don't trust myself for what's to come, either. "I will protect you with my life."

He reaches out with a spindly hand and cups my chin. His skin is cold. Too cold.

"You're afraid, little one." His eyes narrow. *"Good. You ought to be terrified. I am."*

My gut twists into a hundred knots. "Y-you're afraid, Father?"

His hold on my chin tightens. *"Speak to me in your head."*

There it is. The expected chiding.

I swallow against his palm brushing my throat. *"You're afraid?"*

Something volatile flashes in his wan features. He lifts his free hand to gesture to the dead *argot,* whose body is already covered in a thin layer of frost. *"We are about to be as vulnerable as that creature. More, even."*

And I'll be the only one standing between Father and the others—the Hollow Ones who hunt us like animals. Cursed creatures who create no heat of their own, so they hunt us and carve the warmth out of our people.

They are ice-borne nightmares.

"Exactly." Father's voice growls through my thoughts. *"You know the Hollow are ruthless."* He spits to the side, as we always do when speaking of them. *"We can hardly trust you to protect us when you bumble into a hunt. Maybe I should stay awake."*

I don't realize how much I've been hoping to hear him say those words until they thaw through the tightness in my chest. He lets his waxen hand fall from my face.

I whisper, "Could you stay with me?"

If Father stayed awake, he could help me protect the rest. As we have always done.

He could help me think the right way.

Help me push away the fear that shuts me down. Makes us vulnerable.

If Father stayed awake, his voice in my head would help me be safe.

He'd tell me when to move.

I trust my head if his voice is there.

From the way his silver eyes flicker over my face, I can tell he's considering it. He knows how dangerous the pulsating heat inside of me can be. To anyone around me, even to myself.

Our people have grown more used to me. Tempered to my flame—he made sure of that. But it's still unpredictable.

The fire in my blood doesn't lead to the *aethor* sleep—a fact we discovered when I was just a child. That part of me still terrifies our people. But since I am the only phoenix who doesn't need sleep, I am also the only one who can protect them.

"I'll think on it."

But even as he speaks, I can see the weariness in his eyes. The thin veins that carve through his pale, sagging skin. Father is sick. He has been awake too long.

The longer he stays with me, the sicker he gets. Can I let him choose to risk death for me?

CHAPTER TWO

Father brings his wings in, curling them around himself and tucking his razor-sharp feathers through an inner layer of his large coat. Wrapped snugly as an extra shield of insulation and protection. Plus, flying low enough to scout is dangerous these days. Too easy for a Hollow to spot us and send out a hunting party.

"I'll discuss it with the others. Not whether you are ready—" After helping me tether the *argot* with a stretch of cord that makes it easier to carry, he limps away from me, in the opposite direction of our temple. *"But, whether we can trust you. Whether you can control your flame."*

That is the question.

Burrowing deeper into my jacket, I quicken my pace, boots crunching over the snow. *"Where are we going?"*

He glances over his shoulder. *"To give you another chance to prove yourself. Our people still need their last full meal. And you'll want to dry your own supplies."*

If I let those words stand alone, let them drift in the chilled air, I can almost believe he does trust me. That they do have faith in me.

I squint up at the dull crimson fireball in the sky. We used to navigate using the sun, but every day it grows more dim. Like it, too, has been awake too long.

As if *Sol* itself struggles for breath.

Sol, the creator of our sun. A deity my father doesn't even believe in anymore.

The sun's slow death has made it nearly impossible to find enough food to keep our people alive. Some say *Sol* is to blame for the Hollow stalking our every movement. For the frozen rivers and starved wildlife. But anger at a mythic creator who abandoned the sun and our world doesn't change anything. And, as Father says, all the old gods are dead now. Even their names lost to time—*Sol*, being the only echo of an ancient memory. But that name will fade as well, just as everything does out here.

"Mara?" Father's voice is softer now, and I speed up to trot beside him.

"Yes?"

"Help me find the nearest haja. We'll set our trap where we know prey will be."

This I can do. This I usually do.

Father used to be able to find these *haja*, gaps where warmth rose from the *nemior* tubes beneath, easily on his own. But as he and the rest of our people have been awake longer, and have grown more sickly, it is increasingly difficult for them to sense where the magma tubes carry a bit of warm air through to the surface.

So they let me help find *haja*. Sometimes when we're hunting, and sometimes when we are searching for a place to hide our people away when they must sleep.

I am the youngest. The only young, actually. The first *nora*.

The first female child ever created. Ever found.

I've only existed for about two hundred years, still a youth on the cusp of full adulthood, while Father and the others were coaxed to life with the dawn of this world's sun. In that time, I've aged at a slow, vulnerable pace all my own.

Father was born with the dawn of this world—but, from the looks of it, it won't be long until he also sees the day the sun dies. When that day comes, it will only be a matter of time until we all freeze like the *argot* slung over my shoulder as we walk.

It's cold and stiff as a rock, but I keep hold of the rope I've tied to the dead creature, now leading just ahead of Father.

Every few steps, I let my eyes fall closed, reaching out. Letting that pulsating fire buried deep inside search for the pockets of warmth around me. But so far, everything is just—cold. Frigid. Lifeless.

I angle north. We skirt around a sprawling, dark ravine and keep heading into the incoming icy wind.

"Are you sure you want to go this far, little one?" Father's spindly hand clamps onto my shoulder. He's worried about the Hollow.

I glance back at him. *"I think I sense something ahead. Something larger. Maybe a* **lyran***?"* Not shaped like a hunter.

He gives the slightest nod and we keep moving. *I'd better not be wrong.*

We walk for another dozen steps before I can really sense it. The air rising from below, warming a small, frigid section and letting a few stubborn weeds grow.

Where plant life manages to survive, there are always animals nearby.

Father gestures for me to be quiet. He inches ahead, slowly letting his wings unfurl again. Ready to fly, if that's what it takes to win this fight.

Moving in tandem, booted feet whispering over the ice, we creep around the edge of a large boulder piled with snow—and we see her.

About sixty paces away stands a beautiful, slender creature on all fours. Her back reaches about as high as my chest. The beast's thick coat is a shimmering, the pale blue shade all the females share, with soft spots for camouflage. A *lyran*. She's already shed her antlers, but the silvery stubs are starting to grow back. Padded paws gently scrape at the ground as she lowers her snout to pull at rough patches of grass.

Stunning. It's been over a hundred sunpasses since I've seen one up close.

And this one seems pregnant, from the gentle curve of her belly.

"Father . . ." I whisper, and he lets his wings slowly lower and settle back around him.

"We won't kill a pregnant creature. Young are too rare. We're not that desperate."

Respect glimmers through his expression as he watches the *lyran* quietly graze.

I drift closer to Father, my shoulder bumping against his. Instead of pushing me away, he reaches out, pulling me in. He rubs my shoulders to keep me warm.

"You did well, little one."

That single phrase comforts me more than any warm blanket or meal ever could. Letting my gaze fall back to the pregnant *lyran*, I whisper a prayer for the small ones in her womb. Someday, they will probably lose their mother like I did. Very little survives out here.

But if they do, I hope they find a safe pack to join.

Suddenly, as Father and I watch the regal creature—lightly camouflaged behind a slope of icy drift—something *zings* through the air. An arrow imbeds in the *lyran's* chest. She shrieks, making a desperate gurgling noise that echoes my own silent scream.

No!

My body goes numb, the world blurring as I watch several forms descend upon her. Tall creatures wearing armor made of patches of animal skin and pounded metal. Their faces are covered in gaping metal masks with sharp prongs that spiral the outside of the helmet. Jagged and tipped with poison, just in case anyone tries to go for their heads.

Fear burns under my skin like frostbite.

But it's not the warriors' fearsome masks or raised spears that make bile rise in my throat—it's the blood that coats their armor. The gleaming, cobalt blood that licks across the metal plating and pools in pockets stitched inside. There are a few hints of golden blood there too—like mine. Like Father's once was, before the cold stole the warmth of color from even his liquid flame.

These creatures are dripping with our blood. The blood of my people.

Possibly even the blood of my mother.

Slathered across their bodies like a warning.

The Hollow Ones are soulless creatures clinging to this desolate wasteland by cutting apart the last glimpse of safety and beauty and life that exists in this world.

Just like they cut apart my mother.

Just like they're attacking this innocent *lyran* now.

With raised spears and bloodcurdling shrieks, they set upon the gentle animal's body. Unable to watch, I flinch away from the gruesome sight. Only then do I realize Father's voice has been howling in my head, ***"Mara! Run!"***

But I can't. The numbness spreads over my body, my legs immobile. The panic is crippling. Those savage Hollow Ones would sooner get their hands on us than that *lyran*. I can only imagine how quickly they would cut us open.

Carve out our blood.

I try again to force my boots across the snow.

But something else resounds in my head. A memory I burn alive daily. A memory I'd tried to bury deep in my *ero*, under layers of pain hardened like volcanic rock. But it keeps coming back, bringing fresh terror, trying to consume me.

The memory of my tiny self hiding behind piles of furs and animal skins, frozen, as a hunting party of Hollow discovered my sleeping mother. Watching them unsheathe knives. My mother's flickering, golden blood pouring into buckets.

She was deep in the *aethor* sleep—but I could hear her screams.

They echoed in my head.

Just like they echo now.

The Hollow Ones took my mother. Cut her apart like an animal.

And now they'll slaughter us too.

CHAPTER THREE

Get out! Get out! Get out!

The words ricochet in my head, every heated pulse of my heartbeat telling me to run. But I'm frozen in place. Father is shaking my shoulders, trying to pull me out—but panic batters at my ribcage like an *argot* trying to fly away as my mind becomes a prison. Trapped in the memory. I can *taste* it. The same fear that has haunted me since I was a child.

The unwanted memory flays me open, surging up from that raw, boiling place deep inside.

"Hold it back, Mara!" Not even Father's voice, slicing through the pounding in my head, is enough to dam the flood.

I'm a child again, barely old enough to form words, and certainly not old enough to lose my mother. But we had been on the run for a dozen years. Hiding. She never dared let herself sleep. Until the day she carried me over a frigid mountain range where we almost froze to death, into an abandoned camp––and allowed herself a single day of rest.

A single day where she made sure I stayed safely inside while she slept. While she healed. While she regenerated. A process that should have taken years—but she only planned one sunpass for. Her body haggard and spent, desperate for rest. As she slept there, sunk deep into sleep, I could still hear her voice in my head. Keeping me company. The flicker of her subconscious reaching for me.

Only, somehow, the Hollow Ones found us.

"No!" I scream internally, digging my fingers into the icy ground. Trying to escape reliving it. I refuse to release a scream and put Father in any more danger than I already have. He's grabbing me, dragging me away from our hiding place.

I can still see the intruders in my mind's eye, overwhelmed by the memory of them bursting through the door, ripping it off its hinges. Three Hollow warriors in those wretched masks, shrieking in victory and carrying curved spears. I crawled under the bed where Mama slept, curled into a ball, furs pulled around me, hands clamped over my ears—but I could still hear her screams consuming my thoughts.

I couldn't move. Couldn't protect her from the monsters. Only hide till it was too late.

Then my last shred of terror ignited. Lit the boiling heat trapped inside my chilled, shaking body.

I was barely old enough to walk the first time I razed a Hollow One's house to the ground. Left it nothing but ashes.

The same day the hunters ruthlessly ripped my mother apart in front of me.

"Aaagh!" I bite out a gasp as Father drags my limp body over the bleak terrain. I force my legs under me to keep up. My hand strays to my shoulder blades—fingers burrowing into the scars there. The ones Father said were necessary. The scars he said ground me to this world. Remind me what it takes to survive. The numbness starts to recede, my vision sharpening. Legs growing stronger. I wipe away the dribble of warm blood leaking from my nose.

But even as I drown the memory in that well of fire in my chest, the heat churns deep in my gut. A raw, open wound. Volatile.

I try to focus on the sloping mountains in the distance as Father and I trudge across the snowbank, deathly quiet. Try to rivet my attention on the frigid wind crawling over my flushed nose and cheeks. Try to ground myself in the snow melting beneath my palms, cooling the heat pulsating in waves over my body. Boiling just under my skin.

"Run! They've seen us!"

Father fills my vision with his dark hood and fierce eyes. Grabbing my arm and picking up our pace. We race across the icy ground, even as the thudding feet of the Hollow hunting party pursue on our heels. We're their new prey.

"Focus, Mara!" Father screams into my head. *"You can't feel this."* The sentence is a command. One that whiplashes through my *ero* and numbs the dangerous emotions bundled deep. But the force of it slices through my thoughts with a pain all its own.

Father is right. I led us into a trap.

I should have sensed them. I should have stayed away.

He tried to warn me.

I cannot let him down again.

If Mama hadn't already been dead, my first explosion would have killed her. The fire that burns hotter than any other and scars even our own people. I sometimes wonder if—like Father—my mother was running to hide me from the world.

I won't let my volatile body hurt anyone else.

My *ero* is mine. I can control it. I must.

Forcing my body to stay upright and my quivering legs to match Father's pace, I ball my fists. *Shut it down.* My nails bite into my palms—and break skin.

Oh—oh, no.

I hadn't meant to press that hard. To let it out.

But the release feels strangely good.

Thin streams of *alia,* blazing liquid lifeblood, run in rivulets down my shaking hands. The golden-red fire flickers and gleams as it traces thin paths, and then splashes against the icy ground below. It immediately sizzles, burning through the ice and showing bits of dark, volcanic rock underneath.

I focus on my breathing, on the nipping wind, focus on letting those shallow wounds close.

Father's tense shoulders soften slightly, and he gestures for us to take a hard left. Toward the ravine we walked around earlier.

We only stop running when we come to the edge. I glance over my shoulder. We're faster than the Hollow Ones on foot, but they're still gaining on us. The glint of their spears cast pricks of light across the frozen landscape. They're only seconds away.

"Father?" I peer down into the ravine, trying to catch my breath. The deep chasm fades into nothingness, crusted by snow. Only one of us can fly.

He shakes out his wings again, stretches their dark, crystalline breadth, and reaches for me.

"Hold on tight."

One arm wraps around my waist, and then he's throwing us off the edge. He shudders mid-air and we sink for a painfully long moment, crashing back into the wall behind us. I lock the gasp inside and cling to him, his body dangerously gaunt. *"Come on, Father!"*

He grunts, sweat running down his face. He beats his wings with several powerful strokes and we start to gain height. His entire body thrashes as he forces his wings to lift us up over the ravine.

The edge of the other side flashes beneath me and his wings stutter and give out. We both fall into the hard-packed snow.

I struggle to my feet and reach for Father. He's shaking, his wings splayed at a weird angle. He pulls them back in, a cough wracking his body. I grab his arm and help him to his feet.

"Father?" I'm not sure what to ask, but he leans against me and forces us to keep moving. My breath comes in quick, pained beats. But we're safely out of reach of the Hollow. For now.

As we gain speed trekking across the frigid landscape, I chance another glance over my shoulder at the hunting party tailing us. The small group of Hollow Ones is stopped on the opposite side of the ravine, cursing behind their helmets and thrusting their weapons into the air. A few of them try throwing a spear across the divide or shooting off a volley of arrows.

The weapons clatter against the edge of the ravine and fall into the darkness below.

"Mara, we must keep moving." Father grips my arm and pulls me, his words viscerally shoving away my own darker thoughts.

It will take the Hollow far too long to traverse the ravine and find our tracks again, and by then we'll be long gone. But he isn't taking any chances.

We blur our footprints as we walk, and another flurry of snow comes along and helps to further hide us. The cold starts to stick to my lungs, and it takes us painstakingly long to double back before heading in the direction of the temple.

Father is being careful. But the damage is already done.

I practically led us into an ambush. And then I froze.

The undercurrent of fear ripples off Father in waves. He's not making eye contact, just trudging through the snow. Angular shoulders shifting beneath his ragged coat. If I lean in, I can make out the echo of his mounting dread. At least, what doubts he lets me graze past.

Ashen whispers swirl deep in my *ero* like a mounting snowstorm. That cryptic voice I bury, along with all the fears that seem to rise like sparks from a spitting fire. Why are the attacking thoughts always the loudest? *I hid when Mama needed me most. What if I freeze up when Father and our village are vulnerable too?*

"We're here, little one." Father's voice is soft, tinged with a note of sympathy. His tone pulls me out of the swirling blizzard dampening my mind.

I lift my head to see the familiar stretch of almost-translucent frost that always forms over the entrance to our home. This particular channel of magma tubes is buried deep beneath a small valley of jagged, snow-coated hills. It's so dark, I glance up to make sure the sun is still there.

The dim crimson ball still dangles precariously over our heads. But every day it dulls a little more. Dying like the world around us. As a child, I used to beg Mama for stories of how the world used to be. Myths of the flaming, flying creatures who could kiss the sun.

I watch Father's frail form bend and press a hand to the mirrored ice beneath our feet, see him strain to force heat to his skin.

The sun isn't the only thing dying.

Father is too. And what remains of our people, if they can't have the rest they need.

Freezing from the inside out.

CHAPTER FOUR

I duck around Father, kneel beside him, and rub my hands together. Glimmers of fire dance over the lines of my palm. I press it against the chilled surface, and my heated blood starts to sizzle. Cracks spiderweb across the ice, and the thin sheet groans around us.

We take a half step back and then Father slams a boot into the splintered section. It gives way, falling through a dark hole rimmed in charred, volcanic rock. An entrance to a *nemior*—a magma tube.

This is one of the largest entrances we've found to the interconnective maze of magma tubes deep beneath our feet. They run all over this planet, and in the myths, used to flow with magma and connected to the fire-breathing cones that towered above the plains. Now, our volcanic world is as barren as the animals struggling to survive—but at least the thick walls of these *nemior* keep in just enough warmth for some creatures to do so.

Until the last tendrils of heat run out along with our sun.

"Ready?" Father asks. There's a sense of finality in his tone, and I swallow. Once we step inside, there's no going back. We'll have to explain why the only fresh hunt we have is the lone *argot* and handful of small *reiva* Father caught before I found him. Why we'll have to stretch the food again, dried meat and the spindly moss that grows inside these tubes.

This is my fault. I will face it.

"Keep up." He jumps into the *nemior*. Father lands hard, and his pained grunt echoes back to me. I leap in after him.

We walk quickly through the curving, softly heated tunnel. Even a few steps in, the subtle presence of warmth starts to filter in through my heavy coat. I undo a few knots and let the hood fall away from my face.

As we get closer to our little encampment, slowly my *ero* fills with other voices. The comforting, familiar tone of our people. The *fior-errans*, as they call themselves. Forsaken by this world, but remembered by each other. Our little flock. Warm and loud and chattering. A soothing chorus of different tones all speaking to each other and around each other. Animated. Excited.

Expectant of our return.

"The child is back! She found him!" I know it's Hana's voice, even before I can see her. She'd been nervous for me when I snuck out to find Father.

Now she and the others are going to really wish I'd stayed home.

Father lets out a long sigh, limping beside me. He was limping when I found him earlier too. *"Were you hurt, Father?"* I push the question directly into his thoughts.

He gives a sharp shake of his head. *"It doesn't matter."*

As we round a bend in the tunnel framework, the chorus of voices in my head grows louder. Welcoming.

Two more steps, and the tunnel widens, opening into a sprawling cavern easily a hundred feet high. The volcanic rock is smoother in here, the walls softened from years of wings beating against it.

We've hidden here for the past fifty years. Before that, we'd lived in a nook high in the mountains.

The best part of this place is the temple carved out of the volcanic rock itself, rising from the dark floor. Covered in carvings of myths and narratives, four pillars hold up the domed roof and walls of the ancient structure.

While a small place of worship, this temple was once a flourishing hub and trading post. The magma would freely bubble up from these tubes, turning to lava that ran in rivers through this planet. A kind of heat that didn't endanger our people and brought warmth to the tropical land. It's said that even the jungles that grew around the pooling streams of lava knew how to feed off the golden canals and not be burnt by them.

Now, the walls are missing chunks, and straggly weeds crawl over most of the pillars. Any ceremonial items that used to be here were long since stolen, leaving behind only strange, spiraling markings in the cavern ground, with deep drainage holes every several feet. I can only wonder what the ruts were once used for.

Water? Gifts from the worshippers? Something else entirely?

My boots pad softly across the pockmarked surface, heels skimming the curve of a shallow trench that curls outward from the heart of the temple. The voices in my head swell with excitement. The cavern is filled with two dozen of us—tall, spindly creatures with dark wings draping from their shoulders. Crystalized wings that flicker with liquid fire trapped inside each jagged feather.

The *fior-errans*. Forsaken Ones with Wings, the name they gave themselves when the Hollow Ones forced Father and the rest out of their homes in the mountains and into the icy cold of the Forsaken Lands.

At least we Forsaken Ones still have each other. They've already packed up most of our supplies, the woven baskets piled in a corner. Each of the worn-looking creatures has prepared for their *aethor* sleep. There are piles of furs on top of coats and jackets set out in a semicircle.

Awaiting the flock's rest.

Just seeing the dozens of makeshift beds makes my stomach twist.

"Mara! You made it." Hana is the first to look up from readying her bed, and she sweeps toward me. She always looks fragile, her pale face, skeletal cheekbones, and dewy eyes set against the wisps of dark hair that escape from her thinning braid and rim her face. But in the flickering light of this cavern, lit only by the soft glow of my people's wings, she seems even more delicate.

She reaches for me with quivering, bony hands, then pauses. Eyes widening. And glances up at Father.

"What happened?" she asks us both.

He looks away. *"There was a hunting party. They took our larger prey. They almost got Mara."*

Hana purses her lips. *"Shael! They are getting closer and closer to finding us."*

Father places a thin hand on my shoulder.

"We must be even more careful. I don't believe the child is ready yet. She nearly got us both killed." His words rain down around me like a hailstorm. His breathing is labored. *"I will stay awake one more cycle with her. We will protect our people together."*

I lift my eyes slowly and take in Father's downturned mouth. The crease of his pale forehead.

It's the most logical decision. I don't deserve his trust.

With his voice in my head, he would help me protect our people. He would help me drown that haunting echo of screams. He would help me shut out the writhing fury in my chest.

But I can't ignore that Father is very sick. He almost didn't make it across that ravine. Sleep may not be enough to heal him. If Father stays awake with me and dies, then his death really will be on my hands. In the past, he would trade off – sometimes Hana would stay awake with me, sometimes Father, as the others slept. But now, they are all far too sickly. And I only have to sleep after I explode – so as long as I can keep my flame in check, I can keep watch over them. Something that terrifies Father more than he'd admit.

But, I can't let him risk himself. I've already lost one parent. I can't risk the family I've found.

I lift my shoulders a bit, raise my chin, and meet his eyes.

"Father, you need sleep."

His expression turns dark in a way I've never seen. But I've never challenged him like this.

My breath falters, but I keep going. *"I promise I can do this."* Even if it pushes me to the breaking point – I know the consequences if I freeze again. *"I will make my mind strong like yours. I will protect you all."*

I'll prove to him somehow this was the right choice. That I'm still a good daughter.

CHAPTER FIVE

"Mara." Father's wings arch around him and he descends on me, words quick and cutting. Searching for my weakness. *"You cannot make this decision yourself."*

Hana gives me an apologetic look, but drifts away, knowing she can't get in the middle of this. None of them can.

My eyes burn as I turn to face him. *"I know. I know I'm not ready, Father. But if you don't sleep"*—I bite my lip—*"I'll lose you too. And I can't lose you."*

As the devastation marring each quivering word settles over him, fading into the reaches of his mind, his wings soften back around him. His hackles lowering as he realizes I'm not asking to override his authority.

I'm asking to stop hiding. To protect him, as he's protected me.

"I would sacrifice anything for you. To keep you all safe." I tell him, echoing the same words he's told us over and over. *Sacrifices keep us safe.* The scars along my spine twinge at that, but I lift my chin. I will not lose my family again.

"Please, let me do this."

His eyes narrow. He searches inside my thoughts with such force that the tug of his consciousness makes my head hammer. Finally, the tension in his sharp jaw eases. *"I will leave you behind on one condition."*

I hold my breath. *"Yes?"*

His next words fill my head with such ferocity, they drown out the other dozens of phoenixes in the room. *"You must promise me the Hollow will not capture you alive."*

My knees almost buckle at the intensity of his voice, his words splintering through my head. "Father?"

"Promise me, Mara." His hands clamp my shoulders. *"They will creep into your* ero. *If they attack you—or worse, if they discover what you are . . ."* His eyes are intense, frantic. *"We are all doomed. You are better off dead than captured by the Hollow Ones. Do you understand?"*

I just stare at him. "I-I think so."

He now grips my arm so firmly that I gasp in pain. *"Do you understand?"*

With every word, he reaches deeper into my *ero*. His telepathic link is an extension of the fingers he's digging into me. His thoughts root around in my mind and dredge up the screams I've worked so hard to lock away.

He pulls the memory to the surface like a clap of thunder. I fall to my knees, arms over my head, trying to block it out. The bloodcurdling shrieks.

My own mother's cries for help.

"S-stop!" I beg, clawing at my head, clawing at him. "Make it stop!"

But Father doesn't. He simply kneels, facing me, and shakes me again. *"If you trust the Hollow Ones, they will take everything from you. If you let them find us, our screams will drive you mad. You must do whatever it takes to keep them away from us. And from yourself."*

I'm trembling. *"Yes, Father. I'll keep them away. I promise."*

As Mama's screams echo louder and louder in my head, churning with Father's forceful words, that bubbling fire deep inside starts to spill out too. Heat pulsates through my body, turning my skin a flickering orange. Father abruptly lets go of me and staggers. His eyes flicker, taking in my trembling body. Thin lines of flaming blood start to drip from my palms where I'd accidentally cut myself earlier.

I feel the blood run down my shoulders, pouring from the raw wounds along my spine that never quite healed. My own fire is making my body ache and spasm.

"Mara, calm down." His voice is steady, but it's a façade. I see the fear in his eyes. *"This is not the time. Settle your fire. I only meant to remind you."*

"I'm trying," I spit out through clenched lips. I bend over to plant my palms against the cool, volcanic ground. Trying to orient myself. To push all the boiling, fiery pain back into its box.

I'm trying, Father.

I wipe the dribbles of gleaming blood off on my coat, lifting my head to find the rest of the phoenixes huddled in one corner of the room, watching through their pale irises.

They've seen this before. They know what will happen if I let the fire out.

Even Hana stands with them, body tense. Their voices are uncharacteristically quiet and dull. I try not to listen in, but I can't help hearing the snatches of words and emotions. Their uncertainty. Their whispers. *"What is she? Is her power growing?"*

None of them were ever this volatile.

And none of them were ever a child. I am the first of our kind to age, and to start out so tiny, so young. A baby Mama said she found, hidden in a crater. Far too full of flame to be anything other than full-blooded phoenix—but also, nothing like the rest of them.

My flame doesn't bring me into a peaceful *aethor* sleep. It just burns everything in its path to the ground.

Deep down, my flock still doesn't know how to fully trust me.

Their thoughts chorus through my head, over and over:

"Shove it down. Shove it down. Shove it down."

But I've been shoving it down for two hundred years. Shoving away the pain. The grief.

I'm not sure how much longer I can.

Has my own *ero* already betrayed me?

"Listen to my voice, nora . . ." Hana's soft tone drifts into my thoughts like a welcome breath of air. I lift my eyes to search out her kind ones, even as Father takes a few more steps back. He's repeating

for me to stave off the fire, to control it, but it's Hana's words that actually start to cool the raw wound cut open deep inside. The raw wound that bleeds fire.

"You're safe, **nora,***"* Hana whispers in my *ero.* She steps closer. *"You're safe here. And so are we. No one is hurt. You can breathe. You're safe."*

Her words start to slow the racing of my heartbeat. Start to cool the heat raging over my body. Start to soften my panic.

"What is your name, **nora?***"* Hana asks, picking up a blanket as she comes toward me. I can hear the rest of their voices telling her to stay back, but she reaches for my hand.

"Mara." I answer her question through cracked lips. "My name is Mara."

She helps me to my feet and gently drapes a blanket over my shoulders. *"And who are you, Mara?"*

The question should be easy to answer, but any response lodges in my throat along with a choking sob. The fire has almost completely ebbed, leaving an empty pain in its wake.

"I'm not sure who I am. Especially without you and Father."

Hana gently smooths my hair back. *"You're our* **nora,** *that's who you are. A* **fior-erran,** *one of us."*

As I sag against her, Hana's words echo through my head, pouring relief into the shattered places. She keeps brushing my hair, and I hear a shuffle as the rest of our small flock detaches from hiding behind the temple walls and moves closer.

Out of the corner of my eye, I can see Father watching. His expression is hauntingly stoic.

Hana tucks the blanket around me. *"You can let out some of that fire later. For now, we need your help with the* **aethor** *sleep."*

I wipe my dripping nose and blink back the blur in my eyes. A part of me feels ashamed at even showing this kind of weakness in front of her, but it helps steady my pulse. "Alright."

"Are you stable?" When I give a hesitant nod, Father leaves me leaning against a temple pillar and quickly joins the circles of whispering phoenixes.

I take in the room of Forsaken Ones. The temple is practically empty. Everything we own stuffed in the woven baskets and locked away in a storage room. The main courtyard is now filled with rows of makeshift bedding and furs.

I'll have to drag each of them onto those beds when they start to reform.

There are fewer than thirty of us left, and even fewer that are well enough to hunt.

My back against the carved surface of the pillar, I focus on the warmth from my flock that hums and swirls around me. This deep in the *nemior* passageways, I can also feel another source of heat, living and breathing beneath my feet. The core of the planet simmering and humming with energy.

I watch my little family buzz with activity as they gather up their beds of furs and move them closer together. A bead of sweat runs down my temples as I watch them bind up a handful of open wounds on each other—gashes left from recent fights with the Hollow. Fights with weapons that leave wounds not easily healed.

And they mend more slowly than ever these days. *How long will it take them to wake up this time?*

A shiver sweeps me—*how long will I be alone?*

Most of our people are covered in scars, wings drooping from their shoulders. The fiery blood inside them is already dimmed in a way I can physically feel. I watch them bundle up, even here, in our own home. Fighting not to freeze from the inside out.

It's ironic. The Hollow Ones hunt the phoenixes to use their blood as a source of warmth—but these flame-creatures are starting to lose their heat just as much as the rest of the world.

I run my fingers over the carvings etched into the pillar. Old stories of when the world wasn't consumed by ice. When there were jungles and seas and waterfalls. My eyes trace where the curve of the pillar drifts to meet the domed roof and remnants of the temple.

This catacomb used to be a place of warmth and worship. Father once told me the Hollow would come to them from miles away to get a glimpse of the fiery creatures with wings. To lay treasure and prayers at their feet. To bask in their glow.

And then the sun started to die.

And the Hollow Ones began to hunt the creatures they'd seen as gods.

All of that was long before Mama found me as a tiny baby. This is all I've ever known.

CHAPTER SIX

A deep pang of homesickness cuts through me as I watch the small remnants of a once mighty race feast on scraps of dried meat and the roots and shrubbery found inside the tunnels.

As difficult as their lives have always been, they found me. Took me in.

Their bent, haggard forms and chaotic, loud voices in my head are as comforting and familiar as a warm coat in a storm. They let me be one of them. They've risked their lives countless times for me.

I'm one of their flock.

A *fior-erran.*

I wish I could freeze this moment. This familiar bustle—voices chattering in my head as they eat our last stores of food. The jokes and stories and tending to each other.

It's so vibrant. So alive.

But by the end of this night, it will all be gone. And I will be alone. Again.

Tears well and my throat feels thick. I blink quickly. Hana sits against a temple pillar across the room, bracing herself. She's working to rebandage a wound on her shoulder, but struggling to reach it around her sloping wing.

I go to her and crouch down. "Here, let me help."

She lifts teary, exhausted eyes with gratitude. **"*Thank you*, nora."**

She always calls me that. *Child.* But with gentleness, not the touch of forbearance Father has when he uses it. I take the salve and strip of material from her, leaning in for a closer look.

"When did this happen?"

A nasty gash runs between her wings where they taper out from her shoulder blades. I wipe crusted blood away from the wound, the dark color similar to the tone of her pinions. Each of her crystalized feathers flicker with a bit of liquid blood boiling inside.

"Two days ago. A Hollow with a **reer** *blade."*

I wince. I hadn't noticed her come in after going hunting. But even hearing the words *reer* blade makes me nauseous. Only our own feathers are sharp enough to cut the skin of a phoenix. So when the Hollow Ones hunt us, if they can't fell an entire creature, they will go for our wings. Splinter our crystallized lifeblood from our bodies.

Use our own feathers to cut away our wings.

Phantom pains rip down my back, white-hot, and I grit my teeth. *Focus, Mara!*

I start to apply the salve for Hana, but her big, silvery eyes peer at me closely. "Do your scars still hurt?"

I don't answer at first. I layer on the salve and then wrap the strips of cloth around her shoulder and chest. "'A cut from a *reer* blade never truly heals.' That's the way it works, right?" Father's warning flashes through my thoughts. I try to sound casual, unworried. Well-adjusted.

Like I don't hate having to do it every few years.

Like I don't panic any time I think I feel something starting to grow along my back. The faintest hint of something pressing through the skin along my shoulder blades.

But she's not accepting it.

"Would you like me to help you with your bandages next, *nora?*"

Hana is the only one of our flock I've ever heard speak aloud—and it's become like a shared language for us. Her coaxing me to not be afraid to use my voice is part of why I've fallen into the habit even around Father.

I shake my head. "No, it's alright. I'll need to redo my bandages on my own while you're in the *aethor* sleep anyway."

I've been bandaging my own wounds since I was small.

Hana studies me for a long moment, strands of her dark, stringy hair falling over sharp cheekbones. "And you'll also have to check the bandages of the village every ten sunpasses."

I finish tying off her wound, take a step back, and repeat the details Father has rehearsed with me a hundred times.

"Yes, I'll rebandage the flock, as well as make sure this room stays warm and safe. You won't need to eat."

Using her shaking wings to brace herself, Hana slowly gets to her feet. Her dark, crystalline feathers clatter against the floor. If she were healthier, she'd be able to melt the sharp feathers back into their liquid, fiery form and absorb the blood back into her body, instead of letting her cauterized wings drape outside.

But Hana is tired. Dangerously so.

I see it in her eyes—and the eyes of every other phoenix here. Most of them will just tuck their wings around themselves when they start the *aethor* process. Too exhausted to even absorb the energy back into themselves.

I only hope rest will restore them.

"It will, Mara," Hana whispers into my thoughts. I look up at her. Even in her stooped condition, she's still significantly taller than me. "But it may take us a while to reform. That is a long time for a *nora* to be alone."

And there it is. The truth I've been trying to avoid.

I swivel slowly on my heel, taking in the whole of the room again. Father is helping one of our most frail people settle onto her mat. Other phoenixes are clearing away the last of our boxes and rations.

This room will soon feel very empty. I will be the only one awake for sunpasses—possibly years. The only one who can protect them.

Maybe Father is right. Maybe I can't do this.

A cool hand cups the side of my face, and Hana bends down to be at eye level with me. ***"Your Father worries about a great many things. He has taught you well. You have learned well."*** She taps my temple with a trembling finger, whispering the next words aloud: "Trust your *ero*."

That's just the problem. Father doesn't trust my *ero*, and deep down—neither do I.

The scars that rip across my shoulder blades twinge. A reminder of the first time I endangered my flock. And what I had to give up to keep them safe.

When Father first cut away my wings—

"What if the Hollow attack, Hana? What if they find us? What do I do?"

What if I freeze up again?

She tips her head to the side, speaking aloud, voice low enough that Father can't hear. "The Hollow Ones will hunt us." Her eyes spark and she points a finger at me. "But if they find us, I pity them. Because you, Mara, have more fire than all of us combined."

I sigh. "Fire isn't any good if I can't control it. I could hurt all of you."

My fire doesn't bring healing like true phoenix fire. It only consumes.

I could destroy them all in an instant, wiping out the Hollow and my own people.

She gives a wry chuckle. "When you need to, you will. I still remember the first day your Father found you and brought you to us." Her eyes glisten. "The rest of the village was terrified when they'd heard what you'd done. But I was . . ." She pauses, looking wistful. "I was proud. And I knew that this tiny fire-*nora* needed us for now. Needed us to guard her as she grew. But that someday"—she leans in close again, giving me a gentle smile—"someday, you would guard us back, Mara."

Her faith in me fills my lungs with something almost like hope.

I wrap her in a hug, careful not to overpower her skeletal frame, but burying my face into her chest all the same. "Thank you."

Hana hugs me as well, and then we join the rest of the phoenixes, who have all congregated in the center of the curved room under the domed temple roof.

"Are we ready for the* aethor *sleep?" Father's booming voice echoes through every mind in the room.

Two dozen pale creatures all rise and clatter their crystalline wings in a cacophony of agreement. *"Let us begin!"*

Father shakes out his wings, looking down at me. *"You'll want to hide, little one. Once the ceremony starts, we cannot stop it, and I don't want you getting burned."*

He seems to have made his peace with leaving me behind.

I back up to stand at the entrance to the chamber, where the magma tube curls into a sharp corner. All the phoenixes cluster around each other and form a tight circle, wings arched over their heads and curving around each other like a shield.

Even now, I can hardly believe it's starting. No matter how many times I've seen them do this, how many times Father and I stood guard while they slept, it still haunts me.

At least this time, I'm not at their center. Not the thing they are bracing against.

The phoenixes beat their wings in unison, lifting off the ground, flying several feet in the air, the tops of their wings brushing the dark rock overhead.

An uncomfortable shiver works its way down my arms—this is better. This is much safer than the other times they've had to use their wings to protect themselves.

The times that Father used to set off my own explosion, forcing our flock to stay within reach of my blast. It was to temper their bodies to withstand my heat, he said.

When I was small, I couldn't control it as well. And Father knew if we didn't do something, I would destroy them in their sleep.

So he would have them stand at the edge of my explosions. He'd slip into my *ero*, whisper three words, and then the flames would turn my body inside out.

And they would hover at the very edge of my blast.

I shudder as I watch their mighty wings beat the air. I think of the amount of times I would wake and find them nursing burns I'd unwillingly given them.

But eventually it started to work. And as my flame grew in ferocity, it still had the capacity to burn them—but at least they had tempered their bodies to my fire enough that they could survive.

Hopefully. It's been a while since any of the flock have been caught in my blast.

I can still hear their screams echoing in my head from the hundreds of times Father put them near a tiny child trying to hold her explosive nature inside . . . and set me off.

I almost can't watch them transform this time. But somehow, I force my eyes open.

And then, one by one, they dissolve.

It starts in their wings, the feathers shattering and cracking in a way that must be painful. The flickering, dark blue blood inside spills out through the shards of feathers. And as their wings splinter and absorb back into their bodies, their pale skin begins to dissolve too.

I back up until my body is sheltered around the corner of the *nemior,* my head craned to stare up at them. I hear their moans and shrieks in my head—but this pain is different. It's more like the pain of childbirth.

Of bringing forth something new.

Their pale skin splits open, letting the dull, smoldering blue tone of their blood flow out and cover their bodies. Their forms turn inside out, the lines and frames of their bodies blurring as the dying fire that flows through their veins consumes them. Their silhouettes stretch and fade into the form of a giant bird.

One by one, each of the phoenixes split apart into flame, and soon, their fiery, raging forms fill the entire chamber.

But even seeing them like this, in their true forms, for what is my dozenth time witnessing this process—I can see just how weak they've become. Their phoenix forms are dull and flickering, and much smaller than the last time. Even their *ero,* finally on the outside now, is weak and dying.

The transformation only feels real when I see Hana's body split open. When her eyes find mine a second before she's consumed by the cobalt fire.

Father is the last to let himself transform. As the rest of the flock hover in their air, spiraling beings of flame, he turns. Reaches out for me with his mind.

I can almost feel his familiar touch, like a hand on my cheek, even as the flames of the others in their corporeal forms scorch my face.

"Are you sure?" he asks one last time.

I suck in a deep breath. *"Yes. I promise I'll protect you."*

I promise I'll make you proud.

He nods. *"Be safe, little one."*

I take a few steps farther into the tunnel. I know what is coming, but my mouth still drops open when my father's wings break and twist and collapse into his body. I stare as the fire in his bones splits open his skin and the flames consume his whole form. Devouring him until my father is unrecognizable, leaving behind a blazing bird of seething blue flame.

And just like that, with every phoenix now fully transformed, they all arch their bodies, beaks pointing at the roof. Their voices are a loud chorus in my head for a final time—

"No er, elion del aethor!"

No fear, we rise in sleep!

I turn and flee from them.

But I can still hear the blast as they all explode. The heat spirals at my back even as I race down the tunnel. This must have been how they felt when I would ignite—dashing away to stay at the edge of the carnage. A crack of blue fire spirals through the cavern like a comet and singes my coat.

Boiling flame chars the volcanic tube, sustained for a stretching minute—and then collapses. Vanishes. Fading, like they have. It's over.

I inch back into the cavern.

The walls are scorched an even deeper black, and every single inch of the temple is covered in pale ash. It coats the floor and walls and pillars.

The sight turns my stomach, but I force myself not to look away.

These are my people. It will take a few days, but eventually, their bodies will start to reform. Regenerate. And they will need me here to drag them onto their bed mats. To watch over them. To bind any wounds.

They are most vulnerable while in stasis.

In the meantime, I will keep watch.

Using a thick piece of rawhide, I bind off the entrance to the temple, closing them in, and then go to find my pack of supplies where I'd stowed it deeper in the magma tube.

I haul my pack back to the entrance and hunker down outside the temple, tucking the blanket Hana gave me around myself. It's so quiet.

Deathly quiet.

The stone doesn't even breathe around me. No chatter of the flock in my head.

I curl up outside the temple, waiting for my father and the others to rise from ashes, and shiver as a sharp chill races down my spine.

For the first time in two hundred years, I don't have Father's voice in my head.

For the first time, it's just me.

I'm alone.

CHAPTER SEVEN

I don't like my head when it's quiet.

My thoughts rattle around, bouncing off each other and spiraling into haunting, dark places. Dangerous places without Father there to temper me.

I try to hum, try to fill the silence, but it's not as comforting as usual.

What if something is wrong? It's been over ninety sunpasses already—they should be healing faster.

The doubts niggle at the back of my *ero*. That inner-place where the other phoenixes listened and Father set up camp. His consciousness so near he could hear my direct thoughts as audibly as if spoken aloud. He was always there, hovering, soothing, covering my doubts with his whispers and softening the pounding fire in my veins.

What if I am somehow hurting them? If Father were here, he'd know what to do.

My mind forever circles back to that.

Even though I've run through the process a hundred times—even though I have been bandaging wounds for weeks now as the phoenixes slowly regenerate from ash, their bodies tender and healing painstakingly slowly.

Still . . . something doesn't seem right.

I shake off my uncertainty and step away from the cave wall where I've been standing nearly motionless for hours. There at the edge of the temple chamber, just watching them. Watching the deathly still figures that I've covered and wrapped, lying on the makeshift beds I moved them onto as soon as they had reformed enough to be safely lifted.

If I squint, I can just make out the shallow rise and fall of their chests. But their skin is grey and translucent. Their fiery blood murky in blue veins under their pallid complexions.

I cross the cool stone floor, barefoot to remind myself of the general temperature of the stone they are lying so close to. I should look to Father first, but instead my eyes are drawn to Hana. To where she lies on one of the softest beds I could find, tucked in a slightly warmer area of the room, where the heat is trapped a little closer.

She seems to be doing the worst of anyone.

She has always been frail, but her body is far too skeletal, especially this far through the process. I've been tending her wounds daily, trying to soften the rawness of her skin knitting itself back together. Tissue reforming over bone and muscle.

But none of my flock are healing fast enough.

I can't even hear their heartbeats.

And with every day that passes as I stand by, watching and waiting and doing what I can to make them comfortable, the terrifying silence in my head grows more and more painful. The emptiness inside seems to claw at my last shreds of certainty.

What if they left the wrong person awake?

I wish Father were here. Wish he could whisper in my thoughts and steady my nerves and show me what I'm doing wrong. There must be something. The ache of it, of how devastatingly incapable I must be, crawls under my skin.

Tugging the threadbare blanket up around Hana's pallid shoulders, I lay a soft kiss against her forehead. *I'm trying. I really am.*

I just don't know what else to do.

I cross to kneel beside the bed of layered blankets and animal furs where Father lies. He's silent as death, eyes closed like in sleep. But even when he slept—a rare occurrence, at that—I could still hear him in my head.

But this time, when I reach out, softly whispering his name,

"Father? Please talk to me," there's nothing. Just that aching silence. A kind of aloneness that I haven't felt since I lost . . .

Since Mama.

I press my fingers into my closed eyes, rooting myself in the steady pressure. Trying to slow the skittering pulse of my heartbeat kicking up. The flush of heat swells from my suddenly tight throat and streams over my body. My pale skin starts to take on an orange hue as the fire inside flares to the surface.

I launch to my feet, hurrying out of the cobbled-together infirmary and duck around the corner of the magma tube. I press my entire body against the cool, curved wall and strive to soak in the chill, to ground myself in the uneven feel of the stone.

"You are here," I whisper to myself, attempting to pull my thoughts away from those raw, broiling emotions that sit like a flickering coal in my core. "Father is here, even if you can't hear him."

But the words echo even more hollowly in this empty chamber.

My attention flickers to what Father was so afraid of. Out there. The Hollow. *They must have a camp somewhere.* I wonder where. I could go see.

I cover the top of my head with my hands. My own brain has gone a bit mad from the silence.

That is the *worst* idea.

I shake my head at myself. Go out there? Go looking for the Hollow? I squeeze my eyes shut. What if I led them back here?

Just the possibility starts to make my blood boil again. My joints ache. What if I let the same thing happen to them that happened to Mama?

Bile fills my throat as panic starts to rise. What am I doing? What am I *thinking?*

You're needed here. Stay here. You are here. Stay here.

The chant starts to form proverbial threads to tether me to this place. To the world outside my head. Away from my own doubts and thoughts. To the day I'm living now—not the night that always tries to pull me back.

Father would slide inside my head in these moments and brush aside the memories. The ones that swell when I least want them. That bring the nausea and numbness. He was always there, inside my head, keeping me safe.

Am I safe with only my own voice inside?

I don't want to know the answer.

My stomach growls unceremoniously, and I cling to the distraction like a warm gust during a frigid hunt. I head further down the *nemior* tube. Light glints off the walls from the small bits of flickering, flaming blood still pooling in some of the deeper crannies in the pockmarked walls. Leftover dribbles from the countless flaming wings that used to beat against them.

But even the gleam from the liquid fire grows duller every day.

I take another turn and enter a small side alcove where I've packed away my stores. Handwoven baskets filled with dried meat and shriveled greenery that tastes like char but is at least something. One of the baskets holds a tiny herb garden that Hana managed to coax to life and is nearly as valuable *as* life. She spent hours showing me how to tend it and make healing pastes out of the leaves and stems. She foraged the plants over the years – and has been cultivating this tiny garden as if our lives depend on it. With every passing moment they sleep, I realize she was right. They do. I don't dare even lift the cover off the tiny store growing until it's time to water and sun the plants.

More bits of fire ricochet off the walls in here, illuminating images etched in the rough volcanic rock. Drawings carved with a small hand years and years ago. An echo of a much younger Mara.

I measure out a small scrap of dried *argot* meat and a palmful of withered cavern-plant leaves, and ladle out a bit of water from melted snow. It will barely make a dent in my hunger, but it's better than nothing.

I'll need to go hunt before the next moon-change.

It will only be the third time I've ventured out of these caves for food—and I may need to hunt farther than the last two times.

Pulling out my own folded pile of woven blankets and settling cross-legged on them, I force myself to eat the dried meat and leaves slowly, savoring the improvised meal. I let my eyes fall closed, settling into a fantasy of this moment where the room is filled with some of my flock. Imagining Hana sits beside me, eating fresh-made bread from wheat we haven't been able to grow in over a decade, and telling stories of the days when the world was young.

I take another small nibble of my dried meal, bringing their voices to life so loudly in my head, I can almost trick myself into believing they're real. That they're actually here. Whole and safe and filling my small world with warmth.

In these moments, as I hide inside the memories, letting them fill the empty space, I can almost believe I'm not alone.

That the world hasn't abandoned us.

That this couldn't last sunpasses, let alone years.

That I won't slowly lose parts of myself to the quiet the longer I stay here without them.

"Father?" I manage one more feeble time. Pressing my thoughts toward where I know he is in the other room. *"I . . . I miss you."*

I miss them all.

And the longer time passes without their voices in my head, without their steadying tone to help me sort through the clash and clatter inside my own head, the more I begin to miss myself.

Their voices in my head were a comfort. A familiar presence. With them, I knew who I was.

Now, it's just my voice, and the haunting echo of something that feels like it could hurt them again.

Now I'm not sure of my own voice.

I don't trust my own mind.

And that's most terrifying of all.

CHAPTER EIGHT

I slowly open my eyes and take in the patterns scribbled along the wall in a childlike hand. Charcoal swirls and silhouettes that I'd drawn on the curved, dark tone of the magma tube. When we'd first ventured down here to live decades ago, I'd been uncertain of the entire situation. The winged apparition I eventually came to call Father had found me in the wreckage of the Hollow village I'd razed to the ground. I was covered in soot and tear streaks, hands colored with my mother's blood.

And rather than being afraid of me, as the rest of the phoenixes had been at first, my father had gently ventured closer, knelt in front of a tiny flame-child who had just unleashed a blast that had leveled everything within a mile radius . . . and he picked me up.

He slowly lifted me out of the ash and charred wreckage, cradling my toddler-form in his arms, and carried me away from that place. Facing the handful of other phoenixes who'd been out on a hunting trip with him.

He'd met their eyes and told them I was one of them. That I was staying.

I hadn't trusted him at first, but he brought me to these same *nemior* tubes and wrapped a warm blanket around my shoulders. Father and the other phoenixes welcomed me to their hideout—one we had to flee years later, only to migrate back when it was safer. When that generation of Hollow had died off and no longer knew our hiding spots.

It was during that first visit when I drew these shapes and scenes on this wall.

Licking the last taste of the sparse meal from my lips, I move closer to the pockmarked surface and let my fingers travel over the faded scenes. Images of a hauntingly familiar motherly figure holding the hand of a small girl. The first time I'd even been able to speak of my mother since her death, I'd done so without words.

Other drawings are etched into the wall, too. Of trees and a flock of *argots* and of the mountains we'd hidden in at one point. But the largest scene is in the center—a collection of winged creatures floating off the ground, surrounding a child in their midst.

The way I'd seen myself. Surrounded by their ranks.

These phoenixes had quickly become my guardians.

And when I was first brought here and spent long days curled into a ball crying for the mother I knew I'd never get back, that's when Hana had first started caring for my soul in the way Father cared for my safety. She'd scooped me into her arms and rocked me close as I cried.

She'd helped me learn how to cry. How to let the tears fall without them turning immediately to steam. Without grief igniting my body all over again.

She had grieved plenty herself.

And, slowly but surely, she began to teach me how to use my fire too. I'd only been with them for about fifty years when she had taught me how to press enough heat into my finger to singe the wall and draw in the malleable rock that would melt under a hot enough touch.

I continue to trace the lines I'd scorched into the rock eons ago— lines much smaller than my fingerprints now. Where tiny fingers had needed a place to let out some of that fire.

I'd used char to draw a likeness of my mother first. Of us standing hand in hand on a safe mountaintop somewhere. The lines of that drawing were especially shaky, telling more than words ever could have.

And later, I'd drawn the larger scene—the child surrounded by her protectors.

My back aches just looking at the curve of their wings. A form I'll never be able to replicate again.

For their protection, Father whispered so many times, when I missed them. Missed the wings that I'd started to learn how to let drape from my shoulders as a child.

But my wings were flaming, uneven, untamable creatures. And I'd burnt my flock multiple times when they'd sprouted unbidden from my back and began to grow, a massive flaming wingspan that dwarfed my tiny form. It was as if they almost had a mind of their own. But those flames burned too bright.

And I couldn't fly without endangering our flock.

Father said there was no way to tether them and my wings had to be cut away to protect us. All that is left of the muscles that would have supported my dripping, flaming wings are the scars that never heal.

And deep down . . . it still hurts. Even the ghost of those wings hurts.

Especially when, every several years, my wings start to regenerate. New ghosts of feathers trying to grow out from the scarred skin.

Feathers Father would force me to keep from growing.

That was always significantly more painful than the bandages I've had to change every day since I was old enough to create these pieces of art. It had been Hana's way of helping me channel my flame. Turning pain into art. The older I grew, the more my fire grew, and Father said it only confirmed that if I had kept my wings, I'd have eventually burned our caves down.

Shaking my head to rid it of any thoughts of the sparking coals buried deep in my chest, I stow away the rest of my supplies and lightly pat the cover on the small herb garden. Next, I reach for the heavy coat I'd folded nicely atop my bed of blankets. After putting it on, I pull on my boots and take two slender knives, hooking them to my belt.

Might as well go hunt now. Better than just sitting here in this quiet, dredging up emotions that won't do me any good.

I head out of the small room, aiming back toward the temple chamber where my father and the rest of the *fior-errans* are, but then stop. I hear shuffling. The click of something against the stone. The scrape of claws.

The hair on my arms stands on end as I silently draw the jagged knife from my belt. Half-crouching, I inch through the narrowing magma tube toward the sound, the opposite direction of where my flock is hidden.

I will die before I let anything threaten them.

I keep close to the edge of the wall as I turn the corner, hand clenched around the knife handle, eyes narrowed in the darkness. The further in I go, the darker it grows as the light from the flickering wingbeats imprinted on the walls fades behind me.

More scraping sounds. A faint growl.

Animal. Not the Hollow.

The tension in my shoulders lessens slightly. I prowl around the next bend, and suddenly catch sight of something large and furred filling the curving tube ahead. A gaunt, four-legged creature with fur almost as black as the walls and eyes that glint gold in the dark. Large ears taper out of its head and its muzzle spreads in a low, guttural growl.

A seren. They used to hunt in packs down here, but I haven't seen one in decades.

This one growls again, but the sound is weak and its limbs tremble. It's putting up a good act, yet looks starved. Desperate.

Feral.

And I'm probably the best dinner it's seen in a while.

It's so beautiful—I'd hate to have to fell it.

"Trust me, friend. This is not your hunting ground." I stow my knife, lift both hands, and press them against the walls on either side of me, this area cramped enough I can brace myself between both.

Then I breathe into those simmering coals deep inside. Just a bit of heat to swell through my torso and funnel up into my hands. In a quick move, I curve my fingers and scrape them across both walls, letting glints flare from my fingertips and shoot off down the tube. The flaming sparks explode off the wall and ricochet.

The *seren* yelps and quickly backs up several steps. But it doesn't turn tail and run like I'd hoped.

Instead, it narrows its gleaming gold eyes on me as its lips draw back into a deep snarl.

I've made it mad.

The gigantic creature lunges at me.

CHAPTER NINE

I roll to the side at the last moment, scarcely evading the *seren*. But it doesn't pause, doesn't turn its massive maw toward me—instead, it bounds forward, down the tunnel, toward the storage room I'd just left.

"Stop!" I scream at it in my head, only to realize it can't hear me. I try to race after it, but I'm too far away. It's moving too fast. And the blade in my hand is far too small, even if I could wedge it past the thick, bristled fur overlapping the creature's skin like molten lava.

It will destroy the last remains of food I have.

Once it's done there, where will it hunt? The temple courtyard where my flock is helpless?

It could kill them all.

I force back bile as I race after the *seren*. It rounds the corner and starts through the doorway into the storage chamber. *You're too late!* I throw my hands out in front of me and do the only thing I can think of.

"Aaaahhh!" I scream at it, pouring every ounce of pent-up feeling into the war cry. And with the shriek, my pulse takes off like an eruption. My blood heats up in a split second that even catches me off guard. The pulse rips through my body. Through my veins. Rips my palms open. Fire pours out of my open wounds. Raging toward the *seren*.

It makes me go lightheaded, and the flames wash over the half of the *seren* not quite inside the room yet.

I expect to hear it yelp. To hear it scream in agony. To watch its coat start to melt and bubble and its skin ooze underneath. To hear it shriek—like those Hollow did, the night I burned their cabin down as a small child. When they murdered my mother.

But when the dust and smoke settle, the *seren* isn't torn open in bubbling burns. Instead, it pokes its head out of the chamber to look at me. Its glassy, gold-red eyes find mine for a moment. And then it gives a little shake, dislodging any drops of my fire left, and passes into the storage room.

The walls of the cavern around me are scorched and bits of flame pool in small pockets, but the *seren* seems completely unphased.

That's new.

I don't have time to be shocked, don't have time to wonder how that creature could just shake off my flames. It's the first creature I've seen, including my flock, that wasn't damaged by my fire.

I go after it, flexing my fists as the open wounds across my palms start to seal up on their own. I stop short. In the scant heartbeats it's taken me to follow the *seren* in, the creature has already laid waste to all of my supplies. The woven baskets holding meat and dried vegetables and everything I was hoping to eat for the rest of this week lay ripped open and strewn across the floor. Even blankets and some of my weapons have been ripped to shreds or pounced on and broken to splinters.

But the *seren* isn't done. Its massive body is wedged into a corner, head bent, large tail swaying happily. *What is it . . . ?*

And then I see the final basket it's gotten into—the one I'd always made sure was fastened up tight. The one I'd meticulously cared for. Watered. Given what scant bit of sunlight I could find.

Hana's herbs. The very herbs I'd been treasuring away and using to make pastes to heal her and the others' wounds.

The herbs that are keeping Hana alive right now.

And this massive beast is scarfing them down. Consuming the only thing I have to ward off infection as the flock heals.

Rage boils up inside. At all this. Being left to fend for them by myself. At this frigid world that seems to try to take from me every chance it gets.

I almost expect to hear Father's voice in my head again. Tempering the edge of my anger. Cooling that fury always churning in my gut. But he's not in my head this time—it's just me.

And I'm not going to let anything steal Hana or my flock away from me.

I scan the floor of the chamber and settle on a particularly large chunk of a spearhead left jagged and bent against a corner. In two steps, I've scooped the makeshift weapon up.

The *seren* gives a low growl, its shaggy coat bristling. I can see around it just enough to confirm it has eaten every last scrap of leaf and plant I'd gathered in that basket. A few thin, green leaves dangle from its maw.

All Hana's herbs are gone.

Before the massive creature can set its sights on me as its next meal, I run full-speed ahead. Bracing myself with one hand, I vault onto the *seren's* back and thrust my right arm around in front to poise the spearhead at its throat, pressing the jagged edge of metal up against the *seren's* soft under-neck.

I feel it tense beneath me. Its breath catches.

I tighten my grip on its back with my knees, and, leaning over, I press the blade in a little closer. *Take the kill.* What Father would say if he were here. I even let the jagged edge part the thick fur on its neck and clip the skin underneath. A thin trail of blood streaks down its throat.

Finish it off, Father would say. And he would have.

But as those beautiful amber irises lift to meet mine again, as this ancient creature who may well be the last of its race looks me dead in the eyes, I find my hand trembling.

It's probably been alive as long as I have. Possibly seen more.

What right do I have to end its life?

A question Father wouldn't even allow me to entertain. He'd say what he always does: *Either we survive, or they do. It's that simple.* If it came down to protecting my people or letting this creature live—I know without a doubt what I would choose. But it's not this moment yet.

The creature that stares at me is gaunt. Its breath beneath me ragged. It's starving. Like the rest of us.

My eyes follow the small path of blood that runs from the edge of my knife down the *seren's* rough, shaggy hide and along the bony curve of the creature's chest. I suddenly see a tiny head poking up. A small snout, but big, bright eyes. They peer out of a pouch on the *seren's* underbelly.

My jaw drops. *It's a mother?*

I'd only ever heard of small creatures carrying their young in pouches. Though it would explain why no one had ever been able to find a nest or spot where the elusive creatures hid their young.

But this *seren* pup seems remarkably healthy. I notice it's chewing on something—the herbs the mother found.

The *seren* raided our storage to feed its young.

A quick survey confirms this creature is a female, not a male with a pouch. I glance back up at the mother's face and let the pressure of my knife fall away slightly. There's no food clinging to her muzzle—I wouldn't be surprised if she hasn't eaten anything of what she found. All given to the pup.

I'm frozen on the back of this large, ragged creature, just staring down at that healthy, plump pup whose mother's ribcage I can feel between my knees.

Father said this icy world turns everything ruthless. That no creatures hunt in packs anymore. That the Hollow Ones don't have souls. But this creature . . . this large, myth of a four-legged animal shows more compassion than I've seen in the past several dozen years.

Other than Hana, I have never seen a creature give of themselves for another like this.

Is this what it is to be a parent?

I can't kill this *seren* and orphan this pup. Slaughter it like I've seen the Hollow slaughter my own people.

I can't be responsible for another defenseless creature being left alone in this icy world.

CHAPTER TEN

The strength has completely left my muscles and my eyes burn. My skin burns. Every joint, from the knuckles grasping my knife, to my bent knees, aches like a hundred tiny sparks are trying to invade tissue. My own flame eating at my body like a disease.

Taking a choking breath, I let the knife fall from my fingers. It clatters to the floor. In a fluid motion, I slide off the *seren* and take a step back.

Hana's herbs are gone, so I will stand between this creature and my flock for as long as it takes. But if it will leave them alone, I will give it the same courtesy.

I continue to face the *seren*, even as I slowly back up to the room's entrance and position myself at an angle so that I face the direction of the temple chamber.

The *seren* roots around in the ripped-open baskets for another few seconds, its lifted gaze locking on me every few heartbeats. It finds a stray scrap of dried meat and clips it between its teeth. Breaking eye contact, the *seren* bends its powerful head to give the meat to the pup poking its head out. The pup gulps down the food and then curls up deeper in the pouch, so only its pointed little ears stick out.

My entire body vibrates nervously as the *seren* turns toward me. It stands a good several feet taller than I am, slinking low to walk through the storage room. It pads closer until it stares directly down at me, its amber eyes flickering with just a hint of fire. Something eerily similar to the color of my eyes and the other phoenixes.

What exactly is this creature?

I match its unblinking gaze, prepared to dart around the bared claws that might swipe at me, but instead, it drops its head in a gesture of thanks. Then it lets out a puff of breath that skims over my already tousled hair and gives a low grunt.

The *seren* turns and lumbers out of the storage room and down the *nemior* in the opposite direction of my flock. Her fur makes soft swishing noises as she moves, and within a few seconds, the hulking creature fades into the inky blackness of the shadowed tunnel.

I don't realize I'm holding my breath until I take a deep, choking gasp.

My entire body starts to shake and I collapse against the tunnel wall. The room spins and I try to get my bearings and breathe again.

I'm alive. I'm safe. *Everyone is safe.*

I glance down the hallway toward the chamber where Hana, Father, and the others slumber on quietly. For now, the *seren* let them be. But it may not next time.

Like Father says, we're all just trying to survive. Trying not to starve.

I go back into the storage room and start sorting through the wreckage. *Please, Sol, let there be something left*, I whisper a quick prayer to the maker of our dying sun, desperately hoping some of my stores survived. I'm on my hands and knees soon, fingers filtering through the shredded bags and baskets and blankets. While I salvage some of the dried food that the *seren* pup didn't eat, I can't find even a single leaf of the various herbs Hana collected over the years.

Her entire garden is gone.

I can't breathe again.

They'll be fine, they'll be fine, they'll be fine, I think to myself, over and over. Shakily, I get to my feet and stand staring at the drawings I'd carved into these walls. Claw marks jaggedly mar the largest image, the one of my father and my flock surrounding me.

In a daze, I finally move. I unhook one side of the wide, thick blanket I'd pinned over the entrance to the temple courtyard. I'd originally created it just to keep the heat in, but this scrap of fabric won't do much good in keeping the *seren* or any other hunters out.

That's what I'm here for.

Once inside, I let my eyes adjust to the darkness and take in the rows and rows of beds filling this room. I'm surrounded by soft murmuring that lifts from my flock. The quiet whispers of pain as their bodies try to knit themselves back together. A slight coat of flame covers them, but it barely manages to protect their exposed bones and organs as they heal. One of the many reasons I have to bandage and shield their shredded forms with blankets as they slowly repair themselves.

I wrap my arms tightly around myself, dismayed by how cold this room is. With this many phoenixes in one place, it should be steaming as they heal. I drift over to Hana, splayed out on her bed. Her eyes are closed, lips broken and chapped, whole body pallid and raw and bubbled with open wounds that struggle to close on their own. She's most recognizable by the familiar scars crisscrossing her palms—from catching a blade once to protect me.

I should change her bandages now.

Even the newer wounds are now soaked with crusted, gleaming blood and ooze. Her particularly bad ones, those that always reoccur when she regenerates, need to be packed with herbs. Or else they will become infected.

And I must pack my own wounds on my back with herbs every other day.

A process I am numb to at this point, but used to scream through as a child.

A sacrifice to protect our flock. Father's voice always rises whenever I think of those wounds, but his words don't bring the same comfort they used to.

I look down again at Hana. Father and I had to lance one of her wounds once when it progressed into a large boil that was oozing pus. That infection from an unhealing wound left by a Hollow's weapon almost killed her. And if I can't bind her wounds again, such an infection will kill her this time.

And the others will succumb to infection, as well. Nearly every phoenix in this room has a wound from a Hollow blade.

Bandaging them isn't an option. It's survival. Or I will lose all of them while they sleep.

A shudder ripples over my body, and I sway on my feet.

Think, Mara, think!

For now, leaving the old bandages on with the remnants of paste made from the herbs is better than nothing. But I must change Hana's bandages soon. And everyone else's.

I gaze over the courtyard, eyes latching on Father, and go to him. I drop to my knees beside his bed, one hand nervously tugging at the corner of my shirt, the other hand reaching for his.

His almost translucent skin is far too cold.

"What do I do, Father? What do I *do*?" But he doesn't answer. He can't.

None of them can.

They're in too deep. Healing too slowly. And the room is so dark I can't even find comfort in watching the rise and fall of their breaths. Father's hand is icy.

It's all too much.

Do something, Mara. Anything.

I squeeze my eyes closed and tilt my head up at the ceiling.

Sol, help me.

I need to get more herbs. That much is clear.

But they hardly grow wild anymore. It's too cold. It would take months to collect the amount I need. There's only one place I can get the herbs to make a paste to heal my people. Only one place where they are actually grown. Gardened.

"But Father would absolutely hate that," I say aloud.

I try to find an alternative option. Wrack my thoughts for any other way of helping them. But ultimately, I always return to the same thing:

The only place those herbs still grow is with the Hollow Ones.

I need to sneak into a Hollow village and steal from the same creatures who dealt the wounds threatening my flock.

And soon, because Hana will not survive longer than a full sunpass.

CHAPTER ELEVEN

My mind is at war. Thoughts chasing each other back and forth—

Go. **Stay.**

Run. **Hide.**

Remnants of Father's voice doing battle with my own. Even when Father isn't awake, echoes of his words are still there. But one single piece of truth cuts through the rest. The inevitable.

If I don't find more of those herbs, I will lose Hana. And right behind her, possibly my own father, who isn't holding on much better than she is. Their bodies are shutting down and deteriorating before my eyes.

I have to go.

Bending down to wrap Hana a little tighter in her blankets, my eyes blur with a sudden rush of tears.

"I've told you a thousand times—you can't survive out there on your own. Not for long." Memories of Father's warnings flood my head.

I swallow, surveying the sickly lights scattered throughout the temple ruins. I steel my spine. *The Hollow will not stand between me and the antidote.*

Let them just try.

And like that, I find certainty to stand on. I push to my feet, and the next half-sunpass moves quickly. I scurry around, making sure every single one is secure on their cots and that their raw skin is as bandaged as I can manage. I drip water across their lips, though they don't actually need it. Their healing swells from the inside out. At least, it's supposed to.

I push aside any large rocks that could shift their way, make sure none of the temple ruins are sitting too precariously, and check to be sure there are no deep cracks in the walls that could leak in cold. Finally, I position all of their cots in a semicircle around the deep grooves in the floor, so that they follow the odd spiral pattern.

I have no idea if this is what they're used for, but seeing the way my fire had scorched into the walls earlier when I was trying to scare off the *seren* has given me an idea. Rubbing my hands together, I crouch in the center of the spiraling grooves and press my palms to the floor. I try to drain some of the roiling heat within me. But while my skin grows so hot my mere touch singes the molten floor, none of my blood actually drips in the crevices.

"It must be easier to set something on fire when I'm about to be *seren* food," I mutter to myself, and then glance around. I still need to find a way to keep them warm while I'm gone.

And I have two injuries that have never closed.

My throat tightens just thinking about it. A hand strays absently to my back to brush my shoulder blades.

This is going to hurt.

I bite my lip, tilt my head back, flex my shoulders, and lean into the familiar sting down my spine. Curving from the top of my shoulder blades to my waist. Two long scars that never fully heal.

I reach under my heavy top, find the corner of the thick bandage wound around my ribs, and begin to unravel it, loosening the packed herbs from the thick, jagged slices that still ooze down my back.

The work of a Hollow blade fashioned with one of our feathers. A wound that can never reseal. The only time we'd ever used a blade like that on one of our own.

"You are not safe to our people," Father had told me as he reached for my left wing. **"After this, you will be."**

He took part of me I'd only begun to understand. A part of me that my mother had coaxed to life.

But at least the Hollow never found my broken wings. So it was not my own feathers they wielded when they cut into Hana or when one of their spears sliced Father's shoulder. Or the dozens of other wounds to my flock.

I can only imagine the kind of destruction the Hollow could do with my wings. My fire.

The heat inside that's been trying to self-destruct is enough. For the amount of pain my own body has brought, the least I can do is bleed for them.

So I rip the last shred of bandage away from my spine, gasping sharply as the heavy material takes with it a tender scab.

Then I grit my teeth and shove the fire from where it boils and burns and force it up. Like bile rising into my throat, I let my lifeblood drip from my raw shoulders. From the wounds scorching my skin. From the shredded bone and muscle where the edges of my wings used to connect. I can feel fire searing lines through my shirt, but I don't care. I'll change it before I leave anyway.

With a cry, I lean back, arching my back and feeling more of my blood drip and drain and pool onto the swirling ditches in the floor. My blood burns a hotter, more golden color than the thin, almost bluish tone of my father's blood. The fire in my veins quickly fills the grooves in the floor and starts to spread.

I rise shakily to my feet, watching as my blood fills the strange spiraling symbols on the floor. Watching the heat pool around the blood, safely collected in the little pockets several feet away from the sleeping phoenixes, where it can keep this room warm but not singe them or their bedding.

I take a step back to look at my handiwork. At the way my released inner fire flickers and glimmers and casts shadows as if the floor were filled with a thousand tiny candles.

It almost looks peaceful, bathed in this soft orange hue.

But the cost for that blood was not small. And the cost will only grow if I cannot get what I need and return before our dying sun has dipped beneath the icy ridges.

So I use the same bandage to wrap my ribcage up again, to apply pressure to the two long slices, and quietly leave the room. I pause in the doorway one last time to look at my sleeping flock, and then stretch the woven cover down to fully block the entrance to the temple courtyard.

But hiding them behind a woven cover won't be enough—especially not with a *seren* on the prowl.

So I spend what feels like an eternity hunting down all the good-sized boulders and chunks of molten rock I can find and stack them in front of the temple entrance. Higher and higher, until I'm throwing smaller chunks of pockmarked rock at the top of the stack. It balances precariously and won't last for long, but I don't need it to.

I've thought about this before. Too many times. What I would do if I ever had to seal my people in to protect them. And the only answer I ever found was the same one for my mother when I buried her.

I was only a small child, crouched next to her lifeless, terrifyingly pale body, when I started building a grave around her. I'd taken every rock I could and covered her with them like a blanket. Placing them around her face was hardest. I couldn't even see from the tears streaming down my cheeks.

I couldn't feel the stones in my hands from how numb I was. I've never been that cold.

But I couldn't leave her there to be found by the Hollow Ones again if they came back for the rest of her. As if draining her body of all her flickering lifeblood wasn't enough.

Once I'd covered her in a rough, obsidian blanket of lava rock, I finally let my own tears become a flood. That one time I cried fire. My tears cascaded down my face and dripped onto her grave.

And as I cried, as those fiery tears of a phoenix child desperately missing her mother washed over the lava rock, it melted. And hardened again. My flaming tears poured around and in between the rocks like liquid gold poured into a cracked piece of pottery.

The fire melted and reforged the rocks around her. Forming a funeral pyre that would protect and encapsulate her forever. One that not even the Hollow Ones could break with their axes. Forged in phoenix fire.

Forged in my grief.

CHAPTER TWELVE

A similar kind of fiery grief swells inside as I stare up at this massive wall. At the place where my people sleep quietly—cut off from me. Silently trusting that they will wake up.

They *have* to wake up.

I don't cry tears of fire this time. I've locked that kind of soul-deep pain so far away it can't ignite my body the way it used to. But I can still generate some.

So I take a step back, my shoulders still stinging and burning and raw, and lift my hands out in front of me. And lean into that churning grief.

And like an instinctive reaction, the fire barrels out of my palms with force as it washes over the pile of molten rocks and boulders, and immediately they begin to melt into each other. They collapse into the curving roof and sides of the tunnel and form a new wall between the outside world and my flock.

But getting the fire to stop is the hard part. The storm that has started only continues to build inside. I give a guttural scream and clench my fist.

"Back in!" I scream at my own body. To pull all the heat and flames back inside me and stow them back inside this person-shaped tomb.

After a few moments of struggle, the fire evaporates with a *whoosh*, and I collapse on the floor. Panting, I stare up at the wall of molded and molten rock.

I'll have a hard time getting back through, let alone the Hollow Ones or a *Seren*.

It makes me feel a little better about leaving.

My entire body throbs as I drag myself back into the wrecked storage room and shove the few scraps of food left into the only leather bag that escaped unscathed. I add to that a few steel knives and sharpened lava rock, some lengths of homemade rope, and the last thing—a mask. One that Father had taken from a fallen Hollow warrior, should it ever prove useful.

Just seeing the rough-hewn, barrel-like shape, with spikes mounted around it and a terrifying expression carved across its front, makes me nauseous.

But I still stuff it inside the bag. If I'm heading into the enemy's land, I may need a disguise. And unlike my father or most of my people, who stand several heads taller than the Hollow and whose long, slender forms would be too recognizable, I'm still small. Still young.

The only young.

Which works in my favor. The Hollow have never seen one of us that looks like me.

Though I'm not sure they could even assess something like that. They seem to only be focused on hunting anything that moves.

And I'm about to walk right into their land.

I pack on as many layers as possible. Three pairs of fur-lined breeches, three lengthy woven tops, two coats, three pairs of socks, and my heaviest boots. And then I wind a thick scrap of material around my head, only leaving my eyes and nose uncovered.

Slinging the bag over my shoulder and letting some heat lift into my skin and warm the insides of the coat, I'm ready.

As ready as I can be to head out into the frozen wasteland to infiltrate a race whose sole purpose is to drain the life from my people.

CHAPTER THIRTEEN

I trek off down the magma tube, heading out away from where the *fior-errans* are hidden, down the curving and winding tunnel. *I will return*, I vow. *You will not be forsaken by me.* I follow the massive pawprints of the *seren* for a short way before they fade as I leave the gleam of flame behind.

It's pitch black this far in, without the pockets of phoenix blood carved into the wall to light the way, but I don't light a spark. I just keep walking in the darkness, hiding in these tunnels for as far as possible until the magma tubes start to wind the opposite direction than I need to go.

I pat a thickly covered hand against the curving, familiar wall. "Thanks for keeping me company this far," I whisper to the tunnels that have saved our lives more times than we can count. The only natural place on this planet that can trap heat.

I venture a few more feet through the tunnel, my eyes glued to the roof. There. A spot where the obsidian surface seems lighter. Shallower. The tunnel now is so low and narrow here, I'm able to reach up and hammer a fist at the soft spot a few times, and then it gives way. A large chunk of shale collapses, letting in the harsh glint of a dying sun.

A cold gust of air also blows in, sending snow into the tunnel.

My nose is already running and I haven't even climbed out.

With a deep breath, I clamber out of the magma tube and take a few determined steps in the snow.

Trying to catch my bearings, I raise a hand to shield my eyes. The sun wavering in the sky looks even more sallow than I remember. A sickly red color, the ball of flame flickers and does nothing to cut any warmth through the roiling cold stretching out around me. I shiver.

But somehow I take one step. And another. And another. Soon, I'm hiking at a good pace across the rippling, snow-ridden wasteland. Shelves of ice tower over the powdery snow. Mountains rise to the west, blocking out the sun by the sheer scale of their icy reach.

I only know what direction to tread in because of the number of times Father has told me not to go this way. To never pass those wintery, rigid shelves that look like two broken bones, sticking out of the snow. To never hike directly into the sun and to never head south around this ravine.

And certainly never to get close enough to see smoke rising in the distance.

After trekking for so long that the sun has changed its feeble position and my feet have gone totally numb and my nose is practically frostbitten, I see them.

Tendrils of smoke. Telltale signs of a Hollow camp ahead.

I force one heavy boot after another, through the snow, trudging closer and closer to the camp. Humming quietly under my breath, body vibrating with uncertain anxiety. Soon, I can make out the shapes of structures. Ramshackle tents made of splintered wood—something I haven't seen in four decades—covered in animal skins stretched thin and held in place by metal spikes. Snow covers every inch of these draped constructions, so thick that most of the animal skins underneath are hidden.

Some of the tents are small, some large, some nestled into gouges carved in the edge of the icy mountain they're backed against.

Even from this distance I can see flickers of fire. Flickers of *our* fire. Our lifeblood. They're feeding off our very existence, as always.

Surviving off the bodies of my people.

Nausea fills me so intensely that I come to a complete standstill. I pull the material away from my mouth just in time to retch to the side. Spilling what little was left in my stomach all over the white snow.

The last time I was this close to a Hollow camp was the day my mother died.

We found an abandoned campsite to hide in.

For me to stay safely out of the icy wind while she slept.

Only, it wasn't abandoned—and neither of us were safe.

I start to shake. As if the cold that bites and whips around me has soaked through my coat and is turning my insides to ice.

My vision starts to go dark. Pulse speeds up. Gut twists.

I can't do this.

Swaying on my feet, I almost lose my footing. And then I see something. A small shape comes out of one of the hovels.

What?

I can't believe my eyes. I can't process what that tiny silhouette seems to be.

That's impossible.

CHAPTER FOURTEEN

As if tugged by an invisible rope, I creep across the snow, angling behind the nearest rocky edifice protruding like a ghostly finger. Still not close enough.

I spy another chunk of ice protruding out of the frosty wasteland and quickly dart to hide behind it. I'm finally close enough to make out the details of the Hollow village that spreads out in front of me.

There's something stark about their camp. The sharpness of the icicles that jut from the overhanging edges of their sloping roofs. The way misty sheaths of frost coat their walls. Even the bowls that hold our blood, suspended from elongated spears buried resolutely in the snow, look rough and sharp.

A place made for survival. For war.

But it's not their frigid, sharp world that shocks me—it's the tiny form that has slipped out of a tent and now stands on its tiptoes to reach for one of the lanterns. The little creature is wrapped in the heavy, blue coat of a *lyran*, but its hair is the color of the palest fire. Like a beam of sunlight—but almost white.

And it's tiny. *She's* tiny. And she has features like me. Two eyes that peer up at the flickering flames. Not the color of mine—no, even from here I can see that hers are a rich brown. Not flickering orange and red like a phoenix.

But she has small hands. And a little mouth that is screwed to the side in a concentrated expression.

This is a . . . *child*.

A *Hollow* child?

I didn't even know the Hollow could have children. I always assumed they were like the phoenixes. That they just *were*.

And not only is she a child, she looks shockingly like us.

No. No. There's no way the Hollow . . .

I creep a little closer and crouch in the snow, the hood of my coat pulled up over my head, and stare at the little creature. The child starts to shiver.

She's acting as if she was just caught in a blistering snowstorm. My brow furrows, and I unwrap a hand to sense the cold against my bare skin. I can barely feel it, but she is shuddering like the ice is invading her bones.

The child pulls the fur tighter around herself, but even as her tiny fingers reach again for the lantern flickering with warmth, I suddenly realize her fingertips are starting to turn blue.

A gust of chilled wind blows through, and the child screams in pain, trying to dart back inside the nearest building. But she seems to have trouble moving.

I don't understand.

Then a flap on the building opens, and another figure steps out. This one much taller than the child. With long, dark hair. He's definitely the size of a full-grown Hollow.

But this one isn't dressed in armor. Instead, he's also wrapped in a heavy fur. The coat of a *seren*. This Hollow gives a loud gasp and races toward the child, scooping her up.

"Eloa!" The Hollow grabs the lantern from its swaying position on the pike and thrusts it into the girl's arms. She collapses around the small, metal container. He speaks to her in rushed, low words I can't make out from here. But his worry for her is obvious. She wasn't supposed to be out in the cold.

Before the Hollow carries her back in, he lifts his head and looks around—toward where I'm hiding. I duck lower, but not before I see his face.

And what I see shakes something deep inside me.

His face is deeply sunken. Part of his nose is gone—claimed by frostbite, possibly. Dark circles are under his eyes. But something even in his skeletal face still seems hauntingly familiar.

In all the years of running from the Hollow, I never expected *this*.

I never expected them to look like us. Like my people when we aren't in our full forms.

And not only that, but the Hollow have children. Little ones like me.

CHAPTER FIFTEEN

I cover my gaping mouth with a quivering hand.

I used to dream about meeting other children when I was younger. Dream about having a friend my size. A friend to grow with me. Father told me it was silly. That there was nothing out there besides him and our flock.

He told me the Hollow were monsters that only hunted us out of their own thirst for cruelty.

But the small scene I've caught a glimpse of shakes something inside me.

Because if my eyes are true, not only are the Hollow like us—but they are far weaker.

Far weaker even than my father in his haggard state.

That tiny Hollow almost lost her fingers just being out in the cold for a few minutes. Maybe not every Hollow hunts us just to watch us scream. Maybe some of them are like that child.

Maybe they hunt our warmth, because without it, they wouldn't last a day.

They would starve, freeze to death. Like the *seren* cub. Like me.

CHAPTER SIXTEEN

I keep low, boots crunching against the snow, inching closer. I circle the outside of the camp, scanning the buildings, just waiting to be sighted. But none of the Hollow venture outside. They don't expect anything to attack. Especially us.

Why would they? We always hide.

And any predatory animals have already learned that the Hollow will cut their throats and wear their skins. They're the hunters out here.

I never imagined it was because they are so fragile.

Slinking around the edge of the camp, I move cautiously toward the building on the outskirts. The one the child was taken into. Curiosity flashes like a dangerous beacon. Closer, closer . . . until I'm at the edge of the tent. I lift a hand, fingers poking out of the material wrapped around my palm, to skim my fingertips over the thin sheet of ice coating the stretched-out hide. I can feel the warmth humming inside the small structure, feel the frost melting beneath my touch. See faint lines of smoke wafting up and out of the channel positioned along the roof.

Pulling my bag closer against my back, ignoring the way the layers of material rub my rawness, I cautiously skirt the tent and peer through the flap where the child disappeared. The opening is fastened tightly with some kind of sap. Something I didn't even know could be found out here.

Where are they finding felled trees to stretch these hides across? Or standing ones, for that matter?

As I gaze at the outside of the Hollow tent, a part of me tugs at my feet to back away. To run home to my flock. To not attempt this insanity.

But, I've made it so far—I cannot leave without finding the herbs for my flock. For Hana.

Not to mention I've just discovered the Hollow's weakness. And if they don't wear armor inside their own camp, this might be the safest place I can be.

They aren't immune to the cold. And I doubt they're fireproof.

I am nothing *but* fire.

As if to prove my point, the edge of my hood sparks and I quickly brush a thumb over the tiny bit of flame to put it out. Then I rub my hands together, letting more warmth rise to the surface of my touch. Gently, I drag a finger along the fastened bottom of the tent flap. I watch the sap start to soften and run. The opening begins to separate. I continue to drag my finger up it until I've opened a seam in the tent about the length of my hand. Then I peer through.

The floor of the structure is covered in the massive, thick fur of a *lyran*. Actually, several *lyrans'* furs stitched together. The middle of the tent harbors a basin, carved out of dark volcanic rock, holding a large pot. Something boils and bubbles inside. A Hollow One crouches beside the pot, ladling out whatever is being cooked.

This Hollow is so bundled up, it's hard to make out any features—but when it leans over the basin, I see the flicker of bluish fire leap from inside and splash dancing colors across a female's face. Her skin must have once been a rich caramel color, but now it is sallow, and deep blue veins stand out.

These people have not weathered the cold well.

She hands out the cups of ladled broth to others in the room, and only then do I realize how many Hollow there are here. At least a dozen. Haggard, lumbering creatures, draped in the fur of the animals we've both hunted.

But my people whisper a thanks to the lives that are given for us, and would never wear the carcass of a *lyran*—instead, spinning their fur into wool. The Hollow have no such concerns.

They bear the skins and bodies and blood of their hunt with what seems like a kind of sick pride.

All throughout the tent I see the remnants of my people—blue feathers woven through the roof to lend light and warmth. Fiery sapphire blood dancing in the basin that they cook over.

The child is here too. Clutching the lantern filled with flickering, reddish-orange blood that may have once belonged in one of our flock's veins. Hana said our flock's blood and mine was the same color once. But as the cold siphons their warmth, it also drains the tone of their flame. Now, Father and the others' flame has faded to a cobalt.

The little girl is nestled on the lap of one of the other Hollow. Wrapped up nice and tight.

Tears burn.

My mother used to hold me like that.

Leaning in a little closer, still hidden behind the tent flap, I try to take some of the weight off my knees that have started to ache, and strain for a closer view of the room. They must sleep on the thick floor, all circled around the flame in the middle of the chamber, as I don't see anything resembling the cots we use.

Heavy packs are piled in one corner, but even as I strain to understand what bulges inside them, there's no hint at leaves or plant life. Once I've finished my survey of the tent, body tensed and ears perked for any sound outside that might put me in danger, only then do I pause to actually listen.

They're speaking loudly over each other. Rich voices raised in guttural tones that I cannot understand. Words I do not know. A language I don't speak.

I may look like them, but I don't have their tongue.

I won't open my mouth if I get caught.

But they're so full of life and intelligence and reliance on each other. Not the terrors I was told hid behind those cavernous masks.

It is eerie how similar they seem to my flock. Especially like this—sitting in a communal tent, eating together and telling stories to the child in their midst.

"Mara!" Father's warning rears up inside my head like the strike of an ancient snake. Sharp and piercing. ***"They would tear you apart in an instant."***

They probably would. If they glanced behind and caught sight of me. If they knew what I was, they'd grab one of the spears leaning against the wall and bury it in my chest. Pour my lifeblood out onto this icy terrain.

They'd drain my body without a second thought, because in this wasteland, there's only one thing that matters: survival.

They may look like us, but they are still predators. Still bloodthirsty.

Silently letting the flap fall closed, I rise to my feet. Walking carefully in the icy drifts, I skirt around the back of the tent and over to the next one. My shoulder blades skim the edge of the towering mountain they've pitched their tents alongside. Powdery snow litters my coat.

In this next tent I find a sliver of a tear, even though it's been closed over by ice. I melt that shard in seconds and peek in. This tent seems to be a weapons store of some kind. And the place where they skin their hunt. Half-skinned bodies of *argots* and other animals litter the room. A dull rainbow of different-toned blood mingles across the floor.

My stomach turns when I catch sight of the familiar, flickering blood of my people interlaced with the remains of the other creatures inhabiting our world.

We really *are* just prey to them.

Anger and terror spike through my quivering hands.

If they capture me, I'm burning down this tent.

My breathing becomes tight as I cross to the next tent. This time, I melt through a section of the ice coating the fabric, and then cut my own hole to look through.

This one seems to be another chamber focused on sleep, as dozens of their bodies are buried beneath furs and worn blankets. Only two Hollow warriors remain awake, sitting upright, weapons in hand. They must be keeping watch from inside the tent, but by the mercy of *Sol*, none face my direction.

It's . . . it's like my flock.

That realization makes my chest tight.

Quickly, the curiosity of how these creatures look so much like us starts to fade to disgust. How *dare* they rip apart creatures so like them?

We may not have known they resembled us—but *they* knew.

How dare they slaughter us and then crawl into these tents to sleep around a fire made of our lifeblood?

Father's right. They really are soulless, merciless creatures.

Maybe they deserve to freeze.

CHAPTER SEVENTEEN

Luckily for them, I find the right tent on my next try. This time, when I melt a section of frost glassing the thick hide stretched over the worn skeleton and cut an eyehole, I find the most unusual chamber yet. A room with a hole in the roof—covered in a plane of ice that lets faint drops of light in. Lanterns are set in a circle around the room, providing heat while the sun offers a bit of natural light.

My jaw drops at the sheer number of plants growing inside this tiny paradise. There are a half-dozen large, round basins. But instead of being filled with our fire like in the other tents, these are filled with soil. *Soil.* Rich, brown, and warm. I have not seen dirt that soft and malleable since . . . ever. And out of those basins grow a wide array of plants and herbs. Some fruits and vegetables even bud on vines.

It's a whole garden.

I've never seen a garden, only heard of them from Hana.

How did they do this?

I'm tripping over my own feet to scurry around the other side of the tent and quickly melt the sap locking the room. My swift entrance brings in a gust of air. I bind the tent entrance behind me as best I can, then pad further into the wonders of this room.

I loosen my pack from over my shoulder and start gathering as much of the herbs and vegetables and fruits as I can. Leafy greens and small, plump berries quickly move from my hands and into my sack. I try to pack them as gingerly as possible, but I'm trembling with excitement.

"I've found it!" I whisper, elated, to myself. "I can save them."

Father will be proud of me for this.

I've almost filled my pack, humming ever so quietly, when suddenly the thud of footsteps stops me. I freeze, one hand midair, gripping a small, velvety cluster of leaves.

I shove the last of the plants I could grab into my bag as I turn to the tent entrance. I haven't ransacked the whole room, just taken a quarter of everything here. What could fit in my pack.

But before I can determine an escape route, the tent is ripped open and three large Hollow warriors stand there. They wear their armor, either having just returned from a hunt or about to go out. Hoods shadow their faces, but none of them wear their helmets.

Their furrowed brows change to looks of shock when they see me.

Snap assumptions play across their faces. They aim words at me—words I can't understand, but from the tone seems like a question.

Desperate, I tug my own hood off, letting my dark hair spill out. Hoping it does enough. Hoping my dark hair and chapped skin can convince them I'm one of their own.

I flash an embarrassed look at them and nod like I have any idea what they're saying.

Then I push forward. I aim right between them, fully expecting their shoulders to tense—for them to move closer and block my exit. But instead, they step aside.

The Hollow Ones let me pass. They let me through.

My heart rate speeds up, and without glancing back I walk quickly away from the tent and aim for another one. Hoping they'll believe I'm going to the structure where I belong. Just a confused young Hollow.

Then, at the last minute I dart around the edge of the tent and pass behind several others. Eyes focused ahead. I practically race behind their weathered camp, my shoulder brushing the slope of the mountain they've set pitched tents against.

Five more steps. Then I'm past. Then I'm free.

But suddenly, I hear a shrill yell. Followed by a warcry. And another.

I know that sound.

My blood turns to ice.

It's a hunting cry.

And the heavy snow underfoot starts to shake with the pounding of boots racing after me.

I vault past the last tent and start to run, feet churning the powdery snow. A glance over my shoulder shows there's a small army of Hollow Ones chasing after me. Some covered in armor, some just wearing heavy furs. All wielding weapons and looking ready to tear me apart.

They must have discovered I stole from them.

I force my feet to carry me faster, farther, but they're gaining on me. Splitting up and cutting off any of my escape routes to the east or west.

They're all charging my way. Hemming me in and forcing me toward the large outcropping of ice that rises out of the endless white expanse ahead. They've got me cornered like a scared animal.

Chest heaving, gasping for breath, I decide to hold my ground before I'm fully backed against the ice. I slow my desperate pace, pivot, and plant my boots firmly in the snow. The cool wind picks up, nipping at my nose and stinging my eyes. It pushes my hood off and I don't bother to pull it back up.

I face the Hollow that close in on me and scan their faces. Eyes of an array of colors I've never seen. Skin in a variety of tones—but all too pale from lack of sunlight. Most of them look haggard and older than they probably are. Even the young men littered throughout the group who lift knives and metal spears and narrow their eyes at me, even they seem to have lost a piece of themselves out here. Out in this wilderness.

I exhale a long breath, watching it turn to a puff of white. I lift my hands on either side of me to brace myself, curling my fists.

If they want a fight, then they're going to get one.

The fire starts in my knuckles, first. Sparking over them and catching the scraps of material wrapped around my hands. It starts to lap up my sleeves, tongues of red and orange and gold that climb up my forearms.

I watch their uncertain expressions turn to shock.

But before they can lift their weapons any higher, someone shoves through them. Shouting even louder than the sharp tones already being exchanged back and forth.

And some of these words I can understand.

"Put out your fire! They'll see it!" and then a volley of words in the Hollow tongue. Lastly, more phrases I can catch, "Stamp out your flames!"

And then I can see him—a young man who elbowed to the front of the line, past the battle-ready men at the head of the hunting party. He's wearing a coat made of woven fabric that resembles mine more than their armor, with a hood lined with red fur. A scarf winds around his neck, and the thick, snow-dusted curls falling over his ears are the same color as the lava rock buried beneath our feet. But his eyes look hauntingly like mine—a deep, flickering brown with a bit of copper that dances around the edge of his irises.

His expression carries the first sense of kindness I've seen since Hana went to sleep.

And he's speaking a language he shouldn't know.

CHAPTER EIGHTEEN

He reaches one hand out, palm up, and then places himself between me and the hunting party, gesturing at them to lower their weapons.

"Put out your fire!" he whispers tersely, and for some reason, I listen. I quickly absorb the flames, and make a show of tamping it out of my sleeves. I pull my hood up to better hide my face. I try to cover the eyes that flicker far too much to let me pass as one of the Hollow.

The young man gestures to the rest of the hunting party. He speaks to them in their language, and they nod, starting to lower their weapons.

"What are they saying?" I ask him quietly. *And how do you know our tongue?*

He glances back at me. "I'm telling them you traveled here with me and that you come from one of the villages far out east. You don't speak their language and hadn't seen a garden like that in years." And then he's back to pouring words at them.

None of the hunting party seem particularly happy, but the Hollow warriors slowly start to nod. Most of them lower their weapons further. When the few that seem too stubborn to do so try to start a fight with this strange newcomer, he pulls something out of his pocket. A pouch. He tosses the leather bag at one of them, and the Hollow mutters something under his breath and turns around.

And like that, they all start to walk away and slowly head back the way they came.

Run, Mara. This is your chance—run!

But if I leave, I'll never know who this strange young man is that speaks with the tongue of phoenixes. Who just paid off the Hollow to leave me alone.

So instead I ask, "How do you know our words?"

He glances at me, the last of the hunting pack now well out of earshot. The ripple of snow is broken by the fresh tracks the Hollow left behind, shelves of ice that rise and dip and the distant outline of their skeletal village. The tents of stretched animal hide are practically hidden by the snow mounded on them. Even the receding backs of the Hollow war party almost blend in, with their dark furs dusted in freshly gusted snow.

If I didn't know what to look for, I'd think we were alone out here.

The strange Hollow takes a step closer, his cheeks flushed and skin warmer than seems possible. Something almost heated flickers in his eyes. A knowing.

"Probably the same way as you—one of *them* taught me."

I tilt my head, studying him, yet still primed to run. "Who are you?"

He narrows his gaze on me. "I could ask you the same. You're not fully human, are you?"

Human? What is human?

A little shiver zings down my spine. I lick my dry lips and try again. "Are you a hunter? Like those others?"

He shakes his head. "No, and sorry about them. Not every village lives this on-edge. But they are so far to the north, survival hasn't been kind to them."

Nothing he's saying makes any sense. "You're . . . not a hunter?"

That coaxes the smallest smile to appear. "No, I don't have the stomach for that." He shifts, his rust-colored coat adjusting on his broad shoulders. "No, I just travel from village to village helping as I can. More of a peddler." He extends a hand. "My name is Eli—what's yours?"

I cross my arms. I'm not naive enough to answer that.

"How do you know my tongue?"

Overhead, the sun gleams an eerie, bloodstained color.

Eli pulls his sleeves over his bare hands and I briefly notice some scars in the process. He doesn't answer, but presses on with his own questions. "Where are you from? The southern pass? It's pretty common for people to know the fire-tongue up there. Though that's not where my parents learned it. They taught me."

Southern pass? Northern villages?

How many of the Hollow were there? Did they all use our blood to survive?

But this conversation is already carrying on too long. I have everything I need in my pack—I should get back to the other *fior-errans*.

"What did you give the warriors to make them leave?" I ask him, curious, as I start to back away.

He reaches into a pocket and pulls out another small pouch. This close to it, I can sense the warmth and see the way it's carrying something liquid.

My pulse becomes erratic. *He was lying.*

"Just what everyone wants. I sell the liquid fire in all the villages I can hike to—anywhere they need it to survive." He tugs open the top of the pouch and I can see the gleam and glisten of the strangely golden, flowing blood inside it.

The lifeblood of a phoenix.

Blood he took from my people.

He said he wasn't a hunter. This must be a trap.

I back up faster—but this time I bump against the edge of the shelf of ice. I angle away from it, eyes still trained on this Eli.

Was it a Hollow like this who killed my mother? Who snuck in so quietly while we both slept? Who laughed as she screamed and her blood spilled on the floor?

"You *are* a hunter!" I spit at him. His mouth rounds in shock and I spring forward.

I will not be his prey caught in a trap. No matter how big and coppery-brown his eyes are.

No matter how well he speaks my tongue. Or how calming his voice is.

I smack the pouch of fire out of his grip. Most of it spills to the ground, but droplets of flame spray against his hand that was holding the pouch. It will leave a mark—may even bubble his skin and leave a bad burn.

But I don't care. The pain filling me doesn't care.

How could he carry this around and act so nonchalant?

How could he butcher my people?

I hear him intake a quick breath as I spin around and begin to run away. I barely catch his muffled shout calling after me. But, I don't stop – feet thundering against the ground as I flee. I double back a few times, just in case the Hollow are following, and then aim straight home. Around icy spines and past the chasm Father never wanted me to cross.

My boots churn the hard-packed snow, until I can sense a *haja* just ahead. The pocket of warmth that always precedes the entrance to my familiar maze of magma tubes.

I don't stop until I kick through the hole in the roof of the *nemior* that leads to the temple ruins harboring my people. Only once I'm inside the familiar warmth and musty scent and curving walls of the magma tube do I pause.

Placing both hands against the wall, I lean forward till my forehead is pressed against the cool, pockmarked stone.

And I let out an echoing, guttural scream that shakes my entire frame.

CHAPTER NINETEEN

"I sell the liquid fire in all the villages I can hike to—anywhere they need it to survive."

Eli's words taunt my mind. *Anywhere they need it to survive.* Something about them especially haunts me. The double-sided blade of it. How one creature's lifeblood can keep another alive—but at the greatest price.

This is like some cruel joke of the gods.

I pace across the rocky floor of the magma tube. Maybe Father's words are true—maybe we are gods in our own right. He believes we deserve survival more than the creatures who hunt without mercy.

But the Hollow certainly had mercy for each other.

Yet we were made to survive here. Our very blood keeps us alive.

As the world withers and the sun dies a little more every day, sickly pale in the sky over our heads, I wonder if perhaps no one survives. My father would say the idea of *Sol* is just another way of making peace with a world shriveling around us. As our god dies, as the Hollow freeze to death . . . maybe we're next. Maybe survival really is all we have.

Or maybe we will do what phoenixes have always done best—rise from the ashes of a world that should have destroyed us.

My stomach growls, and I lift my eyes to the towering wall of charred and twisted rock I'd built over the chamber where Father and my flock are hidden. I've been pacing in front of it for far too long. I haven't even bothered to set my pack down.

Because I can't get that Hollow's words out of my head.

. . . anywhere they need it to survive.

It makes my skin ache, this newfound awareness. The Hollow aren't just soulless creatures haunting their gratuitous armor. Underneath the metal and spikes and devilish expressions—they look like us.

They have children.

Like the *seren* and other creatures do. But my father and our kind—they were never born. He said they awoke fully-grown, never aging, just existing.

Until me.

I may have awoken in the center of a crater, as if a drop of sunlight catapulted to earth, but I was tiny. Fragile. Growing.

I've never seen another child that looked anything like I did. I'm still aging, very slowly, a youth compared to my father—but I thought I was some kind of curse of nature.

Aging oddly. Burning too brightly. Not as wise and controlled as the rest of my people.

But the Hollow didn't seem frustrated or shocked at the tiny ones. Instead, the one had seemed especially protective of the child. Scooping her up and out of the cold with care.

I can't quite fathom it. Wouldn't a child just be a burden? Especially in the cold?

I give my head a shake, but more questions and thoughts chase through my mind.

What would it have been like to play with someone my age? Someone whose body grew and morphed and who saw the world anew like I did? What would it have been like if I'd had someone to grow with?

Did Eli start out small too? Do all the Hollow?

I spin around again, stalking in quick steps that have started to wear a rut in the floor.

What was it he called them? *Human?* What does that mean?

An uncomfortable shudder starts along my spine, but I ignore it. *The Hollow are the enemy. Focus on that. He was selling our blood.*

But he had gentle eyes. Not the eyes you'd expect from a monster. Eyes that look more like ours.

"This changes nothing," I tell myself. "Nothing."

But my thoughts spiral like a tempest picking up speed, round and round, causing my blood to heat up. Beads of sweat roll down my temples. Drops of glowing orange blood singe the floor underfoot. The two deep scars along my spine spasm as blood oozes from them.

Calm down, Mara, calm down.

My palms are clammy, heart racing like it's trying to escape my chest. Each breath feels so heavy it's hard to remember how to inhale.

Dark spots start to litter my vision. The room spins.

No matter how desperate, they've still slaughtered us. Slaughtered Mama.

I shrug off my pack and collapse against the molten wall I'd created to protect my people, to cut them off from the outside world. To cut them off from me.

I should do what Father left me awake for. I should bring down this wall and step into their tomb. I should stand watch over them, silent and wakeful and ready to burn anything that gets too near to a crisp.

I should ignore the pounding in my lungs and the twinges of hunger I felt earlier.

All that matters is my flock. I already left them for too long. I shouldn't have spoken to that Eli.

But this tunnel is much too hot. And dark. And damp. And closing in on me.

I can't breathe down here. And I won't be able to breathe in there with them.

Get out! Something inside me urges. *Get out!*

So I do. I grab my bag, with most of the plants I'd stolen, and head back down the magma tube toward the hole I'd carved open. I find it, covered in a thin layer of ice that I break through in a second.

In that moment, I can almost hear my father's voice telling me to stay behind. To lock away the panic attack swelling inside and just listen to his voice. To let him drown out my doubts about the Hollow.

But the cool relief of the frigid air outside breezes over my hair and skin. And it comforts the fear inside in a way Father isn't here to do.

I quickly climb out of the magma tube and onto the snow once again. Inhaling deeply, I let the crisp, icy air crawl down my throat.

My father hates it out here. Hates the stretching, blinding wasteland of ice. He would ridicule the dimming sun—claiming it's the closest thing we have to a god. A dying one. **"We are the only gods left out here, little one."**

But as I slowly cross the snow, each step either hitting a slick patch of frost or crunching into a small drift, I realize I don't hate this the way my father does. Not the blistering wind that immediately brings my temperature down or the wind that catches strands of my tangled obsidian hair, whipping it around my face.

Finally, I can take a full breath and inhale deeply enough to feel the blissfully icy air inflate my lungs. Hunger gnaws at me.

I hike a small distance away from our underground haven, searching out the warmth of *haja* pockets that might carry some prey. I've hunted on my own several times since Father fell asleep, but he wouldn't approve of me leaving now. But other than bandaging their wounds, how much can I really do?

I reach out, letting the bubbling flame inside my veins search for other reaches of warmth that rise from the magma tubes crisscrossing beneath the icy terrain. I find a pocket of heat pretty quickly, and after taking a blade out of my pack, I start toward it.

The wind rages more fiercely as I clamber across the ice and over a large drift toward the *haja*. I pull my hood up and wrap my scarf around my face.

Ten more feet and I spot the area where snow has melted, and several sprouts poke up from ashen ground. A few small fowl that resemble *argots* but aren't quite the same species hop around the exposed ground, trying to peck up the slight bits of greenery with silvery hooked beaks. Bright green ridges crown their heads.

Keeping my steps as light and as quiet as possible, I stalk closer to them, eyes blurred from the frigid wind, pulling my other knife from its sheath with my left hand. *One, two, three.* I count down the steps in my head until I'm close enough. Then I crouch, whisper a prayer of solidarity to *Sol,* and lift my blades to spear my next meal.

But then I hear a low growl right behind me.

CHAPTER TWENTY

My entire body freezes. Carefully, I turn my head to look over my shoulder and come eye-to-snout with a massive, shaggy creature. Large ears taper out of its head and its narrowed, gleaming eyes crackle like the lava this creature is named after. The faintest bits of flame still linger in the very edges of her fur.

It's the *seren* from earlier.

My eyes quickly dart to her underbelly, and from what I can tell, she doesn't seem to be carrying the pup with her anymore.

She growls again, but this time the sound is a little softer. It's followed by a snort that puffs air into my face. Realization strikes.

Understood.

I drop onto my knees and pull my legs and arms in so I'm as small as I can be. Head bent, peering up at her from where my arms shelter my face. She leans down to sniff me one more time, and her muzzle actually brushes my ear. Her nose is wet and warm.

She huffs at me one more time, and then leaps over me in a quick bound. The force of her jump carries her the five feet, to where the furred birds are squawking in an awkward little pile.

The *seren* lands on two of them at once. Her monster paws spear three and the rest are crushed under her heavy girth.

The magnificent creature moves, and I see one of the fowl somehow survived. It dazedly bobbles around out from under her. She playfully bats at it with her paws, then rips the fowl open with one swift swipe. It's dead in an instant.

Next, she scarfs down several of the fowl. She prowls away from the scrap of earth and ice slathered in green blood and circles closely nearby but doesn't quite touch me. Though she does meet my eye, and gives the slightest nod.

I blink and look at the section of heated earth and realize she left one behind. Its neck is broken, but it is hardly touched.

At first, I wonder if that bird was sickly, but when I pick up my knives and venture closer, I realize it looks perfectly edible.

Did she leave it for me?

I glance back at the *seren*. It saunters away, ignoring me but staying within eyeshot.

Interesting . . .

Before preparing it, I whisper a quick prayer of thanks over the fowl, the same chant my father always uses. A hush of gratefulness that this time, in the give-and-take of our world where few things last past the night, this creature has given itself for my survival. Even unwillingly. That gift is still worth honoring.

I quickly pluck the fowl and clean it with snow the best I can, saving the furry hide in my pockets for later use and tucking the body under one arm. When I stand and turn, I'm shocked to find the *seren* is still there about twenty feet away. Her tail is to me, but her great head is swiveled just enough to track my movements. Those fiery eyes flicker for a second before she looks forward again.

And then she starts walking, and I can't help but sense that maybe she wants me to follow her.

I hang back several feet as I trail closely in her tracks while she treads in the direction we came. I'm able to pour enough heat into my hands to toast the fowl even as I hike, and sink my teeth into the stringy flesh when I can. I didn't realize I was quite so hungry until I had something more than scraps of moss and pellets of dried meat to eat. I quickly finish off the animal and drop the bones into my pocket with the feathers. I'll use them both for padding and tools later.

Suddenly, the *seren* stills, body going stiff.

My heart drops. Instinctively, I crouch behind her, using the creature's girth as a shield against whatever threat she's sensed.

The hair on my arms stands on end, pulse uneven. *Thud, thud, thud . . .*

The *seren* raises her head, ears back, sniffing the air. She then lets out a loud howl and starts racing forward. She moves so quickly that even at a full sprint I can't keep up.

As I watch her become smaller the more ground she covers ahead, I find myself glancing to the east, wondering if I should just go home.

Curiosity wins out. I start jogging at a steady pace in the direction the *seren* has now disappeared. But soon I notice the number of prints has changed. Beside the heavy, splayed tracks of the *seren's* giant paws is another pair of prints. Ghostly and faint, several hours old. Large and clunky and a little jagged from being made of boots cased in metal.

Hollow tracks.

My head jerks up to take in my surroundings more closely. The faint outline of the sun casts shadows over rising, icy peaks. One looks like a four-pronged spear emerging from the ripple of ice. That means I'm only about a thirty-minute hike north of home.

What are the Hollow doing this close to us?

My heart rate picks up and I pour as much speed into my tired muscles as I can and race across the icy landscape. Soon, I make out the towering shape of the *seren* not far ahead, and just beyond her, a small parade of Hollow. Maybe ten of them.

They're aiming slightly away from where my people are hidden, facing into the sun, but just seeing their tall forms covered in pounded metal laced with glimmers of our blood makes me nauseous.

I hear the *seren* growl, low and dangerous.

She doesn't slow her pace, but neither do they. The Hollow must notice her, but their attention is locked on a small protrusion of dark, pockmarked rock that juts above the earth. A hollowed pocket where lava must have once bubbled out of the tubes that create lacework beneath our feet.

I wonder why the Hollow are so intent on this small cave, covered in snow and barely visible above the ground.

As the hunters reach the small molten outcropping, the *seren* gives a loud, belting screech and bolts for them. Ears flattened back against her head, she closes the distance to the hunting party in seconds.

She barrels into the cluster of Hollow warriors so fast she splays several of them out. Snarling and growling, she positions herself in front of the small cave. Her fur is raised, hackles up, protecting.

And then it dawns on me. *Her pup.*

My stomach churns. They're going to kill her baby. Or the mother—in front of the child.

My angry, burning tears blur the icy landscape as I run faster.

Part of me wants to escape the other direction. To hide. To curl up and block out the screams pulsing through my head again.

But I've seen this scene before and I can't hide this time.

As I close in on them, I watch the Hollow try to deal with the *seren*. They slash at her with their weapons. They seem desperate to get at whatever is inside that cave.

Before I've fully registered the decision I've made, I'm barreling toward them. Weapons raised, shrieking at the top of my lungs.

But as I draw close, I can hear the screams, screams of the Hollow. Only now do I realize they're carrying massive sacks that they've tossed to the side. Brimming with whatever they hunted before they came here.

They hack at the frantic, furious *seren*, jagged blades slashing into her skin. One cuts at her knees. Another blade wedges in her massive shoulder. She screeches in pain and goes for the warrior's arm. She catches it in her giant maw.

I watch the *seren* rip the Hollow warrior's arm clean off, armor and all.

She spits the arm to the side and bristles as she faces the rest.

I can see their fear. Their anger.

Several of them try to bear down on the mama *seren* together, but then I'm there in front of them. My knife blades lift and catch their two spearheads against my molten weapons.

The tips of their spears are made of a flickering, dark blue feather. One of my flock's.

I growl at them, blinking back more acidic tears.

"Those are not *yours* . . ." My voice cracks. I lower both hands at the same time. Their spears bob in the air for a second, and then I swiftly bring my twin blades back up with such force they slice through the wooden shafts of their spears. The feather tips fall to the snow.

Behind me, the *seren* snarls at them from over my shoulder.

I brace myself, knees bent, weapons ready. Four of them are still in fighting condition.

"This is what you call survival?" My chest heaves with each word, tongue feeling thick in my throat. "Attacking an innocent cub while its mother is away?"

The four warriors exchange glances, and while I can barely make out their expressions behind their grotesque masks, their body language is clear. They begin to take careful steps back, two of them turning to help their comrade, who is trying to wrap his stump of an arm with a scarf to stop the gushing blood. Most of their party is bruised and bleeding, bite marks marring their armor, showing gaping wounds beneath.

They seem to swear at me in their language, but pick up their heavy sacks and slowly back away. The mother *seren* and I are shoulder to shoulder, bodies tense, standing guard in front of the cub as the Hollow warriors retreat. Once they're far enough away, they turn and run.

As they should.

Pulse finally slowing, I feel the strength drain out of my muscles. I slump against the *seren*. "We're safe," I murmur, only to realize she still has a knife sticking out of her shoulder.

Before I can help her with it, she limps away, back toward the small cave created from the bubbled lava rock.

She hisses in pain as she gets down on her haunches and gently nuzzles inside the cave.

There's a yipping sound, and when she lifts her head again, she's holding her cub by the scruff of its neck. The tiny thing is all elbows and big ears and eyes, with rough, dark fur like its mother. She bends her neck and nudges it inside her pouch. It settles into the soft pocket, pushing its small nose out to peer at the world.

Carefully and with deep respect, I go around her, to get a better look at both mother and pup. But that knife is still sticking out of her shoulder.

"Can I help you?" I whisper, hesitant.

Gingerly, I move closer and reach for the part of her shoulder that isn't wounded. I let my fingers skim her coarse fur and trail my hand down. She watches me with narrowed, wary eyes, but stays very still.

I run my hands up and down her shoulder a few times, until she becomes less tense beneath my touch. *I won't hurt you.*

After a few minutes, I unwrap my heavy brown scarf from my neck, let her sniff it, and then wind it around the section just below her shoulder where the knife still protrudes.

The *seren* winces when the scarf brushes the knife, but she still doesn't move. Just gives the faintest warning growl.

"I'll do this fast. Promise," I murmur and reach for the blade. I pull it out in one clean move. As soon it's free, I loop the scarf around the now gaping wound several times. I tie it tightly to stop the bleeding.

She yelps and backs up a few steps. She then sniffs at the bandage and turns her head. I stand on my tiptoes to try and meet her eye level. "I'm not like them. I know how much it hurts. I want to help."

Miraculously, the *seren* lets me clean her other deep wound. I only have to determine for a moment whether I have enough herbs stored away to share some with her—and soon decide it's enough.

I can't just leave her.

After disinfecting her wound, I apply a bit of salve I make on the spot from crushing some of the berries in my pack. She even eats the bit of wormwood root I give her. "I know it tastes horrible, but it'll help with the pain."

My fingers work fast, calloused and with a mind of their own— bandaging wounds like this is one of the few things I can do by instinct now. Knowing where to gently apply pressure, how to disinfect and pack a wound, and where to start the stitching process to help a gaping wound heal.

Once I'm content with my care for her, I hoist my bag over my shoulder.

"Alright. Now I've got to get home and do that for all of my people."
She just blinks and I give her a small smile.

I ever so gently pat the side of her head, and she grunts softly.
You're welcome.

With one last little wave at her pup, I start out away from her,
across the snow, angling toward my people.

Only . . . I hear the soft thud-crunch of large paws churning snow
behind me. A glance over my shoulder shows the *seren* is following me.

Immediately, the tension filling each muscle relaxes.

I forgot how comforting it is to not make this trek alone.

Though, as I glance back at her, I'm not fully sure yet whether she's
going to keep me company or feed me to her pup.

My legs are in agony by the time I can actually see the stretch of ice
and ripples of heat that mean I'm close to the entrance to my network
of magma tubes. But I speed up, noticing that the usually hard-packed
ice here crunches under foot.

That's not normal.

The breath is kicked from my lungs when I get close enough to
realize the section of *nemior* I'd cut through hasn't frozen over with ice
as it should, but is instead a gaping hole in the ground. A much larger
opening than it was when I crawled out.

Not just a *haja* leaking warmth—but a waving flag betraying what
hides beneath.

Then I see the heavy boot prints that circle the entrance to our
temple hideaway.

I start running.

Because the mind-shattering fear I've been trying to keep at bay
ever since I escaped that Hollow village suddenly rises to the surface.

What if I've led the Hollow straight to my flock?

CHAPTER TWENTY-ONE

The next several minutes are a blur—blacked out by the racing of my own pulse.

Get to them . . . get to them . . . get to them . . .

This can't happen again.

Each drumbeat in my ears is a reminder of just how long I left my flock alone. How intensely frustrated Father would be. How angry he'll be when he wakes up.

Tears stream from my wide eyes, sizzling on my cheeks.

But more painful than everything, a deep, shameful anger at myself boils and churns.

I abandoned them.

My racing footsteps echo hollowly throughout the *nemior*. I whip around another corner, lungs screaming for air as I suck down ragged breaths. The surroundings start to lighten, to become the familiar, worn pathways that lead to the entrance of our temple.

The world slows down around me as the temple opening finally comes into view. The desperate breaths freeze in my chest when my frantic gaze latches on the gaping hole that should have been covered in the molten-rock wall I'd built. Instead, the makeshift wall is shattered in jagged shards of volcanic rock. Not just collapsed—actively ripped to shreds by some strong weapon. Something that could pummel apart the safety I'd built like it was a simple rock castle.

The room inside is deathly dark. No glimpse of glimmering, golden blood. No familiar silhouettes of my own sleeping flock.

I couldn't breathe if I wanted to, my lungs shriveling inside my chest. My vision sparks and fuzzes. I stumble as I race toward the gaping entrance to the temple ruins. I tiptoe inside, and my eyes adjust far too quickly to the dark.

In an instant, I can make out just how devastatingly empty this chamber is. The rough-hewn mats that are scattered irrationally about the room. Some of them torn to shreds. I stagger further inside, searching around the columns and half-sunken roof of the temple. Desperately hoping they're still in here somewhere.

This can't be happening!

I spin in a dizzying circle, the ashen shades of the walls closing in around me.

Calm down, Mara. Calm down. I try to calm my own terror. There must be some explanation. I try to find a way this nightmare isn't real.

Maybe they woke up.

That could be why most of their beds are still here. Wouldn't the Hollow have taken any good mats when they took my people?

But then my gaze falls to the heavy lines scuffed across the dirty floor. I stare, trying to take in what the strange patterns mean. The lines that are the width of a body . . . dragged across the floor . . .

My knees go weak.

This room is filled with dozens of them. Thick, hefty drag marks. Several lead directly from piles of blankets, across the carved temple floor, and toward the only way out.

Through burning pupils I study the rubble littering the temple courtyard on this side of the cavern exit, and make out the faintest flecks of blue-flickering blood caught on the sharp edges of the shredded rocks.

Something ripped my people from this sanctuary. Something dragged them across the hard edges of rocks that surely ripped up their frail, still-healing forms.

Tears blur my vision and turn to steam as I count dozens of heavy imprints where unconscious, frail bodies were removed from their cots. Torn from this safe haven we've hidden in for generations.

We may not have built this temple—or been worshipped in it since before the sun began to die—but it has become a place that feels as much ours as the handiwork of those who erected it years ago.

Possibly the very same race that once worshipped us followed my tracks, stole down to our secreted sanctuary, and lugged two dozen defenseless phoenixes through the dust and grime.

What did they do with them? How much time do we have?

My hands have turned clammy, body trying to shut down on me to lock out this devastating reality.

What did I let the Hollow Ones do to Father?

I take one last quick sweep of the temple and head for the side storage room, hoping for some whisper of a hint so as to understand where my people were taken.

But the storage room looks untouched since the last time I was here. Still ripped apart by the *seren,* but there are weapons strewn about. Weapons the Hollow surely would have taken.

Why would they have taken my flock but not the weapons?

I back out of the storage room, searching the main tunnelway for tracks. Drag marks lap over each other, only interrupted by my own incoming footprints.

The proof of their disappearance was here the minute I walked up. And I didn't see.

"Where did you take them?" I cry into the darkness suffocating me. Into the warm, mildewed air that ripples around my body as my own heat turns sweat to steam.

I press my fingers over my burning eyes, and suddenly the impression of that group of Hollow hunters sprouts in my *ero.* The ones that attacked the *seren* and her pup.

The ones that were carrying several very large, very full bags. *No, no, no.*

They would have cut them up and stowed them in sacks. Kept their blood fresh by not draining all of it. Kept their wings intact—if any had managed to reform their wings yet as they healed.

I swing my head to the side just in time to spew the contents of my stomach all over the dark, pockmarked floor of the magma tube. For the second time today. I cough and hack, trying for air. I wipe my mouth on my coat sleeve, but suddenly the coat feels too tight. Too heavy.

I don't want to think about this. I don't want to think about this.

Shoving off my thick coat, I stand there motionless in the dark, curving tunnel.

Please, please . . . I can't do this . . .

Not again.

"This is your fault." Father's voice is so strong in my head that it knocks me into one of the sloping walls. For a desperate moment, I wonder if that really is him. If somehow, miraculously, he's found a way to sink back into my head.

But then I realize it's an echo. An afterthought.

It's just me here. And I am fully, truly alone.

My nose dribbles and I wipe at it with a shaky hand, my whole body hollow and shivering.

I'm all they have left.

I must at least try going after them. Maybe somehow they've done the impossible and survived this attack, even in their most vulnerable state.

I start to drift in a haze back down the tunnel. Back down the same pathway I used when I left my family unprotected just hours earlier. The same pathway I should have been guarding.

Only then do I remember there was a *seren* following me until I started to run. The *seren* doesn't seem to have shadowed my footsteps this far, though. She's nowhere to be seen—the stretches of dark, cavernous tunnel going on for miles unbroken.

I'm numb, in shock. I'm not even sure how I'm making my body move.

It hits me that if I do find them, there may not even be much left to bury.

I'm too numb. All that time, all that danger spent trying to get the herbs for Hana—and for nothing.

To lose *everything.*

That thought starts to consume me, starts to choke me out, starts to close the world in around me. The tunnel really goes black.

Which is probably why I don't see the two young Hollow men that are coming down the *nemior* until they are right in front of me. Shoving a lantern in my eyes—a lantern flickering with the blood of the phoenixes they probably just murdered.

CHAPTER TWENTY-TWO

The Hollow stand there, two silhouettes rippling in the gleam of the popping, churning blood they've used to light their way.

I waver on my feet, trying to remember how to ground myself. How to coax feeling back into my hands.

They're speaking—trying to talk to me. Trying to say something.

"Are you okay?" One of their voices finally cuts through the haze in my mind, and it takes me far too long to register that he's speaking my tongue. That voice is familiar.

Doesn't matter. Nothing matters but getting to Father. Finding out where they took him. If he's still alive.

White-hot pain starts to thaw through the numbness. If I don't point the building fear and anger somewhere, it will consume me. The anger at myself for leaving them.

My entire body is caving in on itself. The grief overwhelming, overshadowing.

Where is he? I can't—I can't breathe without him.

Father . . .

Even before my vision fully clears, I push through the two Hollow to head up the way they came.

I must have pushed with more impact than I realized, because they are both flung backward by the motion.

They were so—light. So frail, even in their armor.

My breathing comes in weighted, convulsing breaths as I pause, uncertain as they get to their feet.

I don't want to hurt anyone. At least not until I can be certain they didn't somehow save any of my flock.

One of them rises shakily. He's wrapped in a heavy coat, with a thick scarf brushing his jawline, but I see enough of his face to recognize him as the one I spoke to earlier. Eli.

His friend's light armor of misshapen pieces of shale and scraps of metal and bone hides all the most vulnerable spots. Cumbersome and undoubtedly bruising.

And while Eli seems unhurt, the same can't be said for his companion. The other Hollow rips off his dented mask and tosses it down, unleashing a plethora of words. Red liquid runs from a cut along his jaw.

What is that?

Blood. Blood . . . without fire.

A little shiver runs down my spine. I've never seen the Hollow bleed before.

My body quivers as I stand there, and I finally gasp out, "Where did you take them?" My eyes blur again.

Eli dares a few cautious steps toward me. "Wait—wait. We don't want to hurt you."

My throat is raw from holding back the sob building. "That's not an answer."

The burning pain inside suddenly bursts unbidden from my hands in a blast of concentrated heat. It instantly melts through the molten rock directly beneath me.

Shocked, I stumble backward as both young men's eyes go round in shock. The one behind Eli is half an inch shorter, with skin that seems to have seen a little more sunlight. They both share the same dark-as-night curls and slightly-upturned bronze eyes.

I try again. "Where did you take my people? Are they *alive?*"

My eyes mist over, the angry tears turning to steam inside the hot *nemior*. All of a sudden, I remember being a child, standing inside this tube for the first time, grasping Father's hand. Strong and firm and warm. He gently guided me forward, into the darkness, telling me that if I clung tightly to him, he wouldn't let go. He'd show me how to get through the darkness. How to find my way in the emptiness. In the hollowness left in my chest and haunting in the outside world now that Mama was gone.

As long as I stayed close to him. As long as I clung to his hand.

But I let go when I left the tunnels.

I let go of him—left them.

And now I may have lost them all forever.

The hoarse sob escapes even as I press a hand over my mouth to hold it in. Something in Eli's expression changes, and for the first time I notice that I can see the veins under his bronzed skin peek out unnaturally.

My gut twists into so many knots it would have forced out the rest of the contents of my stomach if I had anything left. "You must be lying!" I plead at them, words erupting brokenly, and reach for Eli. Hardly aware of what I'm doing as my hands press against him, trying to steady myself, begging for a different answer. Every part of this is wrong. "Your hunters must have dragged them from their sleep! Where did they take them?"

But even as I nearly shake him, Eli places his hands over top of mine. Shockingly gentle. The deep well of grief I see reflected in his eyes stills me.

But he shouldn't be looking at me like that. Shouldn't be pitying me.

He'll make it more real.

"I'm sorry," he says. "Only the two of us followed you. I don't think our hunting party did this."

I dart a glance between him and the other warrior. He can't be right. If he is—

No, no.

"Where are they?" I choke out. I can't give up yet.

This isn't Mama. Not yet.

Father—where are you? You would know what to do.

"I must find them. I must," I say under my breath. Over and over.

Father—I'm sorry. I'm so sorry.

I move away and the other Hollow inches in, clearly concerned about his friend, but aiming his words at me, "You may not believe him, but it's true. If our people did this, there would be a lot more"—he hesitates—"mess."

Eli turns to him. "Jude! You can't—"

"What?" This Hollow called Jude lifts a hand. "It's the truth! If one of the local hunting parties had found a bunch of sleeping fire-demons, they would have drained them for every drop and left their carcasses. You know they can't carry that much dead weight around."

I wrap my arms around myself in horror, trying not to picture what he's describing. Trying not to think about how that is exactly what they did with my mother. Or how Jude makes a good argument.

My skin crawls so fiercely, I have to clench my hands to stop from clawing at my own forearms. I wish I could crawl out of it. Out of my bones. Out of this moment.

But Jude isn't finished. "And the last hunting party had already taken down a snow bison. It took five heavy bags just to transport all the meat."

Nearly five bags. So that's what the *seren* and I saw.

Relief sweeps through me.

Eli shoots Jude a glare but then turns to me. "I followed you back to these caves and brought my brother, Jude, with me," he explains. "But, it's just us. We made sure none of the hunters could track you."

Heat suddenly turns my skin to a burning temperature, and I lurch back several steps, rubbing my hands together, trying to tether myself to the sensation of my own touch. To slow the heat that is growing and spiking inside me.

I've never felt this overwhelmingly afraid.

Not even when I woke to Mama being butchered before my eyes.

I was a child. I barely knew what was happening.

But this time it's different. I left. I left the flock alone and defenseless. I bite my lip. Maybe Eli is right. Maybe the hunters didn't follow me. Maybe something else dragged my people off. Another *seren*, even . . .

But it doesn't matter.

"Nothing survives out here while it sleeps." Father's words echo in my head. *"The only way any of us wake up is if someone stands guard. If we are protected."*

I turn away from the brothers in order to settle myself as the mounting flame and panic swell inside. "I have to fix this . . . I have to do something." Now I do start scratching at my own body to slow the spark setting off inside. *I have to pay for what I've done.*

"I'm sorry . . . ?" Eli's concern fills his coppery gaze. He takes a breath and catches my hands, stopping the clawing as I try to hold the fire in. "If we can help, we will." His eyes skirt between the thin tendrils of flame dripping down my arms, to his own hands and the slender scars crisscrossing his palms and wrists. "Don't hurt yourself. We'll help you find them, somehow."

Something like understanding flashes through his eyes as he glances down at the thin scratches I've left on my forearms.

I blink. "Help me? Why would you help me?"

We are only protected by each other. You can trust no one else. Father embedded that in me. *Trust no one else.*

I pull my hands away. My body is rising to such a heat that I start to feel my clothes sizzle. Start to feel the walls of the magma tube softening. A bit of molten rock drips onto my cheek.

"Now you are here to protect us, like we protected you when we found you, little one."

Father's voice carried so much trust. So much certainty. When he allowed me keep watch, he believed I'd do the right thing. That I wouldn't leave their side. But I did. And I didn't run home as fast as I could—

Because part of me enjoyed being out there on my own. Part of me lingered in that village, watching that child. And even more so when I went out looking for food and found the *seren.* More concerned with the creatures that could be our butchers than my sleeping family.

I was so careless . . .

Father was right from the beginning—*I'm not worth trusting.* I didn't protect them.

Instead, I let my emotions blur my focus.

I should fight the way my blood starts to lift from my veins and thick drops of flaming blood start to pour from my eyes, but I don't have any energy to hold it off anymore.

I can't hold my own grief inside any longer. Can't bury the anger when it's aimed at the one person I can't run from: *myself.*

I force my eyes open and croak one word out at the two Hollow boys staring at me, *"Run."*

Jude instantly races away, but Eli hesitates. "You don't have to do this. This wasn't your fault."

But I shake my head. He doesn't know me. He just doesn't want to be entombed here. Incinerated.

"My own body burning is the least I deserve for what I've done. I can't stop it." My voice quivers, pleading, "Please, do the one thing my flock couldn't, and *run.*"

Something like shock crosses his expression, and then he does what my father probably should have when he first found that volatile little girl on her knees beside her mother's grave. Eli turns his back on me and races away as quickly as he can.

At least that's two fewer deaths.

The faint clatter of their receding footsteps is soon drowned out by my own screaming pulse. The heat inside boils to the surface, bringing with it a searing pain. My skin begins to rip apart, my body pulling at the seams, arms thrown out on either side, head tipped back. All the pain, all the flaming anger, all the loss—it becomes a volatile force that shreds through my bones and tendons, and melts my skin away. I feel the heat erupting out of me, tearing apart the pieces of me that used to exist—feel it all turning to fire.

My flaming blood washes over me, and the constant burning pain I live with becomes almost unbearable as my body turns against itself. The flames run down my arms, consuming them. My clothes burn away, charred scraps that fall to the floor. But it isn't till the blood rips through the twin gashes on my spine that I scream.

The flames rush down my back, and the heat starts to lift me off the floor. Not as far as my father rises with his mighty wings, but several inches into the air, until my upturned face hits the curved top of the *nemior.*

My irises burn. My body burns. Every bit of me is on fire.

I force my eyes open, just in time to see the rippling waves of scalding, liquid fire reach my neck and start to creep upward. Within seconds, my face is covered by the flames too. As my bones and skin and soul splinter apart, my body starts to change form. To morph into something larger. For a single moment, I can feel myself dissolving into a silhouette with curving wings and a wide beak—the brief hint of a form I've never been able to fully reach after I lost my wings.

But I only touch the faintest whisper of my phoenix-form for a lingering second . . .

And as I do, I think I hear the faintest melody filling my thoughts. Soft, almost comforting.

A whisper I've only heard faint echoes of as I heal. A whisper I can't quite make out.

But before it can grow, before I can stabilize my phoenix form, the anger inside reaches a crescendo. The heat building from my core grows so strong I can't hold it back. Can't hold back the devastation at what I've lost. At the world I've just seen go up in flames.

I'm sorry, Father.

And with that final thought, I combust.

Every shred of my being explodes in a flood of flame and fury that shreds through earth and ice and molten rock.

Then everything goes black.

CHAPTER TWENTY-THREE

Nightmares haunt the darkness behind my eyes. Echoes of scorching flame that shreds my skin and consumes my frail bones. A kind of pain that strangles out even the scream in my throat. The heat growing . . . growing . . . growing until its hunger devours every part of me.

Until Mara is gone.

And then the sweet relief of the end. Of my body stopping its transformation. Of feeling myself change and shift. Of becoming something other. Something new.

When my expanding, fiery form reaches its limit, I am swallowed in the silence.

But somewhere between the dying and the living again, bits and pieces of myself start to knit back together. I slowly fight my way to the surface of my own subconscious, through the waves that crash over and over. Waves of memories that begin to surface.

At my most vulnerable, laid bare, I find the haunting moments with Mama—many good, one too shattering to look at for long.

Then, I find whispers of my father too. And something inside me cries out just seeing his familiar, wan face. The memories of all the ways he taught me, all the times he gathered up my tiny, crying form as I grieved a mama I could never have back. The stories he'd tell to distract me.

The ways he would calm my racing pulse when I started to reach a dangerous, swelling heat. The steadying reminders he'd slip into my *ero* when my own thoughts would threaten to erupt and swallow me whole.

I was afraid of everything as child. Afraid that if I closed my eyes, even for a second, the Hollow Ones would be there to tear away everything I'd come to love. That they'd steal away my new family like they did my mother.

But when I was on the verge of such panic, my father's voice in my head would numb those fears. And instead, his truth would guide me. Would guide me out of the abyss of fire and screams that would make me a danger not only to myself, but everyone else around me.

But he isn't here now. Just the memory of him.

Be gentle, nora.

I wonder at first if that voice, cutting through the loop of fear, is Father's again, but it sounds different. Softer. Soaking deeper into my muscles and sinew.

Almost a song. A deep hum. Coaxing me back.

Coaxing me awake.

Be gentle with yourself, Solnora.

And I realize it's not a voice at all. It's a warmth. A heat.

The warmth of rebirth. Of the spark that sets our sun aflame. That pulls our kind back from the grave over and over.

The song of *Sol*.

My father said he hated it. Hated hearing the song when he awoke.

I find *Sol's* song almost comforting. A lullaby softening that soul-deep ache. The soul-deep pain that starts to wake me from the deep stasis my body has been under as it healed. As I started to reform from the same ash I was created from.

I fade in and out of awareness. I'm barely able to decipher the vague forms around me before I'm pulled under again. Lost in the dreamscape, with other, more unusual people here.

For a moment, I think I see three forms around me. Two that seem vaguely familiar and one that makes my chest go tight. A haggard form, bent over, face scarred and eyes gaping oddly.

Another nightmare.

And then I'm pulled back under. Back into the *aethor*.

I don't start to enter into awakeness again until much later. How long, I don't know, but hands and toes are the first thing I become consciously aware of thawing out. And as the pads of my fingertips start to regain sensation, the numbness around my limbs melts—slowly bringing me back, slowly letting me wake up.

It feels like it takes an eternity for me to regain feeling in my face. For my nose to thaw, for me to coax a flicker out of my eyelids. It's like my own skin has become a prison.

What if I don't wake up fast enough? What's out there I can't see yet?

When I was a child, I didn't mind the whispers of nightmares I'd see behind my eyelids as I slept. Because I knew on the other side was my mother, and she'd be there to set the nightmares right. To tell me none of it was ever truly real.

As I've grown older, more and more of the nightmares have been true. And the nightmares that say I really lost everything—those are too terrible.

They can't be true.

So as soon as I can flex my hands, I force my eyes open to a world of whites and browns gradually coming into focus around me. I try to bring the sharpness of the world outside my stasis into view, hoping that maybe this all was another huge nightmare.

Maybe I'll really wake up.

But my entire body seethes in pain as I try to turn my head. I blink rapidly, and shapes begin to crystallize, but my brain lags at translating what I'm seeing.

I breathe out, and the scenery unfurls both around me, and clicks into place inside my head, as I tread the water of that *aethor* sleep I've been held under.

I'm in some kind of room, made of heavy, wooden poles and woven fabric stretched across them. A harsh wind blisters by outside, shaking the walls around me.

Not just a room—a tent.

Every muscle groans as I painstakingly lift myself up. I realize I'm sitting on a cot, covered in layers of soft animal pelts. Lanterns of a pale, yellow heat flicker from where they hang on poles in the four corners.

Lanterns filled with blood.

Which only means one thing.

I'm trapped inside a Hollow camp.

CHAPTER TWENTY-FOUR

My head spins at the ramifications of my surroundings. I sit up, pulling my knees to my chest, scanning the room closely as I work feeling back into my legs and shoulders. Not knowing where I've been, what's outside this room, what I missed while I slept.

My wide eyes try to translate the brown hues of this room.

I'm okay . . . I'm okay . . . I'm okay . . .

I've never felt so laid bare. Defenseless.

I force myself to focus on my breathing. *In. Out. In. Out.*

As soon as my limbs thaw out enough, I can run. It shouldn't be hard to cut or burn through one of the walls of this tent.

I'm okay. I can get out. I can get out.

If I can escape, I won't have to consider that worst-case scenario Father made me promise to him. To fall into my own flame before I would let the Hollow capture me. I may be in a Hollow camp—but I'm not truly captured. I'm not helpless, not yet. I can survive.

Father would want me to still try, right?

I cock my head for any sound of the Hollow. There is a fastened-shut tent flap to my right, but no hint of what's on the other side. Either they're painstakingly quiet, or my ears are still adjusting.

Probably the latter.

Time to get up.

I let myself sit like this for a few seconds longer, settling into my own skin. Nothing really hurts. Nothing but the usual mild burns or aches. I've healed pretty well. I slide off the cot, my bare feet rippling with pinpricks as sensation resurfaces. For the first time, I really take in the visual state of my body. I'm fully clothed in an oversized shirt of thick material and a pair of threadbare pants. Clothes that must belong to the Hollow themselves. My stomach turns as I contemplate how long I was unconscious. How unprotected I've been. At their mercy.

Breathe. In. Out.

Other than the still-healing areas on my arms and shins where it is taking the skin longer to stitch back together, nothing feels hurt or raw. And the areas that are still healing have already been bandaged up with thick strips. When I move, I already feel the soft pressure of herbs and paste beneath the bandages.

I think I really am okay.

Would they have bandaged me if they just wanted to drain my body of blood?

The question feels dangerous.

But the fact that they took the time to bandage up my wounds makes me hopeful that perhaps they didn't drain or cut me in any way while I lay sleeping.

I slowly tread across the icy floor consisting of slabs of wood overlapped and nailed together. A creaking, solid floor like nothing I've seen before.

Where did they get all this lumber?

As I reach the center of the room, I lift my hands in front of me, flexing my fists. Leaning into a bit of the heat still pooling in my joints—I know I could conjure more fire if I needed it.

And run. I can always run.

My chest starts to lock up again.

In. Out. In. Out.

My gaze skirts from the fastened tent flap, to the nearest material wall. If I took the blankets off this cot and wrapped myself in them, I could burn through a wall and disappear in minutes. I can already hear the clatter of a rising storm outside. The patter of snow. Perfect cover, despite how cold it will be.

But I can't stop staring at the tent flap.

If they captured me but let me heal on a bed like this, unchained, maybe the rest of my people are held somewhere here too. I don't have to think twice.

Pressing a bit of heat into my hands, I take quick steps and I make it to the exit, but right as I reach for the fasteners holding the tent flap closed, there's a scuffling sound on the other side.

I freeze in front of the flap as it's suddenly pulled back to reveal a familiar face with dark hair and coppery-brown irises. Eli.

My body doesn't want to move, but my mind forces it to.

Aiming my shoulder at his chest, I barrel into him, pushing him out of the way, and burst into the next room. There's no one else here, but this room isn't made of tent fabric. Instead, I'm now entirely hemmed in by walls of wood. My mouth hangs open. Where did all these trees even come from? The floor is hardwood here too, covered in rugs. Slings hang from the rafters. A fire is centered in the middle of the room, flickering out of a rounded basin.

Rectangular wedges are carved out of the paneled walls.

"You're awake."

My hands are shaking as Eli speaks from behind me. I try to spot an escape. A way out.

Nothing is familiar. Nothing is right.

I have to get out. I have to find Father.

I turn as I search the room and see Eli advancing toward me cautiously, palms up, like I'm a feral animal he's trying to settle.

My breathing is coming in short bursts. And as my *ero* continues to thaw out, the emotions swell inside my head like a dangerous snowstorm that blinds and brings everything into sharp focus all at once.

I must find them. It's the only thing familiar, the only thing that matters in this world.

What if they're here? Hiding in this closing-in room of panels and harsh lines.

What if they're trapped beneath our feet? Or in some other room?

I glance back at Eli. Will he tell me?

Trust no one.

Eli takes another step toward me, but I ignore him and reach for the heavy mat covering the floor. I yank up the large, worn fur, looking for secret compartments.

Nothing.

"Be vigilant always. You should not have left us."

I'm trying, Father.

I won't lose you again. I'll never close my eyes—never sleep again. Never leave your side once I find you.

I push aside small, rough-hewn tables and chairs. And then I find an opening and dash into the connected room.

How big is this place?

Blood rushes to my face, heat pulling behind my eyes and filling my sweating palms. *Where are they?*

"Whoa!" Eli's voice bursts after me. "What are you doing?"

I've started in on the next room, desperately throwing aside hunting weapons and kicking bags of food out of the way. There's a final door in this storage chamber, facing a different direction.

Maybe that's the way out?

I reach for its latch, but Eli is ahead of me, palm against the door. "Wait, it's cold out there."

My entire body vibrates. I move back. "You can't hold me captive here."

"We aren't," he says firmly. "We wanted to make sure you had a safe place to heal. What are you looking for?"

"What room are you keeping them in?"

"There's no one else here but Jude and me."

He said he didn't know where they were in the caves, either.

I face Eli. My body hums as it continues thawing out, that inner snowstorm of emotions building up ferocity. "Where is Father?"

He steps away from the door. "I wish I had a different answer for you. But like we told you when you asked before, we didn't do anything with them. And I even investigated it while you were regenerating—no one in that Hollow camp took your flock."

How does he know we call our small village a flock?

Or did I give that away?

I focus in on this human in front of me. Let a touch of heat pour into my hands, sparks leaking through my clenched fists, just to show him I won't be lied to. That I'm not as small and helpless as I feel right now, cornered in this cage of tree carcasses. "That can't be right. *Something* broke down the rock barrier I built."

But before Eli can answer, another voice breaks the silence.

"Maybe it was that scary-looking *seren* that almost ate us when we tried to recover your body."

I see the other brother, Jude, striding through the door I'd hoped led outside. Snow blasts through the open frame behind him, until he slams it firmly closed with a swift kick. He has some furry creature I don't recognize thrown over one shoulder. Snow dusts the leather hunting gear he's wearing, and the spear in his right hand is aimed at me.

"You'd better put that fire of yours away unless you want to go back to sleep for another five years while you heal from *this* injury."

I blink at him and the droplets of flame soak back into my veins. "What did you just say?"

Eli shoots a cautioning glance at his brother, and then back at me. "Look. There's a lot to discuss. A lot has happened since you fell asleep. But the main thing is this"—his coppery expression takes me in and holds me captive for a long moment—"we don't want to hurt you. We kept you here all this time while you healed to protect you. And we've been trying to find your flock for you while you slept."

I stare at him, backing away from both. "What do you mean? How long was I asleep?"

The cold air that gusted in when Jude barged through the door has dropped the temperature in this small, paneled room, but I'm starting to sweat.

Jude drops his kill on the floor with a thud, and I still don't recognize the species. That's not a promising sign.

Jude's hair is noticeably shorter than the last time I saw him—razored down on the sides. And dull silver studs glint in his earlobes. I've seen other Hollow with piercings like that, but they seem even more fitting with Jude's quirked brow and smirk.

Glancing back at Eli, I realize that his skin seems a little warmer than it did in the caves. And there's a few silver hairs in his lengthier mop of dark curls I never noticed before. They both seem older, somehow. Not just their features—but in their eyes.

How long was I asleep?

Eli rubs a hand over his face. "You might want to sit down."

I'm frozen in place, wavering on my feet. Jude comes to stand beside his brother, eyeing me. "Let's be up front about this. Only Eli has been looking for your flock. But because neither of us could just let you suffocate to death inside that collapsing magma tube as you started to reform, he convinced me to bring you here."

So . . . not captured, then?

Rescued?

I cannot even begin to understand what that could mean. They must want something.

Eli keeps his eyes on me. "We haven't lost all our humanity just yet." His attention drops to my curled, shaking fingers, contorted and turning a deep red. Heat pulsating with each *thud-thud* of my heartbeat. "And I don't think you have, either. What's your name?"

I decide to give them the same courtesy they've given me. "Mara."

Eli nods and slowly ventures around me and through the doorway I came from, beckoning us out of this side room with their weapons and stores. I follow the brothers back into the main chamber with the firepit and piles of warm blankets. There are vials and crushed herbs stacked in one corner where a handful of pots and pans hang from hooks in the wall. Eli settles down on the floor on one of the thickly woven mats. "Would you like to sit down?"

I shake my head.

"Okay, Mara. There's a lot you don't know."

The room swirls around me. I quickly retreat to the nearest wall, opposite Eli, pressing my spine into the harsh planking. *Breathe. In. Out.*

Aloud, I say, "Go on."

Jude stands behind his brother as Eli takes a breath.

"Mara, you were asleep for five years while you healed. Your flock disappeared five years ago. And none of the Hollow know where they went."

Five. Five years.

My knees start to cave in on me. I can't even brace myself against this rough, splintering wall. I miss my magma tunnels. I miss the ripple of warmth inside the pockmarked stone.

I miss my father's voice.

Words form on my cracked lips, but nothing is coherent. Eli gets to his feet, watching me, but Jude just shrugs. "Honestly, I still think they were probably eaten by that *seren*. It looked hungry and was territorial of that whole area."

The *seren* I helped? The one that snuck in and managed to eat our whole store—and I still let escape? No—no. The wall was intact when I first returned—and when I left to hunt, the *seren* was with me. She would have had to be devastatingly fast to get around me and into those caves.

I shake my head violently. "No. The *seren* couldn't have done that."

But both of their expressions say she could.

"You must be wrong. There has to be another option."

Jude glances at Eli. "You have to tell her all of it."

Eli's face pales, but something gleaming and determined seeps into his expression.

I don't know if I can survive hearing more. But I have to. *For Father.* I swallow. "What else is there?"

Eli rubs the back of his neck. "When you exploded, Mara—" He gives his head a shake. "I've never seen a blast that big. You turned the entire valley into a charred wasteland. You even scorched the edge of the Hollow village."

An aching waterfall of chills sweeps my body, eyes rounding. "I did *what?*"

I knew my explosions were catastrophic—the Hollow village I'd destroyed when my mama died was evidence of that. I'd seen what happened when Father triggered my flames, especially when he was tempering our flock against them. One of the main reasons he had to always be in my head. I was too dangerous.

But I didn't know I could do damage like that.

I should have known.

Father was right. He's always right.

Jude's tone carries no animosity. "If your people were anywhere near that explosion, especially if they were still asleep—"

They wouldn't have survived.

The gravity of that feels like it should crush my bones. I curl in on myself, head between my knees, trying to get so small I dissolve.

Because even if the Hollow didn't kidnap or kill my flock, I still led a predator right to them.

There's only one common denominator here. I really am the greatest threat to my people.

Just like my father always said.

CHAPTER TWENTY-FIVE

Father used to tell me stories of hunting blinds the Hollow would lay for us—traps set out in the icy tundra. They'd garnish a piece of meat and set it over the top of a deep pit they'd dug. One with frozen water and spikes of ice they'd let form at the bottom. The floor of the pit was sloped, so that when one of our people reached for the bait they would fall in, impaled by the spikes, and die a slow, gruesome death.

Their blood would trickle down the spikes, dripping to the floor of the cave. By the time the Hollow returned hours later, a dead phoenix would be frozen to one corner of the icy pit, body limp and ash-pale in death. The poor creature's flickering, flaming blood would have drained to the other corner, sitting in a seething pool that melted away.

Every inch of my body may be dangerous, and my mind even more so, but there is another possibility here.

Eli and Jude are Hollow and this may be their hunting blind.

Am I the bait? Or are my people?

I cannot fathom the possibility that my explosion destroyed any last trace of them.

Slowly rising from my hunched position on the floor of this large wooden prison, I try to coax some air into my ribcage to lessen the tightness. To just be able to breathe. The baggy shirt that I guess is probably Eli's, from the pale blue matching the shirt he's wearing now, hangs loosely on me.

They must be lying. They must be. I've lost more than I can process if they aren't.

Panic starts to build again, and a kind of frenzied, feral instinct rises like an *argot* caught in a trap. One willing to gnaw off its own limb to escape.

I inch along the rough wall at my back, aiming for the door leading to the other room Jude entered from. I don't know if I believe them, and I'm not even sure where I am, but I can't stay here.

I have to get out.

But Jude springs forward and makes a grab for me. "You can't—"

Instinctively, my body flares. My skin turns brand-hot and Jude lets go with a pained hiss.

"Don't touch me," I growl.

But when Jude lifts his hand, the burn mark that coats several of his fingers and palm has already fileted them, and I cringe.

I didn't mean to hurt him. Not that badly.

And if that alone burned him—how did he and Eli survive my other explosion?

A shiver runs down my heated skin. How can these brothers— virtually strangers—stand here unscathed when my own people are missing? Possibly destroyed themselves?

None of this makes sense.

Jude glares at me, those silver studs in his ears glinting. "Can't you see we're trying to help?" He utters a curse and rushes to try and soak his hand in a basin of water beside the fire.

But still my eyes spark. "You have to be lying."

Eli has positioned himself in front of the exit and I try to break past him. His hand catches my shoulder and holds on even as I watch his face tighten from the pain.

"Mara. Stop. I know you're afraid. I know nothing makes sense anymore. But you're safe here. We won't hurt you."

I pull out of his grasp. "Your people have ripped mine apart. You expect me to believe you?"

Eli's attention shifts to his brother, a decision hovering behind his eyes.

Then he lets go of me. "We won't keep you here."

He goes to his brother, tearing a strip from his own shirt and taking a salve from a hand-carved bowl nestled on a shelf beside the fire. Eli binds up his brother's burn with the ease and efficiency of someone used to mending others.

I know that sensation. The way your fingers work with a life of their own.

The light from the fire reveals scars visible beneath Eli's torn shirt. Silvery lines that etch across his chest. Scars that rival some of my own.

My whole body is a taut nerve, humming and quivering. "I won't let you harvest me," I mutter.

Eli's eyebrows rise, but he finishes wrapping Jude's hand. "We aren't going to *harvest* you, Mara. We saved you."

My eyes narrow. "Why would you do that? The Hollow only hunt us."

Jude lets out a frustrated breath. "Did you really just almost burn my hand off because you thought we brought you here to kill you?" He gestures behind him with his good hand. "You think we gave you your own room and bed and looked out for you all these years just because we wanted to eat you later or something?"

I gape at him. "You eat us?"

"*No!*" The brothers' voices rise in unison.

Eli groans. "Of course not. We kept you here because we wanted to protect you. To keep you safe from any Hollow that might want to drain you."

He's making my mind distort itself. "Where is here?"

Eli shares a long look with his brother, then his eyes turn to me. "We told you the truth, Mara. When you exploded, you destroyed the entire *nemior* system for miles. We were barely able to find your body when you started to reform. We had to get you out of there. The whole Hollow village knew there'd been an explosion—and they were hunting you. We had to find some place where you'd be safe."

Jude gingerly brings his bandaged arm close to his chest. "We have to keep moving a lot, anyway. Eli can't stay in one place long, or else—"

He's abruptly cut off by an unintelligible sound from his brother. Jude clamps his mouth shut.

"What Jude meant to say," Eli picks up, sending a sharp glance toward his sibling, "is that we are nomads and travel from village to village selling flame. We brought you with us. But instead of carrying your sleeping body from one place to the next, we wanted to find somewhere you could heal in peace. So, we brought you here—to our home. In the Riveria Mountains."

My jaw drops, "We're in the Riv Mountains?"

That's several sunpasses' journey away from where our temple sanctuary was.

"You've kept me here for five years? Just . . . in your house?"

Eli's face reddens. "We, uh . . . actually, we built this place around you. It was just us looking after you at first, but the longer you slept, the more we realized we needed help."

I take in the rough-hewn cabin tucked around us. They built this whole thing for me? "Help from whom?"

Eli's reply is simple. "From our father. And others. We'll introduce you to them when it's time."

I blink, trying to take all this in. "You kept me in a secret cabin you built around me for five years?"

Eli gives a hesitant nod. "It seemed the safest option. We didn't want you too close to our village in case you exploded again." He reddens a little more. "Other than changing a few bandages or washing your bedding or clothes, neither of us ever touched you. We had women from the village come help change you most of the time."

I look down at the baggy clothing covering my tall form. My voice suddenly sounds very small. "I've been at your mercy all that time."

I see a kind of pained understanding flash through Eli's coppery gaze. Like he understands that kind of fragility.

I guess that is what being Hollow—or as they call it, being *human* is. Being fragile. At the mercy of the world around you.

But Jude just snorts. "Would you rather us have left you in the same smelly clothes for five years?"

Eli elbows his brother. "We made sure you had as much privacy as possible. We didn't know what else to do."

I touch the cool wood of the wall behind me, fingertips digging into the fibers of the panel. No wonder this house looks different. We aren't in the same area of the world I was when I went aflame.

The entire world is upside down now. These Hollow saved my life. I can't ignore the fact that I am alive.

That they let me fully enter the *aethor* sleep after I fell to ash and let me heal. The only time I ever have to sleep—when I explode. No Hollow has ever done such a thing that I know of. And if they were honest about this, what else could be true?

These Hollow brought me to a safe place to rest, while I destroyed the temple ruins that had protected my flock for decades. Somehow, calling them by the name Father chose for them, *fior-errans,* doesn't feel quite right anymore. Too distant. Too honest.

Forsaken Ones with Wings.

Haunting me. Laughing at me. That no matter how hard I tried, I still lost them.

But my flock are not forsaken. Not yet. Not by me.

Heat swells inside my bones again. Steam cresting my skin.

A pulsating that begins deep inside. A kind of grief that isn't fueled by the same panic as last time. Instead, this grief breaks me. A reservoir opens.

The fire is a flood that starts to rise through me.

I need to get out. Out of this house. Out of my head.

Jude's and Eli's gazes are locked on my skin turning a deep crimson, like coals sparking to life.

They both look terrified. They've been here before.

But before they can run, I say to them, "Thank you for not killing me."

Then I walk as quickly as I can through the storage room, my entire body seething and shuddering even as I force the aching fire back down. I reach for the door I saw Jude come through earlier, the knob melting beneath my fist. I burst out of their house into a flurry of white, blistering snow.

Then I run.

CHAPTER TWENTY-SIX

Nothing about this world wants me. From its icy ferocity to the sun that has become a dull heartbeat over my head. Sickly and dying like everything else here. This planet tries to snuff out any bit of heat it can find.

I wish it would snuff me out now.

Wish it would snuff out the deep ache that swells from the farthest reaches of myself. Wish it would snuff out that overwhelming loneliness. The shame. The guilt.

As I run through the snowstorm, barefoot and in strange, threadbare clothes, I don't even feel the cold. My limbs are generating so much heat that the snow sizzles on impact, creating a wave of red-tinted light all around me as I run.

I scream for Father and throw my body into the storm, the winds whipping around me so forcefully they keep my aching form upright, even when I fall forward. Fire pours from the pain inside and scorches the icy world outside.

The liquid fire starts to crack through my skin like molten lava pressing up through cinnamon-colored earth. It begins to coat my body.

This must be a nightmare.

But, I can't wake up. I can't wake up. I can't wake up.

The fire covers my arms, dripping between my fingers, melting the snow around me. Cutting through the wind and the peppering of snowflakes.

My flock is dead, and I can't wake up.

The flames that emerge from the twin wounds in my back start to thicken, cauterizing even as blood flows down my spine. The grief is overwhelming. Hot and numbing at the same time. Pouring out of me with deadly intensity.

I wish I could escape my own body.

I can feel that ticking clock start. I'm on the verge of another explosion. I should keep running. Get as far away from those brothers as I can. But no matter how far I run, I can't escape myself.

Pain and volatile fear pops and hisses inside me like the flames that pour over my form. My clothes have burnt away, but I'm now covered in a dress of dripping, dancing flame. The fire scalds at first – and then my body starts to adjust.

I stumble forward a few more steps before my knees give out. My flaming tears drip into the snow, even as the wind starts to lessen. The snow swirls around me with a little less intensity—the massive amount of heat I'm generating is starting to combat the storm.

I'm on my knees in the snow, the flames pouring down my body pooling around my knees like the train of a dress. My hands scrape at the heavy snow layer, trying to feel it. But all I can feel is fire. Heat. Pain.

All the loss.

So, I arch my back, fists buried in the snow, body buried in the flaming ache, and let out one last scream. Haggard and broken and desperate.

But as the scream tears out of my body, as the pain and fear rips from my lungs, I feel the fire pouring from those two wounds in my back suddenly react in response. The molten flame spilling from my scars begins to crystallize. To harden. The raw pain creating a crucible that solidifies the dripping fire into something else—something hardened and sharp.

I slowly lift myself to glance over my shoulder.

Shimmering, jagged spikes protruding from both of the wounds that drag down my shoulder blades and reach nearly to my waist.

The wounds from the first time my wings were cut off when I was barely more than a child. When Father had taken a knife to my back, saying it was the only way to protect our people.

I am stunned at the very fledgling appearance along my shoulder blades. Tiny, fragile, but there. Rough and angular and gleaming with the hint of flickering fire still inside them—

Feathers. Like tiny, orange-tinted icicles protruding from my back.

I reach around, hardly daring to touch them.

My heartbeat speeds up as Father's voice echoes in my head. ***"Cut them off!"***

It's been over a decade since my wings last tried to reform. And I've never seen this many feathers at once. Three, pressing up through the skin.

My eyes blur. I hate what I have to do to them to keep others safe, as Father always said. Just one more part of me that's impossible to keep in check without him.

I reach back and try to pull at them, but gasp at the pain. The feathers poking through my heavy scars are rooted to the muscle and sinew curvature of my wings.

I can't just tear them off. Not right now. Not like this.

So instead I collapse into the ashen snow turning to water beneath me. The anger and writhing pain inside starts to soften into more of a dark, dull ache, bringing down my body temperature with it. My form coated in a thick sheath of ash.

As the blood that pours over my body settles, so does the raging storm. For the first time since I ran out of that house, I tilt my head back and look up at the sky.

The sun is barely visible, almost eclipsed by the cascading mountain range. The icy slopes rise out of the pale landscape, reaching upward toward the faint beat of red in the sky.

The sun almost seems to blink out for a second and then stutters back to life.

Something about its glint reminds me of the wave of flame that sputters and flickers around me.

Nothing about this world is familiar except for that sun. And even it is about to die and vanish.

Plunging everything into darkness.

CHAPTER TWENTY-SEVEN

As the raging wind dies down, everything aches.

The world is blurred and numb as I drag myself to my feet, leaving behind steaming footprints as I force one limping step after another through the snow. The ash that coated me has hardened into a kind of second skin, so thick it resembles lava rock. An interconnecting kind of armor, formed around my shuddering body, fragments of hardened shale splintered through with thin rivers of flame. The suit shelters me from the storm, glimmers of flame still tracing trails down my form.

Everything is blank and lifeless without my father's voice in my head. Nothing is right. Not the harsh sting of the chilled air against my face. Not the unfamiliar, craggy mountains that rage at the sky like they want to blot out the last shred of sun. Not the way I can't sense any *hajas* out here or feel the vibrations of *nemior* tubes under my feet.

Not the three tiny flits of feather that shiver against my spine, haunting me.

My own pain leaves behind deep, sizzling paths in the snow as I pause at the base of an enormous mountain. The wind has started to pick up again—not the furious snowstorm I walked through earlier, but a blistering breeze that peppers sharp flakes of snow over my reddened face, the only part of me not cloaked by the ash.

And as if catching a spark, my flaming blood starts to heat up. Not just pouring down my body, but flickering and glowing and dancing.

"You are dangerous, little one." Memories of my father's voice fill my head again. The nickname he used for me feeling like a slap across the face now. *"You have too much fire inside you. But I can help . . ."*

Flames arch up and around my arms, pushing past the ash forming a scab over open wounds. The fire presses through ragged cracks in the layers of shale that cling and hide all the vulnerable places. Like molten lava splintering through obsidian rock. I am a dormant volcano unable to settle—the flame too untamed. The ground shaking as the chain reaction sets off again. My whole body begins to rise as the fire continues to turn me inside out, leaking from cracks in my ashen armor, cracks in my soul.

"I can help you hold it in. I can protect everyone from you."

Tears burn my irises as my eyes fall closed, fire arching up my face. Even as my body reaches skyward, in my mind I fall backward, into myself, as my fiery pain consumes the remnants of a girl locked within.

My toes lose contact with the icy snow, my body rising into the air again. And just as my chest begins to crack apart, pain shooting over me as the fire building screams for a way out—

"Mara!" Eli's voice cuts through the thought in my head. But I don't want to hear it.

I'd rather dissolve and pray I don't wake up.

"Mara," Eli's voice sounds closer now. "I'm *sorry.*"

And that word, plus something about the sincerity in his voice, forces my raw, blistering eyes open. He stands in front of me, a heavy coat wrapped around him, but his hood pulled back to show that beautiful earth-toned skin and thick, jet-black curls. His nose is a raw kind of red, and I watch him shudder from the cold—but he doesn't lose eye contact.

"I'm so sorry, Mara. I know how painful this kind of loss is."

My lips are cracked and raw, but I manage to round them into a question, "How could you possibly know?"

"Because we lost our village too." His voice wavers. "And our mom." There is a crunch across the snow nearby, and I see the other brother slowly approaching from the opposite direction. He's darting harried glances between me and the foreboding mountain just behind us.

"Mara?" Eli's voice is soft, coaxing.

My head feels heavy and I slowly force myself to turn back to him.

"I know there's no reason for you to trust us. But I'm out here because I want to try."

My toes hover several inches off the snow, just above the pool of flaming orange-crimson dripping from my body. "Try what?"

"Try to convince you to stay."

I suck in a breath. "Why? What right do I have to stay when my flock is all gone? And it's my fault."

Eli's brows wrinkle in confusion, "What's your fault?"

I wave a blistered hand through the air, "Everything! If I'd just stayed in the tunnels like Father said, I could have protected them. They would have been safe. They would have woken up."

Eli's face pales. He opens his mouth like he wants to say something, but no words surface. In my peripheral, Jude stays significantly farther back than his brother, continuing to glance up at the mountain behind us.

Eli makes a motion as if to calm me, "Just take a breath. We'll wait. We can talk this out."

I shake my head, droplets of fire spraying everywhere. "It's too late." I glance down at my body that continues to evaporate into the flames, hovering midair. "I can't stop it once it's gotten this far."

"It's your own body, Mara," Eli says. "You aren't as powerless as you feel."

There's a nearly imperceptible stirring across the snow as Eli moves closer. "What do you think of this mountain range, Mara? It's breathtaking and quiet."

I know he's trying to distract me, but I don't entirely mind it.

I slowly lift my head. The mountains really are beautiful. Glistening almost crystalline in even the faintest shreds of light from the sallow sun overhead.

My body lowers a fraction of an inch toward the ground. The tender pain ebbing just a bit.

"Focus on the ice, Mara," Eli's voice breaks through. "Can you feel the cool sensation around you?"

My gaze drops to Eli. Capturing the bits of frost that cling to the broad shoulders of his coat. I try to focus on what he must be feeling—the way he rubs his hands together to stay warm.

Trying to feel the same cold breeze he does.

I start to sense the faintest whisper of cool air coasting over my raw burns. My fire flickers for a moment. Is it working?

I tilt my head. "How did you know this would help??"

The coppery tone of his irises flicker like flames again. "My dad had to do it for me. He taught me how to steady myself."

I think maybe I'd like to meet their father after all.

"You just think, like . . . really cold thoughts." Jude makes an attempt at being helpful that earns him a sharp look from his brother. Jude darts another glance at the mountain behind him and mutters, "And we can all get out of here without anyone getting hurt."

That's when I realize what he's been so preoccupied with. Despite what Eli said, something about the mountain looks unstable. Bits of ice are shifting and eroding. Cracks are forming in its surface as bits of snow sizzle and pop.

Melting. From the physical heat of my presence?

"Focus on the ice, Mara," Eli murmurs again. "Can you feel the cool sensation around you?"

My stomach twists. No wonder they are both treating me like a fragile animal caught in a trap—my body has basically become a living torch. My figure hidden by the sheath of flame and ashen rock and ripples of heat coating me. And my nearness to this icy mountain that hasn't even felt the sun's rays in decades could create an avalanche.

Just being here could bring this entire mountain collapsing and bury them.

"I'm putting you in danger." The words are breathless as I turn wide eyes from the mountain to the brothers, and back again. "Father is right. I just bring destruction. First to my people—and now you."

"No. No!" Eli speaks so forcefully it catches me off guard and my dipping flame falters. He locks eyes with me and something in his expression shifts. A kind of determining. Whether I'm ready for what he says next . . .

"Your flock would have died whether or not you were hiding down there with them, Mara. Your father was suffocating them."

CHAPTER TWENTY-EIGHT

At Eli's words, the flames that cover me suddenly flash, and a blast of heat radiates unbidden. My shock explodes in a vault of warm air that barrels dangerously into the mountain. The snow creaks and moans, but I barely hear it. The flames flicker and dance around my body, holding me suspended, the sparking blood cauterized in an instant.

My eyes rivet on Eli. "What?"

He watches me guardedly. While the blood has softened its pulse under my skin, it still races in time to my thundering heart. I hover a few feet above the ground, covered in ashen armor like some kind of volcanic creature, not even feeling shy as I stare down at him.

Instinctively, I press in toward his thoughts. The way I would if he were one of my people. I'm shocked to find I can catch a hint of the tone of his mind, if not his direct thoughts themselves. He's second-guessing what he revealed.

"What did you say?"

His voice is quiet as he repeats, "Your people were dying, regardless of whether you ever left the magma tubes. They needed heat— sunlight—to heal. By keeping you all hidden away underground like that, your father wasn't helping save them . . ." Eli pauses a moment as steam rises off my shuddering form. "He was starving them, Mara. Suffocating them by keeping them sick."

I shake my head vigorously, trying to dislodge his words. "Why would he do that? How can you possibly know any of this?"

He licks his lips. "My dad. He knew a lot about the creatures of this world. And when you've traveled as much as we have, you see and hear things. So we kept you in the sunlight. On this mountain. As close to our dying sun as we could manage." He gestures to the spirals of steam radiating around me. "Do you feel any stronger than usual?"

A shiver ripples over my ribcage and down between my shoulder blades, where my feathers have started to sprout. There is some truth to his words. *Maybe I'm more resilient than Father thought.*

I gaze at the sky. With the snowstorm subsided, I can make out the lonely silhouette of the dull sun dangling over our heads. It's a sallow grey color, with the faintest hint of the tainted orange it used to be. But even still, as I lift my face toward the faint scrap of heat that filters down, something inside reaches up. Out. Toward the sunlight.

While the ice that covers this harsh landscape is hard and unforgiving, I don't feel the chill. I lower my gaze to Eli. "Even if I did believe you, why would a Hollow like you care about the survival of my people? You've literally been selling our blood."

Eli raises his brows but says nothing. He glances behind him at the quivering mountainscape. "Perhaps we should find someplace safer to discuss this."

But I drift closer, the fragile feathers spouting from my shoulder blades flickering. "How do you know so much about us? Where is this father of yours?"

He shares a quick glance with Jude, and they both look back at the shivering mountain which has now started to shudder. A chunk of ice breaks away and slides toward us.

"You should leave—but I'm not"—I stare down at the sheath of ashen rock covering my body and the ripple of fire that still licks and dances around my hips and fists—"I'm not sure how to quench this."

Eli reaches up and skims the hardened ash coating my shoulder. His touch is surprisingly firm. "We can guide you back. Just put your feet in the snow."

I don't realize I'm doing it at first as I pull the flame back in and will the blood to dissolve into my skin. I've floated downward until my feet touch the ground, and I'm standing in front of him, body quivering as the liquid fire starts to recede into the ash covering me. As my blood soaks into the hardened surface, I sense the rock starting to thin. Ready to break apart and come loose.

Before I even have to ask, Eli tugs off his coat and extends it to me, turning away as I slip in.

"The fabric is mixed with *fire-quell*—it won't burn," he explains, still offering me privacy. "We were going to give it to you anyway."

"Thank you," I murmur, fastening the soft coat tightly. The lava-rock-like layer sheathing my curves dissolves around me. Falling to ash, and for the first time . . . the only wounds that twinge are the ones on my back.

Every other scar is gone. And my skin is a richer brown than I've ever seen it. Always so pallid in the caves.

Ash still peppers my body, but all blisters are healed.

As I tuck deeper into the softness of Eli's coat, there's a loud *crack!* from somewhere above us. I look up just in time to see a shelf of ice come loose and fall toward us—and with its disintegration, the rest of the mountain starts to crumble. A flood of ice chunks, disrupted rubble, and heavy powder pours our direction.

"Run!" Jude yells, racing forward.

Eli sprints after him, but I've already taken in the scene well enough to know it won't matter.

How many times has Father told you not to release too much heat? Especially not at the base of a mountain like this?

It wouldn't be my first avalanche. You don't survive in an icy wasteland as a living ball of fire without melting the wrong places. I also know how quickly they move and how the thunder of snow hurtling down will rip anything in its path.

The brothers will not be able to find shelter. Not fast enough. No matter how quickly they run.

So, I do the only thing I can think of. I race toward them, catching up in seconds, and wrap my arms around both. I pull them to the ground behind an outcropping of rock, one hand on Jude's shoulder, the other against Eli's neck—and let my eyes fall closed.

I am fire . . .

The whisper fills me, and I press it toward my chest and palms, facing away from the brothers and toward the storm.

I am rebirth . . .

All around us, we can hear the swell of the snowslide barreling down on us. But my body has started to heat up again. I squeeze my eyes even tighter and feel that flame inside grow in intensity. Pulsating, faster and faster, matching my racing heartbeat and swelling like steam reaching a boiling point.

I only have two goals as the spray of snow and ice and rock crashes over us:

Don't burn the brothers. Don't let them get buried, either.

Stand between them and the destruction I've brought down on them.

I'm on my feet, towering over the brothers. The outcropping of rock comes to my waist as I extend my hands out in front of me, body already coated in flame and skin a heated red.

Survive.

The avalanche hits us right as I unleash the blast of flame. It's so strong, so forceful it blows me backward, but the channel of fire bursts through the cascade of snow and rock.

I land on my back in the snow, whole body aching and sizzling, but the coat somehow still intact.

I slowly get to my feet and take in the sight around me. My blast has catapulted a path straight through the avalanche, turning a large section of it to steam and stifling the movement of the rest. The snow is mounded up in tall walls on either side. Relieved, I find the brothers exactly where I left them.

Alive and unharmed, huddled beneath the large cleft of rock.

None of us say a word until we are out of the pass and safely where another snowslide couldn't be triggered.

Then, my legs completely give out, my last bit of energy fully sapped.

Eli slows my fall, arms circling the singed coat and lowering me to the ground. He props my head up against his chest. "What are you?" he breathes. "I've never seen a god-born that strong."

My eyes start to blur and roll, but he gently taps me. "Stay with us, Mara."

Jude whistles. "And you think that the Hollow are a threat?" He shakes his head in disbelief. "You think your father was hiding your people from *us*?" He glances up at the steam-filled valley and melted ice showing a hint of dirt underneath. "When you have the potential to do *that*? No. We aren't the threat he was hiding from."

I feel Eli nod in agreement. "The Hollow couldn't even land a blow on a phoenix. Not if your flock was healthy and strong. But they were kept weak and afraid." He shifts carefully. "It doesn't make sense."

I don't trust these brothers yet. I don't know if I fully believe them. But if Eli's right, I was set up to fail. There was no way to keep my people safe. There was another threat I didn't know about. I'm curious how they know so much about phoenixes.

I subtly reach for the knife I see sticking out of Jude's boot. I slide the blade free and in a languid movement make a very light nick Eli's hand.

Startled, Eli yanks away and Jude utters a curse. But I'm the one who gives the biggest gasp as I watch flickering, flaming blood ooze through the cut on Eli's hand. Flaming blood that no Hollow should have.

CHAPTER TWENTY-NINE

ELI

Mara is going to get us all killed.

I glance at the sparks of blood. I wipe them away, ignoring how pale it's become. The gleam so many would kill for.

I would kill *not* to have it.

Flexing my stiff joints, I look up to catch Mara's shocked expression. *Well. I wasn't sure how long I'd be able to keep this a secret.*

Jude is muttering, but she doesn't hear him. Coal-dark irises stare at me.

Assessing me, deciding.

I don't dare breathe, letting this little firebird make her decision.

Slowly, the sense of wariness and distrust that has filled her sharp features softens. Until now, she's stared at us with the desperation of a trapped and wounded animal ready to take a swipe to escape.

I used to look at the Hollow the same way, before Jude and I found a home among the migrating villages. Before our father built a village around himself.

But now, she is regarding me differently.

As if we might have more in common than she thought possible. I hope we do.

"How can you have that?" Her voice is unsteady.

It's still almost miraculous to hear her talk. I'd grown so used to watching her impossibly still body in quiet sleep. Grown used to sitting beside her bed and telling her stories and bandaging her wounds—even admitting secrets about years gone by that I haven't told anyone.

I grew protective of her. If anyone else could understand what it felt like to despise your own blood—it would be her.

I prayed so many days that she would wake up.

And sometimes I wondered if I should pray she wouldn't. I wasn't sure what kind of world she'd wake to.

I was jealous of her ability to close her eyes and become harmless. No longer painfully aware of the ticking time bomb of her own body.

The heat in your veins that could help a whole village survive, but instead, makes your heart pump. Keeping you alive at the cost of so many others.

And I've found so many dead. No matter how many villages Jude and I get to, or how much of my blood I give away, it's never enough. There are always people we miss.

And yet my heart keeps pulsing. A reminder that I survive out here only because of a connection to the very creatures who doomed this place to an icy grave.

How do you overcome the guilt of something like that? The guilt of your own heritage.

But Mara softened some of it, looking more human than phoenix. She has their firepower, but also their vulnerability.

She's other somehow. And there's hope in that.

I rub my hands together. There may even be redemption in that.

Mara is watching me, tightening the nearly fireproof coat around her, awaiting an answer. But how do I explain the nightmares and scars and years running?

And how do I tell her how familiar she has become to me? How these five years kept me closer to home than I've ever been? Dad certainly appreciated it.

I slowly rise to my feet, my head immediately going light as I straighten. The cost of never having enough blood coursing through my system.

"Are you alright?" she asks.

My vision slowly clears. "My body doesn't heal as fast as it used to. Nowhere near as fast as yours. And it's really cold out here."

Mara's eyes flicker with concern, but she reaches out and touches a blood drop on my arm. It sizzles against her index fingertip as she asks for a second time, "How do you have blood like mine?"

The chill of the icy breeze is starting to batter me. A shudder sweeps my body again, and with it comes a blast of bright lights behind my eyes. My head goes light again, and I sway on my feet. Mara steps back, alarmed.

"We need to get him inside to warm up." Jude is always my defense. He reaches to quickly feel my forehead. "He's colder than the ice out here."

Mara's lips pinch to the side. "How is he so cold if he has . . ."

"If I have phoenix blood in my veins?" The three of us walk in the direction of the village, and our cabin set up on the outskirts. Closer than we cared to let Mara know. We were lucky she ran the wrong way. It's only when the cool wind slows and our cabin rises into view ahead that I'm finally ready to answer her.

I meet Mara's flickering, volatile eyes with fire dancing in them. Eyes that remind me of my own. Eyes so filled with light. But that light fades out here eventually. Everything does.

"Because we're alike, Mara," I murmur. "We're both god-born. I have fire for blood the same way I suspect you do—because I'm half human and half phoenix."

The half human side allowing me to age nearly at the same rate as my brother and blend in almost seamlessly as we travel from Hollow village to village.

She shakes her head. "The phoenixes would never . . ."

"You're right," I agree. "None of the phoenixes in your father's flock would ever touch any of our people. But not all phoenixes are like the ones you were raised with."

"How do you exist?"

I tilt my head, not quite understanding the question. And then it slowly starts to dawn on me. Why she has been in such shock at all of this. Why she would trust us so little. Why she was surprised the Hollow even looked remotely like her.

Jude swears under his breath beside me.

I stare at her. "You don't know, do you? Your father never told you?"

We reach the cabin and pause outside. Mara rocks on her bare heels, hands stuffed in the coat pockets. "Told me what?"

I tug off one leather glove. I lift a hand and coax a flicker of golden, dancing light to appear in the center of my palm. "I'm not related to the Fallen Phoenixes. The ones who raised you. My father is a Golden Phoenix. I think maybe one of your parents could have been too."

Her face goes white. She opens her mouth, but no words come out.

Jude raises a brow at Mara. "Your father never told you that there were other phoenixes?"

The shake of her head is so slight I almost miss it, but the way her entire body starts to quiver is far too familiar.

Jude cocks his head. "He really locked you away, didn't he?"

Locked you away . . .

There's something there. *I'm missing something.*

Suddenly, my head snaps back up. "Mara—what if your dad hasn't been hiding you and your flock from us?" From the Hollow. If he really feared us, he'd let her people have more access to sunlight and just destroy us all.

My fingers twitch, wanting release from the reminder of those responsible for my existence . . . and for torturing my father. The only decent Golden.

The creatures who raised Mara only wanted control. They all do. Leaving me to repay a debt I never asked for and had from the minute I was born. And doubled the first time I let a human die because I chose not to give them the heat source in my veins.

"What if your father was hiding from something else?"

Mara turns away slightly. "Maybe he was hiding from *them*."

I nod, rubbing my hands together and feeling the tongues of fire licking over my palm and up my knuckles. The dangerous truth in a world not built for the fragility of humans, but where the vulnerable are treated like playthings. Even by their own kind.

"Yes, and maybe the Goldens finally found him."

CHAPTER THIRTY

The humming in my head is growing so loud it's incessant. This coat feels like it's starting to strangle me.

They could be alive . . .

My breath comes in short bursts as Eli hands me a change of clothes. He and Jude vacate to the other room, though I notice that Eli seems to be limping. I instinctively lock the door after them. Quickly shedding the coat and pulling on the thick pants and long-sleeved top, I brush my hands over my burning eyes.

Hana could be alive . . .

It's all I've ever wanted—but not like this.

They could be alive, if these Golden Phoenixes haven't killed them yet. But, *still.* Some chance is better than none.

I let the brothers back in and they step around the hunt Jude brought in earlier, that I hadn't even noticed.

Eli's wearing another coat now, and he sags against a wall. He doesn't look good.

I sway on my feet. Even the air feels disorienting, alien. A world I thought I knew.

Now I'm not sure I know anything.

We were never the last ones . . .

Jude's quick glance sweeps from his brother, to me, and back. "You both look terrible." His tone is less grating than before. The three of us venture quietly back into main chamber where the firepit is now nothing but coals. Jude helps Eli sink into one of the stacks of cushions situated around the firepit. Eli grits his teeth as he settles on the floor.

"What's wrong with you?" I ask, awkwardly aware that was blunt.

Eli motions for me to sit. "I'll try to explain everything."

Cautious, I settle cross-legged on the nearest stuffed mat. But my pulse is racing so fast, blood pummeling the insides of my veins. I need to find a way to slow it down.

"The Goldens are—" Eli begins. I lift a hand and cut him off.

"Wait. I need . . ." I rub my vibrating hands together. "I need a minute."

A minute to orient myself. To find something familiar to root me into this room.

There's a stretch of open, coarse flooring between us and the firepit, so I reach forward and take a piece of charcoal from the embers lying at the bottom of the basin.

Pinching the charred piece between my thumb and forefinger, I start to sketch. The familiar sensation of dust against my fingers and the scratching of the rough strokes—it's the first thing that's felt like home.

The eager, skittering sensations flow into my fingertips, sketching the whispers that represent each piece still not fitting together.

I deftly mark out the curve of a wrist with drops of flaming blood dripping from it. Then I ram the charcoal against the floor in dozens of small lines, bringing to life the arch of a wing—until the charcoal snaps.

Father would want me to cut away those three tiny feathers clinging to my spine.

If my wings grow any further, any more dangerous, I'll clip them. *I promise, Father.*

In the meantime, I want to understand more about this young man who shares my blood.

I'll let him believe I'm like him, if it will keep me safer.

If it makes him fear me less. See me as less of a threat.

I've barely drawn the rough outline of his face when I finally look over at Eli, where he watches, silent. "Tell me about these Golden Phoenixes."

He absently traces a finger up his cuff. "They live on *Rekren,* an eastern mountain a dozen sunpasses' journey away from where your flock camped out." He pulls his coat tighter around himself. "Our mother went searching for them when Jude was little. I wasn't born yet."

I turn that over in my head a few times, sketching the small form of a woman with a baby slung on her back. "Does that mean Jude's not like you? Half and half?"

"I am fully human." Jude answers for himself, walking back into the room. He's holding a loaf of something that almost looks like bread in one hand and a container of gleaming blood in the other.

He tosses the bread to his brother. Eli catches it and breaks it in half, offering me a chunk. I almost refuse, but my stomach is growling violently, so I give a slight nod of thanks and take it. I nibble on it slowly, trying to get the food down.

Jude's fully human?

Different parentage. That would explain why the curve of his eyes and shape of his jawline and the hue of his skin is slightly different from his brother. The more I see of the Hollow—well, the humans—the more I'm struck by how unique and vibrant they are. An array of expressions and shapes and tones.

"How are you brothers, then?"

Jude coughs a laugh. "My dad died when I was a baby. Our mom had nowhere to go. So, she went to the only place there were rumors of heat—"

Eli continues for him. "She found shelter in the village at the foot of *Rekren,* the Mount of the Gods, the volcano where the Golden Phoenixes live. The Goldens let scraps of their flame trickle down the mountain, and it's one of the few places warm enough for anything to grow."

Both the brothers' expressions seem haunted.

Eli's voice has dipped lower and lower, until it's almost inaudible. "The cost to live there is worse than freezing to death."

Jude's face contorts. "The Goldens saw us as playthings. Specks of dust that would be gone the next time they blinked anyway."

I start to shrink in on myself. "What did they do?"

Jude's expression grows stormy, those silver studs glinting darkly. "A lot. It wasn't just what they did—but what the villagers would do to try and appease the creatures they saw as gods. My mother and I were almost one of those appeasements. The villagers thought our lifeblood was what the phoenixes wanted, since we needed their blood to survive. A trade. So, they tried to sacrifice us at a temple. I was barely five."

I stare at him. "What happened?"

Jude doesn't answer, but Eli does. "My father. Haven. He was the Golden Phoenix that the human village most feared. Our mother became the first human who wasn't afraid of him. He saved them."

I look at both brothers. "Why were they afraid of him?"

"Oh, you'll see soon enough," Jude replies wryly. "He didn't get along with the other Goldens. It was only with our mom he felt at ease. They fell in love and married. He built a home for us on the outskirts of the mountain, farther away from the Goldens. Everything was fine for a while. But, then Eli came along."

Every inch of my body is humming with a strange kind of excitement. I didn't even know places like that existed, let alone that there were instances where phoenixes and humans could live in peace.

At least, some attempt at peace.

It sounds like a dream to me. But everyone wakes up eventually.

"Why did you have to leave?"

Eli shifts, adjusting the coal, voice unsteady. "When the Goldens found out mom was pregnant with me, they asked our father to hand me over to be raised by them, to show his allegiance to them."

Jude, hefting a large jar of flickering, flowing blood in his hands, crouches beside Eli. "Haven said no. They decided to punish him for it. They waited for years, then came for the only family he had."

Charcoal fallen unheeded from my fingertips somewhere in the middle of their tale, I wrap my arms around myself, brow rippled.

These brothers know how difficult family allegiances are too.

"Haven took all three of us and tried to run," Jude continues, one hand scrubbing at his hair, buzzed shorter on the sides. "Eli was ten, I was fifteen." Jude's eyes turn distant. His next words are hollow. "Mom didn't survive."

My skin goes frigid and my heart sinks.

"We don't have to talk about it," I whisper.

Jude doesn't seem to hear me, and Eli gently pats his brother's shoulder before finishing the story. "It took us months to find a place the Golden wouldn't follow, but eventually, we were able to build a new home together. It wasn't long before other humans found us." Something wistful crosses Eli's face. "It's gotten pretty big since then."

Jude rejoins the conversation, taking a bite of bread. "Once we created a safe, warm place for people to come, Eli and I realized that others needed heat too. Eli and I started taking fire to other villages farther on the outskirts about a decade ago."

Eli nods. "It's what Mom would have wanted," he says.

But Jude shakes his head. "I think we can both agree it's gotten a little out of hand." He unscrews the lid and peers at his brother over the top of the jar. "I'm half-tempted to try and shove most of this back inside of you and see if it would help."

Eli tries to laugh it off. "It's fine. I said I've got it sorted and I do." He turns his head to me. "Your father really never told you about the Goldens?"

But rather than answer, I turn my eyes on Jude. I'm missing something. Something important . . .

"What's gotten out of hand?"

"It doesn't matter—"

"No, she's like you." Jude interrupts Eli. "If anyone understands, it would be her. Plus, you said you were laying off for a while. Or would find another way." He stands. "You don't look like you're taking a break. Did you talk to Haven?"

Taking a break from what?

Eli sends an uncomfortable look my way and then turns back to his brother. "He doesn't need to know."

I put down the bread, intent on trying to understand what's being so clearly said—and also not spoken at all.

Eli pulls his sleeves up over his hands. "I'm not talking about this anymore. It's my choice."

Jude gives an exasperated sigh. "We aren't just going to let you kill yourself over this, Eli. There are other ways."

"Not enough. And I can't just do nothing, Jude." He slowly gets to his feet and takes the jar from Jude's hands to tip it so flares of the flaming liquid spill out and coat the pile of logs. But instead of immediately catching, the flaming blood pops quietly against the logs, and almost instantly I can feel heat radiating from the firepit.

It's as if the flames could softly flicker like this for a very long time, not needing to consume the logs for kindling, but rather coating them and pouring heat into them. And out to us.

Heat that must have come from somewhere. Flaming blood that I don't think they hunted for.

I stare at Eli. "This is your blood, isn't it?"

A part of me has suspected it for a while. But it's different giving it a voice.

He settles back down before replying. "Yes. I'm the longest lasting solution we've found to fight off the cold."

Jude has taken a seat on the other side of the firepit, prodding its flames.

Further confirming why Eli has looked drained and weakened since I first met him. He's been slowly bleeding out for years.

"You're selling your own blood in those pouches at each village . . . ?" I cannot even imagine how much blood he would have to give in order to meet the needs of even a fraction of the Hollow villages.

They're both quiet for a moment, then Eli clears his throat. "It's all mine. I have to give back the heat the Golden Phoenixes took. It's all I can do to help save any of the humans."

I lean back a bit to take in his gaunt frame. "How much blood do you even have left?"

Jude gives the stick he's using to stoke the fire a violent thrust. "Not a healthy enough amount. But he won't stop, no matter what Haven or I do."

This is worse than I'd even expected. His bloodshot eyes. The way he sways on his feet and the weakness of his grip.

"But *why*?" I blurt. "Why would you do that to yourself? You're . . ." I bite my lip. "You're slowly killing yourself."

The room goes very, very quiet. Jude bends his head low as if to hide his face.

He has probably said those same words to his brother before.

Eli is shivering again. His body is shutting down on him, just like I've seen my father's do. But my father was sick because of how isolated he was from the sunlight and the world around him, whereas Eli is sick from giving more to the world than he has to offer.

The muscle in Eli's jaw is tight.

Without even realizing I'm doing it, I nudge a thought into his head. *"What are you running from?"*

He must catch the telepathic whisper because he jerks upright and stares at me.

Oh.

I forgot what this was like. Being heard like this—both our minds overlapping.

So intimate. Like a secret shared between just us two.

He seems to get caught up in my wide-eyed gasp for a moment, and then finally lets out a breath.

"Not from—running *toward.* Some kind of atonement. The Goldens have done terrible things I have to make right. They've let millions die by watching the sun fade and doing nothing. They hurt my parents in . . ." His tightened fists quiver, and his voice rises. "Unimaginable ways. There's too much pain. I can't fix it fast enough. But, it's a blood debt I can at least make a dent in."

I lean toward him just enough for my fingertips to skim his clenched fists. Out of the corner of my eye, I can see Jude frozen in place, bent over, barely daring to breathe.

"Is losing yourself actually solving anything?" I press the next thought into his mind. *"I don't know what the Golden Phoenixes did to you, but isn't that their fault? Not yours?"*

Eli gives his head a shake. "I've seen what happens when I don't share my flame. I couldn't forgive myself if I let that happen again."

"What happens to them after you've bled yourself dry? Is buying them a few more days really worth dying for?"

Jude sends me an appreciative look. I'm probably not the first person to say this. Yet I can hardly believe I am doing so.

But I've lived like this. I've shut out every part of myself to try and protect others. But watching someone else do it?

Eli's tone is stubborn. "Some sacrifices have to be made."

I pull my knees to my chest. "That's what my father would say."

That's what I've always believed, too. Now, as I look at the sacrifice Eli has been making all these years, I'm not so sure.

If cutting out parts of yourself is what it takes to protect others in this world, something is very, very wrong.

The familiar scars across my spine twinge and ache. It all hurts. The pain of my feathers pressing through skin, rising to the surface—and the agony of cutting them off, disentangling myself from the weapons that could slice others around me.

But one pain, from new feather growth, almost feels like mending. Like a broken bone healing.

Like rebirth. Renewing.

The scars crossing the bend in Eli's arms, the way he drains his own life to try and give others theirs—that pain is a weight no one can carry for long.

I bury my face against my knees. Father will surely have an explanation, right? But if these brothers' story is true. If there really are other phoenixes out there—

I tilt my head to look up at Eli, at the gauntness in his brown cheeks and the freckles that texture his sharp jawline. A young man carrying the wrongs of a world that stole his mother from him, like it did mine. Yet instead of hiding away and hating them, he's made it his purpose to help it in some small way. He couldn't get his mother back. Couldn't save his father from the Golden Phoenixes' wrath. They just had to run.

But I'm done running. Done hiding. Finally, I can do something for my family.

But the only way to rescue my flock might mean dragging Eli back into the very world he has been trying to carve out of his veins for years.

CHAPTER THIRTY-ONE

Jude warms some kind of stew over the top of the firepit. He ladles out broth for each of us, to go along with the bread. It warms my insides and calms the uncertain pace of my pulse.

I'm finally about to venture another question after eating my bowl of stew, when Eli finishes off his third bowl and gets to his feet. "We need more firewood." He gestures to the firepit. "I'll get it. A bit of fresh air might help."

I instantly force myself to my feet too. I have to ask him about the Goldens . . . and about helping me find them. I pull my jacket back on. "I'll help you."

Jude pauses, ladle in hand, and looks at his brother. "No way. I'm not letting you go out and get wood when you look this sick."

But Eli holds his ground, "I'm fine, Jude. You can't spoon-feed me soup all day. Besides"—he glances at me—"Mara is going to help."

Jude studies his younger brother for a long moment. "Alright. But quickly. It's getting even colder tonight."

Eli heads out the door into the blistering wind, and I follow. He walks quickly around the side of the cabin to a pile of neatly stacked firewood covered in a thick sheath of ice. But before he can dare thaw it with what little spark of flame is still keeping him on his feet, I dart in front of him.

"Let me do it." I set my bare palms against one side of the thick shelf of ice coating. Within seconds, it begins to melt away and reveal the heavy chunks of firewood.

"Thanks." Eli nods, reaching for two pieces and hefting them. I grab a few logs myself, and hurry to keep up with him. For a sick guy, he's fast.

"You said the Goldens might have taken my people," I begin. "How do I get to their mountain?"

He pauses in front of the cabin door. "I knew you were going to ask this."

"Wouldn't you?"

His lips draw tight. "To say it's dangerous is putting it mildly. Just getting to *Rekren* could kill you." He hefts the firewood a little higher. "If your father and the others somehow survived, the Goldens won't just—"

"Imagine if it was Jude," I interrupt. "Could you leave him there?"

He considers my question for a moment, and I see the war waging in his eyes. He wants to disagree but he can't. Because family goes far deeper than blood for us both. And I understand that part of him in a way that perhaps even his own brother doesn't.

"Just tell me something—*anything*," I insist. "How do I get there? Draw me a map."

But Eli has seemingly lost interest in our conversation. He turns away from me, shoulders stiff, eyes glued to the chunks of ice and snow coating the cabin.

"Are you listening?"

He hushes me. "It's back." He gestures to several sets of the faintest prints in the snow circling the cabin, so covered in the fresh flurries and spread by the wind that I almost don't recognize them.

But there is something strangely familiar about the pawprints that curve around the brothers' shelter.

Eli drops his firewood and takes hold of my shoulders to pull me close.

He's trying to protect me, eyeing the churned snow around us.

I know that. But from the growl that suddenly echoes out over the icy wind, I don't think *she* knows.

My head turns to find a large *seren* crouched on the roof of the cabin. An extremely familiar *seren* who seems older than the last time I saw her, and far more feral. Her hackles are up, teeth bared, and when Eli tries to push me toward the door—she pounces.

The creature bowls Eli over before I can warn him, her claws bared.

He gives a yell, and I'm thrown to the side, hitting my head against the wood slats of the cabin. Through my daze, I'm able to make out a devastating scene in front of me—

Flickering orange and red blood splashed across the white snow as the *seren* pins Eli to the ground and rips open his chest with a swift swipe of her claws.

His screams blot out every other sound.

CHAPTER THIRTY-TWO

The giant form of the *seren* growls, and I slowly advance toward her.

"Stop! He's not a threat!" At my raised voice, the *seren* pauses, lifting her massive head. One bared claw still rests on Eli's torn chest. His blood sparks against the snow-coated ground. It only singes her fireproof fur. Without a shadow of a doubt, when I see her amber eyes, I know it's *her*. The *seren* I helped back near our *nemior*.

I race to throw myself between the *seren* and Eli just as she takes another swipe at him. The edge of her massive claw catches my torso as I bend over him, and white-hot pain tears across my ribcage, but I refuse to move.

"It's alright! He's not going to hurt me!"

Another voice pierces the chilled air. "Keep talking to her. Tell her you're safe. Tell her she can ease up."

At first, I think it's Eli—the rich timbre of the voice is vaguely similar to his. Yet it's much deeper and has a strong quiver.

I look around and see someone coming from the opposite direction I'd fled earlier.

The figure is covered in a thick, russet coat, and bends over a staff in one hand as he crosses the patterned snow toward us. "Calm her, child! She's protecting you. Tell her you're safe."

I obediently lift my hands, keeping eye contact with the massive creature and maneuvering around Eli. "I'm safe. Let him go—he's not a threat." Her rippling gaze locks on me, hackles raised. The wind is sharp and biting as it cuts across us. I watch her retract her claws, and then she takes a half-step back. The *seren* looks at me, then to the approaching figure, and then back at me again.

I hear Eli choking on his own blood. A glance over my shoulder shows he has one hand over a particularly large gash, trying to stanch the blood flow. His eyes are impossibly big. With effort, he cranes his neck to see the newcomer who has paused just behind the *seren*, close enough I can see him out of the corner of my eye.

Relief fills every plane of Eli's agonized expression.

"Tell her to come to you," I am told.

I slowly step away from Eli, trying to coax the *seren* to follow. Thin rivulets of flame catch bits of my coat from the gash at my side.

Right at that moment, Jude bursts through the door of the cabin, bolting toward the *seren*.

"Get off him!" he shouts, a large knife in one hand. But before he can reach the *seren* or I can yell for him to stop, the hooded figure moves impossibly fast and slams his walking stick into Jude's chest. Jude practically bounces backward off the staff. He rights himself and his jaw drops. "Dad? You're here?"

I blink and regard Haven with a new kind of understanding.

There is a nod, and he says, "Steady, son."

Jude takes a breath and a cautious step back. His father shifts his attention to me. "Call her to you."

I swallow, then meet the *seren's* narrowed gaze again. "Come here, mama. Come protect me here." I reach for her, taking another step backward—

The *seren* freezes for a moment, turning to look from me to the others standing behind me, and then down at Eli. Finally, she eases away from him and ever so slowly pads up to me.

Eli's chest has three massive claw marks and is coated in so much liquid flame, it's hard to tell where the small river of paling fire stops and the young man begins.

Out of the corner of my eye I can see Jude and Haven making their way toward Eli. The *seren* tenses, trying to sidestep me, but I quickly move closer and block them from her. My eyes stay on the *seren* as Jude and his father come around us and crouch next to Eli. Jude tears off his coat and presses it to his brother's chest to try and stop the bleeding.

The mother *seren* in front of me has her teeth slightly bared, but she doesn't snap as I gently reach out and brush my hand over her rough face.

"Thank you for looking out for me," I murmur to her, "but they're not the enemy."

I cautiously stroke her muzzle. "I'm safe. You've done your job well—I'm safe." Slowly, ever so slowly, I watch her hackles lower and she leans into my touch. I glance down at her pouch, expecting to see the pup poke its head out. But her pouch seems empty, and there is something very . . . grieved about the *seren*.

I can't explain how I know, but I just know.

On instinct, I lean in against her and brush a hand over her back. "You lost your baby, didn't you? While I was asleep?"

She gives a little shudder, and I wonder if the emotion somehow gets through, even if the words don't. The *seren* utters the softest, lowest little whimper, and I bury my face against her.

The anger, the fear I felt an instant ago as she tore into Eli fades into a kind of understanding. She lost her pup and was protecting the only other creature in this wasteland who showed her mercy, who she had reason to care about.

I continue to gently soothe her until I finally feel her taut muscles relax. Her rubbery lips now cover her sharp incisors.

I hear Eli gasp and bite off a cry.

I glance over my shoulder to see their father gently patting Eli's shoulder as Jude tries to apply more pressure to stop the bleeding.

The walking staff stills. "The wounds are too deep."

Jude looks up, eyes pleading. "Can you help him?"

The man turns toward me, and I see a faint glint of flame under the hood. His eyes. "Come closer. I'll need you for this."

I shake my head. "That's not a good idea. I'm not any good at fixing wounds. I'd only burn him."

He gives a low huff. "I'm not afraid of you, child. But I do need your hands to help."

Not afraid of me?

Something about that simple phrase settles in deeper than I expected. I whisper a few more soothing things to the *seren*, and then go over to the others. The *seren* paces back and forth uncertainly behind me.

"I'm fine. I'm safe," I keep whispering into her thoughts.

Now next to Eli, I finally take in the full extent of the damage. The three massive gashes seep flaming blood that has all but burned through Jude's coat. Haven's hands, bent and knotted, interlaced with unusual jagged scars I don't recognize, press over the gaping wounds.

Eli's normally browned skin is as white as the snow and his eyes are rolled back.

This is not good.

I sink to my knees in the mixture of snow turned to steam as Eli's hissing lifeblood collides with it. Even his fiery blood has become murky and languid, starting to fizzle out. I can feel his pulse beginning to slow when I reach for his wrist.

My father's words flood through my head. ***"Assess the damage. Find the fragile areas. Find the deepest wounds."***

"Cauterize."

"What do you need?" I ask. Jude's hands are bubbled with burns from trying to press his jacket against the massive gash torn over his brother's chest. With the jacket gone, we can now see torn flesh and the white of ribs showing through.

"Cauterize the wounds," Haven says, echoing my father's words. "I'll do the rest." His words are low and steady, but there's an unmistakable note of worry interlacing them. The tenderness he uses as he brushes Eli's wounds betrays just how much he cares about his son.

But his calmness reminds me how ancient this phoenix must be—and how often he's surely survived situations like this. I can only hope his son is as resilient.

After shooting one more glance over my shoulder to be sure the *seren* is staying where she needs to, I place both my hands over Eli's chest.

I close my eyes and let the flickering liquid slide between my knuckles, and then press as much heat as I can find roiling inside me to the surface. I pull the heat into my hands and let the warmth turn my skin almost to flame—but not quite. I want to cauterize his half-human skin, not burn it to char.

Eli gives a hoarse scream, his entire body jerking. *Be fast, be fast.* I keep my hands where they are until the blood boils and hardens and the open vessels shrivel at the ends, stopping the flow of blood.

The Hollow are so fragile. Even one who is only half-Hollow.

The moments stretch on, but finally the bleeding stops. Eli shudders and hacks for breath, but he's no longer a spout of flame.

"Well done." Haven reaches out and places his own hands over Eli's chest. As he does so, he leans forward, and his hood falls back to reveal long, dark hair hanging around his shoulders hiding his features. Dark hair the same shade as his son's. But it's the gleam that begins to swell along his bony hands that takes me aback. The bit of flame and light that flows down and over his knuckles and coats the massive wounds on Eli's chest.

I feel my own flame reacting as if answering a call.

The fire that Haven lets wash over Eli is lighter than blood, almost like a breath. It settles over the jagged cuts and bone-deep gashes. Blurring the exposed arteries and muscle.

I hold my breath, waiting for the burns to become apparent, for Eli to scream—but instead, Haven's flame seems to do the opposite. I watch, stunned, the broken bone pressing out from his ribcage begins to move back into place, flesh knitting back together.

It almost looks like—regeneration.

"How are you doing this?" I manage.

Haven keeps his focus on Eli, but answers, "There once were those in our ranks who were proficient at sharing their healing. I was able to learn a few tricks from the best healers before it became a lost art form."

It's like the stories Hana would tell me. Of the many seasons, eons ago, when our people were in their prime and could offer their flame and regeneration freely. When Hana was one of the greatest healers in her citadel.

By the time I met her, she'd become so weak she could barely share her healing. So she taught me to use plants and poultices instead.

She was the last person I saw use flame like this. She mended a cut on my leg when I was a small child. Father never let her explain how.

Father never healed like that.

But Haven is tenderly pulling his own child back from the brink.

Entranced, I lean forward and place my own hands beside Haven's.

I feel my flame react in unison with Haven's. Something ebbing deep inside pushes to the surface—a strong desire to see the warm, brown tone return to Eli's skin.

As if watching a miracle, I see Eli's body continue to heal. Wounds start to fade and muscle mend. *This should be impossible.*

And as I watch that same warm glow that coats my people's bodies as they sleep and regenerate bring the same kind of new life to Eli's shredded form, I'm left with one desperate question: If we have the potential to heal each other like this, why did Father hide our sick away? If *I* have the potential to help with regeneration, why did he never let Hana teach me? Why did he force them to survive my flames, but never teach me how to use my fire to heal?

Father told me I was a threat that needed to be controlled.

Haven isn't afraid and has drawn out a part of myself I didn't even know existed.

CHAPTER THIRTY-THREE

I finally lean away from Eli. Jude and I both stare transfixed as Eli slowly pulls himself into a sitting position. His face is no longer ghostly pale, it's now flushed a deep chestnut, the tone of richly-churned earth, like the day I met him.

Their father lets out a long sigh and slumps to the side. Jude is there in an instant. "Hang on, Dad. Let's all get inside."

My chin is propped on my knees drawn to my chest, panting. My body is completely sapped of energy, but I can't stop staring at Eli. At how . . . renewed he looks. Eli lifts a hand, palm up, and kindles a perfect, flickering flame reminiscent of the one he showed me only earlier today when he revealed his unique parentage. But this time, the fire seems to burst out of his skin, smooth and languid, like it belongs there. Like it's a part of him that has remembered how to burn. How to glow.

The fire is reflected in Eli's coppery-brown eyes, and for a moment, I think it's the continued reflection of the flame in his hand, but then I realize there is fire in his eyes. Something seething and vibrant and *him* that flashes across his irises and gives them a gold tint.

He scrambles to his feet, reaching for his exhausted father. Both brothers heft the bent, older figure up and carry him toward the cabin. I step back to hold off the *seren* until they're inside.

I reach up to gently touch her muzzle again. "I'm safe. All is well. I'll be just inside."

She seems to understand and slowly pads several feet away to sink down into the snow, watching me at a distance.

At least she won't attack Eli again.

I watch her for a stretching moment. It feels like it's been an eternity since I was the girl, hiding in that magma tube, terrified that this *seren* had snuck in to steal our stores. Five years may have passed while I was asleep, but in the past day—I've lived a lifetime.

I give a final fond tussle of the *seren's* tapered ears when she dips her head low enough for me to reach and murmur a thank you, then I turn toward the cabin.

I arrive in time to hold the door for the brothers as they carry their father in. I give them some space as they gently help Haven past the entry room, avoiding Jude's scattered hunting gear, and through the second doorway into the main chamber. They aim for the padded cushions beside the fire. Jude offers him some of the leftover stew.

Before he takes it, the phoenix tilts his head toward me. "Thank you, Mara. I'll be restored to full strength soon, and then will answer the many questions I'm sure you have."

I shouldn't be surprised he knows my name. He could have caught it from one of his sons' thoughts, but his voicing of it lingers in the air.

Eli helps settle his father near the warmth of the fire, and quietly sits beside him. In the flickering light, I can see just how similar their features are. The same rounded face and nose. The same weight sitting on their shoulders.

The same fire dancing inside them. A fire that Haven wields so much differently than my father does.

A shiver creeps down my spine. Father would not like me being here.

CHAPTER THIRTY-FOUR

I linger at the back of the room, watching the brothers with their father. Eli sips broth that Jude has reheated, and the three of them converse in low tones.

A dynamic that is eerily familiar.

As I watch them, I realize . . . they are their own flock. Their own family.

It makes my insides twist.

Giving them more privacy, I limp over to the collection of salves I watched Eli use earlier. I rummage through them and find a needle and some thread and a familiar mixture made of *eliberries* and *furn*.

Trying to make myself smaller, so as not to intrude, I gather them and drift back to the supply room we entered through. All that's left from Jude's earlier hunt is a few droplets of blood and some fur staining the floor.

This house that used to feel like it was closing in now seems a little sturdier. Safer. Quiet and solid.

Did they really build all this? For me?

Suddenly, a familiar burning pain cuts through my ribcage. I gasp as I ease down against a wall in a corner of the room. Once again, I'm mending my own wounds.

I slowly unwrap my coat to assess the full damage and scrunch my nose. Not as bad as when I was attacked by that *velian*, but worse than when I fell down a crag.

My flickering blood has already burned through most of the shift covering my torso. I should have wrapped it up sooner.

The *seren* left a slash across the lower half of my ribcage, and while the skin is already starting to pull back together, it could use some help.

Ripping off one of the sleeves of the new shirt Eli gave me after I'd burnt through the last one, I try to wipe clean the area as much as I can. Then I take one of the jars I'd just discovered and pry it open to pour some of the thick mixture into my palm.

I hiss under my breath as I drizzle a little of the liquid from the crushed herbs into the wound. They'll aid the healing process, but it hurts intensely in the meantime.

Once the wound is as clean as it can be at the moment, I use one hand to press the edges together and then pick up the needle with the other.

I bite my lip, squinting, focusing on where to begin.

My body will heal fairly quickly without the stitches, but I've found that the sutures tend to expedite the process.

Holding my breath, I'm about to start sewing myself up when the sound of footsteps interrupts me.

I let out that breath when I realize it's just Jude. He approaches me, carrying a bowl of something and a look of concern.

"What happened?"

At first, I don't register his question, then follow his unsettled glances from the puddles of flaming blood that splatter the floor, singeing the wood, to the needle I have poised by the gash at my side.

The needle in my hand wavers. "The *seren*—she caught me when I tried to help Eli." His eyes go wider and I rush my words. "She didn't mean it!"

Jude lays the bowl on the floor and examines my wound more closely. "You're about to sew yourself up?"

"I didn't want to bother you or Eli."

Jude shakes his head, the longer bits of hair on top becoming even more messy than they already were, while the sides are buzzed so close to his head I'm surprised he didn't try to create some kind of design.

"So, you've just been bleeding out this whole time?" He reaches for the needle in my hand. "I'll be fast. It's harder to do this yourself."

I give a slight nod, holding both sides of the gash together as he quickly dips the curved needle through both stretches of skin, starting to pull the wound back together.

I wince, biting the inside of my cheek as he deftly makes a few crosswise stitches. He's right; it is fast. Of course, he's done this before.

Once he finishes, Jude packs the full herbal mixture around the fresh stitches. He then fetches more cloth from another room and gingerly winds it around my ribcage to cover the fresh stitches.

As he bandages me, I look up at him. "Thank you."

He answers with a slight nod, keeping his head down as he finishes tying off the bandage. Finally, he sits back on his heels and looks at me. "You know, you are a lot like Eli."

I blink. "What do you mean?"

"You both would bleed out if it meant someone else wasn't in pain. And I don't get why. Especially you, Mara."

A chill crawls over my shoulders, "What? Why?"

Jude reaches for the cooling bowl of broth he brought in. "I've seen far too many phoenixes, and other than Haven, they all have one thing in common."

He extends the bowl to me, but I stay still, waiting for him to continue.

"Our deaths mean nothing to them. In my entire life, I've only ever met two creatures with fire in their veins who didn't view us as less than nothing." He gestures to the next room. "Haven, being the first. And then, of course, Eli. And now you. But you are the biggest mystery."

I take the bowl of broth from him. "Why?"

"Because you should be cynical and bitter and angry. You should only care about your own survival." Conflict is on his brow. "You were raised to be a weapon."

My breath hitches.

Jude looks at me more intently. "But I can't figure out how you got out of the cage you were born in, and still have your . . . humanity. You chose to warn us when you exploded and threw yourself between us and an avalanche." He motions to my bandages. "And between Eli and a *seren*. You were raised a phoenix, but your actions . . ."

" . . . are human?" I whisper, something inside withering at the thought. But I can't fully deny it.

Jude just nods. And the room starts to spin again. "Like I said, you're a lot like Eli, but with opposite fears."

This is the most I've ever heard this young man talk. He's surprisingly perceptive. "In what way?" I ask.

"You're terrified of what will happen if you let your flame out," he says to me. "And Eli is terrified of what will happen if he doesn't. If he doesn't drain every last drop of fire," he clarifies.

Jude stares up at the ceiling, taking in a deep breath. "I didn't know what to think of you at first. But you are growing on me a bit." He gives a slight smile that disappears with his next words. "But if you hurt Eli or anyone else—"

"I understand," I assure him.

"Good."

But I can't get his words of compassion out of my head.

You're terrified of what will happen if you let your flame out—and Eli is terrified of what will happen if he doesn't.

CHAPTER THIRTY-FIVE

Jude leaves me to eat my broth alone, taking the medical supplies with him.

I sit against this corner for what feels like a long time, eyes fluttering as my body finally relaxes. The warm texture of the stew is more flavorful and filling than anything I've tasted in many years, pouring down my throat and heating my insides.

Once I finish, I struggle to my feet and limp toward the other room. Eli's worn coat is still tucked around me, over my borrowed shirt and loosened near my stitches. As if he'd been waiting for me to rise, Eli appears in the doorframe. Beads of sweat slick dark curls across his forehead, but he looks more whole than I've ever seen him.

He takes my empty bowl. "How are you?" He scans the bulge of my bandages, expression heavy.

"Just a little dizzy," I admit.

At that, Eli lightly places a hand against my back, gently guiding me into the larger chamber and over to a cushion beside Haven. My knees nearly give out as I settle onto the seat, and I try not to audibly grimace as the stitches in my side pull at the movement.

I let a measured breath out through chapped lips, trying to angle my body in the most comfortable position as I sit cross legged. Haven remains unmoving beside me, his form massive even hunched as he is. The faintest shadow of something lean and feathered spreads out across the rough floor behind him. A wing? Another weapon?

I catch the slight tilt of his head, watching me.

My hands feel clammy. Do I look at him? Say something?

Thank *Sol*, Eli quickly drops my empty bowl into a bin across the room, then settles down on his own padded seat beside me. He's picked up a scrap of some kind of woven material on his way back to me, something that Jude tracks immediately, and I watch the older brother's expression perceptively darken. Eli works the material in his hands without even looking at it, stretching and pulling at the jet-black, interlaced threads as his fingers glow red from pressing heat to their points.

I'm not sure what he's doing, but it's clearly not the first time, his movements are so methodic and routine. Balancing the material on his knee and continuing to massage it, he leans toward me.

Eli clears his throat, voice low enough that only I can capture his next words. "Thank you, Mara. Dad hasn't been able to do healing like that in a long time. I thought I wasn't coming back from . . ." He lets the unspoken linger, and my insides twist just thinking about it. I haven't been awake for long, but already this gentle half-human young man who shares my blood has come to mean something to me. "Healing me like that could have killed him if you hadn't helped. Thank you."

I stare down at the coarse floor, thumb tracing up and down the lining of his borrowed coat. "I had to do something. I hated seeing you hurt. Especially because the *seren* was just trying to protect me."

"Quite the guard dog," Eli quips, but he can't quite hide the quiver beneath. He licks his lips, dark expression catching mine. "Those creatures are usually deadly."

I give a weighted nod. My eyes drift to his father, sitting hunched over beside the firepit. The skin on Haven's bony hands is split open and raw, but slowly starting to mend.

Jude stirs the flame flickering in the pit, and the orange glow reflects off the silver glinting in his earlobes. His brow ripples. "How did you do that, Mara?" he asks, echoing his brother's uncertainty. "I've never heard of a god-born who could actually share regenerative energy."

"I'm more surprised than you," I tell him slowly. "Hana was the only phoenix I'd ever seen do anything like that, and she didn't teach me."

At her name, Jude and Eli turn to look at their father. Haven's head lifts, and his hair falls back enough to reveal the skeletal structure of a face horrendously scarred with deep, jagged wounds that look to be millennia old.

His attention locks on me. "You know Hana?"

Some of his face is still cast in shadow, but I can see enough.

It's clear that his pain is due to both flame and fileting, the kind of wounds only inflicted by one kind of weapon: a phoenix's wings.

I shudder. It's the damage my own wings could do. A reminder of why I need to clip those three tiny feathers clinging to my shoulder blades.

But Haven is alive. Possibly more alive than nearly anyone I've ever met.

My back aches as I sit staring at him.

Only then do I realize I haven't answered his question. "Yes, she's one of my flock. She helped raise me." I look at them all, confused. "You know her too?"

Haven's thin lips curve into a gentle smile. Something about it reminds me of my father—but with more genuineness in his expression. "Once. Another lifetime ago. She was a skilled healer and taught me how to share my flame like you just saw. But she was far better than I could ever be."

A smile tugs at my lips, picturing it. Picturing Haven and Hana. They would get along.

"When I find Hana, I'll ask her to teach me," I vow.

Jude and Eli share a long look, but I can't decipher it. Haven curls in on himself with a low sigh, head bent, resting on his carved staff.

There's something more here. Something to this story. Something wrong.

I haven't fully earned their trust.

Good. I didn't take them for fools. They've barely known me for a day.

The stitches twinge again, and I try to stretch out more, bare toes angled toward the fire the three of us sit around. The sparks flicker across Jude's expression from where he stands on the other side of the pit, pouring what's left of the soup into a container to store. I wouldn't have expected him to be the cook, out of their small family.

Then again, I also wouldn't have expected him to help bandage me up.

He pretends not to listen, almost lurking on the other side of the fire, but his knowing gaze darting up to meet Eli's says he's taking it all in.

Jude is a human who has been taught to see the world more like a phoenix, measuring and molten. Gravitating toward the heart of the flame.

Whereas, beside me, Eli almost seems to be holding himself back from the warmth of the firepit, his hands shaking a bit as he works at the scrap of material balanced on his knee. Suddenly, I piece together what it is—and why his hands glow a subtle red as he works at stretching and pulling the woven fabric. He's tempering the handcrafted material. It must be the same fabric my coat is made out of. He's preparing this stretch for something else – perhaps to be able to hold his liquid flame, his lifeblood. Preparing to give more of it away.

No wonder Jude's mood grew darker when Eli grabbed it.

I move a fraction closer to the firepit as Jude stirs dancing coals and warms his hands over it. That's when I remember he ran out into the cold without a jacket. He must be freezing. He moves around the pit and closer to Eli, lightly tapping his forehead. "You're warm, Eli. Do you have a fever?"

A smile tugs at my lips.

"He doesn't have a fever," I interject. I take one of Eli's hands, leaning toward him. I'd forgotten the sensation of a firebird's warmth when healthy and bursting with heat. He startles, but when I press a bit of fire through my fingertips into his, his body reacts and his entire palm is instantly enveloped in a sheath of dancing flame.

Jude's jaw drops.

Eli's eyes widen, quickly moving the leather he was working with out of reach of the flame. "I haven't had this much fire that I could pull from since . . ." Something clicks and he abruptly looks up at Jude. "Since we were living with *them*."

Jude darts a worried glance to his father, and slides one hand back to his hip, reaching for the knife stored there. The older brother's eyes narrow on me. "What did you do to him?"

But before he can draw the weapon, Haven raises a gnarled finger toward his adopted son. His other hand grips the staff. "Jude, let her be. We both know she's not like Eli. I've told you that since you first brought her to me."

I flicker a glance between the brothers, then back to Haven. His words might be guarded but his meaning is clear.

He knew the truth.

I sneak a glimpse at the younger of the two brothers. Eli's face seems to have reddened slightly.

"No one really knows what to do with a volatile firebird, so I helped them build this cabin around you." He gestures up at the latticed ceiling. "You've become more of a celebrity than you realize." There's a tinge of humor in those last words.

I stare at him. "But why? Weren't you afraid of me?"

Deep down, even Father is afraid of me.

Haven hums softly, a familiar sound. The same one I make when I want to ignore a voice in my head. I wonder if he's trying not to listen in on my thoughts.

Haven tightens his grip on his staff and lifts his shoulders, straightening his surprisingly tall form. He sits about an arm's length away from me, settled near the firepit, coat thrown around his shoulders. Something else lies against his back too. Something oddly bent, but I still can't get a good look at it. Haven lifts his head, and in that movement, I see all that's left of his eyes are the gaping sockets, charcoal holes. Burned away.

He's blind?

He maneuvers so deftly, I would never have guessed. But it makes sense why he uses the staff and walks with slow, measured movements. Why his sons are so protective.

An even deeper sense of respect and awe forms for this gentle creature in front of me. This creature who can bring healing to his son, and yet has seen more pain and wounding than I can even imagine.

Deep scars lace across his face, ragged and still raw in a way that makes the scars along my own spine ache.

Haven adjusts again, and this time, the edge of a single wing falls against the wood floor. Mangled and ashen, but still rippling with heat.

I was right—it was a wing.

Haven was once a like me, but someone has tried to carve away everything about him that resembled a firebird. He was tortured by something with the power to burn a phoenix.

Who could do this to another creature?

I wish I didn't know the answer.

Father would have said it was the Hollow. That they are bloodthirsty torturers. But something in me says that not even the Hollow could damage like this.

Only someone like us. With fire in their veins. My kind.

I find Haven's focus straight on me. "Are you really the daughter of Darkholm?"

Darkholm. Father's full name. A name I haven't heard in a long time.

"He raised me."

"And you said Hana was also with you?"

"Yes," I murmur, desperately curious what he's getting at—and how he knows all this. "She and twenty-one others. Our flock of outcasts."

"Outcasts," Haven remarks. "That's an interesting way to put it." He leans more heavily on his staff and tilts his head in the direction of the brothers. "Let's speak somewhere safely, away from here."

"I won't hurt anyone," I protest quickly.

Haven shakes his head, using his gnarled staff to painstakingly pull himself to his feet. "I am not afraid of you, child of Darkholm. But the discussions we must have may create a reaction, even if you don't intend it. And I'd rather not rebuild this cabin. There is so much about Darkholm you don't know yet."

A chill carves my spine, and I manage a reluctant nod.

There's little else to say.

CHAPTER THIRTY-SIX

Haven limps toward the cabin's exit, and for a moment I'm frozen in place. Not sure I even want these answers.

It would be so much easier to stay hidden here, inside the rustle of Eli's coat, soaking in the warmth of this firepit.

But as the brothers stir and Jude runs to catch up, I know I cannot hide.

"Wait, Dad." Jude reaches for Haven. "You're still really weak—"

Haven waves him off. "I'm recovering. And she has to know. She's awake and—she has to know."

He steps outside, night starting to fall around us, pulling his hood up again. Bare feet quietly padding across the wooden floor, I follow Haven outside. Eli is a half-step ahead of me, while Jude pulls on his own coat and carries up the rear. The minute I step out of the cabin, the chill nips at my nose and the hard-packed snow sends shooting sensations through my bare feet.

It feels good. Real.

The darkness has fallen quickly, the faintest echo of moonlight ricocheting off the pallid icescapes around us. When most of the world is coated in this much white, it lends a glow all its own. My eyes soon adjust, and when I peer up at Eli, I see that his irises also have a bit of a gleam to them. Our eyes reflect in the darkness, another reminder that we are creatures created to hunt and survive in this wilderness. Jude, on the other hand, stumbles a little as he follows us.

I'm not sure how it's possible that a human is having more trouble finding their way across the ice than the blind phoenix leading the way, but somehow Haven takes measured steps out over the snow. He barely turns his head in the direction of the towering *seren* prowling in the shadows beside the house.

She falls in step with our small parade, impossibly quiet paws treading snow and huffing puffs of cool air into the wind that send shivers down my the nape of my neck. She's watching my back. And ahead, Eli sneaks glances at me every few steps, uncertain.

Both of them worried for me in different ways.

Haven has things to tell me about Father. Do I really want to know?

Haven leads us out a good mile from the cabin, slow but steady. He must have memorized the entire layout of this area. We eventually stop near an outcropping of large rocks that lie opposite a fallen tree covered in ice.

Haven sits lightly on the slick trunk, his presence immediately starting to thaw it out. As the ice melts and the coarse bark underneath shows through, he rests one leg against the curving surface.

Eli and Jude perch on one of the boulders scattered about the nearly petrified tree trunk. Jude's leg bounces so quickly, I can make out the blur even in the darkness. Eli's hands glow as he rubs them together, generating a dancing red flame that ripples over his fingers. He bites the inside of his cheek, those gleaming eyes capturing mine. He nods for me to sit beside him, but I shrug.

Not yet. Not now. Not until I hear Haven out.

I stay where I am, standing in front of the older phoenix, picking at my nails, shifting from one foot to the other.

Behind Haven's sloped shoulders, a rippling lake of blanketed snow stretches as far as I can make out. The *seren* paces quietly nearby, watching us through bright eyes, but her hackles are lowered.

Haven finally lifts his broad shoulders, bent wing rippling behind him. I cannot see his features in this darkness, but I can tell he's turned his expression toward me. He continues where he left off. "We wondered when you would wake. And what kind of creature you would be. You could have taken what you wanted from my sons and left them—but you didn't." A quick sizzle of flame flashes across his features, highlighting his empty eye sockets and those painful scars, but his brow is furrowed with something that seems like awe. "It is unexpected to find such . . . *humanity* . . . in a girl raised by the Forsaken. Especially by Darkholm."

I gulp, tongue pushing against a sharp incisor, trying to hold back any external reaction.

I don't want to hear this.

Talk like this is dangerous. If Father knew what I was listening to—

Suddenly, everything about this hauntingly quiet setting feels like a trap. A warm cabin and full belly and the gentle hush of snowfall in the air—all to quiet my doubts. To loosen my tongue.

This phoenix doesn't know me.

I cross my arms. "No more stalling. What can you tell me about Father?"

Somewhere to my right, Jude snorts. "Oh, you don't want to know the half of it."

At least we both agree on that front.

Haven gives his head a shake. "I know him far more than I wish I did. But no, first—I must hear it from you. Why did you sneak into the Hollow village where my Eli found you? And why did you explode outside of your flock's own temple?"

My throat seems to clog. In my peripheral, Eli leans forward. "Mara—we already told Haven everything. We know your people were hiding down there, probably sick, so you stole those herbs . . ."

He keeps going, briefly laying out the nightmarish few days that feel both like yesterday—and another lifetime.

I want to tell Eli to be quiet. Want to pull the hood of this cloak over my head and disappear. I don't want to talk about my failure, my loss.

But as I start to sway on my feet, drawing back into the safety of my own thoughts, Haven says something that catches me off guard. "If Darkholm left you to watch over him, he must have really trusted you. Unusual."

Father certainly tried to trust me, even though he knew what I was capable of.

"Dangerous." Haven's voice drifts past my mind, and I instinctively reach out to receive the thought. Then I realize what he's done—

The telepathy. Directly invading my thoughts in a way I haven't felt since I lost contact with Father. My entire body doubles over, and I fight off the nausea. The dark shadows arc around me.

"What happened?" Eli jumps up to steady my wracking shoulders. I grip his arm tightly, trying to slow my pulsating body, trying to settle myself.

But my pulse has kicked up, steaming tears blurring the darkened landscape.

Though I've pushed my own thoughts into Eli's mind, into the *seren's*, it has been so many sunpasses since I have heard another voice in *my* head, and something about my thoughts being invaded again makes my entire body shake.

Instead of grilling me for more answers, Haven rises and places his worn, calloused hands on either side of my face.

Haven's hollow eyes are so close, I can tell just how burnt his sockets are. But I wonder if he can see more than most with sight ever could.

Bile rises in my throat.

"You have scars too, child," he says. "You have scars like me, but most of them are in here." He taps the edge of my temple. "What sorts of things has Darkholm made you do? In what ways has he cut through your very mind?"

Father . . . Father was trying to help me . . .

But the words feel empty, even in my own thoughts.

Another shudder sweeps through me, and I wrap my arms around myself, backing away from him and Eli. "I'm fine."

No one in this quiet alcove believes it. The two brothers watch me with something like pity. The *seren* has padded closer, lightly pressing her nose against my shoulder in concern.

I swallow and force the words out. "How do you know my father? Do you know where they took him?"

Haven reaches for his staff and leans against it thoughtfully. "When exactly did he disappear?"

I take another step back, trying to fade into the darkness so they cannot see the way my eyes have become misty again. Faint tears turning to steam.

My voice cracks. "Like Eli said, I had to leave them for just a few hours to find herbs to bandage their wounds. When I returned, they were gone." I blink rapidly, stomach clenching again. "When I couldn't find them, I lost control."

Haven nods slowly, and his voice becomes very soft. "And you're certain you exploded *after* you noticed they were gone? Not that—"

My eyes go wide. "That I exploded first? No—no. I didn't make them disappear."

Not directly.

Haven lets out a long breath. "Alright, that was my hope. Good." Then he turns his head toward his younger son. "How large was her explosion? Remind me."

Is that why they haven't had more answers?

Haven wondered if I'd accidentally destroyed my own family?

My knees suddenly betray me and I crash to the snow, catching myself with my bare hands. In a blur of shadowed forms, I can sense the brothers moving toward me, but I just shake my head.

"Stay back."

It's not safe. Not yet.

I dig my fingers as deep into the frigid snow as I can. Try to let the icy sensation spread up through my touch, my skin, cooling the panicked heat searing through me.

I didn't hurt them, I didn't hurt them, I didn't hurt them.

After a stretching second, I shakily rise back to my feet. I can feel the pulse starting to ebb. Eli's eyes flicker in the darkness. "Mara, we don't have to—"

"*No*, I must know." My voice is like gravel, and I aim the next words at Haven. "Keep asking your questions."

He lets out a long sigh, then nods to his son.

Eli thinks for a moment, rubbing his hands together and sending sparks into the air. "Her blast reached about a quarter-day's travel to walk from one side to the other. We only survived because she had told us to run, and I used my fire to brace between the blast and ourselves. Absorbed some of it."

Feet shuffling in the snow, I squint at Eli. He *absorbed* it?

That's . . . unheard of.

He must have incredible resilience to have been able to not only survive that blast, but absorb it and protect Jude. I doubt even Hana could have weathered it that well.

Even in the dark, I study Eli closely. Tucking that realization away. Even if he is only half phoenix, Eli has more endurance than any of our flock, besides Father.

But he's also seen far more of the sun than they have.

Haven utters a prayer. "Thank *Sol* you both survived." He turns his steady attention back to me. "How often do you have to explode like that?"

I can't understand this questioning, but give a labored shrug. "Never. Not like Father and the others need to, so as to heal. Mine happen without warning and are usually set off by something more . . . emotional."

Or when Father slips inside my head and breathes into my fire himself. Igniting my body to protect my people, he said.

Haven traces one of the scars that drags jaggedly from his forehead down his jaw. "Fascinating. And Darkholm knew this? He could set you off?"

"That's not—" I dart a glance between Haven and the brothers, who suddenly look a little ashen. It sounds much worse than it was. "No," I say quickly, fists clenching. "He would help me control it. Let it out in safe ways. He even taught my people how to build immunity to my fire."

Haven blows out a long, ragged breath. His expression has harshened. "He was building a weapon under their noses. No wonder they came for him."

"You mean the Golden Phoenixes?" I shuffle closer to him. "Do you know where they are? And why they took my father?"

Haven pauses, then turns back to the brothers. "Are you sure? I know you have considered this ever since we left. But are you *sure*?"

Eli sighs. "She wants to free her family. And if she can—well, maybe she heals more than herself."

My brow furrows, struggling to even make out their subtle expressions in the hazy dark. My desperation for him to relinquish the information I need intensifies. "Please, just tell me how to reach the Golden Phoenixes. I need to find my flock. Who are the Goldens, really?"

"*Liars*," Haven's voice is like gravity, that single word pinning my bare feet to the icy ground. "They're liars. As is your so-called father. You cannot trust any of them."

A cool breeze whips my hair across my face. I stare at him. "How do you know that?"

"Because I believed them once. I believed their way really was best." He leans against the log. "When they decided they would rather be worshipped than sacrifice themselves for the humans, everything changed." His face darkens. "Before long, it was child sacrifices. They took a sick pleasure in watching the humans kill each other out of desperation. I could not just stand by."

My mouth feels dry. "What did you do?"

"I appealed to them," Haven says, "to stop requiring such horrific sacrifices just for the humans to have enough warmth to live. And then I gave the village some of my fire to survive." He leans heavily on his staff. "They said it was treason. I had betrayed them by giving humans the fire freely. But they couldn't kill me."

Thud-thud-thud —

My pulse grows in my ears. "Because you'd regenerate?"

He shakes his head. "No, there are ways to snuff out a phoenix flame forever. But if they did so, then their own souls would be tainted by it. They would fall too. So, they did the next best thing." He lifts a withered hand to touch his sunken, scarred face. "They took my eyes and ripped my body. One of them tore off most of my wings."

A shiver creeps down my spine. Eli and Jude are silent. But I have to know. "How did you survive?"

"The kindness of a people who we believed were not capable of kindness," comes the quiet reply.

Jude stares at the ground and tugs at one of the studs in his ears. I'm reminded that he is the only true human here.

"The humans saved me." Haven gives his adopted son a fond smile. "They nursed me back to health as much as they could."

Another chill raises the hair on my arms. I know what that's like.

"They gave me a place to stay, sharing what little fire they could still create at that time with me. Their kindness warmed me in a way I'd never felt in the eons I've existed." Haven's single wing arches behind him a bit, the warped feathers still giving off the faintest hue of light. "I lived at the foot of the mountain, mostly keeping to myself for generations, trying to warn any newcomers to leave while they still could. Then, one day, Jude and his mother arrived. She showed me kindness in a whole new way. Eventually, that kindness turned to love, and I swore my eternity to her. Not long after, we had this one." He smiles again as he lifts his staff toward Eli's direction. "At that point, my people said my allegiance had gone too far. They came for my family. I tried to run, but in the process"—he pauses, an ache filling his next words—"I lost her. But I refused to lose my sons. Even without my sight, I protected my boys and we fled as far away as we could. I built my family a new home."

Parts of this story remind me of Father. Of the way he described finding me, and rescuing our flock. Hiding them away from the bloodthirsty humans.

But in Haven's story, it is not the Hollow who are the monsters.

I brush a hand over my face, trying to meld both the pictures in my head. The pain of two worlds I thought I understood, but that now seem at odds.

Either Haven is lying, or—

I gulp, a spark zinging over my shoulders and arms like a flaming shiver.

Or, Father is.

He must be able to explain. There must be a reason for all of this.

Curling my fists till my nails press against my palms and puncture skin, letting thin rivulets of flame trickle down my wrists, I turn a determined gaze to Haven. "Where are the Goldens? Where would they have taken Father?"

I will find and rescue him, and he will set this all to rights.

"We can guide you. But first, you'll need to come to my village. To stock up supplies and see—" He hesitates. Is he searching for the right words?

Before Haven can continue, Eli pushes off of his perch on the rock and takes careful steps toward me. "To see the world your father kept you hidden from. At least once, before we take you to find him."

My heart drops to my toes, eyes shooting wide. "Before you take me?"

Jude snorts. "Well, Eli at least. I'm still deciding how much I want to relive that nightmare."

Mouth hanging open, I dart a glance from one brother to the other. "Really? You'd help me like that?"

Eli rubs at his jaw. "I mean—someone has to take you. And I won't just send you into that trap by yourself."

Another sizzle of flame skims over my body. And before I realize I'm moving, I've suddenly closed the gap to pull Eli into an awkward, brief hug. "Thank you," I whisper, voice breaking.

I didn't know how afraid I was to go alone, until I realized I wouldn't be.

He returns the embrace quickly, and for a fraction of a moment his lips brush the edge of my ear, and my pulse kicks up again.

And then I'm reeling backward, smoothing out my coat and clearing my throat.

What got into me just then?

My cheeks feel hot, and Eli is looking away, but there's a soft little smile on his lips.

"When do we leave?" I ask, trying to keep my voice steady, but Jude is biting back another low snort.

Haven lets my question linger before lightly rising from the stump, taking limping steps toward me. "Tomorrow we will leave for our village. A day or so after, Eli will guide you to *Rekren,* the Mountain of the Gods." His gnarled hand traces up and down his withered staff, leaning forward just enough that his expression now fills my whole view. "Hear me on this—*you can trust no one on that mountain.* Not the Golden Phoenixes, not your father, no one. Those creatures I once called family have become vain and self-seeking. Setting themselves up as gods, and ignoring the purpose *Sol* created them for." His voice hardens. "Darkholm was one of the worst. He led a sect rallied together in their fear and hatred of the humans. They even turned on their brethren—and were cast out for their treachery."

My legs have become shaky, and I sink to sit on one of the rocks beside Eli. He gently nudges my shoulder with his own, but I cannot even lift my head.

Father can't be the madman Haven is describing.

A shudder crawls between my shoulder blades. One thing is very clear—Father was on the run from the Golden Phoenixes.

And from the state of Haven's shriveled form, I don't blame him.

It takes me several minutes to find my voice. I stare at my bare feet, covered in dirt and snow, and finally murmur. "I still have to go find him. I have to get them back."

There's another aching moment of silence, and then Haven says, "We know. They're your family."

I nod, sniffly and aching.

I don't realize Haven has moved closer until his frail, bony hand rests on my shoulder. His grip is surprisingly strong for how bent and broken his tortured body is. "You've done well, Mara. Despite what you may have seen, you've brought life, not pain. Even imperfectly. You have nothing to atone for."

And with that last sentence, I can feel his head turning in his son's direction. Not just aiming the words at me.

But they still sink in deeper than I'd care to admit.

You've done well.

How often I've waited to hear those words from my own father.

The tears—real, saltwater tears—start to silently drip down my cheeks as I can only manage to reach up and cling to his wrist like an anchor. I hold on tightly to this ancient creature who doesn't push me away. Beside me, Eli leans closer, his body steady and certain against my quivering side. Eventually, the tears soften to a blur that I wipe away with a balled fist.

Haven gently lets go and I bring my knees to my chest, chin tucked against them, trying to breathe. Blinking tears away before they can sizzle on my cheeks. It takes me a long time to dare a glance at the brothers, but neither of them are looking at me. Eli's hands are laced in his lap, and he stares at them with a kind of aching understanding. Even Jude is quiet.

I try to speak several times, but no words rise to my lips. Finally, I swallow around the thickness of my own tongue and whisper, "Thank you for not leaving me alone."

Thank you for walking with me into a trap that has laid in wait for decades for you.

And as relieved as I am by the idea of not having to find the Golden Phoenixes on my own, I cannot avoid the foreboding that turns my chest to ice.

There is no promise that my flock is still alive, waiting in that mountain bleeding red with loss and pain.

And I may be forcing Eli to lead me to his own death.

CHAPTER THIRTY-SEVEN

Eli locks the cabin behind us, and I head for the mama *seren*, who restlessly paces around us. Jude and Haven have started out a few steps ahead, shouldering heavy packs, with Haven leaning on his staff for support.

They're taking me to their village. And after that, we can go find my flock.

I reach out for the shaggy muzzle of the creature who kept watch outside the cabin the entire night.

"Hello, mama *seren*." Her dark fur is as coarse as pumice stone itself in some places. She lowers her massive head and I lean my forehead against hers, looking into those flickering, lava-bright eyes. "Thank you for taking care of me. None of these with me are a threat. They're part of us now."

I beckon Eli, and he slowly approaches. I reach for his hand and guide it to stroke the *seren's* muzzle as I carefully step back.

She gives a low growl but lets him touch her. She stills and then leans into his hand and gives a chuff of appeasement.

I'm not even sure how I knew that would work when I tried it with Haven and Jude, but it did. Eli and I follow close behind his father and brother as we strike out west from the cabin. The *seren* keeps an easy pace with us, covering my flank like a guardian of fangs and fur.

I turn to Eli. "How far is the village?"

"A few hours," he replies, glancing at me. "We originally made camp beside a frozen river, and over time, Dad was able to thaw it. The village grew from there as more humans arrived. It is the only place plants can grow for miles."

My eyes round. "Your father thawed a *river*?"

A smile lights up his face. It's hard to articulate how much of a relief it is to see a bit of brightness back in his eyes. I can only imagine how Jude feels. "Just wait until you see it."

I've never seen a running river in all the years I've been alive.

Eli walks at a brisk pace, and I scurry to keep up. The small family must be used to quiet, as we walk in silence for what feels like an eternity. Ordinarily, I'd want to sink into that silence—but with them so close, with Eli just a reach away, it feels like wasting precious moments to hear their voices.

What I wouldn't give for my head to be filled with the voices of my flock again.

Passing the faint tracks of animals, skirting around *haja* pockets and following the faded angle of the sun. Every time I try to start a conversation with Eli, I feel awkward. Even though his father and brother are just ahead of us, it still feels this gentle young man and I are alone in the middle of the frozen tundra. I adjust the heavy jacket he offered me.

A soft whistle fills the air beside me.

Eli's tune is so slight that, for a moment, I think it's just the hollow whisper of the wind cutting across the rigid layers of ice that rise up around us, but then I realize the whistle is rising and falling too cheerily for the wind.

It reminds me of my own rhythmic humming.

I glance over at him. Eli's shoulders are pulled back, head tipped toward the sky, bits of snow and slush catching on his thick dark curls and lashes. He's chipper and has a warmth in his cheeks I haven't seen before.

He's so full of life for someone determined to drain it from his own veins. I don't want to have to say goodbye to him any sooner than I have to.

The thought kind of shocks me, but as I trace the ruddy flush that brushes his cheeks and the laugh lines at the edges of his eyes, and the way his lips quirk at the corners, I realize this quiet, gentle man is the safest person I've ever met, apart from Hana.

Though he's not always very gentle with himself.

Jude sneaks knowing glances over his shoulder at us every so often. I'm reminded of what Jude said about Eli and I being similar. Jude does seem to have adjusted to having me around—something about the slight smile he flashes at me when I catch his backward glance makes my insides warm a bit.

This family is letting me become one of them.

The *seren* follows quietly behind us, her hulking figure casting unique shadows across the ice ahead. Her presence scares away any unwanted interest that might cross our path, along with any prey we might have been inclined to hunt. But we have more than enough in the pack Eli shoulders to feed us for a few days.

Everything looks the same out here. But occasionally the flatlands are broken up by shelves of buried rock that look like giants who died here long ago, leaving nothing but their ragged carcasses covered in snow.

But as we keep walking, ice turns to sludgy snow and bits of green break through the blinding white crystals. *Is this...grass?*

Excitement propels my steps as I start to run toward the sound of water lapping filling the air. *Could it be . . . ?*

I crest a small hill of snow and discover a dense valley spreading below us. Nestled against the curving edge of a towering mountain, faint buildings hide in its shadow. No one would even know any of this was here unless they came up this close.

And below me, rippling and vibrant, is a river. A real, thawed, river!

My boots thud over the snow as I race down the hill and soon the snow is giving way to grass as I near the edge of this winding river. Just hazy spots of green at first, and then it grows to rim the brilliantly blue river and stretches out toward the village now in our view.

The water ripples and murmurs to me, as if the sky had dissolved into the earth. Airy and pale and reflecting the clouds overhead.

Eli's family soon catches up with me, Haven using his younger son's arm as a guide to reach me more quickly without tripping. Though Haven cannot see the look of shock on my face, he must sense it as he lightly chuckles. "Welcome to our valley."

My mouth falls open. Tall plants of some kind sprout out of the ground, hemming the village in and waving their lush green leaves. *Trees.* But not just trees. To the right of the village are rows and rows of other kinds of plants growing. Not in a special tent like in the Hollow village, but bursting from the ground on their own. Flickering tongues of fire fill trenches that hem the field of crops.

How is this possible?

An unfamiliar sensation, not at all unpleasant, spreads through me as I follow Eli, Jude, and Haven across ground that seems to spring beneath my feet. The icy breeze that has followed us this entire way is gone. Everything about this area seems to have this . . . warmth. Welcoming. Like the world here has remembered how to breathe again.

As we draw closer, I see the village is made of wooden houses, almost like the brothers' cabin, but far more elaborate. Some have multiple levels and overhangs and areas outside for sitting. People mill around them, small ones—children—running near the buildings.

Every structure is handcrafted in different sizes and shapes, but there is one consistent factor that makes my gut churn.

My feet abruptly stick in the grass, stopped in my tracks, gaping at the hauntingly familiar glint that seeps through every inch of this village. Every house has a rim of metal around the outside of their roofs, and in it flickers something gleaming and dancing and fiery.

Phoenix flame.

CHAPTER THIRTY-EIGHT

Amazement and confusion battle within me like fire and ice as I take in the impossible sight before me.

This should not exist. Father said the world was too far gone to be revived. That all the trees and plants had died.

Yet here is proof of his lie. The village is so *alive*. Plants spread out over the ground and climb up smooth, wooden walls. Buildings are crafted from planks and stone, looking like they grew alongside the crops that blanket this valley.

The hushed lapping of water mingles with sounds of animals calling to each other. *Argots* perch on roofs, and a cluster of *velian* peek out from their tunnels carved along the water's edge.

But the loudest, most stunning sound is that of children playing. Laughing. Chattering in a way that exudes safety.

The tiny ones with their small legs and little bodies chase each other around, playing a game with sticks and rocks. They laugh and shriek—until they catch sight of us. The children pause, staring wide-eyed in our direction. Then they start racing toward us, cheering and shouting one name over and over—

"Haven! Haven!"

Haven limps forward with his staff, and bends down to welcome the little ones with a wide embrace. Jude awkwardly pats at some of their heads as his father straightens and calls out to the dozens of other Hollow now coming out of the wooden houses. Many wave our way, and some drift closer. Curious murmurs scatter in a language I don't understand. They're all dressed in the lightest clothing I've ever seen— and their shoulders and feet are bare. No need to protect against the snow and cold here.

Eli leans close to me. "They're going to be so happy to see you awake."

How many of these people knew about my sleep?

I glance at the *seren* behind us, her big eyes taking in the area, cautiously treading forward as we continue on.

Eli leads me toward the crowd forming around Haven and Jude, when something stings my feet. I glance down and spot what had lit the flames that are now fading back into my skin.

The earth itself is interspersed with tiny sparks. The ground is a rich, dark color of cooled lava. But beneath the dirt, I can feel the hum of something deeper. Something electrifying and guttural. A part of . . . us.

The scars along my back ripple in a kind of ghostly understanding. *Could it be?*

I crouch and dig my fingers into the powdery earth, carving down into the ground until they touch something sharp and vibrating with heat. Something that is spilling fire through this area.

A feather. An example of the kind of flame Haven has used to bring light and warmth to this place.

The very same flame I can create. The same kind of flame I have been cutting from my back before my fledgling feathers can grow to their full, dangerous size.

Something deep inside aches like homesickness, just seeing this feather buried here. Burning bright and bringing warmth and life.

My father would never use my feathers like this. Instead, I was instructed to crush them up and let them turn to ash to take away their edge, their burn, their bite.

But maybe even their flame, even their sharp edges, could have brought life.

My eyes burn as I take in the people starting to crowd around me. I want to muster a smile in response to their greetings. I want to soak in Haven's words as he explains the way the village is set up and the meaning of the various crops planted on the surrounding hillsides.

But all I can hear is a kind of ringing in my ears. A deep, unsettled tightness in my chest.

None of this should be possible. Hollow smiling at me and welcoming me in—

It goes against everything I've been taught.

These things cannot all exist in tandem. Either Haven's village is some kind of a fever dream and I never truly woke up—or I have been lied to for years.

I'm not sure which is worse.

CHAPTER THIRTY-NINE

I sit on the front step of the house, watching as Eli and several of the Hollow children throw a ball made of intertwined reeds back and forth. The children laugh and tease in their language, but their smiles are universal. They are utterly carefree as their simple clothes ripple in the wind, their long hair braided behind them.

They'd pulled Eli into the middle of their game almost as soon as we arrived. They are laughing as he plays with them. I'm amused to watch him make silly faces and move his feet in funny ways as he pretends to throw the ball to one child, instead tossing it to another.

Just watching them feels like a dream. I know I was small like this once. But I never played like this.

I almost wonder how Eli knows how to do this. And then I realize it's probably because he grew up playing with Jude, with Haven. He had a family who embraced his growth.

He had a childhood. I barely had a chance to bury my mother before Father was hiding me away in a cave. Showing me how to take a knife to my spine. Teaching me how to clip my own wings.

A shiver sweeps over me.

Eli's thick curls are drenched from sweat. Like me, he's left his heavy coat inside the house. The place Haven has brought us to spend the night and restock any supplies we'll need for the rest of our trek.

But Eli told me something, before the children pulled him into their game.

"You could stay here, you know. With Haven and all these families. We'd happily give you a place. You and Dad . . . would have a lot to talk about."

He offered the out so gently, it still rings in my thoughts.

We can stay here—safe. Whole. Healing quietly.

But I replied to him with the same thing I always come back to. Every step of the journey here. Every second I stare at Haven's scarred face.

"I have to go, Eli. I have to know how my father is. If I left my flock to be . . ."

He had looked at me with shadowed sadness. *"To be hunted like Haven was?"*

I nodded my head rapidly, and Eli heaved a long sigh. *"I knew you would say that. But I had to ask."*

I'd just sort of sunk into myself after that. And the children came rippling forward like a small wave of bright faces and futures and eyes not yet tainted by the cold. Not yet made chilled and cynical like the rest of us.

They pulled Eli away before I could say one last thing. One last hope. *"But maybe . . . maybe after we find my flock, I can come back here."*

I can bring Father here.

Suddenly my eyes are filling with liquid as I watch Eli run and laugh with the children. I watch their smiles and the hope that fills their playfulness. They will get to treasure these memories. They won't feel alone. Or know the fragility that would steal the breath from their families. Or know the kind of fire that burns you from the inside out.

They would not have to choose who gets to eat and who starves.

The tears on my cheeks turn to steam as I prop my chin on my knees and continue to watch them through blurred vision.

I cannot even imagine what getting to live like this would have been like.

Who I would be if these were the memories that had built a wall around my heart.

If this had been my childhood, there wouldn't even be a wall.

It would have been a garden. A beautiful place filled with plants and vines and flowers that climb and bloom and reach for the sun. A warm, rich place. A place that's alive.

But instead, the world I've always known is so chilled that even the deepest places inside me, the ones that boil with seething, crackling flame—even those places are cold. I didn't know a sanctuary like this existed.

Father didn't know it could be real, either. I rub a hand over my face. *How would he?*

But now there is the whisper of treasonous thoughts. *Maybe he did know.*

My heart seizes. Breathing becomes labored and fast.

My entire body is caving in on me. I press both hands against my chest, trying to breathe as I go numb.

Panic and anger and fear all lace my veins like poison.

No! No! He couldn't!

My frantic gaze tries to find something to pull myself out of these thoughts. I keep one hand firmly pressed against my chest and press the other against the wall behind me. The textured surface is revealing just how dizzy I've become—I can barely feel the wood against my fingertips.

The world is starting to close in.

He kept us sick.

I can't breathe. I rock forward as tears stream down my face.

"Mara? Mara?" Someone is grabbing my face, trying to get me to focus on them.

Copper-tinted eyes. Dark hair.

Eli.

"Mara? Can you hear me?"

His skin is so warm. Everything is so warm.

We could have been this warm. Hana could have been this warm. Not shivering, shriveling on the floor of our *nemior*. I didn't have to watch her shrivel away in front of my eyes.

The porch spins so quickly, it's an arc of molten colors as my heart thunders in my ears. Each pulse driving home the two words echoing over and over through my thoughts:

He knew. He knew. He knew.

Eli is yelling for his brother, for Haven. But I can't understand the words anymore. Can't seem to hold onto the time.

My body feels so heavy.

I start to fall, but Eli's arms wrap around me. He sits on the porch with me, rocking back and forth, smoothing my hair.

"Mara? Mara, it's alright. You're safe."

I'm curled into his chest, shivering violently. I manage to gasp the words. "He knew. And he still let us freeze. He knew."

CHAPTER FORTY

Eli holds me so tightly that his arms become a cocoon I want to bury myself in. "I'm right here, Mara. It's hard. I know. Lean into the fire. You'll be alright."

I'm not sure what fire he's referring to, and then I see a flicker start along his arms. A bronze spark that doesn't burn me, but brings a softer kind of heat I have missed. That wraps around me and starts to reach deep into my panicked, labored breathing in a way nothing else has.

Through my blurred vision, I can make out that the children have gathered nearby, but not so close that they touch me. They watch quietly, sadly.

They whisper a question at Eli, and even though I can't understand them, I know what they are asking. "What is wrong with her?"

My breathing has started to calm down when Jude and Haven arrive. Haven kneels beside me. He places a hand on my shoulder and leans in to gently rest his temple against the edge of my head. The gesture feels so tender and open.

It draws forth a distant memory of my mother doing the same. Pressing her temple to mine as a physical representation of our ability to press our thoughts to each other.

"I'm sorry, dear one. You have seen more of this world's pain than anyone should."

A hiccupped sob escapes my lips, and Haven keeps speaking

softly to me in a way only my own kind could. *"This is a safe place, nora."* Something breaks inside, hearing him use the same term of endearment as Hana. *"You can stay if you want. We would be grateful to have you."*

There it is again. The invitation. The way out.

But I can't take it. Even now, with these dangerous suspicions gnawing at my chest.

I have to let Father explain. He has sacrificed so much for us. I've seen him place his own body between a spear and our people.

He couldn't have purposefully hurt me like this. He must have had a reason.

I begin to tremble. I lift my head off Eli's chest and look directly at Haven. "I must know the truth. I have to hear it from him. He's my father. He's the only family I have left."

Haven's sightless eyes seem to see through me. "I understand. But, you have a place to come to when you find out what you already know deep inside."

I don't want to even think about that.

Get up, Mara. My own voice suddenly sounds hauntingly reminiscent of my father's and it makes my body seize again. With a gasp, I force myself to breathe.

I push away from Eli and rise unsteadily to my feet, nearly tumbling into Jude.

"Are you okay?" Jude lifts his hands, not to create a barrier but to steady me. Concern fills his voice.

"Yes. I'm fine now." But despite the family's kindness, I can't make eye contact with any of them anymore.

I stumble up the steps into the house. Eli calls after me, but I can't hear him. I don't want to hear him.

I lock myself in the room Haven provided for me. I sink to the floor. I weep until I don't know where the tears are coming from. Or what I am actually feeling. There is a knock on the door, and I can hear Eli's muffled voice, but my head is too stifled to make out the words. I ignore him until he goes away. I sit, staring at the shadows shifting and fading on the walls as the day passes.

Soon, even this room becomes stifling. The tears have subsided, and I'm left with a bone-deep ache everywhere. Especially over my back along the scars. I want to carve them away with the devastating memories that hurt more than the twin gashes do.

I start to peel off layers of bandages that cover my spine and shoulder blades. The heavy scent of the herb paste that Eli replaced before we left the cabin this morning assaults my nose. He said it would keep the open wounds from becoming infected.

As I tear the bandages away and scrape out the thick paste that is packed into the open wounds, my fingernails hit open flesh poking through. The wounds that may have feather growth, but still never heal. The pain feels more real than this nightmare. More real than this village that is too good to be true.

I get to my feet, pull my shirt back on over my aching shoulders, clean my face as much as I can, take a breath, and leave through the door.

It's nearly dark outside, an ambience that feels haunting now. What kind of darkness am I walking toward? What sort of cold world could Father pull me back into?

I try to banish my thoughts.

Jude and Haven sit in the main living space, eating and talking quietly. Haven must have intensely sharp ears, as the minute I creep out my door, he catches on and presses a thought my direction.

"There's food here, if you want any."

I put on my discarded jacket and make for the door. "I'm not hungry."

I don't want more of his questions. I don't want more of his voice in my head. I don't want more reminders of the intimate way my people communicate and of everything I've lost.

I just want to *be* lost, for a while. To have the cold on my face and to stop feeling.

To either be ice or fire, instead of being so raw and angry.

Suddenly, Eli appears before me.

"I'm glad we're going together."

I stare at him. "What?"

"To *Rekren*," he repeats patiently. "I've been running from the Mountain of the Gods for a long time. From the people there." His copper eyes flicker. "No matter what happens, we're all just ash in the end, Mara. Including the Golden Ones. Living is the hard part."

Living is the hard part.

Yes, it is. I think of what he gives so others can live.

But am I just letting him sacrifice himself more by helping me?

In the end, is Father right? Do I only bring destruction?

CHAPTER FORTY–ONE

I expect to find Eli waiting for me when I step outside their little house two mornings later, after having given myself just a little more time to rest. To soak in the smiles of the human children and eat several full meals and finally feel warm and almost whole.

But three days is more than enough. And the brothers are growing restless just as much as I am. I shoulder the packed bag Eli told me to ready an hour ago. But instead of finding the half-phoenix boy's familiar warm gaze and soft smile, I find Jude waiting at the bottom of the steps.

He quirks a brow, one of his silver studs catching a bit of light. "Looking for Eli?"

I give a light nod. "He said he had something to show me."

Jude eyes my packed bag. "He's taking you to the Crag, eh? Before the bigger trip."

He had mentioned wanting to show me something first, but hadn't given it a name. "What is that?"

Jude waves off the question. "Never mind. Eli is in the marshes with Haven. C'mon, I'll take you there."

I almost don't recognize this version of Jude, compared with the one I first met. Somehow, I've earned his trust.

He leads me to the edge of Haven's village, past the houses built from planks and thatch. We cut around a group of men, bare backs glistening in the dim rays of sun as they build another structure here.

The heat that emanates under our feet brings a soothing warmth that causes beads of sweat to ripple over my forehead and prick my bare forearms.

"It's so warm here," I murmur.

Jude glances at me. "Just wait till you see the lava flow."

My eyes go wide. The *what*?

I notice he's wearing heavy boots as we leave the small town and start hiking through the pass between the mountains that rim the edge of this inlet. Soon we've come out on the backside of the curvature hiding the small village.

What we find on the other side makes my jaw drop. We're in some kind of swamp—tall trees grow out of murky, soggy, dark ground. Hundreds of types of unfamiliar plant life spread before me and the air is filled with the chitter of creatures I don't recognize.

I'm alien here, yet somehow my body adjusts to the warmth, keeping pace with the pulsating heat beneath my feet. The pulse of the planet, starting to thaw more here than I've ever seen.

A sweltering gust of heat barrels into my face, but I keep pushing forward.

My heartbeat kicks up, barely daring to hope. Is this what it was like? Long ago, before the sun grew sickly?

Is this the world I was made for?

Something flickers and echoes through the dark, swampy area. It casts dancing shadows across tall, leafy trees with bark made of rippled, ashen hues.

A river of lava, sparking red and orange, languidly snakes through this area.

"Walk exactly where I do," Jude calls back, guiding me toward an outcropping of obsidian graphite. We leap from one rock to another, treading lightly over a fossilized tree trunk turned on its side.

The further into the murky bog we go, the more I can make out. At first, it's just a few splatters of red and gold glimmering underfoot, dotting the sweeping roots of the trees. Then those splatters begin to grow in size, and soon, small, thin streams of lava weave around this thick swamp.

Finally, Jude leads me past a particularly thick cluster of spindly trees, and I gasp as I see where the trickles of lava are coming from.

I gaze open-mouthed at the churning, gurgling lava that flows through, winding and curling and spitting like some massive serpent.

The lava should be skin-searing at this proximity, but while the swamp is thick with heat that coats us in sweat, it's not unbearable. I lean down for a closer look. This lava flow isn't consuming anything. In fact, the trees are bending toward it. Large roots dip in and reach for the mesmerizing rivulet.

These trees with their dark ivy and obsidian flowers blossoming near their roots—even the ashen ground that curves around the lava stream . . . they should all be eroding. Burning. Shriveling.

How are they not?

"Amazing, right?" Jude shoots a grin at me, silver studs glinting from all the shadows cast around us. "Haven discovered it. After he started planting his feathers near the river to thaw out the land, he also thawed out one of the local volcanoes. It was small and mostly underground, but the magma bubbled up and started flowing into lava right away."

I continue following Jude, careful not to step in the pooling lava. But I cannot take my eyes off it. "How is it not burning all these plants?"

"Because they are made for its heat." Haven's voice drifts into my thoughts. I lift my head and spot him with Eli at the edge of a large outcropping of rock that juts out over the lava. Eli is picking dozens of small, snow-white flowers growing from a bush that winds itself around a protruding root that dips into the lava. He gently places the flowers into a small pouch at his side.

Meanwhile, Haven is bent over the popping, gleaming river of lava itself. And he's reaching in . . .

My heart leaps into my throat. "Wait! You'll get hurt!" I start racing toward them.

But Haven just straightens, turning toward me. He points with a bent finger toward the root they climbed down to reach their perch.

I climb down to join them, but Jude hangs back.

It's soon clear to me why. The heat is especially strong here, frizzing my hair and slicking every inch of my body with sweat. But it also feels very peaceful and calming. Cocooning.

"Mara, here." Haven gestures to a place beside him. I kneel next to him, and he nods his head toward the rippling lava. "What do you see?"

I look over, and my heartbeat chases through my veins again. From this angle, I can see . . . creatures. Creatures with fins that almost look like wings, swimming in the lava.

"Those are *nemya*. Aren't they beautiful?" Eli says. "Native creatures to these lava rivers."

I cannot wrench my gaze away from the ethereal, flaming creatures. And all around them, growing in and through the flowing river of lava, are more plants. The most gorgeous flowers I've ever seen—and stronger than iron. Their languid petals, toned in rippling shades of purple and gold, bend and wave in the rapid flow of the lava, but miraculously are not dissolved or torn apart.

"How can this exist?" I breathe to Haven, who smiles at me.

"This is how our world used to be, child. Rivers like this ran everywhere. They don't burn. They bring life. They bring life to the creatures and plants meant to thrive within their reach. Even the humans can live in comfort and safety near these rivers."

I think of the network of caves I've lived in for so long. All I can picture is the magnitude of magma that must have flowed through them at one point, heating the earth and bringing it back to life.

Haven leans forward, reaching into the lava. The skin on his hand grows a little more red, but otherwise, he is unscathed as he touches some large leaves that sprout from the bottom of the river.

I tentatively let my palm hover above the flow of lava. It's warm but not scalding. "How are you not burnt?" I ask, curiosity winning out.

"Outside of its underground home, the magma cools significantly to lava," Haven explains. "To our kind, it will practically feel like a warm bath. But to this world, created for its heat, to be nurtured and brought to life by it"—he gestures around us at the gorgeous, mossy, swamp-like forest—"the lava is a salve to a wound. An old friend resurfacing."

A smile tugs at my lips as I lay on my stomach on the shelf of basalt and reach over. At first, I just let my fingertips skim the popping, boiling river. Again, the heat is soothing and calming, so I press my hand in all the way.

A little giggle escapes me, and I can sense Eli watching me. "You've never seen lava like this before? Not even in the magma tubes?"

I shake my head, drifting my hand through the river, turning it around and splashing a few droplets into the air. A part of me aches to climb in. To be immersed in it.

But Eli has somewhere to take me.

As if hearing my thoughts, Haven gently nudges a thought toward my mind. ***"You could very well swim in this lake, little one. But don't forget, if you ever stumble upon the heart of a volcano itself, or find a pocket of magma inside a tube—it will not be forgiving. The heat of it could pry your skin from your bones. Be careful."***

I nod, bringing my hand back up. "Thank you."

I notice Haven has layered the half-dozen leaves he plucked from the lava bed and is rolling them up and handing them to Eli. "What are those for?" I ask.

Eli stows them in his pack. "They're *fire-quell*. One of the few materials that our blood won't burn through. I use them to make the pouches to transport flame."

Thoughts start to trip after each other. I lift my head and look around. The large trees, toned by the nearness to flame. Tempered.

And then I spot a section of the swamp where many of the trees have been cut down.

"Are the houses built out of these trees?"

Haven nods. "Somewhat. We call them *elio*—born from the heat of *nemioria*." *Nemioria*. The term for the magma that flows through the *nemior* tubes. Tears of the *nemior*. "We are careful not to use too much of this newly revived bog, so we only cut down a few, and instead use their fireproof nature to coat the outside of the buildings as a protective barrier."

They built their village to withstand heat and flame. Possibly even a blast from a phoenix?

It's brilliant and terrifying at the same time.

Somewhere behind us, Jude gives a loud cough. "Eli, if you're going to make it to the Crag before nightfall, you'd better get going."

Eli stands and helps Haven to his feet. "Yes," he replies, "we're about to go. Can you help Dad home?"

Haven's mouth twitches. "I am in much less danger here than you are"—he tips his head in Jude's direction—"but you could give me my staff."

Jude promptly complies.

Eli turns to me. "Are you ready?"

I heft my own pack, pausing for a moment to gaze around, wishing I could stay here for longer. Bask in the warmth and watch the swimming flame-creatures and climb the *elio* with their fireproof bark. Finally, I look at Eli. "Yes, I suppose so. Do we have to hike through this bog?"

"It's the shortest path," he says, then winks at me. "And admit it— you're curious to see it all."

I give him a half-smile. "I certainly don't mind the warmth."

Jude and Haven start to make their way in the opposite direction Eli and I need to go, but I suddenly dart forward and reach for the phoenix's arm.

As if sensing my question, Haven has already turned toward me. "Yes, child?"

"This world was made for us," I say.

Haven smiles and nods. "Yes. For all of us."

The world Father feared so much was right here, with all its possibilities.

Swallowing around the lump in my throat, I continue. "If we could have breathed life back into this world so easily by just planting a single feather . . ." My eyes burn. "Then what was Father hiding us from? Why did he hide our flock away from a world that wanted us?"

The fabric of a world that was literally dying to be revived by just a spark of our heat. The life that has been in stasis beneath all this ice.

Haven stands still for a long time, then shakes his head. "Truly, Mara, I do not know."

Neither do I.

And that scares me to my core.

CHAPTER FORTY-TWO

The sun is just a dull echo above as Eli and I make our way through this lava-bog. As the trees shroud the world around us, the rivers of lava are even more vibrant. Gleaming basins and waterfalls and rivers of rippling orange and reds.

It makes the very blood in my veins hum.

I've never felt quite so at ease, even as Eli and I walk carefully around protruding rocks and large roots that curve up through the jagged ground. Just the layer of heat that cocoons us is welcoming.

My heartbeat starts to settle. Each breath is smooth, filling my lungs. Little droplets of sweat roll into my eyes, or stick hair to my face, or cling to my sleeveless top, but it all feels *safe*.

Here, my heat is welcomed. Even if I exploded, I wouldn't do much damage.

I'm caught up in the riveting gold and orange reflection of the dancing lava against obsidian stone. All around us, gorgeous red flowers have started to open their buds. They gleam in the darkness as if they've captured some of the lava in their unfurling leaves.

This world is so entrancing, I don't notice the large root jutting out just in front of me.

My ankle catches it and I nearly go down—but Eli's there, pulling me upright.

I give him a grateful wince. "Thank you for catching me."

His chuckle is soft. "Any time. Just be careful. I know you're not worried about the lava, but these rocks are pretty rough. They could cut you severely."

I keep walking, and eventually he says, "It will get harder to see." He then takes my hand. "Better to stick together."

I don't mind the feel of his strong, calloused hand in mine as we walk. The packs we carry are annoyingly heavy and feel even heavier with the heat, but I know once we get past this area, we'll be back out into the cold. I'm grateful for the several hours we've been able to spend in this molten swamp.

Eli and I hike in silence for a while, and I wonder why I feel so shy. Then I realize this is the first time I've ever walked this far alone with someone who wasn't Father.

In fact, Haven and Jude letting Eli leave with me alone shows more trust in my ability to not burn him alive than anyone has ever had in me.

A shiver runs down my arms.

"Are you cold?" Eli asks.

I clear my throat. "Uh—not exactly."

He glances at me. "This must all be pretty overwhelming."

I silently agree, having no words for the world around us. As we continue to follow the snaking path of the river, I start to see ice beginning to form on some of the plants. And on the petals of the crimson flowers that are closing up again. We must be nearing the end.

"I've never . . . not felt dangerous. Or in danger," I say, more to myself than to him.

Eli looks down at me. "And you feel safe right now?"

I let out a soft breath. "This place isn't afraid of me. And neither are you. That's . . ."

A knowing look fills his brown eyes. "Like being able to breathe for the first time?"

I nod, and he smiles. "Good. Because we have about half a day's journey still to go. But we should reach the Crag before nightfall, and have somewhere safe to rest before we hike home tomorrow. Hold onto the warmth you feel here."

I can feel the tiredness pulling at my muscles, but shake it off.

Nothing is a short journey in these wastelands when you are fighting against snow and blistering winds. We stand at the edge of the bog for longer than needed, soaking in the warmth, before pulling out our jackets and preparing for the larger portion of our hike.

Eli helps pass the time by telling stories and teaching me one of his whistled tunes.

As we leave the trickle of lava behind, the luminescent bog fading from view, I try to lean into the warmth and heat in my own chest. To hold onto it, to not let the sense of foreboding grow as we once again trudge through ice and snow. The sun slowly starts to dip and dim over our heads as we pass hours just in each other's company, one determined step after another.

There's no need for it anymore, but I still hold onto Eli's hand, both of our palms warming the other. *You're safe . . .*

I force my tensed shoulders to relax.

You're safe . . .

Eli releases my hand. "Have you ever had a snow fight?" There's something mischievous in his tone.

I quirk a brow at him. "No. What is that?"

He then proceeds to show me how to make a small projectile out of snow and regales me with stories of the wars he and Jude waged as children. Somehow, Jude always won—until Eli learned how to melt incoming snow missiles on impact.

I try to live in the stories he tells and to picture them as children, laughing and playing together. To enjoy those memories he brings to life. To not think about how all of my childhood memories are of fire and flame and desolation. To not wonder what it would have been like if I'd had a sibling.

After he finishes some of his stories, I show him how to sense for *haja* pockets, in case he ever needed to hide in the warmth of the underground lattice of caves that tunnel beneath our feet even here. He catches on quickly, so used to sensing the cold that reaching out for the heat seems to be a welcome relief.

After another stretching hour, Eli takes my hand again. "We're getting close, Mara."

I shake out of my reverie and muster a smile. I realize I haven't been cold this whole time. My nose isn't red, and Eli even has a few droplets of sweat on his forehead.

I glance down at our clasped hands. We have been regulating each other's body temperatures instinctively. Fascinating . . .

A quick glance at the sky reveals that the falling shadows are due to the sun dipping lower and lower. Our eyes will adjust to night soon. Up ahead, the blanket of stretching white snow and outcroppings of ice are broken up by some kind of large, dark sliver.

"What is that?" I ask as we aim directly for it.

"That is the Crag." Eli loosens the scarf around his neck. "A chasm cut through the ice at the edge of a stretch of magma tubes. Similar to where you grew up."

My eyes go wide. "People . . . live here?"

He nods. "Yes, a lot do. It's the warmest place for miles, before Dad built his village."

"Why don't they live with your father?"

Eli sighs. "Some of them still don't trust him because he's a phoenix." He gives a wan smile. "But they'll let us bring supplies and fire."

So that's what we're doing here. Eli is showing me his world. What he's chosen to do with the fire in his veins. The flame that Jude said Eli is desperate to be rid of.

But if these strange humans don't even trust Haven . . .

What will they think of me?

CHAPTER FORTY-THREE

Eli pauses at the edge of the Crag, opening his pack and rummaging through until he settles on a pair of slender axes with a sharpened point. He hands one to me, keeping one for himself.

"What are these for?"

"The climb down. You ram the point of the pick into the wall."

I let out a weird little grunt, and he quickly hefts his pack back on. "Don't worry—it'll be fun."

I bite my lip. "Just don't let me slip."

Eli's eyes spark. "Never."

I then see that he's pulled something else from his pack. A long rope. He ties one end around himself, and one end around my waist.

Now tethered together and wielding ice picks and packs, he surveys the few steps ahead. "Ready?"

I've never scaled an icy chasm before. "Can I say no?"

Eli laughs and guides me closer, and I can see this chasm is far deeper and broader than the one that Father and I would frequently circumvent when we were hunting. It's impressively daunting. And there are little spindly waterfalls of lava that drip down the edges every so often.

"That's new," Eli murmurs, catching sight of the lava. "The thawing from Dad's village must have stirred up some of the magma pockets out here."

I stare down the deep cliff face. The dark Crag, with its jutting

artifice, is like a creature's ancient maw wanting to swallow us whole.
There are people in here?

"Eli?" I grab his arm. "Why are we here? Really?"

Why was this the one place he wanted to show me before we left?

"If we help you find your father and your flock . . ." He pauses,
then looks directly into my eyes. "I want to make sure you know what
you're leaving behind. You're not the only one who has been hiding."

And with that vague answer, he slowly moves closer to the edge,
gets down low, and begins to lower himself over.

I stare down at him, shaking a little. "What if I can't do this?"

"You can," Eli says promptly. "You were made for this world as
much as anyone else. Just follow me."

He shows me my first handhold, and where to brace my ice pick to
leverage my weight as I climb in.

It's terrifying, but kind of thrilling at the same time.

Climbing down into the Crag sort of feels like the inverse of
flying. I follow him as he cautiously feels out each step, each ledge,
each nook to place his foot or hand in. As we lower ourselves into the
darkness . . . I'm not alone.

Eli is beside me, but I also feel a kind of warmth. Maybe it's coming
from the flowing spouts of lava that drip at various intervals. Maybe
it's the warmth of *Sol* himself.

For the first time in a very long time, I'm so concentrated on each
step, each handhold, each breath, that I'm not thinking about myself
and my spark of heat. Or whether I'm guarding my thoughts and
whether I'm too close to others. Whether Father is happy.

I just am.

And there's something about the texture of the pockmarked rock
against my bare palms, the way my fingertips scramble for a hold, the
way my toes cling to the small ledges, that is strangely grounding. A
challenge I'm slowly but surely conquering.

"You're doing great," Eli encourages from below me. He keeps a
careful pace, certain to not go so fast that he tugs at the rope tied to
me. "Not too much further."

I take my time as we climb down. I reach out to let one hand brush the odd, translucent ivy climbing the Crag to my right. Or I angle to let a small spout of lava trickle down over my hand when we pass it.

It may be very different from the caves where I grew up, but this space, these surfaces, they all feel familiar. I can still feel the hum of heat through them.

Then I start to hear voices. Low, vibrating through the rock.

My flock?

In my excitement, I try to scramble down faster—and miss a foothold. I slip, my hands coming up empty, pick slashing through the air—

"Mara!"

But in that half-second, my instincts kick in. I wedge one foot into a cranny and slam the ice pick so hard into the wall I've created my own crack in this rock.

But I've stopped falling.

My chest heaves, and I find better shelves on which to plant my feet, one hand clinging to my pick, the other grasping tightly to an outcropping. Panting, I glance up at Eli, who hovers just above me from his position when I fell.

"I'm okay," I huff, but my body is trembling.

I inhale deeply, focusing on just pulling air in. Then letting it back out.

Eli climbs down to me and places one hand over my trembling one, and lightly presses his temple against mine. "You are okay, Mara. You're safe. That can happen and you handled that perfectly. You're alright."

His words help soften my shaking, and I give a steady nod. "Okay. Okay." Deep breath in. Out.

I'm getting better at this. At handling these moments. Thank *Sol.*

I muster a smile for Eli. "How much farther?"

"We're almost there. You can see it."

I follow where he's pointing and can make out a section not too far below where the cliff face curves inward into some kind of large opening. A cave, born into the side of this chasm.

No wonder the Hollow chose this place. There is very little that could reach them down here.

My heart starts to rise into my throat as we get closer and closer to this village's hideout. Soon, we're climbing down the side of the gaping tunnel and up and onto the solid ledge. The voices are louder now.

Not from my flock, but this village. Their words echo through the rock.

The cavern is very dark, and I cannot see a thing until Eli climbs inside first and pulls me after him.

My feet now firmly planted on some kind of worn-smooth surface, I can make out the large, arching top of the cave curving above our heads, so high I couldn't reach it even if I was on Eli's shoulders. Behind us, the Crag continues its steep descent down into darkness. This is the only opening for as far as I can see, and one that no one would know was here without climbing down.

I move closer to Eli, because while I can hear muted whispers, I still can't see anyone.

But I do sense the glint of weapons, even in the dim light.

An angry voice barrels toward us through the darkness, speaking the Hollow tongue I cannot understand. But Eli positions himself in front of me and raises one fist high over his head. He then coaxes some fire out, and his clenched hand bursts to life, becoming a torch with blue-tinted flame flickering over it.

His light illuminates the dark chamber, and I hold back a gasp.

There are dozens and dozens of Hollow Ones gathered. Several brace in front of us, spears raised, dented armor hanging loosely on malnourished bodies.

They have not eaten in some time.

Behind them, I can see more of their men and women cowering in the darkness with children hiding behind them. Small, pale creatures with too-big eyes gaping from their skulls.

But as soon as Eli's light begins to illuminate the space, all of their weapons lower. And expressions of pure relief fill their features.

"Eli! *Noren!*" they shout. Words I can understand. Suddenly,

Eli is surrounded by a dozen of the warriors who were seconds ago pointing weapons.

He seems to know them well. He refers to each by name, smiling and greeting them. Bits of the language I can understand mixed with the words of the Hollow. They know why he's here, and he knows what they need most. Within seconds, they've ushered him into their midst.

I stand awkwardly behind him, hands shoved into the pockets of my coat, not sure what to do.

Eli glances over his shoulder at me, then addresses the room. "This is my friend, Mara. She's like me. She's a *Solnora.*"

The eyes of every human in the room turn on me, narrowed and uncertain. Eli lets his pack slide off his shoulder and brings me into their center. "You can trust her. She's here to help." He glances at me. "Right, Mara?"

I nod mutely, and that's when I see the long, cold stone pit in the center of the room. A huge, curving basin that should keep this chamber warm, but must have run out of heat a long time ago. I slowly walk over to the firepit, and the women sitting around it don't move, only stare up at me in curiosity.

I can see they've tried to burn some of the moss and plant life they could find, but whatever bits of lava they'd been able to burn before has all gone cold and glassy.

"May I?" I ask the woman nearest me, an older Hollow with beautiful grey hair tied back to reveal soulful eyes.

She just nods. I bend down beside their fire pit, cup my hands over top of it, and close my eyes. Eli says I'm here to help. To bring warmth.

These people are freezing.

They aren't afraid of my flame, they need it.

And with that, I feel the heat rising from my veins, blood rushing to the surface and beginning to drip from my skin. It only takes a few small droplets to land in the pit, and soon it is roaring to life. It consumes the scraps of plants left inside and spreads heat throughout the room. I press in more, letting a few more droplets of blood spill.

By the time I straighten again, the fire is roaring loudly and vibrantly. The Hollow quickly place more firewood at its center. The heat is filling this place and the light brings each of their faces, their eyes, their souls to life.

"Thank you," a few of them say to me, and I nod and go over to Eli. He's sitting on the ground further into the cavern, pulling things out of his pack and distributing them.

He's speaking a language I don't know, but what he's offering, I understand clearly enough. He's brought fresh blankets and healing herbs and even some food. They seem to have some scraps left of their own, but haven't truly eaten in some time. Several of their taller warriors carry out prey they've hunted and stored, finally able to prep them to be cooked above the fire.

They must have been eating some of it raw. They take the supplies Eli's brought and distribute them, then begin to bandage the fresh wounds among each other.

"Why do they live like this?" I ask Eli. "Why not move closer to your father?"

Eli keeps his voice quiet. "Because the phoenixes have broken so much trust, it is not something that even a generation could restore yet."

My heart stills a little. "What did we do?"

"*You* did nothing, Mara," Eli responds firmly. "But the Golden Phoenixes did." He sweeps his hand. "Every single one of these humans was once enslaved by the Goldens. They tried to live in the shadow of their heat, just for survival—" Eli's voice grows grim. "Instead, they were basically tortured. Treated as less than animal. When they tried to leave, they were hunted."

"So they hid away?" I already know the answer.

He gives a little nod. "And I'll be honest, Mara . . ." A muscle in his jaw tightens. "Before Haven and I found them, this small town survived because the inhabitants hunted the same creatures that hunted them."

He lets his words sink in.

It shouldn't be a surprise. That these humans—these Hollow Ones—once hunted my people.

But as I stare around, at their depleted forms and hungry, frail bodies, a part of me struggles to be angry with them. They were doing what we all have been doing—trying to survive.

"How often do you bring them supplies and fire?" Already they are placing the small pouches of flickering blood that Eli brought them into various nooks in the walls, distributing it around this cavern so that it will heal and light the area.

"I try to come by every few months," Eli says, then admits, "but it can be hard."

Every few months? I intake a sharp breath. No wonder Jude is afraid Eli is draining his body of blood. He's not wrong. And this is just one village.

"What do they do when you don't come?"

I see the sense of respect in his eyes as he surveys them. "I'm not their savior, Mara. They survived for this long all on their own. They are able to build fire out of very little. I just like to help where I can."

I look at him. "But they don't even believe or trust you. If they did, they would move closer to Haven. Why do you keep giving yourself to help a village that wouldn't offer you anything back? They would probably even hunt your father, if given the opportunity."

"Because they need light and warmth as much as anyone else," is Eli's terse reply. "It's not about them agreeing with me or treating us well. It's just being decent. Everyone deserves a chance to live. I can't let them freeze to death when I can do something to help them."

And maybe that's why I feel safe with him. Because while I know there is a part of his sacrifice that comes from guilt, this part, this heart, that is all Eli.

It's a kind of sacrifice my father would hate.

But one that fills me in a way I cannot explain. It's a kind of giving that doesn't expect you to lose a part of yourself to fill a hole someone has made you responsible for. It's sharing the light that already pours out of your wounds.

The small village readily invites us to join them for their meal, and Eli translates as they share stories. Somehow, several small children end up climbing onto my lap as we sit with them.

I lean back awkwardly, not sure what to do, a little uncomfortable, until they jump up to run away and play. Eli quietly turns to me.

"It's okay if it takes you time to get used to being around this many people. You can see the little ones are especially friendly." He subtly angles his body to help block any other curious children from crawling into my arms, while giving them a genuine smile. "I wasn't sure what to make of people when they started filling Dad's village, either."

I offer him a grateful look. Everything about this is foreign.

They're so . . . loud and alive.

The children laugh and giggle and run around as the older teens eye me with uncertainty.

It takes my breath away to see, in this small group within a confined place, so many stages of a human's life played out around me. From the infant nestled against a mother's chest, to the toddler that keeps trying to catch the spark of flame that keeps fizzing through my hair, to the older woman who still sits beside the fire.

So much life. So much light. Joy in making the most of the world they've been given.

They set Eli and me up on mats covered in our own blankets in a corner of the large cavern, to catch some rest, before we begin the trek back.

As I curl up on my mat with my back against the rock wall, I watch the children chasing each other in circles and the adults deep in conversation or sewing layers of clothing. Something wells up inside.

I want to find Father. I want to find my flock.

And yet I have lived so much life in these past few days than I did in the two hundred years before then . . . I'm not sure what I truly want anymore.

Eli gently taps the floor between us. "You okay, Mara?"

I slowly nod my head. "I think so."

"It's a lot to take in," he remarks.

I nod again.

He looks over at me. "You asked me earlier why I brought you here. It's because I'm not the only one coming with you—Jude is too. And it's not a short trip. We've started prepping supplies and already told Haven we're leaving in two days."

I bolt upright. "What! Really?"

Both of them have agreed to help?

Leaving in two days . . .

My heart pounds. It's what I've been hoping for, but suddenly feels so soon. We'll barely return by nightfall tomorrow, and then we'll be off again, the day after.

This time, for my people.

Eli smiles over at me. "Yes, we'll help you. But I wanted you to see these villages first."

"Why?"

"Because they represent everything your father has taught you to be afraid of. I wanted you to meet them. To see them. Because it's hard to dismiss faces and names."

I look around again at the chattered conversations and the woman preparing a stew over the fire pit and a warrior sharpening his weapons. The mother playing with her children and the father teaching his daughter how to sharpen an arrowhead.

"It's hard to call them Hollow," I admit to Eli, "when I see that they have so much life inside of them."

CHAPTER FORTY-FOUR

The next two days pass in a blur. Eli and I make the trek back to Haven's village uneventfully and spend a day resting and preparing.

We leave the following morning, now having spent nearly a half-dozen sunpasses at Haven's village, before the sun has even managed to drag itself out of the inky mire overhead. The brothers trade a quiet but heartfelt moment of goodbye with their father that causes me to drift toward the back of the cabin, observing the quiet exchange that is almost wordless. Haven's face falls as he embraces Eli.

I don't mean to listen in, but the whisper Haven presses into his son's head is so loud I can't help but catch it—

"I didn't sleep last night, **noren.***"* The word for son in the language of our people. Haven's entire body is bent over, arms still wrapped around Eli. *"I just stared into the sky, thinking. Wondering if I should let you go and what it would mean for you to return there."*

"I'll be as careful as possible, Dad," Eli promises.

Jude is on the other side of the room, lacing up his boots and pulling on his jacket. I should join him—but something in me can't help but move closer to the other two.

Haven places his hand on Eli's shoulder. *"But then I realized it is not the Goldens that I fear most, my son, it is your own* **ero.** *Your mind. The weight you feel—the way you carry my pain. The pain of our people. Of our world."*

Eli's face twists, and for a moment I think he won't listen and turn away. But he holds more tightly onto his father, as his shoulders shake a little.

"I will let you go, **noren,** *but only if you promise me you will come home. You will return to me. And that you will not carry scars that are not your own."*

Eli's voice is thick. "I will."

"Good. You do not need to feel guilty for what I have lost, son." Haven gently eases away to step back and grasp Eli's shoulders. *"All will be right in the end. As* **Sol** *shines, so the world will be reborn. And every tear will turn to steam."*

Eli swallows. "I hope so."

Haven has a half-smile. *"I know so. Our world will be made right in the end. For now, you must do the greatest thing. Live."* He turns toward me, waving Eli in my direction. *"Make your own way and lead this girl with the sun in her veins."*

A shiver snakes down my spine as Eli gives his father one last hug and then picks up his heavy-laden pack. *What am I doing?* Am I about to take these brothers away from their only family and lead them into the same pit of vipers that nearly tortured their father to death?

My gut twists and tightens so strongly that I suddenly can't seem to choke down a breath.

Terrifying thoughts snake across my mind's eye—images of the young men, haggard and bent. Their eyes burnt out and scars lacing their sallow expressions.

No. No. I won't. I'll do whatever it takes to keep them safe—

Jude claps a hand against his stepfather's back and they share a hug. There's a kind of heavy gravity in Jude's expression, and he's the one who whispers a message to Haven this time. I have an idea that he's giving the same promise I'm making.

To protect Eli.

But for Jude, that will be all that matters. Protect his brother, no matter the cost.

With one final goodbye, Jude finishes gathering up his things and turns my direction. I try to lift my shoulders and set my eyes on the blinded phoenix who has lost so much—and who is trusting me to not add his sons to that list.

I approach Haven, and he reaches out to me. "Come here, child."

I put my small hand in his large outstretched one.

"Do not let their beautiful voices lull you back to sleep. You are finally awake, Mara. Do not let them clip your wings again."

"I'm learning . . . how to keep my eyes open," I tell Haven.

He brushes a hand over his eye sockets and this time speaks aloud. "Good. Having those eyes open is a gift few truly appreciate."

Unexpectedly, he draws me in for an almost fatherly hug. My body goes stiff, and I'm not sure what to do with it.

He finishes by giving me an awkward pat on my shoulder. "Be careful, *nora*."

And with that, it's my turn to slip into my heavy coat and shoulder the heavy pack Haven and the brothers put together. It is filled to the brim with supplies, tools, and weapons from this thriving village. I join the brothers at the door, and we give their father one last goodbye before setting out into the icy world beyond this wondrous place.

As we start walking past the village buildings, I hear a heavy thudding sound and turn around to see the *seren* bounding at me. Dust and scraps of leaves scatter over her thick fur, and I can only imagine where she's been burrowing the past day or two. She races up to us, her belly full and a new light in her eyes.

This village has treated her well too.

After greeting the *seren* once more, we all set out.

The warm, grassy terrain shifts from vibrant and alive, breathing in the area that spreads out from Haven's touch, to slowly becoming more snow-ridden the further we go. The further we tread from where these brothers had expected to always stay.

I catch Eli looking over his shoulder, back at the village, as the ground under us grows icier, the grassy knolls underfoot turning to darkly charred ground. Snow is mounding up around us.

"You'll be back soon," I say.

He glances at me. "Or we won't. Either way . . . we can't hide any longer."

My stomach twists at his words.

Eli stoically continues on. I wish I knew what words to say, other than just walking beside him, but Jude seems to find some. Walking on the other side of his brother, he starts to whistle. The same melody Eli whistled when he led me here a few days ago. It coaxes a smile out of Eli, who gives a small laugh and elbows his brother. Behind us, the *seren* lets out a low, good-natured growl.

"Want to hear about the first time I ever took Eli hunting?" Jude asks me with a grin.

Eli gives an exaggerated sigh. "Oh, no, not this story again."

I fight back a smile. "Well, I have to hear it now."

Jude launches into a story about when Eli was barely ten years old. A tale of tripping over logs buried in the snow and accidentally shooting at himself with an arrow that narrowly missed his hand. Every sentence dripping with sarcasm and whisking away the gloominess that had hovered over us like a cloud just a moment ago.

As the brothers banter, I begin to have an idea of why they have survived. They have almost an unspoken language between them, but very different from that of a phoenix.

I don't realize we've left the last ray of warmth from the village behind and are fully immersed in the icy stretches of these Forsaken Lands until the wind kicks up, biting across my face. Even the *seren* crouches against the wind.

Jude's stories slow and Eli's laughter fades as they both pull their hoods up closer around their faces, bodies bent against the onslaught of wind.

"How do you know the way?" I shout at Jude above the growl of the growing storm. Each step sinks into the fresh layer of snow, and streaks of sickly crimson sun drip down the horizon.

Jude tilts his hooded face toward me. "Memory! And landmarks."

The brothers point out the markers to me as we pass them, but for hours at a time the wind is so fierce it takes all our energy just to walk forward. We take turns dropping back to walk behind the towering *seren*, using her bulk to cut the wind a little, but we still need someone in front to guide the way.

After hiking until we are all about to collapse in the snow, we finally stop for the night. The brothers quickly carve out a small shelter from a shelf of ice. Then they set up a portable tent crafted from slats and stretches of material split between our three packs.

With the heat Eli and I both generate, and a few drops that roll down my spine from my twin scars, making my sprouted feathers twitch, we're able to warm up the small area quickly. We pile in the blankets we brought, cluster in close, and I eventually fall asleep in the warmth.

The brothers wake me before I've had nearly enough rest, and we break down the tent and are on the move again.

The days stretch on, and the ice that unfolds around us seems never-ending. We narrowly avoid frostbite, but each of us nurses cramped muscles and feel physically ill from the cold. Our legs are littered with jabs from sharp pikes of ice hidden by the frequent storms we hike through. There are no *haja* pockets here to hide in. No places of warmth marking the entrance to a magma cave.

Eli and I quickly realize we have to hike with Jude between us, so as to use our bodies, as well as the *seren's,* to try and shield him from the cold as much as we can.

It seems like we have been on this trek for years by the time we reach what the brothers promise will be the final day of our journey. The distant memory of a warm bed in Haven's village feels like a fever dream.

Everything is so coated in white my eyes have started to blur. Every step is the same sinking crunch through snow. Treading around miles of drifts and frozen mountains.

My foot skids on something smoother. Something slick.

I pause and look down.

The snow coats the sheened surface, but the area ahead is flatter than what we have traveled over so far. There are stretches of rippled sheets of snow, but no rocks or small hills ahead of us.

What is this?

Jude raises a hand to stop us for a moment. The four of us—*seren* included—cluster near to hear him.

"We're getting close!" he yells. "This is a *fjord* that wraps around the edge of the volcano where they live. It should be frozen solid, but be careful. If anything seems off, stop where you are and tell the rest of us."

My eyes widen. "We're walking *on* a frozen lake? Isn't that exactly what we avoided doing by your father's village?"

Eli puts a mittened hand on my shoulder, snow dusting the top of his hood, "It's the fastest route. If we walked around, it would take us an extra two days."

Every minute counts. I've already waited five years.

I nod.

Jude reaches into his pack and he pulls out a length of rope. We tie it around our waists, one after another, to join us together, so no one can get separated. The blustering storm over the frozen lake seems to only grow worse.

The *seren* treads quietly behind us as the brothers and I wrap our coats tighter around ourselves and keep trudging forward. Foot after foot. Step after step.

My lungs feel dry and angry, but we keep pushing forward. The world becomes a blur of whiteness and flakes that cut into any exposed skin. I focus on the steady movement of Eli's broad shoulders ahead of me, a few of his dark curls peeking out on the sides of his hood. Something about the languid movements of his shoulders is soothing.

After what feels like an eternity, the heavy storm around us starts to soften, and ahead I can just make out the not-so-distant silhouette of a massive mountain jutting out of the blistering snow toward the clouds. A mountain that is bathed in a glowing orange light and a rich, dark color I haven't seen anywhere but in the magma tubes. Even at this distance, I can see spots of green winding around the base—otherwise, the hulking volcano is completely thawed. A dark contrast to the world of white that wraps around us.

"That's it!" Jude yells to us. "That's *Rekren!*" The Mountain of the Gods. "Time to get off the ice."

So we aim away from the ice, crossing out toward the edge where we can skirt back to the mountain.

And we almost reach it, when a massive *creeeak* ripples under our feet. My head jerks downward, to the stretch of ice underfoot. I suddenly realize that the area we're stepping on is completely cleared of snow. Instead of it being a murky sheet of glass, I can make out the discoloration of water below.

Water? The ice is thawing out the closer we get to the mountain?

I guess Haven isn't the only one able to create a pocket of warmth in this wasteland.

As I stare down at the darkening ice, I see a shadow move.

A *large* shadow.

CHAPTER FORTY-FIVE

This must be a trick of the eyes. It has to be.

The shadow moves again. In my field of vision one second, gone the next. I slowly back away, eyes glued on the murky area. The shadow darts past again, and this time the ice shakes.

I grab onto the rope connecting me to Eli and tug at it, trying to get his attention as he hurriedly steps away from the creaking ice—

But then the shadow beneath my feet changes direction, aiming back toward me. Behind me, I hear the *seren* give a low growl.

"I think there's something under the ice—"

Suddenly, the shadow aims directly upward and shoots through the water. A massive creature with scales and a snapping maw bursts through shattered ice. Slush and fragments of what feels like glass spray into my face, stunning me. To my horror, the massive water-creature collides with my frozen body, its coiling, scaled form slamming into my legs as its massive mouth snaps at my waist.

It crashes back into the water, and with the ice under my feet gone, I fall in with it.

By some miracle, the layers of jackets I'm wearing protected me from the row of sharp teeth meant for my ribcage, but the bite snapped off the section of rope connecting me to the brothers.

Numbing water hits me like a blow, and I sink beneath the waves. It doesn't even feel like water—it's nothing like the gentle waves that lapped at the edge of Haven's village. This is like a darkness, heavy as a rockslide, pulling me under. Dragging me to a place where no light ever shines and where my fire will be suffocated.

I try to force my eyes open, desperately holding what breath is left in my lungs. I struggle against the strong pull of the icy depths, trying to strike for the surface, but it's too deep and too heavy. And I've never been underwater before.

The massive fanged creature is swimming back toward me.

I raise my arms over my face. A blast of flame shoots out from my body. But even my fire is instantly extinguished under the water. It does at least startle the demon fish enough that it doesn't take my arm off.

At least not yet.

I try to crane my neck upward, frantically trying to find the crack in the ice where I fell, but everything is so dark.

My ears are so numb, I almost think I hear a splash of another creature.

I desperately claw at the water, kicking my legs, trying to press upward, only to have my head bump a ceiling of ice where any pocket of air would have been. I can feel the water around me splitting as something barrels toward me. I wonder how fast its attack will be. Will it rip me to shreds quickly? Will it savor as it devours?

"I'm sorry, Father. I'm trying—"

I send a last desperate plea his way. So close, yet so far.

And in the silence of the ice swallowing me up, of the demon fish preparing to tear me apart, I hear an impossible whisper breeze into my thoughts. A familiar voice I never thought I would hear again.

"Mara?"

Father! It's Father's voice.

"Father? Can you hear me? I can hear you!"

I struggle against the heavy waves, slamming my fists against the heavy layer of ice locking me away from the air. My heavy jacket threatens to pull me deeper.

"Father! Father—speak again!"

Prove to me that I'm not hallucinating. That you're really here. That you're really alive. Truly real.

"Father?"

My lungs scream from holding my breath so long, but now it feels like I'm holding my breath twice over, waiting for him.

"Father?" I kick violently, even as the underwater creature snaps at me and I fend it off one more time with another blast of heat. *"Father—please!"*

And in that moment of suffocation, as the world closes in, the darkness swallowing up the wingless phoenix with fire in her bones, suddenly, I hear him again.

Faint, but there.

"Mara? Find us."

He's alive!

Maybe they all are. Hana and all the rest of my people.

Hope ignites the flame inside me and I continue to slam fists against ice that refuses to give. A smaller wave comes at me, bubbles erupting. My chest tightens—something else is about to attack me.

I sense the hulking creature before it touches me, and it snaps at the back of my neck. I try to wrestle away from it with my heavy limbs, but then I realize it's grabbed my hood. Its massive paws churn the water around me. I can't quite fathom what is happening as I'm dragged upward, back through the water. I bump into the stretch of ice I'm dragged along. There's a brush of fur at my back, a muzzle against my neck.

And then I'm shoved upward so fast that my body doesn't fully register when my head breaks the surface.

Eli's and Jude's faces are dizzyingly near, arms reaching for my frozen body. Both shout my name.

They ease me from the jaws of the *seren*, and then help her out too.

They roll me over on my side and I hack up water, shivers wracking my body. Once I've started to chokingly pull in a gulp of air, Eli scoops me up and cradles me against his chest as they swiftly get off the ice.

Over and over, I hear them shout my name in my fading awareness. But it's not their voices that have lit something inside of me. It's that snatch of a voice that I heard when I was underwater.

It was Father. He's alive. And he's close.

The fire begins to spread through me, stilling the shaking through my limbs and pulling me from the brink. Out of the corner of my slowly returning vision, I see the *seren* shake off water from her thick fur. The *seren's* hide was far better insulated and resisted the water much more than my coat did.

I curl closer into Eli, shuddering and shaking, trying to get warm. I try to coax more heat into my body, but every inch of me is so cold. My lungs still feel heavy.

Heat emanates from him as he tries to use his unique heritage to warm me. His breath dances across my cheek.

Still holding me, he twists to roll up his coat sleeve, preparing to drip liquid fire from his own veins, but I shakily reach out and put my hand over his. "Don't."

I see the hesitation in his eyes, but then he lets the coat sleeve fall back down.

Instead he asks, "What do you need?"

I'm warmer here.

"Hold me tight."

And he does. He pulls me in closer. The sensation of his body, steady and calm, starts to spread strength into my own shaking nerves.

Jude is on my other side. "Should we get her out of her wet clothes?"

But Eli shakes his head, "Hold on . . ."

I lean deeper against him. *I'm safe. I'm safe.*

I close my eyes and focus not on flame, but on heat. Heat that swells and rights my body temperature. Heat that dries my clothes and breathes life back into my bones. Heat that starts to flow out of me and warms the brothers beside me. The *seren* drifts closer to feel it too.

I don't let any of my blood out—not wanting to risk burning them. But the heat? The heat that constantly makes my joints ache and beads of sweat start across my brow? The way I constantly feel as if I'm running a fever?

That warmth is easy to bring to the surface. Especially here, cocooned in Eli's arms. I cannot even fully explain how soothing it is.

After several minutes, I lightly push away from him. ***"Thank you."***

I could stay there forever, tucked against him.

But Father needs me. And I'm finally close.

I stumble to my feet and head toward the *seren*. Instinctively, she kneels so I can climb on top of her back. I sprawl against her rippled spine and press the heat from my body and skin into hers. She gives a little shake.

"Thank you, girl," I whisper to her. The *seren* gives a low grunt, and I wrap my arms around her neck as the massive creature gets to her feet. I look down at the brothers from my perch atop her.

They have already risked their lives multiple times for me. They don't have to risk more.

I can sense Father now. I'm not as lost any longer.

"Thank you. But I can continue from here on my own . . ." I lick my dry lips, the heat coating my skin already dissolving as more snow kicks up around us. "You brought me to the mountain. You could go home to Haven."

The brothers gape at me for a moment. To my surprise, it's Jude who answers first. "Listen, Mara. We almost lost you. We need to stay together. We've made it this far. And it's unlikely you'll be able to get your whole flock out by yourself," he adds.

Before I can protest, he and Eli start walking again. Silently, I join them, still seated atop the *seren*. We keep trekking forward, around the edge of the lake, toward the mountain that rises out of the earth ahead.

CHAPTER FORTY-SIX

We draw closer to the arching mountain towering over us like some kind of deadly omen. I've started shivering again, but I don't feel cold. Instead, every humming nerve ending is on edge.

The mountain should be calling us. A lure that promises warmth and safety. But something about the hauntingly welcoming vision that spreads out ahead of us feels too perfect.

I lean closer against the *seren* swaying lightly beneath me, crushing powdery snow under her large paws. Eli and Jude walk close beside us, heads bent.

They don't want to be here, either.

The snow starts to fade underfoot, and soon we've crested the edge of the lake and start to descend into a deep valley that rims the towering volcano.

Something about watching the ice fade away and seeing a new tropical world unfolding reminds me of tiptoeing into Haven's village, but the sprawling encampment at the base of the gods' mountain is something else entirely. It makes Haven's village look like a child's attempt, like the art I'd drawn as a small one on the walls of my people's caves.

The world the Goldens have brought back to life doesn't seem real. I have never seen so much green.

The houses that fill the city at the base of the gods' mountain are multi-tiered structures with arching roofs, shingled with slates of chipped lava-rock. Beautiful, stretching murals spiral along many of the walls, and the curved edge of every roof is filled with flickering flame.

My eyes widen even as the heat emanating from this reborn section of our planet makes my coat suddenly feel stifling.

Is this what our world used to be? A small paradise?

Still ahead of us, the volcano rises from a garden of lush tropical foliage, where brightly colored animals dart through the trees and birds with vibrant plumage take flight. Streams of flowing water drip from the lake and snake their way through lush tropical trees adorned with flowers and fruit hanging from every branch.

But it's not just water that flows here—there are also thin streams of flame flowing through this lush paradise. At first I wonder if this flame comes from *nemior* tubes like the lava I'd watched Haven coax back to the surface. But as I watch the flame dripping from the top of the volcano hidden in the clouds, to trace flickering paths down the volcano's dark surface, I realize it's not lava.

These streams are the exact same kind of liquid heat that swells in my veins. But this gleaming fire doesn't act like the burning flame that lives beneath my skin. Instead, it seems to bring warmth and new life. Trees cluster around the edge of these rivers of flame like they would around the rivers of water. It fosters even more life than simply the heat-resistant plants that filled the lava bog near Haven's village.

A thought dawns on me. The phoenixes at the top of the mountain apparently funnel a different kind of flame through this area, the kind that coaxes back to life, instead of bringing destruction.

This fire may not even come from the volcano itself, but perhaps flows from the very creatures that live above it. How much flame must they constantly emanate for this to be their table scraps? The runoff of their wings?

"This is what my people gave up hiding from the Goldens?" I whisper to myself with a stab of guilt.

Eli must hear. "It's not all it looks like. But it is the most beautiful prison you've ever seen." I suddenly realize both he and Jude look slightly nauseous.

"What is that fire? How come it doesn't hurt anything?"

Father said my fire was more volatile than others. Is this what he meant?

Finally, Eli answers. "It's what the Goldens give in return for the human's sacrifices. If their sacrifices are satisfactory, that is."

I gulp, remembering what his family had shared with me of their past. "Sacrifices."

He gives a hesitant nod and lifts a hand to indicate something I'd missed—a curving structure built into the base of the volcano. A structure that is eerily familiar. Several pillars holding up a roof and rimming an intricately carved building. A temple.

Like the one my people found buried within those *nemior* tubes. My stomach sours as Jude withdraws a long knife from his bag. On instinct, the mother *seren* increases the space between us and him.

Eli's face hardens. "To the Goldens, we are nothing. Just specks that blow away in the wind. Here one instant and gone the next. They'll keep us alive if they get what they want out of it. If not human labor or the ability to use us for their sick curiosities, then it's the very thing that makes us different from them."

The temple is about a mile away from our vantage point, but I can tell an aspect of the building that is chillingly different from the temple where I hid the other *fior-errans*. Deep crimson color mars the building. It drips and spills down from its roof.

My stomach tightens. Human blood. "They asked for blood sacrifices."

Eli gives a curt nod. "Exactly. With no care for our lives or what that does to a civilization and the ways it tears us apart. Especially since it's usually children they want sacrificed."

My vision becomes blurry, just thinking about it. How horribly cruel.

"This is why you left. They wanted you. Your blood."

Jude makes a guttural sound. "We *ran*. But it wasn't enough." He glares down at the village. "They still took our mother from us and nearly everything else away from Haven."

Eli has been gazing down at the village. "I should go down there first."

Jude swivels to him, his silver-studded piercings seeming to darken along with his next word. "What?"

"I should go down there first," Eli repeats decisively. "I'll meet back up with you after I see if I can help them."

"*Absolutely not.*" Jude's words are as low and fearsome as a thunderclap. He grabs his brother by the shoulders, glaring at him. "You are not going back there."

"But Jude, they might need help—"

"No. *You* need help." Jude's fists are balled. "I will not let you go down there and nearly kill yourself again to give fire to people who already have it and don't care. They know what it costs." His eyes dart from the foot of the volcano and up its rocky slope. "And unlike Haven, the Goldens won't come after them. Those people aren't forced into anything. They can leave, Eli." Jude glares at his brother. "I don't think this is about what's best for them. It's about what you think is best for you."

A flash of anger sparks across Eli's face. "That's ridiculous."

"Is it?" Jude gives a humorless laugh. Eli pushes back, voice rising. "How is this helping myself?" He points to the scars on his now bared arms.

"Because it's easier for you to be a martyr than face the truth."

Eli's face pales. "What truth?"

Jude gulps and crosses his arms over his chest. "That you are one of the lucky ones who can survive here. That the same blood you feel guilty for being born with gives you the ability to outlive me and Mom and everyone else like us." Jude's eyes glint. "The world isn't fair, Eli. You can't save everyone. You're not helping anyone by draining every last drop you have."

The brothers stare at each other for a long moment. The tension between them thick enough I can feel it resting on the air like ash. I cautiously clear my throat.

"I—uh . . ." I rub my face, unable to ignore my part in this any longer. "I've put you in enough danger. I can still go the rest of the way myself." I slip off the *seren's* back and step between the two brothers. "You risked and sacrificed more than enough for me . . ."

Eli's brows ripple, but the anger and shame that filled his features seconds ago soften. He studies me closely. "You sound . . . different. More like when you first woke up."

Because I'm remembering things I'd forgotten. I've been away from Father too long.

My *ero* has been quiet too long.

"I'm not sure I can watch whatever memories this mountain holds tear you both apart. You made it out and I won't force you back in. Please, go home. You still have a father and a community to return to."

That seems to catch them both off guard. Jude takes a sharp breath, but Eli stiffens. Their expressions silently betray their internal war.

They want to leave this place and its ghosts behind. I would too.

And I expect them to. I expect them to turn around and go home—

But instead, Eli shares a long, deciding look with his brother, then turns back to me.

"If we leave you to face these nightmares yourself, we'd be no better than those people down there who would abandon a child on the roof of that temple."

"That's not—"

"I hate this place more than you can imagine, Mara," Jude interrupts. "It has taken an untold amount from us, from others. And from you." He pauses. "But you've started to show me something."

I blink. "What's that?"

Jude takes a breath. "That maybe not all gods are selfish. And there are phoenixes besides Haven who are capable of some humanity. Some of them may be just as lost as we are." He reaches up to gently stroke the *seren's* neck. "Haven risked everything to get us away. He'd want us to do the same for your family. And if we can rescue Hana among them, maybe she can help heal Eli, maybe even Dad. So there's no question. We have to try." Despite Jude being fully human, I see a spark flicker in his eyes. "Even if we have to burn this mountain to the ground to free them."

I stand silently. Absorbing his words. Their meaning.

I swallow. "Thank you. For being willing to help me get my family back."

Jude awkwardly pats my back. "We might regret it later, but we're involved in this now."

We're all in this now. I swallow down the emotions bubbling up my throat, pressing them back down into my stomach where they continue to churn.

I have no real idea the threat we're about to walk into, but if Jude is right and I must burn this mountain to the ground to get to my father and the rest of my flock, so be it.

If there's one thing I can do, it's light things on fire.

CHAPTER FORTY-SEVEN

We decide to skirt the village and aim for the mountain directly. Better not to draw any more attention than we already will. It's eerily quiet as we creep our way through the jungle as quickly as we can. Even the *seren*, the most silent of all, seems unsettled.

We've stuffed our heavy coats into our weighty packs, wearing fewer layers. Eli and Jude constantly look around, scanning for danger. But I imagine they are not just seeing the lush jungles around us. They are also seeing ghosts.

Ghosts of a childhood they spent in this area, which they thought was normal. Living at the base of a mountain where those they called gods only kept them alive with mere drippings of fire that fell from their wings, and in return expected them to give everything.

The base of the volcano becomes visible through the thick cluster of palm trees ahead. Rippled, dark stone and earth rising out of the ground.

Jude stops right at the edge of the mountain, beside where the fire stream trickles down the steep side of the stone, having formed a deep divot in the side of the mountain.

"Ready for this?" he asks us both, as if hoping we may give a good reason to turn around.

But we're so close.

I pull my shoulders back and meet his gaze, realizing for the first time that this is about more than finding my missing flock. This mountain could hold the answers to questions that have haunted me all my life. Where I came from. Where Mama came from. Why she was hunted and I was left behind.

"I've waited two hundred years," I murmur mostly to myself. "I'm not waiting two hundred years more." Louder I say, "I'm not leaving Father or Hana a moment longer than I have to."

"*Wait*—" Eli abruptly reaches out to grab my arm. "What do you mean two hundred years? It's not possible for you to be that old."

I give a half-shrug. "Haven has been alive for a lot longer than that, right?"

Jude's eyes get wider as he closes in on me, Eli's hand still gripping my arm. "A half-phoenix has never lived that long, or had their aging slowed." Eli bites his lip, studying me.

My brows draw together. "I never claimed to be half-anything. Haven told you, I'm not like you. I don't exactly know what I am. I just know I'm different."

"Haven always told us the phoenixes were birthed by the hand of *Sol* himself, from the heart of a volcano." Eli looks up. "Like this one." He points his chin at the mountain ahead. "Always created fully formed. Full grown, as it were."

He gestures at me. "And yet here you are. More powerful than any half-phoenix I've ever met. Are you sure Darkholm wasn't hiding more than your flock from the Goldens?"

I stare at him. "Why are you asking me all this now?"

Jude lets out a long breath. "Because we're about to climb right to the Goldens' doorstep. Are you sure we're not bringing them exactly what your father was trying to keep away?"

I blow out a long breath. "I honestly don't know the answer to either question. But I was a baby—I didn't wake up fully grown in a volcano. Is that what you're asking?"

Both brothers consider me for a long minute. As if deciding whether they believe me.

Although I am leaving out a pretty important piece of information.

I *am* the first full-phoenix child to ever exist. Mother didn't give birth to me, but she did find me as a baby. Somehow, I am here. Fully flame, yet also able to age and grow unlike anyone my flock has ever seen. Growing stronger and more volatile every day.

I'm sure my father didn't want the Goldens to know about that.

But I refuse to hide away like a dormant flicker kept inside a cave to protect it from flaring up and burning a forest any longer. Maybe my flames are inevitable. Maybe the Goldens knowing of my existence is inevitable.

But so are two other things.

I will leave this mountain with my flock and these brothers safely at my side.

I will not let anything stop us.

My non-answer seems to be enough of a confirmation for now. Jude pulls more rope and two iron hooks from his pack, and then sizes up the sharp mountain face in front of us.

"Ready to climb a practically unclimbable mountain?"

CHAPTER FORTY-EIGHT

We leave the *seren* at the mountain's base and she fades into the jungle before I've even said goodbye. I only hope she will be here waiting when we return.

After tying the rope once again to each of us, Jude starts to scale the mountain. Toward the base, the slope is a little less steep, and we're able to walk uphill for about an hour before the volcano's angle grows more vertical. Before long, we're climbing one foothold and outcropping of rock at a time. We pull ourselves up from one shelf to another, taking long minutes to rest in between. Being forced to use knives as handholds to inch our way up the mountain wears away my calloused hands.

We're about a thousand feet off the ground when we reach a small shelf of volcanic rock. I almost cry from relief when I have at least one foot flat to balance on. Our knives are driven into the side of the mountain up to the hilt. I glance over at the brothers, then up at the nearly devastating distance we still have to climb.

"Are you sure—" But before I can get the words out, the shelf beneath us suddenly crumbles. My entire weight is thrown on the fingertips I frantically dig into the rough mountain face. Out of the corner of my eye, I see Jude scramble for his handholds, but his grip slides off. He drops several feet, pulling the length of rope between him and Eli taut. Eli lets out a yelp as he loses his left grip, leaving him dangling precariously with the weight of both brothers pulling at his remaining grip on the mountain.

"Mara!" He shouts at me, but I'm barely clinging to the cliff myself as I reach for him.

I'm able to grab his outstretched hand, but holding both his weight and Jude's is too much. I only have an instant until my grip fails altogether.

"Mara—fly!"

It's Father's voice. How he knows—I can't imagine.

It's an order he has never given before. The opposite of what he's always told me.

Clip my wings, never spread them.

And like that, my fingers cramp up and release. I fall.

We all fall. Downward off the side of the towering mountain. Down, down . . .

My pulse kicks into action and brings fire from the well inside my chest, through my veins and bones. Adrenaline keeps time with me and I let out an angry yell.

Not here. Not when we're so close.

I arch my back, kicking off the edge of the vertical cliff face as I fall, body suddenly inverted. Fire spreads along my shoulder blades, pressing out from those twin scars on my spine and flowing around the ripple of feather tips pressing through skin.

And all the anger and pain erupts from me in an explosion of flame that spirals out of my chest. The flames coat my body and stop my fall midair. I don't know how I manage to get ahold of the brothers' arms, but somehow I do, even as my body starts to transform.

Flames, not wings, erupt from my scars. This is far more painful than the growth and subsequent cutting of my feathers. My survival instincts kick in and crack my body open, turning me to fire. I can hear the brothers yelling—splatters of my flaming blood singeing them. My grip burns into their arms, but I don't dare let go.

I aim my own exploding body upward, toward the top of the massive volcano. I shoot through the air so fast that the wind cuts past my ears at a dizzying pace.

Faster, faster, faster—

I crest the top of the volcano in a matter of seconds, the world a blur. Then, I catch sight of the ground beneath us. A flat surface.

I force all the flames back in. Force the anger and fear back in.

I let go of Eli and Jude. We all drop together. Rolling and tumbling in the air until we crash into the top of the mountain. I've curled into a small ball, arms wrapped around myself, skin coated in charcoal-like ash as my flames cool too quickly. My body feels raw and raging at the same time. My head pounds when I finally still. Slowly, I lift my head and pat out the last bits of fire dancing across my shoulders.

My ears are ringing, but my searching eyes find the brothers. Jude sitting up, holding his head with one hand, the other marred by the smoking, burnt imprint of my fingers across his wrist. Moaning, but alive. *Thank* Sol. Eli, a few feet away, cradles an arm that is bent at a weird angle, his forearm burnt more than his brother's. But his eyes are fixed on something else.

I look more closely at the source of the stream of flame that pelts the smooth, obsidian surface we've crashed on. That's when I realize we've landed on some kind of road made of polished obsidian. A curtain of fire ripples toward us. Jude and Eli scramble to their feet to get away from the sizzling flood. I slowly raise my head, tracing the wave of flame up to its source.

Five stunning, gleaming, fiery creatures hover midair only feet away from me.

Their wild, feathered wings resemble a firebird in a way I've never seen, rending the air in waterfalls of flame that are a sharp contrast to the burnt, ashy flakes that cover my combustive body. Their wings don't even resemble my father's. His wings were built of hardened, crystalized fire. Like any bit of flame needed to be collected and protected.

But these creatures are so full of light and fire, they don't have to hold it back. It flows from their glorious bodies. Their physical forms are hard to see, as if mostly absorbed into the flame around them, but it seems they all have their arms crossed. Only their eyes are unwavering—twin flames riveted on me.

When they speak, it's in unison, and not aloud.

"WHAT ARE YOU, SOLNORA?"

Their voices ricochet in my head so loudly I double over. I cram my hands over my ears. Trying to block out the sound of their words that fillets through me, searching my *ero* and seeing *everything*.

I can't block them out.

Maybe these creatures really are gods.

Fallen gods.

CHAPTER FORTY-NINE

Fear pounds my temples as I push myself off the ground and rush over to the brothers, who have crawled as far away from the waterfall of flame as they can, almost to the edge of the massive mountain. When I reach them, I plant myself between them and the fallen gods I've practically fed them to. Right now, concern is the only thing circling through my head.

Not concern about how the Goldens knew we were here. Not the name they called me. Not what they are going to do to me.

My only concern is protecting Eli and Jude. In that moment, blood trickling down my face and raw skin still healing—I feel almost human. Not like the Hollows who struck down my mother without mercy, but like Jude and those who welcomed me into Haven's village.

"Don't hurt them!" I scream into the heads of the five powerful, winged creatures floating just feet away. *"Stay away from us."*

The Golden Phoenixes gaze down at me with those fiery eyes. Finally, the one who seems to be their main communicator pushes a few words into my head. Her voice is weighty—almost as imposing and echoing as Father's. *"You have no idea what you are, do you?"*

I startle. What I am?

A week ago, I would have immediately had an answer to that question. *Daughter of Darkholm.* Child of darkness. An outcast from the outside world.

Worthless alone. *Dangerous* alone.

But now I'm not so sure. The patience and trust Eli and Jude have given me have changed everything I thought I knew about myself.

I feel a kind of soothing, yet burning pain press up through my spine and shoulder blades. Not very comfortable, but . . . good. Like the muscle burn after a run. Like the itch of a wound healing.

Like the pain in your limbs as you grow.

The ache of growth.

New growth.

The bud of more new feathers begins to push through my skin, fanning out beside the three longer feathers that have grown stronger every day since I woke up in the cabin built for me.

But this time, the knowledge that my wings are growing doesn't drive me into a panic. Instead, I get to my feet and square my shoulders. "I'm here to get my father and flock back. Where do you have them hidden?"

The phoenixes laugh. Their odd, rusty chortle echoes in my head. *"You will see. We have been waiting for you."*

And then, in a movement that completely shocks me, the phoenix at the center of the group drifts forward to float just inches away from me, her blinding wings dripping rivers of flame that singe and pool over the ebony ground.

She lifts a flaming hand out to me. *"Come with us."*

Instead, I lurch backward. Behind me, Eli's voice is audible and clear. "Don't trust them, Mara!"

The gleaming creature turns her head toward Eli. *"He's hurt. We will heal him."*

And before either Jude or I can do anything, she has drifted closer to Eli, her fire falling in rivers all around him. Jude jumps in front of Eli, trying to cover him with his body and shield him from the flames, but the phoenix lifts a hand to them.

She lets the tongues of orange and red out like a small wildfire over her outstretched arm. Flame drips from her open hand and splashes all over the brothers, bathing them in a kind of gleaming, vibrant flame.

It makes my own blood sear through my veins.

Both wrench away from her, arms over their heads, trying to

shield themselves from the rivers of flame, but they can't escape them. Their coiled bodies stiffen, taut in preparation for the intense scalding pain. But instead, their expressions go from terrified to bewildered . . . to amazed.

I can't help but gasp as her flames wash over Eli's broken arm. I see the bone *snap* back into place, the torn and bloody skin mending itself. I'm pulled forward by a hauntingly magnetic force, my entire body trembling with the impossibility of this moment as I watch his body heal before my eyes.

But, it's not just Eli that she pours healing over. Jude seems to straighten as the shining droplets of light rain around him. The human inhales so deeply, I see the dark circles under his eyes fade. The scrapes and cuts littering his arms are gone.

Both brothers stare up at the Golden Phoenix with mouths agape. "Why did you do that?" Eli asks breathlessly.

The phoenix tilts her head at him, still communicating telepathically, ***"Why not? You have not come to do us harm, have you?"***

Jude coughs, tugging at one of the silver studs punched through his earlobe. "Not after this."

Eli flashes his brother a sharp look, but Jude gives a hesitant shrug.

The phoenix still hovering midair nods. ***"Consider this a debt you can repay by extending the same goodwill to us."***

She turns away from the brothers and shifts her attention to me. Her telepathic link presses each word into my mind with the same force I'm used to only hearing from Father. ***"Your friends will be well cared for. We will show them to a place to rest. Now, you can come with us . . ."***

"Why would I do that?" I kneel beside Eli, gently brushing my fingertips over his healed arm. "I appreciate your help," I continue, "but I'm here to—"

"Retrieve your flock." One of the other phoenixes answers my thought. ***"We are aware. We will take you to them. But first—you must see what you have lost staying with Darkholm."***

The words spark curiosity, but I still take a firm-footed stance, meeting their flaming gazes. "I'm sorry, but I must see my father first."

I've come so far. Part of me is terrified, however, of going with these Golden Phoenixes and not despising what I see.

In all the stories Jude and Eli regaled me with—in all the fearful glances from my flock—no one ever mentioned their flames could heal. Or that Golden phoenixes might treat humans with kindness.

Yes, there were temples. But is it possible the humans created those themselves? Did these phoenixes really ask for their sacrifices?

I shake myself. *All the same, I need to find Father. I'm sure he can explain.*

How do I convince these godlike beings to do as I ask?

What would Father do?

Use the only thing I have—fire.

I lick my cracked lips, coaxing a bit of flame to burst from my veins and flow down my shoulder blades and up over my arms. I try to sound imposing as I meet their glowing gazes. "You let me see my father, or I'll set myself off. It will cause a chain reaction not even he could control."

The words feel foreign on my tongue.

They shouldn't.

Father's said some version of those phrases to me multiple times— made me repeat them back until they were part of my every thought.

My threat only elicits a flickering glance among the five phoenixes. Conversing amongst themselves in their heads, undoubtedly. Then, as a single unit, they swell toward me. Slow smiles come to their unnervingly beautiful faces.

"We are not afraid of you, little one. Not like your father was."

Their words barrel into my chest. I sway on my feet.

But they keep talking, their powerful voices flooding my thoughts, *"Your fire is not a threat here. We are not so fragile."*

Sparks dance across my vision. If they aren't afraid—if they don't need my flame—

"What do you want from me?"

"To show you your birthright. The world you were stolen from. You are one of us, Mara. We have no need to quiet your fire." Their voices rise in cadence. *"Here, your flames are a gift. A legacy. You*

were taken from us so many years ago when your mother ran away.
Now, you are a prodigal returned home."

In unison, they all turn away from me and motion to the curve of
a city that rises out behind them, glimmering in tones of gold and this
obsidian volcanic rock. "*Welcome home,* **Solnora.**"

They know about Mama?

And they called me the same thing Haven did.

I twist my sweating hands together, stomach in tight knots. They
know about Mama.

I have to hear more.

But Father—

I glance over at the brothers, but relay a telepathic question back at
the Goldens. "*If I come with you, will you keep them safe? Promise*
nothing will happen to them?"

"*We swear on our eternity, no harm will come to your fellow*
travelers."

And just like that, I'm standing on the razor-edge of a decision that
could tip me into the heart of this consuming volcano or bring me
even closer to the memory of the only person who ever truly loved me
with no strings attached.

Mama.

I step right up to the phoenixes, unfurling my wings and giving
them a little shake. "I'll come with you."

They almost smile and whisper those haunting words into my
thoughts again.

"*Welcome home.*"

CHAPTER FIFTY

While whisking Eli and Jude off to some kind of medical area, the remaining Golden Phoenixes grab hold of my arms and lift me off the ground. Their wings beat in stunning precision around me, glimmering flame dripping around us and flung into the air by the heavy movements.

Gripping onto their arms with my own as they carry me higher and higher, they angle deeper into the city, giving me an aerial view.

It's a marvel of spires of shining gold and rippling lava and buildings carved out of obsidian stone. It's more beautiful than anything I've ever seen. The city is layered upon itself in a way that makes every floor seem like it's dangling suspended in the air. Each rooftop and ledge is coated in waterfalls of flame. The rivers of warm, scarlet-golden fire run all around us as if the blood of *Sol* himself flows through these streets. Something about that makes me shudder.

Countless gardens filled with tropical fruits and trees are interwoven with more streams of flame, reminding me of Haven's village. Like that small glimpse—this mountain was made for our fire.

I see the phoenixes everywhere—striding through the gardens, like winged, flaming sentinels training, flaming swords flashing.

There is an arena, toward the edge of the stretching city, where youthful ones run and jump and train with swords. Far too young and fragile to be full-phoenixes like those carrying me.

Children with flames rippling over their arms or turning their hair to fire.

God-born, as Eli called them. The offspring of phoenixes and mortals—like him?

A shudder sweeps my body, and the phoenixes hold on even more tightly, aiming away from the arena, but a thousand questions tumble through my head.

Does Eli know? Does he know he's not the only one?

He must know.

Or was Haven trying to shield him from this?

But the youths, even from this distance, don't appear angry or desperate. In fact, I can tell there are smiles and laughter. They're enjoying themselves. Tempered by fire, like the rest of this city.

Nothing here is as heartless as I expected.

And no one bats an eye at me. Here, I'm less of a threat than the volcano beneath our feet.

I have to wonder. What was Father so worried about?

The Goldens set me on the tiered edge of the cityscape. Roofs and rafters are filled with rich, lush foliage.

Most of the phoenixes have slowly parted ways for my little procession throughout the course of their tour, and when I'm finally placed in the center of the garden by the phoenix who has spoken the most, the other two who flank her just nod their heads at me.

"We will see you more soon, Mara, Daughter of Sol. Ra'an will make you welcome."

And like that, their massive, flaming forms rise back into the clear air and they fly toward the other side of this city. Their wings dip into the edge of a flowing waterfall of flame that splashes on their feathers, absorbing into their own gleaming forms.

"Do you ever have to sleep?" I'm not sure why it's the first question I ask the phoenix known as Ra'an. It just slips out as I take in the strange myriad of flaming, seemingly ageless creatures.

Her wings curl behind her, droplets of liquid fire trailing from them and running around my bare feet. It warms my skin like the river of lava near Haven's village. It's oddly soothing.

"No. We stopped needing the aethor *sleep long ago. Our flame nourishes us without it."*

She looks at me with intense curiosity. *"Your father has to rest? Interesting . . . We have also heard that Haven's scars have still not healed. Is that true?"*

I blink at her. *"You know Haven?"*

"Of course," is the reply. *"Darkholm chose to lash out at our own. In defying his very nature, his flame started to cool. As did any who chose violence alongside him. They all became fior-errans."*

My brows suddenly shoot up. "How do you know that name?"

Fior-erran.

Her flaming gaze flickers. *"What did he tell you it meant, little one? Forsaken Ones? Forsaken by the world hunting them?"*

I barely dare to breathe, giving an almost imperceptible nod. Skin chilled at how closely her words mirror Father's.

Ra'an's gaze narrows. *"Not Forsaken for the reasons he undoubtedly wanted you to believe. We named them the* fior-errans. *So all would know they had forsaken their very nature, their very kind."*

I find myself drifting backward, out of reach of her gleaming flame. Stomach twisting in knots. *Father must have an explanation. Somehow.* But—this echoes what Haven said too.

As if catching that thought, Ra'an continues. *"Haven was not hurt by us. Nor scarred by us. That was Darkholm—"* She peers down at me. *"The one you call Father."*

My knees go weak and I stumble backward until my aching spine presses against the curve of a tree behind me. "What? No. He wouldn't—"

Her voice thunders through my head. *"He did. That is why he fell and why his body slowly is draining of life. He hated the sympathy Haven felt for the humans. Though we stopped him before he completed the deed, not even our healers could restore the wounds Haven already suffered by the wings of his own."*

The wings of his own . . .

The *reer* blades. Weapons fashioned out of our own feathers.

Feathers Father used to cut away my own wings from my spine and forced me to do the same.

No wonder Jude didn't trust me. No wonder Eli was so shocked when I told him I carved out my own wings.

My fingertips dig into the rough bark of the tree, feeling the life pumping through it. I try to ground myself and settle the verging panic.

Ra'an just observes me with those flaming eyes.

"I have something to show you."

She gently lifts me again and we fly to the center of their city of towering, tiered buildings and hanging gardens. To a courtyard surrounding a temple that feels oddly familiar.

It's a more glorious, alive version of the temple ruins in which my flock hid.

My feet touch the ground and I slowly cross the courtyard and stop at the threshold of the temple. Through its massive arched doorway, I can see the roof inside curving like a reflection of the sky, with carvings etched across its surface. Bits of shimmering blue flame lap around the edges of the temple and mix with the waterfalls of fiery gold that flow from the channels carved into the floor and down the hanging gardens around us.

Wordlessly, I move in closer. Just being in this place is like revisiting an earlier version of myself. Something is very familiar . . .

"What is this place?"

The flames dripping from Ra'an's reddish-gold form fill the spiraling crevices across the floor. *"This is the temple you were first brought to, Solnora, Daughter of Sol. A child your mother should never have found—but a miracle for our people. We all gathered here to see you with our own eyes. Until your mother had to flee."*

My head tilts back, sparks still caught in my hair and splattering against my shoulder blades. The edges of my very fledgling feathers flicker as the flames drip across them.

The images carved in the roof show a sun that is mightier and gleaming in a way I have never seen, and from the beams of the orb there are sketches of flaming, winged creatures. Born from the sun.

Children of Sol.

"What happened? Why did my mother run?" The words echo hollowly in the room.

Ra'an glides closer, the air around me growing warmer as the flames that drip from her body pool in the room. The phoenix is quiet for a long moment, gazing up at the ceiling, her hair a waterfall of dripping flame.

When she answers, her voice in my head is low and cautious. *"She ran because you were hunted . . ."*

"By who? Humans?"

"No. By her own kind."

My heart seizes and I take a faltering step back, toward the exit. She shakes her head. *"No, little one. Not by us. There are two things you need to understand."*

She indicates the spiraling art above our heads. Images that remind me so much of my own crude artwork, with hints of that blueish flame sparking across them. There is a kind of energy that reminds me of my flock. *"The humans are not our enemy. They are not even worthy to be called prey—certainly not predators."*

I blink at her. "What would you call them, then?"

There is a pause before she responds. *"Atmosphere? There used to be many of them, you know. When the sun began to die, they struggled to survive. We have done what we can for them, but this world really wasn't made for their frail bodies."*

Something about her words are a sharp contrast to what Haven told me about our origins and purpose of our people. I certainly don't trust this Golden Phoenix, but even if she isn't entirely honest with me, I have to ask. I press my next question toward her thoughts, suddenly feeling uncomfortably bare, speaking aloud and sharing that element of my humanness. *"But weren't we created to protect them? To guard over the humans?"*

Ra'an's mighty wings rend the air, making my scars burn.

"That was an old-world religion. It was created to enslave us." Her eyes spark. *"To enslave us to a world that does not deserve our flame or sacrifice."* She rises off the ground, toward the drawings etched above us. *"The humans will destroy themselves if left to their*

own devices. Even the ones that live at the base of our mountain have taken to slaughtering their own children, foolishly thinking that will appease us."

"Can you not stop them?"

"We have tried. We impose peace for a few hundred years, but then several generations of their insect-like lifetimes pass, and they are back to slaughtering each other. We used to carry the weight of believing that protecting them was our duty, given by **Sol** *himself."*

She touches a shimmering image carved into the roof. The one of the sun incarnate whispering the phoenixes into existence. *"But we are no longer so naive. There is no* **Sol**. *The sun did not give us life."* She hovers in front of the image. *"This sun is dying. And yet we live. We truly are the gods of this world. This icy wasteland needs our warmth as desperately as the humans do."*

I stare up at her, at her glistening, golden wings, rending the air like twin waterfalls. She almost looks like a flaming god.

"Do not trust them. They lie." Haven's words resurface in my mind. I lick my lips as I continue to stare at Ra'an's glorious form.

"What about all the humans who are freezing out there?" I take a deep breath. "Even the ones who hunted my flock because they were desperate for heat? What about them? Do they deserve to die? Or go mad from the cold?"

I can hardly believe the words flowing from the deepest parts of me. I'm defending the vile creatures who slaughtered my mother.

The world is not as black and white as I thought it was. Eli and Jude have taught me that much.

"They can come to us for salvation if they choose. Or they can endure the world beyond us. We have offered them safety and warmth—"

"In return for what?" I scream the thought into her mind. All Eli's horrendous stories bubble up around me like popping pockets of lava. *"What do they lose to live at your feet?"*

"Nothing. They are near our glory, that is enough. Sometimes our brethren will take a special interest in a human and invite them to live with us." She gestures to me. *"That is what happened*

in the case of Haven and the human woman who bore your god-born friend."

There's that term again. *"God-born?"*

"A word coined by the humans for a mortal child who has fire running in their veins. They view our mountain as a kind of heaven. A paradise, an afterlife."

"What happens to the god-bo—" I stop myself, feeling odd uttering the word. *"To the half-blood children?"*

"We raise them here, of course. Train them. Most of them." Her smile brings a chill to my spine. *"That child of Haven had eluded our grasp for a very long time. Thank you for returning him to us."*

Alarm erupts like lava. No wonder they healed him and welcomed us with open arms.

I delivered Eli right into their false embrace.

CHAPTER FIFTY-ONE

Heart racing, I start edging toward the door. *"And if he wants to leave?"*

Ra'an slowly swirls toward me, flaming wings flowing out around her.

"Mara . . ." The other voice is faint, but still crackles through my head. *Father.* It's as if the connection keeps faltering, but he is there.

"Mara . . . can you . . . hear?"

Father?

But Ra'an's next words snap my attention back to her. *"The youth can leave whenever he wants. But most like him choose not to, once they see what we offer here."*

I clench my jaw. *"And what's that?"*

She smiles a long, willowy smile. *"Immortality. No more pain. No more death."* She floats closer, reaching out to let her fingers graze my chin. Her voice is overwhelming, thick as smoke, making it hard to ascertain my own thoughts. Making it difficult to even hear Father.

"Your friend is dying. His fire is absorbing the life from his body, no matter how quickly he tries to drain it from his veins. Even if he stopped giving his lifeblood to the cattle, he would find his body failing him. His human skin is not able to hold his flaming blood for long." She drifts closer, flaming eyes narrowed on me. *"But we can help him. We can heal him forever. He can be like*

us. Never needing to regenerate, and always whole. Nothing can taint or hurt us here."

I draw back from her touch. But I can't deny the value of the offer of no more pain. No more regeneration. Never again watching myself and my world burst apart. No more crumbling to ash and pulling myself back together again.

"Mara . . . listen . . ." Father's thoughts invade my *ero*, shaking me from my reverie. I step back from Ra'an, needing my original question answered before I find a way to hide and converse more clearly with Father.

"You still haven't answered my question. What was my mother running from?"

Her eyes flicker and become like stone. Her next words she says aloud, as if to add gravity to their utterance.

"The creature you call Father."

CHAPTER FIFTY-TWO

I gasp. Instinctively, I try to close my mind off from Father. Like latching a door shut. I've never really tried before, but with his distance here, perhaps I can have my mind to myself for a moment to hear this. *"That can't be right . . ."*

The Golden Phoenix continues to speak aloud. "Mara, Darkholm is not your ally, nor your guardian."

Heat builds deep in my chest, sweat dripping down my temples. I hardly dare to ask the next question, but I need to know. "Then what is he?"

"A religious fanatic. A dangerous zealot who not only believed he was a god, but also did not deign to allow humans anywhere near our mountain. He viewed any of us who took mercy on humans as a disgrace to our very race. Especially one like Haven, who fell in love with one."

I think back over the scars and burn marks that cover Haven's body and the looks of absolute fear on the brothers' faces the first time they met me and heard about my father.

I think of the thousands of times Father warned me about the outside world and swore we were the only ones left. The only ones who mattered.

How much he hated the Hollow and said they were soulless, bloodthirsty creatures who deserved the death haunting their footsteps.

I can't avoid this. Not anymore.

I manage to speak. "What did he do?"

"I am sorry for this. We did not want to tell you your history so quickly. We wanted to give you time—"

But she doesn't know Father is in my head too. Trying to listen in. I can feel him pounding at the edges of my *ero*. Trying to get through that locked door.

"Tell me *now!*"

And she does, filling in gaps that once seemed insignificant.

"He gathered a small cult of followers, our own brothers and sisters, who believed his fanatic lies and agreed that humans were a scourge who would someday endanger us." My heart freezes at how her words ricochet and connect with the dynamics in our flock. The way everyone, even Hana, looked to my father. The way he spoke of the humans. The way we hid from them.

The many times he would kill any who got close. Out of self-defense, he said.

But Ra'an is not done. *"He took two dozen of our ranks to his side and tried to challenge the rest of us. Especially any who took mercy on humans. When we would not acquiesce to his plan to let the humans freeze or hunt them ourselves . . ."* Her eyes turn glassy. *"He attacked his own people. He killed some of us and tortured others, like Haven. And so we cast them out—Darkholm and those who sided with him. They fell to the surface."*

The whole room spins.

This can't be real.

All along, I thought I was raised by wounded gods—but I was actually the captive of a murderer and liar.

"Whatever they're saying—it's a lie." Father has finally broken through. His voice is clearer now. *"They're trying to sway you against me, Mara."*

I don't know who to believe. *What* to believe.

But someone hurt Haven. Either my father or these Goldens— I'm not sure what to even think anymore.

I brush against the wall again, making my raw, fledgling feathers burn and hiss. A bit of blue flame singes my collar and I stare up at Ra'an. She's seemingly sympathetic to my plight.

"Your father is very sickly, Mara. We did find him, and we brought him and his flock here for their own safety. And the safety of you and all the creatures on the planet."

My breath catches. She admitted it.

Father's voice persists. *"Mara—come find us. I will tell you everything. Don't let them entrap you. Don't let them inside your mind."*

"Like you are right now?"

There is no response to that. I doubted there would be.

I need to get away from this place. To sort through what I thought I knew about my life.

Something almost liquid in her flickering amber eyes nearly makes me believe she would answer, that she is sympathetic to the thoughts and emotions swirling through me. But these creatures have been alive for thousands of years. Those may be false tears meant to make me trust her.

I slide around the wall of the temple. *"Thank you, Ra'an. I will take time to consider everything you've shared. Can you take me to Eli and Jude?"*

She nods. *"Yes, we will take you to them."*

I quickly cross the remainder of the flame-coated floor to the massive double doors.

As much as it pains me, I have to ask, "Where is my father?"

"Somewhere safe. We will take you to him tomorrow."

I plaster on a smile. "Thank you. That will give me the time I need to think."

"You have taken this all far better than we expected. Well done." She inclines her head.

I nod in return, backing out of the temple. *"I've been wondering where I belonged for a long time,"* I add.

It's not a lie.

Ra'an reaches for me right as my father's clear, terrified voice explodes through my thoughts.

"Mara—no. You cannot wait until tomorrow. They are coming to execute us now. Find us."

I'll come, I just need to escape this phoenix first.

By some miracle – Father catches that thought but Ra'an doesn't.

"No." The fear in his voice is overwhelming. *"We don't have that much time. They will start with me, and then Hana."*

My pulse ramps up.

That can't happen.

While the phoenix who raised me is a lot of things, a cold-blooded killer isn't one that I've seen. He may have hated the humans, but if he wanted, he could have wiped out their villages easily. Instead, he chose to hide us away.

Something about Ra'an's story doesn't make sense.

Ra'an guides me out of the temple, and then the phoenix's golden hands are on my shoulders. In seconds, she's lifted me off the ground.

Ra'an flies with me across the tops of this cluster of buildings and gardens. It is darker than before, as the sun has completely left this section of the sky. I force myself to relax. To not let her sense anything—in my thoughts, or in my body. To drown any thoughts in that inferno deep inside where I used to hide things from Father, too.

I let my eyes close as she soars with me across the amber paradise they've built at the spout of this volcano. I reach out for my father. For that same heat signature I would trace in the ice wasteland. For the hint of where they've hidden him.

There are too many heat signatures out here. Dozens and dozens.

But Father's is different. And while it's faint and flickering, I suddenly catch onto it. And all around him, clustered closely together, I can sense the rest of my flock.

He and Ra'an are both right.

My family is dying. I can feel their life forces draining away.

But, why can I sense them so easily now?

As Ra'an's massive wings rend the air around me, flames splattering across my ash-coated form, my eyes skim over buildings and trees growing out of the rocky ground and perches built into the edges of this top of the volcano—and then I see it. A familiar, dark-tinted tube with an opening halfway hidden by a latched door.

That's it. I'm sensing their warmth through volcanic tubes that interlace this mountain. In the same way I could navigate through a blizzard to get Father and myself home.

But if I can feel the heat rising from my flock through the magma tubes, that means one thing.

The Golden Phoenixes have trapped my family at the center of this volcano.

My pulse kicks up so fast my head goes dizzy.

I found you, Father.

"Sorry about this—" I say to Ra'an, as in one swift motion, I place both my hands on either side of her temples and channel as much heat into my palms as I can.

I expect it to sway her attention—at the most, knock her unconscious. But the flames blast through her head and melt her fiery visage like a snowball falling to pieces. Only her face doesn't melt—it turns to ash. Crumbling in my hands.

With her entire body falling to ash in my arms, we both drop like a rock. Terror grips me, until I see flames sparking across her body as we fall. I've instigated her regeneration.

I don't have much time, but in relief I realize she'll survive.

Midair, I desperately scan to see if anyone has noticed. But by some miracle of *Sol,* there are no phoenixes nearby, let alone looking in our direction.

For once, luck is on my side.

I hit the ground in a roll, rise to my feet, steady myself, and dash toward the covered volcano tube I've managed to land nearby. All around me are enormous buildings crafted of volcanic rock dripping in streams of flame.

I make it to the magma tube and wrench the lid off. Staring into the black abyss where the ground drops away, I take a deep breath.

I wish Eli was here.

Once I get my flock out, we'll free the brothers, and all get off this cursed mountain.

"I'm coming, Father. I'm coming."

CHAPTER FIFTY–THREE

I crawl through the magma tube as quickly as I can, the small cavern pressing in on me with the weight of the mountain. The deeper into it I travel, the more strongly I can sense the familiar heat signature of my father and the rest of our flock. Calling to me. Drawing me onward.

With every inch I crawl, I can feel myself starting to curl inward. The rush of heat in my head is simmering to a low murmur. The boldness I'd gained while traversing with Eli and Jude is overwhelmed by a kind of crawling sensation flooding my skin.

Father is in my head again.

And that shakes me and starts to shut me down, piece by piece.

Once again, I am that child sitting in a corner of our own magma tubes, waiting for him to tell me I can come out.

That I won't hurt anyone.

My bare feet are scuffed up from the harsh texture of the *nemior*, my palms lanced with cuts and scrapes, but I keep crawling. At least the strange mixture of hardened ash and remnants of material that mold to my body like a Mara-shaped cocoon protect my vital organs from the roughness of the tunnel.

But the sheath of ash doesn't protect my body from the trembling that starts in my palms and spreads.

I'm going to see Father soon. Why does that make me so anxious?

I force myself to keep moving. How do the *seren* travel through tunnels like this? I force myself to press a whisper toward the empty space.

"Father? Can you hear me?" I crawl inch by desperate inch.

"Yes, you're clearer now." As is he.

I can make out the faint sound of other voices. Snatches of desperate pleas. Hana and other members of our flock. But why do they sound so distant still?

I finally see a flicker of firelight reflecting off the bend in the pitch-black tube ahead of me. Almost there.

I emerge into a small cavern that doesn't look like it's seen another living creature in years, but the flicker of light is coming from a connecting tunnel on the other side.

I'm coming, Hana . . .

I climb through the second section of tunnel, but this one is much steeper—aimed directly downward. It's filled with sweltering heat that starts me coughing, giving my body a moment to adjust and regulate the temperature the lower I go. I finally enter this last stretch of *nemior*. I brace myself inside it, back against one wall, palms and feet against the other, and shimmy down. I close my eyes.

And there they are. Two dozen forms flicker against a backdrop of seething intensity that seems buried not far below them.

My father's strong presence is most recognizable, but my chest locks up at the rest of the flock's silhouetted heat signatures. They're alive. I have been dreaming of seeing their familiar forms for so long. It's more than I hoped for. More than I deserved.

"I can see you!"

"Where?" Father's voice is nearly as strong and intense as always.

"I'm in the magma tubes above you. Are you tied up?"

"You are close. Hurry!"

I open my eyes and peer downward as I reach the end of the smaller tunnel. Beneath is what looks like some kind of thin, chiseled layer of hardened volcanic rock. But I can still see the flicker of something liquid and heavy roiling under the surface. The source of this stifling, sweltering heat that is trying to make my head go light.

I'm in the center of the volcano.

I almost forget to keep myself braced in the tube from the shocking realization, but manage to make it the rest of the way down as carefully as I can. I cautiously slide my body through the end of the chute.

Careful . . . careful . . .

If I land too hard, I might break through the blackened skin of cooling rock and into the magma beneath.

I drop to the dappled floor as gingerly as I can.

Nerves and excitement spike through my shaking palms.

I'm here. I've found Father. I'm here.

Why don't I feel relieved?

Instead, my chest is locked up, ribcage pinching, throat raw.

My pulse echoing in my ears.

"Mara!" It's not just Father's voice this time. The weak but breathlessly relieved voices of my flock resound through my thoughts. Their familiar warmth fills the space and wraps around me.

Slowly, barely able to breathe, I straighten and take in the room. Tears fill my eyes at the devastating view.

My father and every single member of my flock hang from the chamber's ceiling. Cords of dripping blue fire cover their wrists, wind around their waists, and crawl down their legs. The flames cruelly burn and chafe their bodies as they hang suspended. Secondary cords of flame extend from their ankles and tether them to the volcanic floor.

At first, I think the flames are holding them in place. Cautiously approaching, I meet Hana's large, bloodshot gaze first. Her body is dangerously gaunt and pale.

Thud-thud . . . thud-thud . . .

Breathe. Breathe.

You can do this.

I slowly turn to find Father's boiling stare. He's slightly separated from the rest of the flock, the flaming cords binding him an even darker color than the others.

"Free us, Mara! They'll be here any minute."

My heart falters. No—hello. No hint of joy to see me.

Has he missed me?

"There's time for that after we are safely out."

I should feel . . . alive again. I found them. I found him.

Everything should be righted. The world tipped back into place.

But instead, my chest is still clamped tight. A quiver shakes the unusually cold hands I rub together.

It's fine, I tell myself. *You're just worried about them.*

Thud-thud . . . thud-thud . . .

My own heartbeat nearly drowns out the fragile reassurance.

This isn't what I thought coming home would feel like.

I'm so cold.

"Mara! Move."

I quickly brush away tears and hurry forward to touch the flaming cords binding my father. His nearness should be steadying. His voice in my head should calm my nerves.

But my skin crawls being this close to him.

Just free them—just get them out.

At the first touch, I realize the flames aren't stagnant, they're being drawn upward through the roof above us.

Worry fills my lungs. "What are they doing to you?"

Father's silvery eyes grow darker. **"Siphoning our fire to fuel themselves. Draining us. I told you—you cannot trust them. Get us out, child."**

I wrap a hand around the chain, the rippling flames biting into my knuckles. "How do I cut through this?"

There is a spark in his steely gaze. **"With your own fire. Do what I've taught you."**

What he raised me for.

I'm suddenly very, very aware of the three feathers against my spine—barely a whisper, but tiny sparks of independence he would abhor.

Angling so he cannot see my back, I take a deep breath, reach up, and close both hands around the nearest fire-laced chain holding him in place. I pour a bit of flame into my palms, and then lean into that bonfire within my chest. The heat spirals through my skin, making contact with the chains that tug the fire from Father's body and channel it upward.

The golden-orange tongue of flame that flows out of my touch quickly pushes his weak, blue flame aside and melts through the first chain in a matter of seconds.

It falls to the side almost instantly.

"Yes! That's it! Hurry. There were Golden guards here only moments ago. They'll return with reinforcements to finish the job."

He doesn't have to ask twice. I move away from his torn wrist, burnt and raw, to free his other hand. I burn through that chain quickly and he's released. He stands, towering over me. *"The feet—quickly."*

I shake as I free his first foot. The fire I conjure is fiercer each time, and once I've reached for the manacle around his other leg, I burn the chain to ash in less than a second.

None of this feels real. I straighten and look Father in the eye. But he reaches for me with a light embrace that makes me go stiff. *"You did well, my child. Now help the others. I'll stand watch."*

He barely avoids brushing my feathers when he holds me, and I'm out of his arms as quickly as I can be.

What's wrong with me?

I have dreamt of his voice in my head for so long.

Ached for the ghost of his *ero* so many times on this trip. For him to tell me what to do, make me feel less alone.

But actually seeing him, feeling his familiar, almost-icy warmth and that rich tone echoing through my head, my mind feels hedged in for the first time in many sunpasses. Taut. Controlled.

This is what I wanted, so why do I also feel deeply unnerved?

I rub my eyes, trying to orient myself. Nothing feels right.

I'm going to be sick.

Thud-thud.

Thud-thud.

My arms are wrapped around my chest, and I tap a finger against my forearm in time to my own heartbeat. Trying to slow it. Trying to breathe again.

Father was correct about one thing: the Goldens aren't our allies. They've chained up my people. Drained their lifeblood from their veins—just like every other creature has wanted to. Just like the Hollow Ones.

"There is a reason we hid away, little one. The outside world is not a safe place for us."

I glance at Father as I cross over to Hana next. The Hana who once knew Haven.

Maybe she'll have answers—know what is wrong with me.

Father is facing a round tunnel entrance I didn't notice on the other side of the room. That must be how the Goldens get down here.

I breathe in a lungful of stale, ashen air and tip my head back to meet Hana's eyes as she dangles above me, tied by the same kinds of chains father was. "Are you alright?" I say aloud to her.

To my surprise, she answers with her voice. "Yes, Mara. I knew you would come for us." Her words are shaky and gravelly, but her effort causes another tear to slide down my cheek.

I was supposed to keep her safe. To watch over her in those tunnels.

It was my one goal. One purpose. Instead, I let them be taken and tortured.

"I'm so sorry," I whisper.

But she shakes her head as I quickly burn through the first chain holding her arm. "It was not your fault. No one could have stopped the Goldens when they came for us. Somehow they knew exactly where we were and that you were gone."

I burn through her other chain and gently guide her to the ground. She sits weakly on the rocky floor, the lava-rock beneath us uncomfortably heated.

"They must have been tracking us for a long time." I char through the shackles on her feet, and she gives me a grateful smile.

"Well, they underestimated you. Did you find us on your own?"

I muster a small smile for her myself. "No. I met two brothers who guided me here. One is like us, but only half. Part human, part phoenix."

Her eyes go wide and her breath catches. "And he helped you?"

I nod, gently helping her to her feet and guiding her to lean against the wall near the exit. I keep my voice down, knowing Father is listening in. "Yes. They showed me a whole Hollow village that means us no harm. It's where their father lives. Another . . ." My words trail off when I see out of the corner of my eye, my father has gone completely still.

Idiot! I berate myself. If there is any truth to what Ra'an said, my father would not have forgotten Haven anytime soon. I hope Hana hasn't.

Hana tilts her head at me. "Mara? Are you well?" Her voice is raspy from a tremendous lack of use, but I am proud of her for trying.

"Yes, Hana," I assure her. "I'll have to tell you everything once we are free."

"Mara, get to the others . . ." Father's voice rockets through my thoughts. I drop my head in a low nod.

"Yes, Father."

Stepping away from Hana, I quickly work on the chains that trap the rest of my people, continuing to carefully position my body so that my back is never fully facing my father. Despite the heat pulsating through my quivering hands, a chill still clings to my skin.

"Quickly, quickly!" Father shouts at me, and I blaze through the rest of their chains. My palms are bloody and raw from the amount of fire I've drawn to the surface by the time I finish. Soon twenty-four in all are freed, including Father and Hana.

I help as many as I can over to where Hana rests. Our little group of phoenixes lean or sit against the edge of the room, and being in their midst like that helps slow my pulse a fraction. Despite many of them watching me and the flickering floor underfoot with the same uncertainty, they still murmur gratitude into my *ero.*

But they seem on edge too. Apprehensive.

Watching Father out of the corner of their wan expressions.

He turns away from scouting the entrance to the room, finally addressing me. *"Good, good. I can sense them returning, but they are too late."*

I glance toward the large tunnel, blocked by a heavy door that must lead out of the center of this volcano, and when I let my eyes fall closed, I can see four heat signatures descending on us. Only seconds away.

Two of them seem eerily familiar, but I'm too dizzy to ascertain why.

Trying to steady myself by placing a hand on Hana's shoulder, I peer at Father. "How do we get out now?"

In a few quick steps he's reached me, chilled fingers cupping my face. ***"You."***

CHAPTER FIFTY-FOUR

Me?

His grip on my face is so tight my jaw aches. *"This is the moment you have been training for, little one. The reason why I had you explode so many times among our people—so they could temper their bodies to survive your blast."* His voice drops low. *"So we could survive."*

I stare. "W-what do you mean?"

"You are our savior, my child." He caresses my cheek with sweet movements that make my stomach churn. *"And now you will carry out the very reason I brought you here."*

Brought me here?

It can't be . . .

I glance at Hana, but she can't meet my eyes. She does speak aloud, voice low. "He told them where we slept. He knew you would come find us."

The heat drains from my face.

He couldn't. He *wouldn't*. This is madness.

Father's—Darkholm's hands close around my face again, and for the first time in my years with him, he speaks aloud.

"Madness is hiding like rodents for centuries! From creatures who should have fled from *us!*"

His gravelly voice shakes every bone in my body, words forcing their way into my *ero* again. *"I know these creatures, Mara. They only want to use you. No matter how far we run, they will hunt us. And next time, they will not merely siphon our lifeblood from us. They will slaughter us all."*

He sweeps his hand, gesturing to our flock. *"I have kept us locked away to protect us as long as I could. But the outside world will always be unsafe. It will always clamor to get in unless we can protect ourselves. Unless I can protect you."*

"Protect me?" I gasp out the words like blood gushing from an open wound. The chill spreads over my whole body. My knees nearly buckle as a harsh shudder wracks me.

Through the thunder of my heartbeat chanting a warning, I can finally hear the clamor of footsteps in the tunnel outside. The Goldens are closing in. Nearly to the phoenix-hewn metal door covering the entrance.

"Yes, protect you. Your fire will protect us all. And you will do what you were born to do—" His eyes pierce me. *"Burn."*

I try to pull away from his claw-like grip on my face, but he is too strong. *"You will rid this world of the parasites who hunt us. We will finally be safe."* I push at his chest, but he is unmovable. *"You are our guardian, Mara. Our avenger. Your fire will destroy everything that has ever threatened us."*

The world is caving in on me again. Tears spark at my eyelids and I grab for his shuddering wrists. "What if I don't want to, Father? What if I don't want to hurt anyone?"

But his eyes narrow, pools of darkness now in his wan face. *"You have no choice. This is why I rescued you from the Hollow. You are my instrument of death."*

All the pieces sweep into place like strokes of a deathly brush. A picture I don't want to see, but was always there.

All the times Father would push me to explode and nearly kill our flock. All the times he told me my fire was too volatile. All the times he told me that only he could help me control it—or unleash it—safely.

He was building walls around my *ero*—around my soul, around my flame—so that he could trigger it at will.

And destroy the world he has always viewed as his enemy.

He presses into my thoughts, funneling feelings of panicked fear and rage, flashing images of carnage and my mother's dying body through my mind's eye.

He doesn't just want to blow a hole through the side of the mountain. Or push back the Golden Phoenixes descending on us. He wants me to bring down this whole thing and destroy everything within a several-mile radius.

He's going to force me to annihilate a whole nation. The countless humans who survive in their shadow—and the innocent brothers who trusted me enough to lead me here. "I *can't!*" I gasp, steam rising from my blurred vision. I've always—I've always been what he wanted.

Gave him all my empathy, all my trust—

Believed him when he said he wanted to protect me. Protect all of us.

But now he's cutting me open again—this time not just to carve out my wings. My only escape. But to carve out everything that makes me Mara.

To turn me into the same kind of monsters who took Mama from me.

"Why are you doing this?" I press my sobbing plea into his *ero.* I try to push through his grip. But the fear and pain he's funneling into me is already bringing me to my knees. I hit the floor, feeling a cracked spiderweb beneath me, a hiss of steam rising from the writhing magma below.

I cover my head with my hands. "Please, Father! I don't want to hurt anyone!"

Especially not Eli and Jude.

Panic fills every choking breath in my chest—but more than panic, a deep sorrow weighs down my lungs. This is my father, the one who said he would always look after me. Who claimed to love me.

I believed him.

But again, I was just a means to an end for him. A weapon he sharpened.

In this moment, it feels more real than ever before.

I'm not a daughter to him.

I'm a tool to be wielded as he sees fit.

My throat is so tight, I can't even sob. Can't scream.

I don't have time to grieve, only to fervently plead as tears streak down my face. ***"Don't make me do this!"***

Don't prove that you have forsaken every shred of compassion I hoped you had.

Don't look at me like I'm not even your own child—

Like I'm just a *thing.* Just a weapon.

Just a means to your end.

Don't make me hurt anyone else.

He growls, ***"Those human brothers? They are a weakness, Mara. We have already given too much to the humans. We spent eons of our lives lighting up their world and protecting and caring for them. Sacrificing ourselves over and over for them. And for what purpose? I will not be the prey anymore."***

He says it with confidence, but under his words, I hear fear.

A fear he wants me to inherit.

"This is for the best, Mara," he says aloud, voice rough. "I want to protect you."

I used to believe you.

The Mara he knew in those caves—she would have listened. Even six sunpasses ago, I would have been able to close my eyes and let his voice tell me what to think. Would have believed he was *fior-erran—* forsaken by a world that only wanted to drain and cut and hurt him.

But I've seen too much of that world. The place he taught me to fear. I've felt too much of its pain and seen its joy to let him turn me against it.

There is darkness out there. And maybe he's right about the Goldens having ulterior motives—but nothing deserves this.

We, more than anyone, know that dying is easy. But living? As Eli said, *living is harder.*

I grab his wrists and pry them away from my face. I stumble back, trying to block out his touch from the inside of my mind. His emotions, his fear, his rage that swirls through my *ero.*

Those are *his.* My father's to carry. They are not mine.

I shakily make eye contact with him. ***"I won't do this for you. I*** *know you have sacrificed your life to protect us—"* At my words, I feel him soften. His grip on my mind lessens a little. ***"But I will not do this for you."***

He's built walls around my mind—but that's not the only thing he's taught me.

I can build walls of my own.

Shields around that tiny, phoenix child curled up in those memories, waiting for him to set her off again.

He doesn't get access to her anymore. These memories are mine.

I wrap my arms around my own head, squeeze my eyes shut, and say, "I don't have to inherit your fear."

And I lock him out. It shakes my entire body to slam the door shut on him.

"Mara—"

But I clamp my hands over my ears harder and start humming to drown him out.

Humming the whisper of a song that I hear every time I regenerate. Every time I wake.

The song of rebirth.

It is the only thing louder than his fear.

I'm not sure how long I can hold him at bay, but if I have to slam my head into the wall to knock myself unconscious and give this mountain a little more time, I will.

He does not own the inside of my head any longer.

CHAPTER FIFTY–FIVE

I . . . will not . . . let him . . . in!

My fingertips scrape into the rough stone beneath me with such force that I break skin and feel stinging dribbles of magma press up through the split rock.

By the grace of *Sol*, at that exact moment, before my father's hammering at my temples drives me to anything drastic, several Golden Phoenixes burst through the tunnel. Two tall warriors in head-to-foot armor, carrying weapons. But it's the two figures they shove ahead of them that makes my heart stop.

Eli's curly dark hair and flashing copper eyes are unmistakable. He lifts his head and makes eye contact instantly.

Seeing the relief in his gaze is the first time I've felt like I could breathe since I dropped into the center of this volcano.

Eli's here. And Jude, who has a new bruise on his cheek, but seems unharmed otherwise.

Eli lurches away from the Golden guards. "Mara! Get away from him!"

His eyes flash to my father, standing across from me, but I just shake my head.

It's too late.

There's nowhere to run that the creature I once called *Father* won't follow. And no one he won't burn through to get to me.

Somehow, the Goldens let Eli go, but Jude clamps his brother's arm, stopping him. Cautioning.

A deep *hiss* seeps through the room. My head swivels to see my father's wings unfurling, arched around him in a battle stance. Like a cornered animal with its hackles up. He narrows his eyes at the two Golden guards.

"Don't come closer."

The Goldens share a look. *"Darkholm, don't do this."* One of the voices is familiar. Assessing them more carefully, I realize it's Ra'an. How did she regenerate so quickly? Is this the kind of power the Golden Ones possess? Fully healthy, so close to the sun? She glances at me and grimaces. *"I told you to wait for us."*

In this moment, between the two possible threats, the Goldens suddenly seem like the less dangerous option. Eli and Jude no longer seem afraid of them, either. I suppose there is one singular threat that has united even these age-old enemies.

Father.

He grips my shoulder, fingers digging into my skin. *"No more silly games, child. They have come to take you and chain us up again."*

My attention darts from him, to the two guards, and back again. They couldn't tie Father and all the phoenixes up with just two of them. They can't believe this is enough of a force to contain him?

"Mara," Eli calls to me again, taking a cautious step closer. "Just— step away from him. Come with us."

Behind him, Jude holds a weapon he must have craftily swiped from the Golden warriors.

Something else sweeps into place.

The Goldens aren't here to forcibly take me or to chain my father up again—they look too scared. Sweat rolls down Ra'an's face. Her hands are not steady as she grips her spear.

This isn't a show of force. This is a last-ditch effort to remove a potential explosion from the spark that's inches away from lighting it.

They know Father's plan. They know he wants to set me off.

And they must know that no number of Goldens could stop it once my body ignites.

Eli and Jude are the only weakness they could source to extricate me from exploding at the center of their world.

They're afraid of me.

"Yes. For once—they should be the ones afraid."

No!

I jerk away from him, hands over my head again, reaching for that song once more. I try to let the humming fill my thoughts and help bar the door, keeping Father out.

My eyes desperately search Eli's for answers. But he looks as lost as I feel.

Father's telepathic force is battering at the edges of my *ero*, slamming over and over against the frail walls I've built.

"You must let me in!" he shrieks. And then he closes down on me, his tall form like some towering, shadowed predator.

But I hold my ground, arms over my head.

My eyes are now squeezed tightly shut, so I have no warning when his hand smacks the side of my face so hard my head snaps to the side. He tries to use force to barrel his way into my thoughts, but I drop to the ground and curl up, using every shred of strength to keep his screams echoing through my head at bay. He kicks me. So hard I taste blood.

Monster.

It's the only word that I can see clearly as he tries to shove his way through the walls I'm intently constructing and reconstructing inside my own mind.

It isn't love Father pours out on me. It never was.

His next kick is aimed squarely at the fledgling feathers peeking through my shoulder blades. His foot splits open the deep, lengthy scars there that he never lets fully heal.

I scream as he once again tries to destroy my wings, my personhood, my ability—my very being.

His words spew through my thoughts. **"I told you, even your feathers are dangerous. Every part of you is. And you cannot hide it."**

But before he can kick at my bloody back again, he is knocked away from me.

Between my fingers, I see Eli and Jude both go tumbling as they shove Father away. He throws them off, shakes out his wings, and glares at me.

"Friends of yours?" Then he turns his gaze to Hana and the other fragile phoenixes. *"Maybe you'll finally protect us if you remember what we were all born to be."*

And suddenly, he's withdrawn from badgering my thoughts and bears down on Hana and the rest of the flock. I watch them viscerally react to his presence forcefully invading their minds. Their pale, haggard bodies start to gleam dangerously. Flames crackling across their skeletal frames, splitting open their grey skin. Pain flares across their wide-eyed expressions.

He's hurting them to get to me.

My heart drops to my feet when a scream tears from Hana. Out of my peripheral vision, I see Eli reaching for me. He helps me to my feet, his eyes round with terror. Jude's breathing comes in panicked jolts. Ra'an and the other Golden Guard have backed up the way they came.

Ra'an tries one last time, telepathically bargaining at my father. *"Darkholm! This carnage won't bring back the years you've lost."*

But Father whips toward her, eyes narrowed. *"You will know what it feels like to lose."*

Wings start to crackle down Hana's rent shoulders, and she gasps, "Please, no!"

But he pushes farther. *"We cannot let them hide us away again."*

My vision blurs and blots. I can't pull him from their thoughts. Not all of them. Not fast enough.

Not as he screams a chant into their thoughts that I once thought meant rebirth and relief—but now I realize was only a means for control.

"No er, elion del aethor!"

No fear, we rise in sleep!

If he pushes Hana and the others to explode in their frail state, they may not come back from it. *All fear, he will destroy them before they can sleep.*

His pain is about to destroy everyone he's sworn to protect.

CHAPTER FIFTY-SIX

Hana's wings flicker to life and unfurl around her. Blue flames spill down her cheeks like tears. The Golden guards move further back, preparing for the worst.

Suddenly, Hana forces a step forward. She juts her chin up to look directly into my father's eyes.

"You . . . don't . . ." Her entire body quivers, the words halting and filling our minds. But I watch the flames pouring down her cheeks begin to lessen. *" . . . own . . . us."*

My father's face freezes as Hana starts to de-escalate her own flame. Pulling it back inside herself—and locking out Darkholm's voice. One by one, I watch the other phoenixes behind her do the same. The fire that creates small chasms across their fragile bodies begins to painstakingly soak back into their forms. Skin knitting back together.

They rise to their feet and stand beside Hana, each placing one hand on the shoulder next to them, until they're standing together, shutting Father out.

I watch, stunned.

Jude's mouth has fallen open, but Eli finds my gaze and gives a cautious nod. Maybe we'll survive this still.

My eyes blur watching my flock stand against Father, but bile rises in my throat.

They're standing with me. *For me.* And he will be furious.

His entire body starts to tremble from anger. His wings shift and dark flame ripples out around him. Father flaps his spidery, dark wings, rising off the ground, eyes locked on Hana.

And then he lets out a roar that drives every creature in the room to the floor, even the Goldens. *"No!"*

Eli and Jude stagger against the dappled lava rock, sweat soaking their torn clothes. But the command has the most impact on Hana and the flock. They're too weak, too frail. And try as they might, his voice is too strong, too powerful.

He withheld the sun from them for eons, while he hunted out under its rays to gain strength. To keep control.

And now he's forced his way back into their minds. I watch the flame start to break apart their bodies once more, as they writhe on the floor, begging him not to.

"Stop, Darkholm! This is not what we wanted!" Hana screams into our *eros* as he pours his fear and rage into the rippling flame inside their skeletal chests.

"This is not how you said you would protect the *nora!*" Hana gasps out, but Father isn't listening.

He is intent on only one thing: destruction. However he has to get it.

Eli and Jude have steadied themselves. Jude bracing against the spear he stole from the Goldens, Eli leaning toward me.

"What do we do?" he mouths, turning also to Ra'an, in hopes the Goldens can do something. But Ra'an shakes her head.

"I'm sorry. He'll get through eventually. She's too volatile. They all are. We can only clear the mountain." She looks at us a moment, then she and the other guard finally abandon us, locking the heavy doors behind them.

Walling us in.

With a sudden shout, Jude launches himself at my father, brandishing the spear. But Father knocks him back with the casual sweep of one wing.

Flames swell over Eli's clenched fists, but I sense he's unsure what to do. He starts to move toward Father, like he's going to take a swing at him, even though he knows he's no match for him.

No one is. Not Hana. Not my half-alive flock. Their cries rip through my head as, against their own will, they rise off the ground. Bodies bent back, torn wings rending the air.

There's only one thing I can do.

I grab Eli's wrist, and hold tight until his gaze focuses on mine. "Get my family out of here. I'll hold him off."

That moment lingers as his coppery-brown eyes swallow me up. He knows what this could cost. What it probably will cost.

But they're my flock. I have to.

I manage to capture Hana's attention as I let go of Eli, and within seconds, I've planted myself in front of Father, placing my body between him and the frail creatures he'd brainwashed into following him. Those he'd kept so weak and fragile.

Those he'd turned into weapons as much as he had me.

But I have one thing they don't.

I've felt the sun.

Sol beating down on my shoulders. Filling me.

I know what it is to only have my own voice in my head. My voice—and the voice of hope.

They can't stand right now—but I can stand for them.

CHAPTER FIFTY–SEVEN

I position myself between Father and Hana, where she floats in the air, at the front of the flock. My back is once again exposed to him. The shredded wounds dripping blood, but those tiny, baby feathers somehow still intact. Living proof that I've started to regain my wings, piece by piece.

I catch Hana's eye. "Let me in. I can help."

And she does. She lets me into her head, where Father is filling her every breath with fear and flame.

Maybe I can pull his thoughts back—hide them from the others.

"You are—" I press in against him. Cutting off the words. Trying to pry them back from Hana's mind—or at least let my own body and mind be a barrier between her and Father. His rippling form shudders for a second, confused. He tries to keep going, but I deflect his thoughts away from Hana.

I feel her relief at the release from Father's voice as I solidly keep myself in between them.

His attention snaps toward me and I know his eyes are twin pools of angry flame boring into my back. He tries to push past me, into the minds of the others, but I plant my feet and continue to stand my ground between them. Pulling him back.

Building that same wall, that same shield, between him and them. Weak and frail as it may be, I'm able to pull his words toward me instead. Carrying his anger, his fear, his violence.

"How are you doing this?" he spews at me aloud.

I slowly, painstakingly, turn to face him, still cornering his thoughts before they can reach Hana and the others. "You can try and hurt me—but I won't let you hurt them."

And I'm used to being bombarded with your fear.

Stronger than I look.

"Are you sure they are worth all of this?" He presses in closer, his thoughts focusing fully on me. His mental violence battering at the doors of my mind once again. *"This will hurt."*

I gulp, shuddering fists balled at my sides. Tears spark down my cheeks.

"You've already hurt me."

Proven by the grief that rises inside like flames, the ache that pours through every inch of me. The sadness at what I've lost—what he's completely destroyed.

I won't hurt anyone, won't be his weapon, but I have lost something this day.

"I don't have a father anymore."

That thought seems to shake him, and for a moment, I see a flash of the creature I once believed cared about me return in his flaming irises. All around us, the Fallen Phoenixes drop out of the air, Darkholm fully rescinding his control over them.

They crash to the ground and splinter the thin layer of rock overtop of the lava pit. Bits of liquid magma begin to bubble to the surface. Hana takes hold of two of the phoenixes and heads to the thicker edge of the room.

Eli has helped Jude to his feet, and is already running to the aid of Hana and the others. Even though the older of the two brothers is holding his head in pain, he follows his brother. He and Eli start dragging limp phoenixes away from the spiderwebbing cracks in the floor.

I'm surprised at the way Jude's eyes almost glisten as he helps carry one of the most fragile phoenixes out. I can only imagine how much they remind him of Haven.

Have I given Jude a new kind of sympathy for my people?

That alone ignites a spark of hope in my chest as I watch the human help my flock. A smile tugs at Eli's lips as he continues carrying my people out of Darkholm's direct reach. He and Jude drag the last phoenix over to the edge of the room, and then the brothers start tinkering with the lock on the door.

Leave it to a human and a half-human to unlock a door even phoenixes couldn't burn through.

Always underestimating those they see as weak.

My father recovers too fast from the wave of grief that stilled him in his tracks.

He slowly takes in the scene before him. The flock he has called family now crawls away, cowering at the edges of the room. They wait breathlessly for the very humans my father's taught them to fear to unlock the cage he trapped them in.

The room of torture he's used to lure his daughter into that same trap.

I brush away more steaming tears as he pushes against my thoughts once more.

"Why can't you just let go?"

His body stills. *"Because I will not lose everything again. I lost your mother, I lost this mountain. I won't let them take you too. We'll lose this whole planet if they take you."*

"You think killing them will stop that?"

"If need be."

And then he slams the full weight of his telepathic connection into me. *"You are my child."*

It shreds through the walls I've built, but I ball my fists and force him back out.

"No, I'm a child of *Sol*."

Solnora. Even if I don't fully understand yet what that means.

"You are fire."

It takes every scrap of strength I have to shove the thought back out. The pressure of holding him at bay is starting to erode my body. He's trying to set me off, and fighting it starts to rip my body apart. My skin begins to melt, the fire in my veins rising to a scalding temperature.

Sheaths of flame cutting through quivering limbs, cracking me open like the splintered lava rock beneath my feet.

I grit my teeth, swaying on my feet from the pain, but I still meet his eyes.

"I am Mara."

Flames rip over me, fileting my newly healed skin. But I don't waver. Don't take a step back.

"I created you." Those twin pools of dark flame consume my vision as he presses in.

I grit my teeth as another wave of flame cascades over my body. Burns bubbling over my arms and shoulders and chest. The words stirring a combustion inside.

My body will soon be unable to fight off the physical toll of his lies. But they are lies.

"My mother created me."

"Your mother **found** *you. And then she died—because of you."*

Tears pool again. Still, one thing remains true: *"I still love her."*

My eyes instinctively go to the only family I have left and find that Jude has figured out how to unlock the door and is starting to pry it open. The flock of Fallen Phoenixes clusters around him, terrified.

Darkholm growls, trying to sidle away from me to deal with the others before they can escape, but I push in. Even as my body is rent apart by the force of him trying to reconstruct my mind into his image. As the flames boil up through my quivering form, shredding through skin and tissue, I can feel the healing fighting too. Flakes of ash fill the air around me. Coating the open wounds.

My body shredding apart and trying to mend its wounds at the same time.

But I'm not strong enough. Not fast enough.

Beneath my feet, the frail rock splinters further, my bare feet burnt by the magma just under the surface.

"I am not your daughter," I press at Darkholm, catching hold of his attention and not letting him move toward Eli and the others.

Angry cobalt flame ripples out over his body and skitters down the floor. *"Your own people are abandoning you. You are alone."*

Tears streak my face at how painful it is to wade through his words. And the physical toll they take. The ideas that had once built me now being dismantled as I am torn apart and rebuilt.

But I'm doing it.

Even as it's ripping me apart, burning through my coat and instead leaving me coated in ash and bubbling, popping pools of flame, I'm doing it.

My people are getting out. I steal a glance their way and can see Jude helping them through the exit, Eli carrying one of the fragile phoenixes in his arms as Hana points the way.

And the creature I once called Father is no longer welcome in my head.

"They will finally be safe."

His brows crash together, and he shoves in harder, searching for the flames already searing me with burns and ripping open my body.

"No one is safe. You couldn't even save your mother."

That one hits me like a blow to the chest. My knees give out, and I'm about to hit the cracked ground beneath me. I throw my hands over my face, choking on my own breath, prepared for the spray of magma that is sure to splash up through the floor when I crash through—

But I don't hit. Before my knees meet the ground, strong arms wrap around me, holding me up.

And I know, just from the sensation of that familiar hold, *it's Eli*.

He should have run out. Gotten as far from me as he can. Eli bends down to look at me, the back of my head pressed against his collar. My raw spine and the feathers hanging on by a thread are soothed by the softness of his shirt. Scraps of material and thick chunks of ash cover my body where the flame isn't creating open lacerations.

I can feel Darkholm's anger churn like a mounting, dark storm. His wings try to batter at us, try to knock Eli back.

"How dare you!"

But Eli just draws me closer, holding me up. I'm still not healing fast enough, every inch littered with blistering burns. Over Darkholm's shoulder, I watch Jude help Hana through the exit. The last phoenix to go.

My heart falls. Eli should be with them.

Continuing to fight for breath through a throat that is swelling shut, I peer up at Eli: "What are you doing here? You need to get out. *Please*. Save yourself."

Eli only pulls me in tighter, my sweat-streaked hair sticking to him as he faces Darkholm. He takes in the fury spreading through the air like a tangible sizzle of steam. I can only imagine the horrendous things my father is trying to bombard Eli's mind with, but the young man's feet are firmly planted on the splintered surface beneath us. Even as the stream of magma and flame melts his shoes and burns his feet.

Eli squeezes my shoulders. "I can't fight through this for you, but I can hold you up." Then he leans in to whisper, "I'm proud of you, Mara. You've done well."

For the first time, I can inhale a full breath.

Suddenly, the angry, rending words Darkholm blasts through my head, and the way my own body is being ripped open, softens a fraction.

Eli's touch is like a soothing balm.

I don't have to face this alone.

CHAPTER FIFTY-EIGHT

ELI

How is she surviving this?

I'm struggling to find where to place my hands without pressing one of the open wounds marring her quivering form, but somehow, Mara stays on her feet.

She's stronger than anyone I've ever met.

I've never held onto something as important as this woman in my arms. This creature of flame and warmth and rebirth. I don't know how to help her fight, other than to stand here, holding her up.

"Don't listen to him," I whisper, eyes darting for any kind of weapon to push him away.

But there's nothing here in the center of this pit but the three of us. The monster towering over her—the father she came all this way for, only to find it was a lie.

That he only wanted her heart so he could learn how to shatter it.

But I won't leave her.

The room is so hot, my skin is singed just standing here—but nothing like the way I see her body falling to pieces. Bleeding flame and gaping flesh and bits of bone show through her tattered coat. The effort of propelling him out of her thoughts literally rips her apart.

But even as he beats those huge wings, fury locked on her, I watch as she begins to heal herself. Ripped apart . . . and reformed.

Lesions tearing through her skin, flame bubbling out—and then ash from the flames filling the air around her, falling to coat the open wounds, and beneath the charred sections, the skin slowly reforming.

A thousand lives flashing through her, over and over. A thousand lies to rip her apart—and yet, bits of hope to pull her back together.

Darkholm takes a step forward, lifting a hand to try and grab for her face, but I smack it away. He growls, and tries to come for me, but Mara's voice reverberates through the room.

"*I*..."

She huffs.

"... *am*..."

Her body quivers in my arms.

"... *not*..."

Each word is louder, echoing through my thoughts and shaking the room, more forceful even than Darkholm's telepathic barrage.

"... *your*..."

I feel her straining, lifting her shoulders, rising to stand fully and meet his seething gray eyes.

"... *pain!*"

His reply is also telepathic, but so forceful even I catch it. ***You are desolation.***

"*NO!*" Mara screams back at him, their fight echoing through my head too.

The force of the word halts him. Darkholm is inches away, his hand wavering near her temple, dark fingers tinted and warped. As if their intense battle of the wills has frozen him.

"***You are fury!***"

The battle happening inside their minds is written across the strain on their faces and the way Mara's body continues to melt and sizzle and burn in my arms, and to slowly reform. New skin painstakingly sealing over bubbling flesh.

But it's not fast enough. He's wearing her down.

Dad would know how to help her.

I glance at my own arms, wrapped around her. Turning red and bubbled from touching her flaming body. Usually, my blood can warm, but it doesn't heal.

As I watch Mara's liquid flame stream down her body at the impact of Darkholm's manipulation, I suppress a shudder at that Fallen Phoenix towering over us. I hate the way he brings out whispers inside of my own head.

Those darkest things I'd never admit to anyone. But the truth still stands: *Darkholm is everything I am terrified of becoming.*

Selfish, using his flame only for himself. Letting others burn and forgetting their pain.

Letting his own loss freeze over an understanding of what living without our blood costs others.

Hiding from others' pain because it's easier. Because, deep inside, the power feels good.

Does my own blood make me kin to this monster?

I glance over at Jude, relieved as he disappears through the exit with the last phoenix. That feat alone is nothing short of a miracle. Helping a phoenix escape, especially a Fallen One. But something has changed in him.

Because our dad isn't the only phoenix with humanity. Mara taught us that.

She arches back in my arms, pain wrenching her apart, screaming at her father again, loudly enough I can hear her thoughts. *"I will not let you hurt them!"*

She shouldn't be as she is, raised by Darkholm.

She should be like him. Destructive. Selfish. Hurtful.

But she's not. She's letting her own body be torn apart, over and over, to protect the flock that didn't protect her. To help Jude escape.

To protect me.

And if Mara can fight back and push through to rise past her heritage, maybe I can too. Maybe I can also rise up.

I wrap my arms tighter around her waist.

What does she need?

Not what will make my conscience feel better. Not what will atone.

What does she *need*?

The overwhelming sadness that I find rippling off her is in greater waves than the anger and fear that ricochets from Darkholm, still frozen inches away.

"You are destruction!" He shrieks into her head. He's trying to press something into her thoughts with such force that I catch sight of it. A memory of her as a small child, hiding under some kind of bed. A female phoenix curled up on the cot above her.

Mara's mother. That means—

My stomach recoils and I want to retch.

I cannot even bear to look at Darkholm. What kind of maniac would make her rewatch this to trigger an explosion that will shred her body further apart?

I want to stop seeing it, but somehow, Mara has invited me in. She's sunken against me, clutching to my arms with what strength she has.

"I need to get through this," she whispers brokenly into my thoughts. *"I can't let him hold it over me any longer."*

This is what she needs.

I let my eyes fall closed and hold her, silently weeping with her as she relives her greatest pain.

I feel my entire body start to warm, feel a kind of rich empathy being pulled from somewhere deep inside. An echoing desire unlike anything I've ever felt. I want to soften this for her, to provide relief.

To help her breathe.

She gives a shaky exhale, and relaxes fully into me. Trusting me to keep her safe.

As I hold her steady, an odd humming sensation begins to spread from my touch over her. Eyes still shut, I quietly wade with her into the memory. I hold her through it as Darkholm tries to use her pain to manipulate her.

But as it unfolds, I realize the memory is from an odd angle. As if someone else was watching from a distance. Someone who pointed two Hollow warriors toward the rammed-shut door of the small hut.

Mara realizes the impact of the scene seconds before I do. Her weak head jerks up, bloodshot eyes staring at Darkholm.

Her voice rasps out the words, "No, you speak for yourself. You are destruction."

And in her head, with more strength than her throat could muster, *"I am healing."*

And that's when I realize that she really is. Little by little. And in the places where my skin touches hers, it's happening a little faster. Her open wounds mending.

The wounds inside will be much harder to heal. And take much longer.

But I can try to give her this.

I'm so focused on Mara, I don't realize we've been joined by someone else until a light hand touches my shoulder. "Lean into it more. That heart and heat inside you. It will help you lend her your regeneration."

I look up and find the older female phoenix that Mara seemed most fond of standing by us. Her bare feet are blistered and swollen as she stands on the cracked floor. But she reaches out and wraps her arms around Mara as well. And immediately, a strange kind of gleaming touch spreads out from her fingertips and starts to stream out over Mara. I stare down at my hands, wondering if I can do the same.

"Yes, you can, son of Haven."

I startle. "How did you know?"

She gives a soft smile. "I knew your father well."

Hana. Of course this is Hana. The phoenix Jude and I are here to find. I'd had a feeling she must have been the one Mara was gravitating toward most.

My throat suddenly feels tight. Could she be right? Could I even offer a fraction of the relief to Mara that she can?

I peer down at the woman in my arms, trying to coax that same light out from my fingertips to swell over her blistered limbs. Trying to press some of my life-force into her to keep her body safe while her mind is able to finally cut free of Darkholm's binds.

Darkholm takes a disjointed step forward, reaching out once again for Mara, but Hana doesn't flinch, just keeps holding tight to Mara, whispering to her.

"Be brave, *nora*. You don't have to listen to him. You are restoration."

Finally breaking through the mental hold Mara seems to have

captivated him in, Darkholm lets out a bellow, yanks Hana away, and tosses her small body like it's nothing. She flies several feet back and lands crumpled on the floor.

Mara gasps and grabs my arms to forcefully shove us both out of the way of Darkholm's sweeping wings. We barely manage to avoid his crystalline, deadly-sharp feathers as they rend the air. He starts to rise off the ground. "Enough games, child."

Mara turns to me. "I have to finish this."

I shake my head. "I won't leave you. I can help!"

She reaches up to touch my face, fingers shaking but big brown eyes filled with light. "You already have. But I need to be sure you and Hana are safe. That is also help."

I slowly nod. Understanding.

She manages a small smile. "Get Hana out. Make sure Jude is safe." Then she pushes me toward unconscious Hana. "Quickly!"

So I do. I run over to Hana and scoop her up in my arms. She starts to regain consciousness as I race with her back to the exit. I have a fleeting hope that there will be a whole army of Golden Phoenixes storming down the entrance to help us.

But I know they aren't. They told us they couldn't.

They also told us something about Mara. Something I now only begin to comprehend.

If Darkholm sets her off, no one will survive. And not even their armies could stop her.

Nothing can stop the sun.

As I race up the exit tunnel, I find Jude halfway to freedom. He's waiting for me, blisters from the sweltering heat covering his body, and I place Hana in his arms, my mind racing.

"You ready to get out of here?" he asks.

He catches my hesitation and stiffens. Jude's face falls. "Eli, if he sets her off—"

"I know."

Jude squeezes his eyes shut a moment and takes a deep breath. "What are you planning to do?"

"I don't know," I admit. "But she needs someone to stand with her.

Even on the outskirts. Someone to pick her up and carry her out of the aftermath." I tap his shoulder. "Not everyone has an older sibling as great as you. She needs what you've given me."

I've reached a crossroads. A decision. I have to go back for Mara.

She's like me. But better.

Jude cocks his head and says something that catches me off guard. "You're starting to fall for her, aren't you?"

My brows rise.

She does mean something to me. Something more than anyone else ever has.

I'm not sure what it is yet, but Mara has become a part of me. Like family, and maybe more.

I can't leave her behind.

With a heavy sigh, Jude nods. "Okay." His voice breaks and I know Mara has become special to him too. He gives me a wan smile. "Just try not to die, okay?"

"You, too," I return.

He shifts Hana's unconscious form in his arms and starts back up the tunnel toward the outside and freedom. Toward Dad and safety and the Golden Phoenixes who have been surprisingly helpful. Who were more afraid of Darkholm and of Mara herself than we'd ever realized. Who were just trying to protect their own.

But I turn away from the way out and stride determinedly back into the center of the flaming volcano.

To the girl with the power of the sun hidden in her veins.

CHAPTER FIFTY-NINE

My body feels like a raw, open wound. My legs are shaking. I try to stay on my feet. The room is hollow and empty—left with nothing but Darkholm and me.

The one I couldn't run from. I couldn't escape from. The creature who convinced me to cut apart my own body. To cut away my own wings.

But I stand here. Still on my feet. Still alive.

The very part of me that he was terrified of—the fledgling slivers of crystalline fire dangling from my shoulder blades, those feathers that are just as much my voice as the words in my throat are—those feathers are my way out.

I always wondered why every other part of my body healed, but never those.

Now, I begin to understand why.

Because not even my fear can clip these wings. The purpose I was truly born for.

I move away from him until my back bumps the edge of the curving volcano wall, then I take a deep breath. And think of Mama.

Of her gorgeous, broad, sweeping wings. Of her delight over my very first feathers. Of her celebrating them every time a new one came in.

I think of the way her wings would unfurl around her.

I feel the echo of them ripple through my shoulder blades. I remember the hush of what her full-grown wings looked like—and the whisper of what mine could have been.

Could be.

The creature I once called Father may have stolen Mama from me, may have shown the Hollow where she hid just so I would run into his arms in the aftermath—but he does not get to hide me away any longer.

I'm not afraid of myself anymore.

A soft thrum reverberates through the nubs of sinew my father cut apart all those years ago. I feel the bow of my wings begin to press through the skin along my shoulder blades. Flame and feather growing slowly, slowly from a place deep inside me.

Yes, the sharp feathers stretching and forming hurt, but nothing like holding Father's lies at bay. Or cutting the feathers from my own body.

This pain is different. This pain is more whole.

The pain of growth.

Of healing and expanding.

I peer over my shoulder, watching the feathers slowly ripple out from my scars—crystalline slivers that link from one to the next and grow longer and longer, reaching down to my feet. Arched, curving wings that reflect the light like diamonds.

I didn't know my wings were this big, could be this big.

As they unfurl around me, tears leak down my cheeks.

Oh, yes, it hurts, but it also feels so *alive*.

My father's eyes are rooted on me, a strange kind of fascination in his expression. "You look like her."

My wings stretch out on either side of me, reaching from one side of this small chamber at the center of the volcano to the other. A sharp, gleaming array of interwoven feathers, like dual shields of gold and orange. It's all more beautiful than I could have imagined. And the flame that pours from my body and drips down the crystalline feathers pulsates with something I didn't know I could feel. As if the heat always building in my chest, always aching for release, the pressure I shove back down suddenly has a release.

Flowing like waterfalls down my wings. In glorious, rippling, arched floods.

The wings spill out from my twin scars like a stubborn reminder that even as Darkholm bombards me with his mental barrage, even as my body starts to crumble to ash and I pull it back together, over and over—I'm still here.

"I've risked everything for you, Mara . . ." He lets his tone lower, even as my wings beat the air for the first time. He starts to circle above me, the edges of his bat-like wings of crystalized flame tearing into the arching walls around us. *"All I've ever wanted was to protect you."*

I shake my head at him. "It was never about protection."

As I continue to stretch, to test the air with my wings, I'm amazed at the strength just having them unfurled gives me. The way it immediately stabilizes my weak stance, alleviating the pressure on my feet.

"You're volatile. You're young. You may not want to hurt any of the Goldens, but they won't show you the same mercy. And if it's not them now, it will be that half-breed boy sometime when you don't expect it. You'll lash out. And he'll be the one burned."

I swallow hard. His words resonate—but not fully.

Not while these wings stretching out on either side of me pour out flame that washes over my body and begins to slowly help knit my wounds. A hint at the kind of healing Haven and Hana and Ra'an are capable of.

The kind of training that could help me not hurt those I love.

Like Eli.

A new voice echoes firmly through the room. "We've all been burned. I'm not afraid of Mara."

The floor is so shattered with slivers of flame that Eli has to carefully leap around several large cracks to make his way to me. The ground could fully give way, releasing the magma at any second. It isn't safe for him.

"I told you to leave!" I protest.

But he just shakes his head. "I'm with you. I'll be here for as long as it takes." He grabs my hand and a soft hum that spreads out from his touch starts to spread over me. I've felt this before. Where?

With Hana. When she used to have enough energy to heal me. Could she have taught him in those few minutes she was able to reach me before Darkholm threw her to the side?

The stream of regenerative flame washes down my hand and continues on, slowly breathing air back into my lungs. Steadying the flame pouring down my shoulders.

It's not a bandage to cover all the burns and sores. But it's enough.

It's more than enough.

Because far more than Eli offering me a bit of his life and breath is the truth that he's here.

Unafraid.

He should be terrified. Terrified at the way my wings are continuing to sprout out on either side of me, of the flame continuing to grow inside of me, of the way the flames lick out, covering and cauterizing my open wounds and flowing across the ashen skin coating my body.

Of the fire I've been terrified of. That the Goldens are frightened of.

That even the one I once called father is scared of.

But Eli just stands here, looking into my eyes, utterly unafraid.

It bolsters me like nothing else.

"Why aren't you running?" I whisper.

Eli's tone is tender. "Because I trust you, Mara. I know you won't hurt me. Or anyone here, no matter what Darkholm tries."

He leans back a little to take me in fully. "Your wings are . . . stunning."

Heat fills my cheeks. "Thanks. They're new."

"I know." He gently cups my face in his hands. For a moment I want to pull away, the gesture unnervingly reminiscent of Darkholm. But Eli's touch is gentle and breathtakingly soft. He leans in to lay his forehead against my mine. "I trust you, Mara. You're safe. And I'll be here when you're ready."

I inhale a deep breath. And let him wrap me in a tight hug for a brief moment. I whisper, "Thank you."

And then he's letting me go, and at my prompting as the cracks in the floor continue to expand, races back to that tunnel exit to stand inside it.

I lift off the ground, eyes locked on Eli for one more stretching second, soaking him in. Soaking in the memory of those gentle coppery-brown eyes, and then I lift my face, where the demon-creature who raised me is hovering. My wings rend the air, surprisingly strong, taking me fully airborne with very little effort.

I shoot upward faster than I expect, and am nearly at eye-level with Darkholm in just a few wingbeats.

The steady stream of flame finally burns through the full layer of rock underfoot. The rippling magma bubbles to the surface and begins to fill this chamber. Starting to rise. Not enough pressure built for eruption, but enough flame to force me higher into the air.

This chamber is small. Barely enough space for my father's wingspan and mine.

But I hover in the center of this volcano, staring at Darkholm across from me. The flames continue to pound inside me as if my pulse has become a drumbeat.

The fire flowing in continuous sheaths drips down my slender, crystalized feathers, turning my wings into twin waterfalls of flame and crystalized daggers.

He's set something off.

The deep, raging anger and pain inside.

"There it is. There you go. Let it out—let all the pain out."

Darkholm and I circle each other, and he beholds me like a proud father. That look is all I once lived for. To look at me like I'd done well.

"You are fire . . ."

He starts the process, and instead of fighting it like I have been for what feels like an eternity, I let the words wash over me.

I am fire.

My flame is a part of me.

The flame seeps out from my chest, boiling up through my veins and turning my body inside out. Creeping down from my newfound wings and swelling over me.

A hauntingly familiar sensation. The start of a process that I'd been weaponized for.

But now I know. Now I'm awake.

"You are destruction . . ."

The flame continues to creep up my torso, my wings starting to swell and the shape of my body blurring. I close my eyes and lean into my phoenix form. Into this part of myself that I've only ever been able to hold for a short period before the explosion caught up with me. Into the part of me that was always connected so deeply to the wings he wouldn't let me spread.

I am capable of destruction, yes. But I'm also capable of healing.

You're safe, Eli said. *You're safe.*

"You are rebirth!" Father screams into my mind.

At the last phrase, the flame swells fully through me. Licking up toward my face. Crawling up over my mouth and turning my hair into coils of heat.

I can hear the *beat-beat-beat* of Darkholm's wings. He's certain he'll survive this. He's tempered himself to survive.

But this time, my body is my own. My mind is my own. As my flame is my own.

My wings are my own.

And I'm safe.

I suddenly open my eyes and I look straight into Darkholm's seething, hollow irises. Hungry for the next part.

"You say I'm rebirth?"

I flick my gaze down to where Eli is still standing at the exit to the chamber, gazing up at me. Something almost like glory reflected in his eyes.

His features are lit up like he's in broad sunlight.

"Yes, I am," I say aloud to Darkholm, wings continuing to beat the air.

I lean into this extended part of me, to the glorious twin suns arcing out on either side of me, and bring them inward. I've never unfurled them fully before, so I never knew how they could provide an outlet for the flame washing over me in wave after wave.

How my wings channel the fire I haven't known how to control. How they use the pressure and power to keep me aloft. To build into a combustion I can hold within my own form.

No wonder he wanted me to cut them off.

I didn't need Darkholm to help me control my explosions.

The wings I was born with were meant to grow with me, and all of the fire inside could lift me off the ground, turning my body into a beacon.

I'm not a weapon. I'm a reflection of the *sun*.

Solnora.

It's like waking up for the very first time.

This is what we were created for. This is why I was born with wings and flame—

To thaw this world when the sun could no longer bring light.

Maybe the one who hung the sun knew that one day it would die. And he gave the humans us.

I curve my wings in front of me, aiming their tips, and let the flame loose.

I let the wave rise inside me, let my body evaporate into the soaring form of a firebird, wings closed around me and pointed at the one person who wanted my power, but not my personhood, and unleash the fury of flame directly at Darkholm.

I aim all the grief and anger and fire and hope at him.

If he wants my fire, he can have it.

The force of the explosion knocks a hole through the side of the volcano, launching Darkholm through it and slamming me backward into the other side of the chamber.

I hit my head so hard the world goes dark in a detonation of white-hot color.

CHAPTER SIXTY

I awake to find myself in the cratered shell of the volcano. Darkholm is gone but my first thought isn't of him.

Heart in throat, I try to sit up and call for Eli—until I realize I'm cradled in two achingly familiar arms.

He's already here, holding me close to his chest, carrying me out of the mountain's remains.

Relief crashes over me. Just being in his arms has coaxed my regeneration out faster, the same way being around Haven lifted it to the surface once before. I stare down at my own body reforming even as he carries me.

"How'd you survive the blast?" My tongue feels thick, but the words somehow manage to be comprehensible.

Eli nudges a strand of sweat-soaked hair from my forehead. "Your flame went up, mostly, and through the left side of the mountain. It didn't come anywhere near me or this tunnel."

My mouth drops in disbelief. "It really worked? I controlled it?"

A bright smile lights up his whole face, reminding me of the look he wore seeing me in my full phoenix form. "Yes, you did. And Mara—" His smile becomes almost shy. "You looked incredible. I couldn't take my eyes off you."

My face warms, and I stammer. "Um, well, that's what happens when you're an incarnate explosion."

He just chuckles, and I curl into his chest a little more. I let out a long breath. "We did it."

"Yes." Eli rests his chin on the top of my head again. "We survived. Wait until you tell Haven about all this."

"Your dad won't believe it," I say. "Neither will Jude."

Eli gives a small snort. "Oh, Jude will be jealous and more impressed than he'll admit."

Our relieved, exhausted banter fades as we emerge from the volcano's shattered dome.

The remnant of the Golden city is nothing but fileted carnage. Ash and soot and the roiling residue of flames coats everything. Buildings are shattered and broken, their hanging gardens charred. Not a single living thing in sight is not turned to ash.

My stomach churns. I've destroyed their whole world.

I hope they all escaped before the explosion.

My head is spinning as Eli slowly sets me on my feet. Eyes wide, we both survey the area. Jude and any remnants of my flock are long gone. Not even Darkholm seems to have stuck around—if he survived.

All that is left here is the wreckage that the creature I called Father and I have created.

"Mara," Eli says suddenly.

I follow his pointing finger and see that, spread out around the corners and nooks and crannies of this mountain, the Golden Phoenixes are shaking the charred residue of their world from their glorious wings. They rise all around us, pushing aside toppled beams and lifting from under caved roofs.

Breath coming quickly, I spin around, seeing more of the Golden Phoenixes emerging from every direction. Their wings rend the air violently, eyes sparking. Some of them are carrying weapons.

I raise my hands, and my wings begin to unfurl again. I position myself in front of Eli as best I can. The wings now spiral down my back. Pools of dripping flame, like a void deep inside has been rent open.

The Golden Phoenixes slowly circle me, closing in. I couldn't possibly feel more desolate than I have today when Darkholm tried to detonate my flock against me, but this is unnerving.

I steady myself as I lift my hands. "I'm really sorry. I didn't mean to do it. Don't touch us—"

But they float closer, and instead of raising their weapons against me, they all drop them. Their weapons clatter to the ground.

The entire nation of Golden Phoenixes starts to cheer.

My jaw drops.

"You did it! You truly are the daughter of the Sun! **Solnora!***"*

My eyes nearly pop out of my skull. *Not what I expected . . .*

"Thank you!" Their voices echo through my head, but I couldn't be more lost. I search for a familiar face, and spot Ra'an a few feet away, her helmet discarded and long, golden hair hanging past her gleaming features.

"But I destroyed everything." I aim the thought at her, and Ra'an only smiles, coming close to me, those eyes of twin flames almost lick my skin.

"All will heal over time. What you have done is far more momentous. You have awoken the mountain—and breathed life back into our sun. You truly are **Sol's** *daughter."*

At her words, I finally look up.

That's when I see it. The spiraling ball of flame hovering in the sky, always so sickly pallid, has taken on a new orange gleam around its edges.

"You think I did that?" I ask incredulously, and she nods emphatically.

"We knew the daughter of the Sun would arrive one day. To bring life back to our world. And now you are here." She touches my face. *"And now you can rest,* **nora.***"*

"Rest?"

"You have done many hard things today. And now, you are finally home. Join us as we rebuild. And rest."

It does sound nice. Refreshing.

"I can just . . . stay?" I glance at Eli. "Can we both rest for a little bit?" I ask.

"Of course. You both are welcome. Your journey is at an end

here. *Let your weary body have its much-needed rest. We will watch over you.*"

I practically collapse against her. I'm so tired.

"Alright," I say. "Just for a while. And then we need to go find Jude and my flock."

"*They all got off the mountain hours ago. I saw to it they were safe.*"

I look at her in the sunlight, and Eli speaks up. "Why would you help them?"

She smiles and speaks aloud. "You are one of us, child. Both of you are." She looks Eli up and down. "Even you, child of Haven. We have already spoken of this."

I raise a brow at Eli and he gives a slight nod. "They treated Jude and me well and took us seriously when we told them you were going to get your father out and needed help."

A little chill crawls down my spine, but I ignore it. A part of me has missed this, being a part of a flock. And they were right about Father.

"Yes, we'll take your offer. But just for a bit," I say again. "We must be on our way."

Ra'an beams. "Wonderful."

Suddenly, four Goldens appear, reaching for Eli and lifting him into the air before I even have time to blink. "Wait! Where are you taking him?"

Eli starts to struggle, but the Goldens reassure him. "*We have a safe place for you to rest. The Daughter of* Sol *must be shown the temple first. It's ceremony.*"

Eli's face is a mirror of mine—questioning in our eyes, uncertainty etched across our brows.

I relent. "I guess that's fine. Once I see the temple, then you'll take me to where Eli is going?"

Ra'an nods, and with that, the Phoenixes fly Eli away. As soon as he's gone, my body goes cold. No longer soaking in his steadying warmth. No longer able to sense his thoughts nearby.

Taking a deep breath and trying to shake off my nerves, I turn back to Ra'an. The remaining Golden Phoenixes curve around me in a semicircle. They trail behind Ra'an and me as she guides me around the edge of the enormous crater in the center of the volcano that is still spewing smoke and ash, and toward the temple she had shown me earlier. Somehow, it has managed to survive, those spiraling floors with the same curving designs etched in them that our own *nemior* temple had. And the designs etched above us too.

"You will be able to rest in here."

Ra'an leads me in, and I glance over my shoulder at the other Goldens. They've gathered in front of the massive double doors, watching us almost hungrily.

"What about the volcano? Shouldn't we get away from here?"

"No. The volcano will not harm us. We know a way to settle it. To rebuild."

I stare at her, sudden chills spiraling down my spine. Darkholm may have been insane—but he was sincere in his mistrust of these creatures. As was Haven.

What am I doing?

As if snapped from a trance, I spin around and scan the floor. I'd barely given thought to the burn marks scorching the curving hollows before, assuming they were just from the number of Goldens that had flown into this room, wings radiating heat. But there's more to it than that.

My heart stops. This room didn't remind me of the temple where Darkholm had camped out—it was familiar for another reason.

I've been here before . . .

As a child. Right before Mama grabbed me and ran.

My wings whip up to curl around me like twin shields and I race toward the exit. But the Golden Phoenixes swell around me and block my way. I'm screaming, fighting, yelling. I try to pull away from the crowd of golden creatures dragging me back inside the temple. Back into the room where I first exploded as a child.

The room where they first tried to kill me, when I was barely a year old.

The night that mother lifted me up from the ashes, wrapped me in her arms, and ran.

She wasn't running from the humans. She was running from the Goldens.

So was Darkholm. He said they had other plans for me. Dark plans he was protecting me from.

Could some part of his twisted *ero* have actually been trying to protect me from this?

I bellow at them, wings sweeping around me. The droplets of flame from my waterfalling feathers singe the Golden Phoenixes' bodies and burn through their armor.

Their screams and cries echo through my head—voices filled with rage.

They're afraid of me after all.

Where is Eli? Is he okay?

What do they plan to do with me? To us?

Even as I struggle, they force me back into the temple room and throw me onto the floor. My wings thrash through the air, slicing and burning and trying to curl around me like twin shields.

But Ra'an jumps on my back, pinning me to the ground. She grunts in pain as the fire dripping from my wings singes her.

"Quickly! Her flame is growing brighter!"

A dozen Golden Phoenixes bear down on me. They wrap their wings around mine, holding my wings steady on either side. Splayed out like a bent and broken bird.

And then they unsheathe their curved *reer* blades.

"No! Stop! Why are you doing this?" I scream at them.

Ra'an just looks down at me. *"Because we need you to rest, so that we can live. The fire we could siphon from the Fallen Phoenixes only lasted so long. But the fire we could drain from the sun?"* Her eyes flicker hungrily. *"It could keep us young forever. We will never need to be reborn ever again."*

And with that, the phoenixes on either side of me start to slice through the wings that spill out from my shoulder blades. They slice through the new feathers and the section where the flame connects to my shoulders, the sinew. The wings I fought so hard to regrow.

And now they are cutting through them again.

The pain is excruciating, but the knowledge of what they are doing is even worse. Angry tears stream down my face.

As they rip through my bone and sinew and blood rains down around me, my head goes light and I drift into the moment when this happened before.

Only it wasn't the Goldens that time. I was a young child. It was merely a year after losing my mother.

No. A different creature tied me up and took a ragged *reer* blade to my fledgling wings, ripping through my back. Not stopping no matter how I sobbed at him. No matter how many times I asked him to stop. The creature I called Father.

He clipped my wings the first time. And then forced me to do it every time after.

To keep me hidden away. To keep me from flying away.

And now these creatures who call themselves gods are doing the same thing.

By the time they've cut through both wings, my whole body is so exhausted and in so much pain, I collapse, heaving for air and sobbing.

"Why?" I scream up at the phoenixes who just moments ago told me I was one of them. All I've ever really wanted. "Why?"

Ra'an takes a heavy chain and wraps it around my wrists, other phoenixes wrapping chains around my legs. They drag me across the floor and my back absolutely screams as my flaming blood soaks the world around us. It pools in this room and falls through small holes throughout the curling pattern in the floor.

"Because your blood is our salvation."

Something about their selfishness makes me think of Eli. Of him being so ashamed of his own heritage that he would drain the golden blood from his veins to give life to others.

But the price he was trying to pay was impossible to meet.

And when he stopped trying so hard, he discovered a kind of healing he didn't even know he was capable of.

Whatever these insane creatures think my blood will give them . . . it won't.

They can't hide like this forever.

I shriek and thrash as they drag me across the floor, toward the very center of the room, where they open a rounded hatch I hadn't noticed before. The Golden Phoenixes drag my bleeding, wounded body through a devastatingly familiar tunnel. Downward. Deeper into the heart of the volcano—and within moments, we're back in the center chamber I escaped barely an hour ago. But deeper—past the hole I blasted through, into the very heart of the volcano.

But this time Eli is nowhere to be seen.

Their wings beat the air and they rise above the flowing, angry magma, lifting me with them. Holding me suspended by the chains looped around my wrists, ankles, and chest.

"What is this?" I shout through a split lip.

Ra'an maneuvers around the other warriors holding me suspended and hovers just in front of me. She grips one end of the chains binding my ankles and ties them around a massive piece of metal. The chains melt against the hefty, dark piece that's sharpened like the immense point of a spear.

"This pit is the lifeblood of our entire city. We can pull enough healing energy from the phoenixes we've tethered here to never need to sleep again."

Bile rises in my throat. That's why the temple had traces of blue flame—my people were tethered directly beneath it. And they were probably the latest in a line of phoenixes that the Goldens banished to the heart of this volcano for threatening them. Do they plan on doing this to Eli too?

Whatever that temple was made from must have blocked their heat signatures and funneled their regenerative fire upward, through those chains.

"And you, **Solnora,** *will give us a strength we cannot even imagine."*

Flames spark over my exhausted, raw body, but I still have some fight left. "No. Just try and—"

But then they do the unthinkable:

They drop me into the magma.

Ra'an lets go of the massive piece of metal she's holding, and that's when I realize it's an anchor. It hits the magma a second before I do. My body slams into the swirling, angry lake of flame and swallows me whole.

The chains are unbearably heavy, immediately pulling me to the bottom of this seething pit. When I try to strike for the surface, skin already melting off, the heavy, melted mesh of chains below holds me back and pins me down. An anchor melted at the bottom of this pit of torture.

My lifeblood gushes through the river of fire all around me. The chains fastened around my wrists don't melt. They are made of something much stronger than the ones that were around my flock, and I feel my wrists wrenched upward. More pain bolts through my body as the chains around my wrists and torso start to pull. Start to tug at my own healing fire desperately trying to protect the skin that is burning away.

They're siphoning away my regenerative flame and keeping me suspended in the one place where I will never be able to fully heal. It will take all my energy just to stay alive. If I fall to ash here, I'll never come back. This fire will consume the fragility of my form.

They've trapped me in a world of fire that screams I cannot escape.

"We are sorry to resort to such means, but we cannot be too careful with the Solnora. *You were born to destroy this entire planet—including us."*

What? What is she talking about?

I try to crane my neck upward, but the slight movement lets the magma break through the thin layer of flame coating my body. The burning liquid tries to eat at my face. I press as much flame as I can from that angry place in my chest out to coat my body and keep the magma away. My lungs ache for air. Every inch of my body screams as the burns cover me.

"This is the best way to keep us, this planet—and even you— safe, Mara." Her voice has softened to a coo that makes me want to spit in her face. *"This is what's best for you. This is protecting everyone. This is the sacrifice you were meant for."*

A raging scream rips from me only to be swallowed by the liquid magma that presses in all around me. Trying to push past the flame I'm desperately using to shield myself. Drops of magma seep through my shield and my continued screams ricochet through my *ero*.

They leave me in that pit of flame, my own blood and flesh burning and mingling with the raging magma. I'll be locked away for what could be an eternity while they drain my life for themselves rather than share it with the world beyond these walls dying of frostbite.

Slowly, so slowly, I calm my raging heartbeat. Steady my own thrashing body and let myself hang suspended in that sea of fire. I focus on thickening that shield of flame coating my skin and holding back the magma just enough.

Just enough that I'm not consumed.

My own fire, the flames I've been so afraid of, are now the only thing keeping me alive.

Maybe that was the purpose all along. Maybe that's what Haven meant.

That my fire wasn't created to be held in. To be hidden away—

Maybe my flame really is a thing to be unleashed.

You're safe, Eli had said.

The very thing Father tried to weaponize is keeping me safe.

The chains wrapping my body try to drain away the healing flame that slowly mends my own bones. But for every drop they take away, I find there is more fire inside to replace it. To turn my body to flame, even beneath that magma. I find a place somewhere between awake and asleep, between human and phoenix, where my fire is a war cry.

The voices of the Golden Phoenixes splinter through my *ero* like a growing roll of thunder. They try to drown out my own voice.

"Sleep!" they bellow in my head. **"Sleep, Mara!"**

They want me to stop fighting. To become a barely alive shell. Suspended here where they can siphon from my soul forever.

They want me to be their silent little weapon.

I've been there before.

You'll . . .

I curl my fists, magma pressing in on all sides, starting to, one by one, lock out their voices.

. . . you'll have to do better than that.

I've spent decades with Darkholm's voice in my head. I let him cage me away. When really, I could have been freer then than I possibly imagined.

But now, as I'm trapped in this pit, unable to even try and swim upward without the magma prying my skin from my bones, as the Golden Phoenixes bombard me with their voices, trying to wrestle my sanity from me . . .

. . . something is different.

I may be more trapped than I have ever been. But my mind?

My mind is awake. And free.

Something else is awake too. Something deep inside. A fire I didn't know I had. A coal that I'm no longer afraid of stoking. No longer hiding. A voice I no longer fear.

A song always at the crest of living and dying. A song of regeneration.

It may be centuries before someone finds me down here. Or I may breathe my last in this pit of flame and darkness. But it doesn't matter anymore. I've always feared myself most, but for the first time, I'm not afraid.

Those who truly matter—they see I have the power of the sun inside me.

And I'm finally ready to *ignite.*

ACKNOWLEDGMENTS

The book in your hands has lived a thousand lives.

Very much like its author. I've been working on variations of this story since I was a teen—almost a decade now. And nearly everything about it has grown and changed and shifted. But the core theme has remained:

A story of a young woman learning how to step into the truth of who she was created to be, unafraid to spread her wings.

I hope this novel reminds you that even your scars can bring healing. That even when we may be afraid of our own fire, our voices and passions and weaknesses and faults—there is still beauty.

Even in the brokenness, we rise.

But I couldn't have told it without the help of so many—

Thank you, firstly and with my whole heart, to my wonderful husband, the Disney boy, David. I adore you. Thank you for championing this book, and for being proudest of me. <3 I couldn't have done it without you.

To my family—Swansons, Matsumotos, Rands, and Navarettes—I love you all. Thank you for loving me, walking alongside me, growing with me. Mom and Dad, thank you for seeing my gifts and wings and encouraging me to spread them. Aunt Terri, thank you for loving Mara even when she was named Noel—you taught me to dream. To the moon and back <3

To my community at Enclave—thank you feels so small compared to all you have given me. Thank you, Steve, Lisa, Trissina, Jamie, Lindsay, Avily, Sara, Kirk, and so many others. Thank you for pouring into this story and helping me craft something beautiful. I am beyond grateful to each of you. Thank you to Steve especially, for waiting patiently for this story to take shape and seeing a place for it here at Enclave. And thank you Lisa for your tender care with the themes in this one. And thank you to Morgan, Tricia, Victoria, Gillian, Nadine, Jill, Candace, Lisa, and so many others of my Enclave author family. I am so honored to be a part of something as special as the community of stories we have cultivated here.

Thank you to my readers, for becoming friends and falling just as in love with Peter and Claire as I am. Your fan art, letters, videos and messages make my year. <3 You are my favorite.

To my beautiful author community—Nova, Lorie, Tosca, Stephanie, Mary, CJ, Victoria, Erin, Steph, Ruthie, Lauren, and so many others. I am beyond grateful for you and the chance to grow and learn and cheer for the incredible stories and lives you are all living. I want to be you when I grow up.

To Alex, for lighting a spark with your brave, brave heart and unwavering kindness.

To Cynthia, for bringing Mara and all my other characters to life. And being one of my oldest friends. <3

And nearly last but certainly not least, my Author Conservatory family, to my safe people, coworkers, and friends. Truly, I have the best job in the world, with the best people. I am blessed beyond measure to be able to come to work every day and spend time with people and students that I just adore. Each of you has such an incredible voice to share, and so much compassion and wisdom. You show me kindness every day, and make me a better person while also championing me. This book would literally not exist with you. Without your insights and wisdom, Brett. Without your feedback and storytelling genius from concept to finished draft, Katie. Without your notes and polishing, Jen. Without your unique perspective having read all the incarnations of this story and your cheerleading, Bri. Without your excitement, Naomi, Sydney, Marielle, Ruth, Calissa, Elena, Cheyenne, Anna, Charis, Rhianna, and all the other amazing students who offered feedback. Each of you are powerhouses in your own rights, and I cannot wait to see you rise. I'm also so grateful for the support of the rest of our team, who has cheered for me and stepped in to hold down the fort when I had to make a tight deadline—Amy, Joanne, Lauren, Katie W, Cassie, Abi, Kellyn, Faith, Josiah, and Diana. Not to mention all our YDubs family.

Thank you, thank you, thank you.

May we not only teach our students to craft powerful stories, but continue to help each other rise into the stories and lives we have to tell as well.

Finally, thank you to my Jesus. For crafting beauty from brokenness and giving all of yourself—and still rising. For never leaving me, no matter how alone I have felt.

For being my wings, my hope, my sol.

Here's to all the stories left to tell.

ABOUT THE AUTHOR

Kara Swanson writes stories about fairy tales and fiery souls. She spent her childhood a little like a Lost Girl, running barefoot through lush green jungles which inspired her award-winning Peter Pan retellings, *Dust* and *Shadow*.

She is also the cofounder of the Author Conservatory (authorconservatory.com) where she has the honor of teaching young writers to craft sustainable author careers.

You'll find Kara with her toes in California sand as a SoCal resident, belting Broadway show tunes on weekend drives to Disneyland with her delightfully nerdy husband, or chatting about magic and mayhem on Instagram (@karaswansonauthor).